YANKEE PASHA

Yankee Pasha

The Adventures of
Jason Starbuck

by

EDISON MARSHALL

FARRAR, STRAUS AND COMPANY

New York   1947

CL

PRINTED IN THE UNITED STATES OF AMERICA

To PAUL R. REYNOLDS
Mainbrace of this book

CONTENTS

BOOK I

CHAPTER ONE

The Clansman

I.

I, Jason Starbuck, would not have you know my parents, Reuben and Prudence Starbuck, because you would quickly love them and quickly lose them. And do not learn to love, as I did, one-armed Pierre—once a voyageur in Quebec—who had lived with us on the Adirondack frontier as long as I could remember.

It is enough to tell that my father was a lean, ruddy man, markedly handsome among the frontier folk, not stupid like the Palatinate Dutch nor grim like the Scotch. Perhaps he was not so good a farmer as the foreigners, but a far better hunter and rider; so when they moved in to blast at the deer with their blunderbusses, we moved on. He was tolerably sober too, by the western standard. Partly this was the happenstance of his having almost no bottom, a demijohn that would throw two Dutchmen giving him only a happy heart and a huge appetite for supper; partly it was real temperance, for he would never trade for strong drink when my mother needed gingham, and all of us yearned for coffee, tobacco, and sugar.

Why, I had known him to pass up a jug in favor of books! Some he rented at the settlements for Indian curios or pelts; once he went all the way to Schenectady to buy a batch from Captain van Rensselaer, and a wonderful bargain he made for a bale of beaver skins. True, once the patroon looked him over, he did not offer him any dull or even pious works. The library included *Arabian Nights* in French, which Pierre could read aloud to us of an evening, a dictionary, *Robinson Crusoe,* Chaucer's tales, and a big, close-printed volume of Shakespeare's best-known plays. My father was very eager for me to read quickly and well. My mother, who could not write her own name, cared even more. After I had got my nose in Robin, I needed no caning to keep me at it, and soon no dunce cap for the long words. Not many young men of sixteen north of the Mohawk had read and relished *Macbeth!*

3

On the night of May 16, 1794, my father was indeed a little tipsy. He had just returned from selling some furs and deer pelts at the trading post at Plattsburg and, having got a good price, he had included among his purchases a jug of whiskey. The Scanlin brothers and their young wives, our nearest neighbors, had ridden four miles to help celebrate his return, so my sweet mother did not blame him for a little excess joviality and indeed became blithe and prettily flushed from a glass old Pierre fixed for her. I took a teacupful or so in the course of the evening—having been counted almost a man since I was thirteen—and all in all we had a most happy time. Feasting on wild turkey, venison, cornbread, and molasses, the Scanlins became so high spirited that they teased my father about being a "Downeaster" and an "Old Salt." I had known that both my parents were from Massachusetts Bay, but I never had a wish or thought to see it. Our faces were turned toward Lake Ontario and the great Northwest.

The guests spent the night, the little cabin holding eight—nine, counting a new Scanlin baby—as easily as four. All were up and their horses saddled before dawn, when I rose to go hunting. Old Pierre decided to go with me, for we were short of meat, neither he nor I having dared to leave the homestead during my father's absence. Just before we left a young squaw came wandering down the mountain trail and begged my father for sugar. Evidently some of her tribe, trading skins at the settlements, had seen him pass with his bulging saddlebags.

Pierre and I started southwest, intending to hunt out some woods nearer the west branch of the Ausable. Finding only stale, sparse sign, we turned straight west into Indian country. When about ten o'clock we climbed a high ridge, Pierre's quick eye noticed a dark-blue cloud of smoke in the direction of our cabin. We had looked at it an instant when the need came to look at each other. I do not know what was on my face, but I saw what was on Pierre's. It was more like flint than flesh, its very hatred of a stony, implacable kind that my young heart had never learned, and a terrible resolve already glinted in his granite-gray eyes.

"It may have caught fire by accident," I stammered in French.

"That squaw," he replied. "She reconnoitered the ground, and signaled in a war party."

I was already wheeling my horse. The old voyageur stopped me.

"Wait, Jason. We mustn't make one wrong move. Our horses mustn't be seen on the skyline—they think we're away to the eastward, and must continue to think so."

4

"Then tell me what to do." And I would have thanked God then, if my mind had room, for having spoken French all my remembered days. All of us had had to learn a little, to talk with our companion who spoke no English, and since Pierre was well-born and educated, my French was better than my native tongue, a mixture of Yankee and New York State.

"Don't give up hope," he told me. "Maybe the fire caught from the chimney. But if so, there's no need of haste, for there'll be nothing but ashes left of the cabin. If the fire was set, there's likewise no need of haste. There'll be nothing but ashes and blood."

"Let's do something." My voice was shaking but Pierre would not lose faith in me on that account.

"We will, never fear." He was testing the wind now. "Never fear for that, young one," he went on. And as his voice died away, I knew he was doing the most important thing possible now—thinking. Those thoughts were icy as his eyes. They were like a clear, sparkling river fed by a thousand rills from two score hills, and the hills were his years among the painted people. He was looking down at the configuration of the land.

"Come, Jason," he said at last. "I'll tell you the rest as we ride."

He did not have to tell me twice. When the redskins struck, the law for white people was ancient and inviolable. It was to save lives if possible, and for every one lost, to take swift and full revenge. It was a wonder to have reached the age of sixteen without yet fighting the painted devils, and I had known it would come sometime, like drouth or flood.

If redskins had raided the valley, they were likely renegade Mohawks, he said—the squaw we had seen certainly was—and had struck from their spring lodges on the Saranac lakes. Even so, it was a most bold stroke, probably by a small hunting party of young braves suddenly taking the warpath without the consent of the wer-o-lance, for we were at peace with the Iroquois Nations, and there had been no powwows. That meant they would hit and run. They would streak for the big timber by the shortest trail, which would lead them through a rocky defile that Pierre and I called Eagle Pass.

"If I'm wrong, and they take some other trail, it will be too late to change," Pierre told me in a low voice.

"I don't think you're wrong."

So we rode to Eagle Pass, swiftly but not wildly, taking care not to loom on the skyline. If Pierre was right, we had enough time, for redskins would hate to leave the scene of their triumph until the flames burned low. When we gained the defile, Pierre tested the wind again. Then we tied the horses up-current from the trail—so they would not smell the enemy band and snort at the drying blood that streaked them—and of course behind heavy growth. Then the old voyageur gave me some last-minute instructions.

"You'll take your stand on one side of the pass, nearest the horses, and I'll take the other side," he told me. "But you must give me time to shoot, before you touch trigger." I had almost forgotten that his left arm was a stub thrust into a wooden horn with an iron hook at the end, good tackle but not as handy as a hand.

"I will."

"I'll have a dead rest, so can account for one, sure. The others will charge me with tomahawks, and still you mustn't shoot—not until I've grappled with the devils—to give you a good head start when you run for the horses. You can't miss at that range. That will make two, sure."

"No, I won't miss, Pierre."

"Two at least. Poor pay for your Pa and Ma, but something. And I hope to get my knife into one, amid the melee. That will make three."

"That isn't enough," I told him, my teeth chattering.

"Hark to me, Jason. Monsieur Reuben—" so he always called my father—"will have laid low others—one or two or three—unless taken wholly by surprise. And it's not good for a line to end, for a family to be wiped out root and branch. For me—it's no bad thing. My time's short now, and I'd like to end it with the pride I knew long ago—and even my arm was lost to me by a poisoned arrow. When you've shot, run like a wolf, then ride like a hussar!"

People who dwell in a softer land might wonder that he had let me stay even this long. I was sixteen, in many respects no older than Valley youths of that age. The answer was that in matters such as this, I had been counted a man two years or more. He would not question my standing, since we had hunted and ridden and been woodsmen together so long and far. He had seen boys of twelve stand up with the men when the war whoops sounded. I had shot nigh a hundred deer, and wild turkeys past counting. Anyway I was taller than Pierre and a good deal stronger, a better woodsman than half the Yorkers in the Valley and all the Dutchmen.

Folk of a later day might wonder too at Pierre's clean, clear thought and noble language. I did not, knowing how the wilderness had called some of Europe's best. He had chosen the life of a voyageur in

6

Quebec instead of an officer's career in Louis' armies, and I reckon had lived a bushel to that peck.

"Goodbye, Jason," he told me, faintly smiling.

I started to cry but choked it back. He gave me a little lick with the side of his wooden arm.

Just then we heard the distant knock and rattle of a stone rolling downhill. It may have been dislodged by spring seepage, and again a too hasty step might have loosened it. The sound had carried a good half mile, and I saw that Pierre's ambush was well laid before I looked to my own. One-armed save for the iron hook, he might have needed me to move a log, or help him to break a branch in silence. As it happened, he found a perch behind some thickets, and a rest for his rifle as handy as though provided for his express use. He was the only Frenchman I ever knew who chewed tobacco—they are fastidious fellows, even on the wild, white rivers of the north—and when I left him he was chawing away, yet with a certain daintiness.

2.

My ambush was the top of a big rock on the other side of the pass. Some high grass growing in a crack provided a perfect screen whereby I could watch the trail for a furlong below us; and one bound would take me to the hillside, forty yards' run from the horses. Blessedly, we had not long to wait, although perhaps I could have waited long and yet shot true, so fixed was my post. More than once I had waited two or more hours while deer fed all about me; and more ticklish than deer, wild turkeys. You would think it a different thing entirely, yet all frontiersmen find out they are cut from the same cloth.

Around the bend into open forest came the war party. They were not driving or leading prisoners—they had taken none. Well, it had never been more than the shadow of a hope, which Pierre had not broached—which I had not uttered to him. I counted them with care. There were five braves and one squaw, the latter the same who had come to our door. We had not guessed wrong about their swift retreat. Unable to run up the steep slope, the warriors paced like wolves, and the squaw could hardly keep up because of her heavy burden. The two leather saddlebags were the same that had lain last night, full of new provision, on our cabin floor.

Five was a small number of braves to have attacked one lonely cabin. It was reasonable to suppose that there had been a couple more, that our little fort had not been wholly surprised and there had been

7

time for its garrison to bolt doors and gain loopholes. If so I thought that God had had mercy on my soul. Old Pierre, with his good arm in position, his iron hook ready, had made the same count. It seemed I heard him spit.

The three hindmost braves were armed with bows and quivers, but the two foremost carried rifles, one a heavy, awkward-looking piece such as thrifty Hollanders used to sell to the Algonquins. The other looked like the long flintlock that had hung on our wall, the last of the three firearms our cabin boasted.

The party forged swiftly nearer. The braves were naked, save for their accouterment and war paint, and some of the red streaks and smears on their dirt-colored hides were not mineral pigment. Then I saw something that brought bitter slime into my mouth, one sick wave that seemed to unbrace my bones, but the weakness quickly passed off. Even to shoot a turkey I knew how to freeze within. My boyhood was far behind me on this trail.

So I looked carefully at the fresh scalps a-swing on their deerhide belts. There were two, of course. The one flaunted by the first brave had rather short, black hair. The other, worn by his follower, had long hair, once the color of wheat straw in a September sun.

The party moved into the defile. The foremost warrior appeared to stumble, my eye catching the movement a perceptible instant before I heard the roar of Pierre's piece. Pierre would naturally take the leader, and the brave who carried the black-haired scalp would naturally be that leader; yet I felt something like exultation that the second Indian, not the first, fell to my portion. Pierre's fellow had been head shot, the old voyageur not considering any other target at such close range.

The others let go a howl of fury and fear, louder than the gun's roar, and converged like a pack of wolves on Pierre's ambush. I saw him rise up and his knife flash as my rifle leveled. My target was clean and clear, the shaven back of a head. Since I had learned to shoot in the frontier fashion rather than the military—no holding and tickling the trigger, but firing the instant the mark came into my sights—his violent movements could not throw off my aim. Then I saw the black spot made by the bullet as plain and neat as on a birchwood chip at a shooting match. Before he hit the ground I had swung around and leaped off the rock. Then I ran for the horses.

We had tied them in a certain way—mine to be loosed with one jerk of the rein, Pierre's with a long thong to my saddle. Soon for my skin's sake I was up and bounding downhill, the rocks rolling and clattering behind me. When the redskins had finished killing Pierre —it would be too costly in blood and time to take him for torture— they would stand with their topknots high for a few seconds, listening to my clamor. Both of us would thus be accounted for, the old paleface lying in his blood, the other fleeing toward the settlements. Such sound carried far in the still noon.

What they did not know was that one terror-stricken horse may sound like two. When heavy forest had screened me, I looked for a moist deer trail running across the hillside. When one came handy, I freed Pierre's horse and sped him on his way with a cruel thrust of my rifle barrel into his flank. Then I began a long loop to carry me back to my enemies.

Was this a high order of cunning? Believe me, I would have been capable of better than this, if this were not enough. Pierre had taught me some real 'cute tricks, if the need for them arose. It was not even superior courage, only tolerable, so great was its need; boys younger than me and men less obligated had played thinner chances in the Indian wars. Pierre had likely killed two of the war party—no bet could hardly be safer—which would leave only two and the squaw. That old French wolf might have sunk his teeth into one of these in the last set-to. I could attack by surprise, and my nag show them clean heels if my plans went wrong.

I stopped and reloaded the rifle, then pushed my dun mare Minx as fast as she could tear to the top of the ridge. I hardly hoped for any hunting so close to our kill, but one glance at the trail changed the outlook. It was streaked and spattered with bright blood, different from the dark kind as every hunter knows; and an old voyageur smiled down at me from heaven.

Keeping to moist ground parallel to the trail and dodging sound traps, I soon came in sight of the wounded man, now forsaken by his comrades in redskin fashion. Although still on his feet, he was reeling and staggering and streaming war paint; and I had no notion of wasting powder on him and alarming his mates with the blast. When he saw me, he tried for a war whoop—a brave act—although he managed no more than a strangled bleat which did not carry far. As I rode him down, he raised his tomahawk, only to drop it when I banged him across the head with my gun barrel. It was not a heavy blow, for a hunter learns to take great care of his piece, but it felled him, and he lay quivering. There was a great rip under his arm where Pierre's hook had caught and yanked. Leaning far out of my saddle—for I

9

had tightened my cinch—I thrust my long, keen, hunting knife into the base of his neck, turned it, and drew it out.

Only two of the foe remained—one brave and one squaw. This the trail told plain. Thus four had been sent to Manitou—not a bad account for two dispatched to heaven. No, there were three of my party gone. The brave fleeing on ahead paraded a scalp with Pierre's gray, sparse hair. But truly I need not count scalps for heart to go on with the hunt. I need not consider that if I stopped now, I could not tell the tale to other Indian fighters without their making allowance for my youth. What hunter whose larder is bare will stop with one turkey, when others gobble just over the hill? The larder of my heart was woeful bare.

I rode on, again keeping to silent ground, and fast as Minx could go. Before long I saw two saddlebags left on the trail. For this the squaw could expect to be beaten almost to death if she reached the lodges, but she had not liked the smell of things. Things had not gone as well as she had intended when she saw Pierre and me ride off across the valley and signaled in her pack lying on the hillside. Any kind of beating was better than the beating wings of the birds of death.

Before long a straight reach of the trail gave me a distant glimpse of her and her lone companion. They were traveling fast, although sometimes glancing over their shoulders—and to see them do it exulted me, now that I had them. Beyond lay open woods, where even a turkey could not run unseen. I closed the distance slowly until they were well in its pretty shade, then, as Pierre had bade me, rode like a hussar.

The pair saw or heard me a little short of good rifle range. At first they tried to leg it, then seeing the folly of this, the brave ducked behind a tree. His flintlock came poking out. I changed my course to his flank. Pierre's lore of Indian fighting had not been wasted on me. Not good shots to start with—they cannot grasp the science of the rear sight—redskins are easily flustered, despite their wooden looks. The trees flitting between him and me would not only break his aim, they would greatly tend to break his nerve, and cause him to jerk the trigger.

It worked as pretty as a new jack-in-the-box. Pierre's smile in heaven turned to a roar of laughter. The brave's bullet flew so wide I could not hear it whistle, and now he was in my hand.

To give the devil his due he charged me bravely, his tomahawk high and his war cry resounding. I need only check my mare—she had been taught to stop on a door mat—and, with the redskin coming on my left and a little in front, wait until he was in point-blank range. I did not take the head shot though, and was content to place my bullet fairly midway in his sweat-wet, painted chest.

The squaw gave me a run through the woods. She dodged like a chicken in a barnyard, back and forth, wonderfully quick at turning, and screeching high. Once she tried to hide in a thicket, but I flushed her out like a turkey with a broken wing. Gobbling and cackling, she darted about, often whirling around trees, until once I guessed her turn, rode her down, and caught hold of her long hair. She turned like a wildcat to fight, but riding full tilt, I yanked her off her feet and dragged her alongside until I could slip my reins over the pommel and draw my hunting knife. Then, reaching back, I cleanly cut her throat and let her fall.

That made three gobblers for Pierre, two and one hen for me, and that was a bag indeed for a summer morning.

3.

During the hunt, the thought of the future or the past had hardly crossed my mind. I had lived for the instant's scratch and bite, like a bobcat at bay. I had not thought of anything save hunting or being hunted, and my heart had been bucking too hard to let Sorrow get on and ride. Now, in the silence of the forest, amid the dappled sunlight and cool shade, with only bloody carcasses where my enemies had run and fought so lively, all that was changed.

I was bitter lonely, woestruck, and afraid. I dreaded lingering here another moment only a little less than going homeless home. What I must do, I did quickly, the first task not troublesome to me of itself—taking the scalps of my slaughtered redskins—the second task most horrid and almost beyond my will-power to perform. I had to remove the brave's three trophies from his belt—one he had taken from Pierre at Eagle Pass, and two he had stolen from his fallen comrades there—and carry them farther into the woods to bury. The clansmen of the slain would greatly crave the paleface scalps. Retching and sobbing, I did the job, and then ran swiftly so that my vomit would not mark the spot.

Riding swiftly on the trail to the pass, I stopped twice. Once it was to pick up the two saddlebags the squaw had dropped, and once to lift a scalp that belonged to Pierre, I having merely retrieved his death-wounded turkey. At the pass I collected three more, two for

Pierre and one for me, and also removed his knife thrust deep in the brown breast of his second man. Then I slung Pierre's body—three scalps fastened on his belt—behind my saddle and tied it well.

My worst task was yet to come, although I felt more equal to it than before. Anyway it could be delayed no longer. There was a sight that the sun should not see, and no one left but me to dispose of it. All danger from redskins had passed for now; the swift flight of the raiders showed that they were renegades far from their clan. No out-lyers were about, or they would have run off with Pierre's pony grazing free beside the horse lot.

One mercy was granted me. As I cleared the last ridge, I saw two horsemen advancing warily across our corn field. It did not take me long to recognize the Scanlin brothers, our guests of last night. No doubt they had seen the smoke of the burning cabin, and after sending their wives to safety, had advanced to give what help they could. I wanted them to come and meet me, and tell me the worst, and be with me when I went to look, so I rode slowly. Men's pride grows tall on the frontier, but loneliness strikes deep, and they learn the good of neighbors.

They gained the cabin when I was yet two furlongs off. They moved about, and stopped, and moved again, and then when I hallooed, came riding fast. It was the place of the older brother, Noah, to tell the news. Instead the younger brother, Amos, did so, he being handier with words.

"We've got bad word for you, Jason Starbuck," he began, when about ten paces from me.

"I'll hear it, if you please."

"Your Ma and Pa been killed by Indians."

"I know that part. Did they die by torture, or quickly?"

"Quick. Your Ma by a musket ball, and your Pa tomahawked."

"Well, I'm glad of that." As I started on, they wheeled their horses to lead the way.

"They was scalped—bound to be that—but the red niggers didn't hack 'em to pieces as they might've," Amos went on. "I reckon they was in too much a hurry to light out. We'd hoped both you and Pierre was safe, till we seen you toting him home."

"Only I was saved."

"They didn't get off cheap, by God they didn't. Two was lined up dead outside the loophole, and one, what was left of him, in the ashes of the cabin. I reckon he got inside where your Pa knifed him."

"I didn't expect there'd be two outside. There was only one gun."

"Your Ma was a right pert 'un to load, while your Pa braced the door. And three plays even for both of 'em and Pierre too."

"We played more than even." I pointed to the scalps on Pierre's belt and on mine.

"Tarnation glory!" Noah, the elder brother broke out, and you would have thought that lightning played upon his face. "A whole passel!"

"Three for Pierre, all bucks. Two bucks and one doe for me." They would not think I was bragging, and the thought could not come to me either. It was only telling the score.

"I'm glad, I'm mighty glad." Noah's look, and the way he sat tall in the saddle told more than his words. "That was good, Jason, for a young feller."

"A growed man couldn't do no better," Amos told me. "That must about cleaned out the party, from the sign."

"It did clean it out."

"Nine who won't do no more prancin' about their fires. That was good, Jason. All o' ye done good."

We were now only a few paces from the battleground. All of us dismounted, but I looked first at the dead redskins. Still, there was no fort, no bush to hide in. The only mercy was, I had seen Indian butchery before, usually bloodier than this. All who dwelt at the fringe of the forest had to consider such sights, to see or to be seen.

We three men dug three deep graves in a row. The task took the rest of the day and a good part of the night. In the moonlight we buried my three dead; and Amos Scanlin, who was better with words than Noah, said some over them. If our Bible had not been burned in the cabin, he could have done as well as a preacher. Then we replaced the dirt, packed it well, restored the sod, and hid all traces of any digging, because the redskins might revisit the scene before long. By the time we had lashed the three "good" Indians together and I had dragged them with my mare Minx to lay a feast for the buzzards, morning came cool and sweet and scented over the river.

The war party had not taken time to burn our barn, or to round up and kill our oxen and milk cow. Since our corn was well seeded and sprouting, there was no reason I could not yet make the crop, before setting off on a journey. So after caring for the oxen, the poultry, and farm tools, I carried only our cow and Pierre's red gelding Rouge to the Scanlin farm, of course in addition to his knife, the leather bags, and the four firearms, three of ours and one Dutch piece, lashed lengthways under the flap of my saddle. After supper that night, sitting on the fence of the Scanlin's horse lot, Amos Scanlin asked what were my plans for the future.

"As soon as our crop's made, I thought to go and live with my Pa's folks, Downeast, to Salem."

"That's a good piece from here."

"I reckon more'n three hundred miles."

"They say them codgers and Yankee traders are a consarned lot o' folks."

"I reckon so, but my Pa and Ma came from there, before I was born."

"So your Pa told me. Do you know any of his kinpeople?"

"No, Amos, I don't. But he wrote a letter one time to his brother Samuel there, and Ma got one from her brother, Dan'l Todkill, posted at Boston. Pa read it to her." When talking to our neighbors instead of to my better-spoken father, I naturally fell into an easier vocabulary. My mother's speech had been good for a woman who could not read or write, but spiced with queer expressions that had made Pa laugh. She was a real blue-water sailor's girl, he said.

"I reckon you'd find cousins and sech a-plenty."

"I didn't hear any mention of 'em."

"I wouldn't say a word to bend you, but Noah and I allowed if you wanted to stay on with us, we'd like it fine."

"Thank you kindly, but I'll go."

"We could work both farms, and arter we got ahead a piece, sell out and go down to Mackinac."

"That would be good, and if you want me to stay here till the crops are in, I'd like it fine. After that, I'm bound to go to my uncle's. I've got no kinfolk around here, and need to be with some."

"That's right, Amos," Noah broke in. "A feller needs kinfolks by him."

So that was settled, and I stayed throughout the summer with the Scanlins, we working both farms. It was a very strange time, in which I never felt wide awake or quite alive. When I hoed weeds or did other chores on what had been my parents' homestead, my heart became a hard lump insensible as a clod, and there was a fence across part of my mind that thought could not jump over. The last days of July the corn talled, and I turned seventeen. Yet even after the crop was in the barn I stayed on week after week, through winter and till sap was a-running, hunting deer for the Scanlin's table, jerking the extra meat for their summer use, and running a line of traps along the creeks and the shores of the mountain lakes. It seemed best to have a poke-full of money when I began my journey to Salem.

It came March, and I told the Scanlins I would leave on Easter Sunday.

"We won't try to hold you no more," said Amos, speaking for his tongue-tied brother. "Noah and me talked it over, and his wife and mine puttin' in, and we reckoned maybe it might be the best thing for you, arter all."

"I'll be sorry to leave you all."

"Well, the next thing's what you figure to do with the farm and the crop, and them horses and cow and oxen, and tools and guns and fur?"

"I figured to take the horses and two guns, and sell all the rest."

"What do you figure to ask, 'ceptin' the fur that you'd sell at a trading post?"

"A hundred dollars in gold for the farm—we've got title to two thousand acres, with ten acres fenced—and a hundred for all the rest, 'cept the fur."

"Noah, does that seem fair to you?" Amos asked his brother.

"Plumb fair."

"Well, then, Jason, we'll make the bargain, if you'll take part payment in fur. Noah's wife brought him o'er a hundred in gold, and we've saved a mite. We'll reckon our fur at what 'twould bring at MacDonald's trading post. If you'd carry it to Salem with your own, you'd realize a heap more."

"That's agreeable to me."

"Did your Pa leave a will or something, so there'd be no trouble about the papers? Noah and me was a-feared maybe they was burned up in the fire."

"No, they're all at the courthouse at Plattsburg, and if you or Noah will go with me, I reckon we can fix 'em all right."

So riding Minx and leading Pierre's gelding Rouge packed to the eyebrows with pelts, I set out on my travels. From our farm to Plattsburg was no piece, even in winter weather, and from there to Ticonderoga, spring was in the air thin as wood smoke a mile from home, but plain. Across country to Sand Hill on the Hudson, and then in no great hurry—entranced with the new villages and fertile farms—deciding to see Albany, second city in the state with five thousand head, I enjoyed every reach of the road and turn of the season. The inns being buggy and bleak and somewhat costly besides, some nights I bivouacked in the woods and fields, well nourished on smoked venison and parched corn, and snug in my saddle blanket as a coon in a hollow tree. Mainly I put up with farmers, sometimes three abed with their young ones or on the floor by the fire. The more crowded, the better I liked it.

One night I traded a few kisses with a plump and pretty daughter of my host, neither of us feeling cheated by the bargain, and could have bundled with her in a week, had I accepted her father's offer of a job on his farm. At Greenfield, Massachusetts, the hotbed of Shay's Rebellion, I almost got in a fight in defense of the Downeasters, for my parents' and kinfolks' sake, when the rebels said they were a pack of skinflints and thieves. But I remembered Pierre's warning never to start shooting even my mouth off, until sure of my mark and an open path behind me.

It was a long way to Reading, through a long-settled countryside. There were children by the road who had never seen a painted Indian, and who hung on the fence to watch a frontiersman pass. Still I did not put on store clothes, to be muddied and spoiled—deciding to stay a mountaineer until I could become a real, fine Yankee—and rode into Salem clothed neck to foot in buckskin. The seams and the sleeves were fringed, in the Indian fashion, for my mother had liked to have me go gay as our rough world afforded. My coonskin cap had a ring-tail tassel, and my Indian-black hair I wore long in a tight queue. This too was the western style for Indian fighters, to show a scalp worth taking to the painted devil man enough to take it.

Still I was glad that lamps were lit and houses shut and the long street nearly empty as I rode down. As it happened, the sight of a mountaineer in this long-settled city was not as rare as I thought, long-hunters and beaver-trappers occasionally bringing their pelts here to get the seaboard price and see the sights; however, the town watchmen kept them under close surveillance, lest they raise a rumpus. When I stopped a young man to ask for the house of Samuel Starbuck, he gazed rather wistfully at my outfit, but with no great amazement.

"Why, you don't look much older than me," he remarked through his nose. "I'm twenty-one this comin' August."

"We're about the same." I was eighteen, come July.

I followed the youth's directions to a house smaller than some of the mansions near by, but a palace compared to our cabin. That just suited me, for it was sign of a strong kinsman not so rich that he would not need a young nephew to work hard and help him in the business. But when the door was opened by a middle-aged man carrying a candle, I thought surely I had barked up the wrong tree.

"Well, what is it?" he asked, in a peevish voice.

He had not seen me well yet on the dark stoop—he could have taken me for a beggar. But I could see him quite well in the light of his lifted candle, and I decided then and there he could not be my Pa's own brother. If this was the right house, I thought, he must be some boarder or a relation of my aunt by marriage. Although hardly any older than Pa, at most no more than forty-five, he was thin but not lean—two different things—a dry husk instead of a long, yellow ear of corn. He was not graceful like Pa. His eyes did not hold the same kind of light nor his face the same lively expression. He had a sharp nose instead of a high, bold one. All I could say for him was, he was dressed very fine, with a gold watch chain across his belly.

"Would you please direct me to Samuel Starbuck?" I asked.

"I'm Mr. Starbuck," he replied. "What do you want?"

I wanted my first impression of him to be mistaken; I wanted my hunter's eyes to be unable to judge a real Downeast Yankee. Before I could untie my tongue he looked past me to my horses dimly visible in the moonlight at his hitching post, then held the candle nearer my face.

"Why, you're a Westerner," he said quickly, in a much more agreeable tone. "I haven't my spectacles on and didn't notice."

"Yes, sir, from the Adirondack Mountains." I could not burst out that I was his nephew.

"Do tell! Someone gave you my name, I reckon—"

"No, sir." This was quite true, to my sudden worry and wonder. Even in his will Pa had not proposed that I find his brother Samuel and make family ties with him. "But my father mentioned it."

"Who was your father, young man? Doubtless I'll recall him—"

"Reuben Starbuck." Without my knowing it, my head had shot up higher so that I was looking down into his face.

Any blood kin I could picture would grab my arms at that, his face lighting up, and holler. Uncle Samuel only sucked in his breath. It appeared like he was never going to speak, but it was his turn, so I waited. He glanced quickly up and down the street, and from the look of him, his thoughts were scurrying like mice.

"Why, I had a brother by that name!" he ventured, exactly like a mouse sticking its head out of a hole.

"He was the one."

"And you're his son! Well, well, this is a surprise. Traveling through, I suppose, and stopped in to see your Uncle Samuel! Come in and meet Aunt Levina." He was making room for me in the narrow hall.

I knew then there was more room in any mountain cabin than in all this big house. It cramped my chest so I could hardly speak.

"Yes, sir, I just came by to say how-de-do."

"Your father's in good health, I hope?"

"No, sir, he's dead."

My uncle paused in his busy step. "Now there's a pity. I'm sorry to hear it, I do vum!" Sighing, he opened an inner door. "But 'In the midst of life we are in death,' the Good Book says. And we've been parted twenty years—"

I did not care now about the fine sitting room, with its fine chairs and curtains and a table just for looking at instead of eating off of and an expensive whale-oil lamp. I looked at the woman sewing on a quilt without eagerness of heart, not surprised, not even caring, to find her mean and purse-proud, sharp-featured and sour. When my uncle introduced me, she gave me a sharp look that became an astonished one as she took in my clothes, but there was nothing childlike in her eyes, as in Pa's and Ma's when they saw something new from the city. She thought the buckskins outlandish, and wrinkled her nose at their racy smell.

When she said I might sit down, she pointed to a chair without a cushion.

We sat and conversed awhile, and maybe they thought my queer-sounding, shaky voice was the one I was born with. Aunt Levina was not surprised, she said, that my father had been killed by Indians, since he had chosen to make his home in the wild west. She trusted that he had left me well provided for. Hearing that I had my own way to make did not surprise her either—Reuben had not been famed for his thrift. Was my mother well?

"Thank you kindly, but she too is dead," I answered, hardly knowing what I was saying.

She and her husband exchanged quick glances. "Why, I feel for you!" But I hated hearing her say it, and suddenly I was as steady as though out hunting.

"Do any of her folks live in Salem, ma'am?" I asked.

"None ever did, that I know of. I believe she came from Medford —fisher folk, if I'm not mistaken. Samuel, are any of them left?"

"Only Dan'l, I believe."

"I did not mean him, Samuel. You should have known that."

"Will you direct me where to find him?" I asked quickly.

"Young man, it's our duty to speak to you about your Uncle Dan'l Todkill. He was in the Caribs, the last time he was mentioned, and the less you have to do with him, the better."

Stiff-backed in her chair, her hands folded primly, she proceeded to tell me quite a little of my family history. I listened carefully to every word. Although the Starbucks were not the equal of the Salem merchant families—at that her husband bleated "My dear!"—some of them were whalers sailing their own ships out of Nantucket. Even some of the Todkills had been honest folk, although of humble station. But it had been very hard on my Uncle Samuel, having virtually a pirate in his own brother's family. However, having made connections with the best people, my good uncle was well thought of in Salem and getting along well.

"By thrift and prudence," he explained. "While I've no ready money on hand—all of it invested in Mr. Featherstone's ventures—no doubt you've heard of him—"

"No, sir, I haven't."

"I can hardly believe it. The richest merchant in Salem, save possibly Mr. Derby."

"My mother loved her brother Dan'l," I told the woman, holding my voice as steady as a rifle, "and I want him to know of her death."

"Then you may write a letter and leave it at the customhouse. Some ship captain will consent to deliver it."

"Thank you, ma'am, and as it's getting late—"

"I'm sorry we can't put you up for the night, but our spare beds are undergoing spring cleaning. There are some taverns on the water front—they charge cheap enough if they don't know you're Samuel Starbuck's nephew—and no doubt you want to make an early start."

"Yes, ma'am, as soon as I sell my furs."

For the first time I heard a grandfather clock ticking solemnly in the corner. Then my uncle asked, "You have furs?"

"Yes, sir, a heavy horseload. I put 'em inside your fence, while I made the call."

"Some of 'em wouldn't be beaver, would they?"

"All are prime beaver."

"Good lack, they might be stolen." Uncle Samuel was already on his feet and quickly led the way through the hall. The big deer-hide bales had not been tampered with.

"Why, you must have more than a hundred," said he, hefting one of the bales. "In that case, I'll—" he stopped, a little embarrassed. "Do you know, my boy, you haven't told us your given name?"

"It's Jason, sir."

"Why, the same as your Grandfather Todkill, and a good Biblical name!"

"No, sir. It's from Ancient Greece."

"To be sure. Well, Jason, I can look after your skins tonight, and if you've time for my wife to make up the bed—"

"I'll stay at the inn, Uncle Samuel, and won't trouble you with the fur."

"Why not sell them to me, here and now? 'Twill save you a load of trouble. It's a pity the demand has fallen off so sharp, but I'll pay you the top price."

"What would you give for 'em, sir?"

He hefted all four bales. "You guarantee they're prime?"

"Every one. I'd too far to go to bother with small sizes and such as that." As a matter of fact I had given the off-prime skins to Noah Scanlin's wife to make a bed robe.

"Well, I'll say in round figures—taking my chance on the market, and remembering you're my brother's boy—a hundred dollars in gold."

I could have got more than that at Plattsburg, but did not tell him so. For the first time since he had answered my knock, I was enjoying the visit.

"Thank you kindly, but I wouldn't want you to lose on 'em, just because I'm your nephew. Tomorrow I'll show 'em to all the buyers, and take the best offer."

It was a pleasure to watch him squirm, as I lashed the pelts to Rouge's packsaddle and then got astride Minx.

"I'll make it a hundred and twenty in gold," he told me, almost panting. "After all, if I lose by 'em, it's in the family."

"I wouldn't sell 'em to you if you'd make it a thousand," I answered, with a sudden, painful heave of my chest.

"What's that, nephew? What do you mean, young man?"

"I don't mean for you to make a penny off them, if I have to give 'em away. But I'd given them to you gladly, if you'd needed them in your business, and had treated me like a kinsman instead of a beggar."

Then Minx must have been surprised how I dug my heel in her ribs and jumped her away, hauling startled Rouge behind us. The beat of their hooves on the cobblestones covered up some womanish sounds I would not let Samuel Starbuck hear for all the world.

CHAPTER TWO

Horseflesh and Horse-of-tree

1.

That was the most I ever had to do with my Uncle Samuel and his peaked, ugly wife. And I ought to be glad to be shed of him so soon, seeing he was not only mean as a wolverine, but a piddling man besides. If he had been at all 'cute, he could have made a show of welcoming me at least until he found out if I was worth skinning. It would never have entered my head that kith and kin—a man's trust and mainstay in the West—would turn on their own. Too, he ought to have known that a white man, not an Indian, smart enough to take fur, had some notion of its value; he had taken me not for a man but a backwoods lout. I reckoned he would never amount to very much, and he never did.

What was I to do now? My first thought was to go back to the Adirondack Mountains and live with the Scanlins. I do not know why it was so repellent to me, in spite of loneliness deeper than a flowing well. Shame of defeat had something to do with it, and pride of name, and never wanting to see an Indian again lest I should try to kill him, and a perception that a man like me would never get very far on an Ohio farm. I had to go tremendous far. I was obliged to get rich and marry the prettiest and toniest girl hereabouts, and have fine children by her. Having no kinsmen worth holding by, I had to make some fine ones. Partly this was for my parents' sake, Pa's and especially Ma's, partly for old Pierre's, but in a great part for never standing again, alone, with a dead heart, under tall, dark trees. Thomas Jefferson had written, and my Pa had fought for it, that all men were created free and equal in the United States. Yes, but they didn't stay free and equal, and I must climb near the top.

Instead of going farther west I would like to see some countries overseas. The riches being piled up by Salem merchants came out of the sea, and it was in my blood-and-get to be a sailor. So lying in my buggy bed in a cheap tavern—I had bought a pound of sulphur at a ship chandler's to sift into my buckskins and foil the pestiferous devils—I came to a great decision.

In the morning I sold my fur to Mr. Derby, the foremost Salem merchant. He paid me two hundred dollars in gold without batting a keen, blue eye. That swelled my poke to three hundred and fifty, which two years before would have made me feel a Croesus, but the profit on one of Mr. Derby's ventures had once amounted to a hundred times that sum! Then I had a chance to swell it a little more by his admiring Minx. He had spotted her outside his countinghouse—his eyes did not miss much—and when he had paid me for my pelts, he walked out with me to take a look at her.

"A tol'able piece of horseflesh," he remarked. "And in good condition, considering your long ride."

"She had good rations and plenty of rest all the way."

"It's a pity she's not as good as your fur, or I might buy her off you."

"Sir, there's not a horse in Salem that's her match." And that was not only a foolish remark but a mighty rash one. I did not know that rich Salem merchants took great pride in their stables, importing the best horses from Virginia and even from England, and lately the town was agog over racing them against one another.

"Would you like to run her against one of mine, winner take both?"

When you find yourself up a tree, Pierre had liked to say, take a good look at the scenery. An older man would have wiggled out of the trap, but my boy's pride would not let me. Anyway, by taking Pierre's advice—thinking hard and quick with a cool head—it seemed I might turn the trick. Mr. Derby was waiting patiently, with a faint and quite pleasant smile, for my answer.

"I'd have a go at it, sir, with stipulations," I told him.

"Stipulate all you please."

"You know the tracks hereabouts, and I don't. I'd like to pick the course."

"Any course you pick will suit me well."

"I'd not want your horse, and want to dispose of mine. If I win, will you pay me fifty dollars for Minx, and twenty-five for Rouge, and sign me on one of your ships as man 'fore the mast, and let me put my capital in the venture?"

He stopped smiling now, and stared. "Why, blow me down," he exclaimed presently, "but you talk turkey!"

"I'd work for you faithful, sir."

22

"That I don't doubt, and I like a lad who don't putter about. But a mountaineer going to sea is a new thing."

"I'm a Starbuck, sir, and my mother a Todkill."

"That's good salt blood, and no better, and I'm glad you mentioned your Ma's name, for I've respect for it. But skipping to the tops in a full-reef gale is a different thing from climbing a pine tree to scout Injuns."

"I've climbed some tall ones, sir, and in wicked weather."

"I've a venture toward, but it scares me, e'en though she's only one bottom to risk, and me safe on shore. It's around the Horn and to the nor'west and then clean across the Pacific. I've no notion when she'll be home, if ever."

"That would suit me fine, sir."

"It would, would it? It would have suited me once myself, but now I'm too fond of my easy chair and my hot punch. Do you know I'm having trouble signing good hands?"

"No, sir, I didn't know it, but there'll be none about signing me."

"Well, then, I'll take you, and if you put your capital in small bulk—say Medford rum—I'll furnish it to you wholesale and stow it at cost in ratio to the invoice."

"I'd thank you kindly."

"I like the way you dressed your fur, no fat, and no rot. You'll ride your own nag, of course."

"Yes, sir."

"Well, I won't ride mine, for I like my neck, but there's a young man in Salem new home from Harvard who fancies himself a gentleman rider—the son of my chief competitor—and he'll jockey for me."

"Is he much lighter than me? I'd race him the same—"

"He's full your weight and tops it, but I warn you, if the report's true, he's a good hand."

"I thank you for the intelligence."

"You're welcome, and give him a good run. If you do, and lose anyhow, I'll take your plugs at your price and sign you on the 'Hattie' though with a different deal as to your goods."

He gave me till sundown to pick and report the course, named ten o'clock of the second day for the race, and went into his counting-house smiling. I rode at once behind the town, looking for the roughest country I could find. To my great joy, there were some heavy thickets, with plenty of thorn and berry vine, a steep-banked brook or two, rocks, high rail fences, and cut-over wood lots. I chose a stretch of about two miles, between one farmer's gate and another, with no kind of a trail between them, and to go by the road would be at least four miles. This I reconnoitered on foot, so not to leave a trail my rival might follow when he scouted the course tomorrow. Not always taking the shortest cut, I picked the ground over which Minx could make the best over-all time.

You would think that Salem, with its beak nose in account books, would pay no mind to a private horse race. Instead the meets between gentlemen had been its chief diversion lately, and by sundown next day everyone knew of the match. Indeed it captured more interest than most, being a rough-and-ready steeplechase between a mountain horse and a thoroughbred, and a mountain man and the son of a merchant prince. Besides that, many remembered my father kindly, and meant kindly toward his son. Report had it that backers of Mr. Derby's horse had no trouble placing bets, and quite a few people partisaned me with no money at stake. Perhaps they saw me as the underdog in this contest. There is something about Americans, and the English before us, to make them like to see the low man win. Mainly though, being common folk, they did not care as much about my winning as my opponent's losing. Nor was this a grudge against Mr. Derby, whom everyone seemed to like. Rather it was the hope I would humble his gentleman rider, Dick Featherstone. The latter, son of Elisha Featherstone, a rich, crew-starving, bargain-driving skinflint, apparently gave himself airs.

Among those who laid on Dick was my Uncle Samuel! So rumor told, and I did not doubt it, as he worked for Elisha Featherstone. But I was glad;—it was the spur I needed to ride like a hussar! If I won, I wanted to see his face.

It happened that the end of the course was nearer town than the beginning. When I ambled by on my way to the starting post, at least forty men were standing about on the high ground, some of them very considerable to judge from their dress, and some with long marine spyglasses in their hands. A few called encouragement or good-natured jests; all took a good look at Minx. Some shook their heads, for she was not of ancient lineage, although no scrub. In that she was like my mother, I thought, seeing no impropriety in the comparison.

Mr. Derby was there with a spyglass and a big gold watch. "I've set the piece with the starter's, on the second," he explained to me, when he had waved me down. "You see, I've bet on the time, as well as on my horse."

"Are you betting on the fast side or the slow?" I asked.

"Fast. A six minute run, I put it, and my 'ponent six minutes three seconds."

"I'll try to win that bet for you, sir, to soothe you for losing the other."

"Leastways the harder you crowd my nag, the better I'll like it."

But Mr. Derby had doubtless scouted the course, and would never have picked six minutes unless Wilkes, the stallion he had pitted against Minx, was a wonderful beast. When I came to the starting gate and saw him, that guess became a surety. He was two hands taller than my mare, powerful, with a proud head and fierce eye and doubtless a fighting heart. Wilkes was a good name for him, I thought, doubtless after John Wilkes, our fieriest friend in Parliament in our quarrel with King George; and maybe the big bay stud resembled the Lord Mayor in another way. He took a long sniff at Minx to make sure she did not want another rider besides me, and if she had, I would have been in a fix.

My mare would have trailed him woefully on level, open ground, and her only advantage would be her schooling on rough ground. Even so it was so slight that my best hope of winning hung on his rider—Dick Featherstone's seat, hand, heart, and judgment. The first two of these were patently excellent. He looked nearly a stone heavier than I—the latter only fair to me, since Wilkes was so much taller and more powerful—and all rugged muscle and good bone; he appeared lithe and had good balance. He was devilish handsome, I thought, but in no way to weaken him. His skin was oddly pallid in contrast with his chestnut hair, and that was not nervousness, only nature. He had what Pa used to call a marksman's eye, close lidded, intent, and very bright. I would know more about his heart at the end of the race, but already suspected it was strong, and his judgment good unless he lost his temper—no doubt high.

"How do you do, sir?" I addressed my opponent politely. "It's a fine day for a race."

He looked at me for some seconds before he answered. I think what he meant to convey was that he was used to riding with gentlemen, and although he would oblige Mr. Derby by beating me, he wanted no familiarity out of me. He wore a red coat, such as English fox hunters boast, not uncommon in Virginia according to report, but the first I had ever seen. Neither this nor his twill breeches would rattle thorns.

"It's a fine day," he said. "I hope it will be a fair race."

The starter had us stand abreast before the open gate, between the posts of which stretched a white string. The stallion cavorted and pranced, not taught to stand statue-still lest he betray his master's ambush in Indian country, but Dick Featherstone mastered him well. Minx stood with her ears cocked forward, her body poised for flight, for she knew by my tight rein we were ready to go.

"One—two—three—go!" the starter cried.

Minx bounded through the open gate. We had gained twice her length before Wilkes got his hooves under him to run. The first furlong of our course was open, level ground, and before we were half across it the stallion drew abreast. His tail was two yards in our van when he breasted the thickets.

We did not try to overtake him here. Instead we turned uphill, slower going now, but faster later. As the brush thickened on the slope, it thinned on the ridge, and when we came out in a pasture we were again two lengths ahead. This distance he closed before we reached the rail fence, which we sailed over side by side.

And this was the pattern of the race for three-fourths of the course. On open ground he made a monkey of me, but I returned the compliment across rough country. Minx knew how to wiggle through briar and bush, weave through thick scrub, and wind up steep hillsides. Knowing her abilities well, and having scouted the course as none but a hunter could—as I never could have, save from Pierre's hard school—I knew just where to guide her. Especially she shone on steep declines, for she was sure-footed as an Adirondack stag, and I could take her down full-tilt without thought of my neck.

We were staying even with the stallion, and his rider was disagreeably surprised. We were crowding him hard, as Mr. Derby bade us, and Dick Featherstone was surely losing his temper and might yet lose the race. His face appeared paler than before, livid almost, his jaw muscles tense. Maybe the thorns we had crashed through had not helped his humor. I had minded them not at all, in my tough buckskin, and Minx very little in her seasoned hide, but they had played hob with Dick's fine riding suit. From his not knowing how to ward them, they had scratched his face severely. Even so, he was nearer to winning at this moment than at any in the race. While not liking to face the fact, still I must not flinch from it, or my cake was dough.

The last part of the course was generally more open than the first part. After a boggy place, which I intended to skirt, we would come into a road flanked on each side with a thicket-grown fence leading straight to the finish line. Unless we had a long lead when we hit the

26

track he would surely overtake us and reach the gate before us.

We led him through the last wood lot and he was gaining fast as we took down the bank of a brook. It was a steeply cut bank with a boulder-filled bed six or more feet below, and as he came level with us, he saw his chance to put me out of the race. Possibly he had schemed it beforehand, if the contest proved close. More likely it washed into his head on a wave of fury.

He deliberately swerved against us, to knock us over the bank. We were saved only because I had guessed the move at the very start, and checked Minx enough to miss the brunt of the blow. One thing she could do in a hurry was pull up, almost hurling me over her head, a trick all good mountain horses know. Even so, for a second or two we hung on the very brink—luckily no deep-bedded stone gave way— before we swung behind the stud on solid ground.

Dick could have won the race without trying to break Minx's leg and like as not my neck. I had been close to despair a moment ago, for I had counted on a long lead at this place, to be cut but not quite lost at the finish line. Now, because he had fouled me, he might yet lose this race.

All thought of losing passed out of my head. Out for bear, as we say in the mountains, I was thinking cold and fast how to win. I pushed Minx through a boulder-strewn swail I had intended to dodge—a fine place for a fall—and the short cut fetched us a length ahead of Wilkes as we hit the brink of the bog. Then instead of skirting it as I had firmly decided on, I plunged straight across.

Everything hung on his following me. If he kept cool, perceived that the long way round was the shortest home, I was done. If he plunged in behind me, my much lighter animal could surely outdistance him in the mucky ground and give me a fighting chance on the homestretch. If Minx and I floundered, which was well within my reckoning, we would at least have high-class company.

As I had hoped, Dick could not stand the sight of the long loop. Fury at my passing him and fear I would beat him yet caused him to give the horse its head and lose his own. The stallion's instinct was to follow the leader until he could take the lead, and Dick did not turn him.

Across the swamp we lighted out, and thank heaven I was ahead, because Minx's hooves threw mud worse than a bogged bear. Plenty landed on Dick until he was out of range behind us. The big stud could not begin to keep up with my trim mare in going like this, and we were a good three spans ahead when we gained the bank.

27

We tore down the road toward the finish line. But we had not won yet against that superb beast and his furious rider, and now the track was open, hard, and flat. Shouts rose, but did not drown out the nearing thunder of great hooves.

I laid whip to Minx, no common thing. Tired as she was from plunging through the bog, she laid her feet faster and lighter. She opened wider, bless her stout heart, as when we had raced for revenge. But Wilkes's great head came into view from the side of my eyes. I could see the fit of his neck on his powerful shoulders and in a second or two more he would be abreast of us, with some fifty yards to go.

Then I sucked in my breath and let go in an Indian war whoop. It was one of the most prized accomplishments of my boyhood, and once I had fooled Pierre with it, proof of its fine ring. Truly it is a most harrowing sound even to people who don't know what it means. Neither the stout stallion nor his enraged rider had ever heard it before.

If Minx had been inclined to lag, the war cry drove her on. But Wilkes shied from the blast in his ear and swerved toward the fence. Startled half out of his wits, Dick was a second late in jerking the hellion's rein. We broke the string across the gate with half our length to spare.

2.

Amid the shouting a weazened little man I had never seen before made his piping voice heard. It pricked my ear like a pin.

"I cry foul," he squeaked. "You heard that mountain rascal scare Mr. Derby's horse."

The crowd instantly quieted, for many bets hung poised over various pockets. Every one looked at Mr. Derby.

"On my part," he said firmly, "I've no complaint. But others are interested parties, and I'll leave it to an impartial judge. Jason Starbuck, do you agree to that?"

"Yes, sir, I do."

"Do you, Richard Featherstone?"

My mud-plastered rival wiped his face with a fine, cambric handkerchief. "Why, for my part, I agree with you, and admit to a fair beating," he replied—a stronger, steadier man than was healthy for me, if we were to run any more races. "But in respect to the wagers, I refer the matter to an impartial judge."

"Will Mr. Baker suit all concerned?"

Since all eyes turned on Mr. Baker I had no trouble identifying him. He stood out of the crowd on account of his dress—somewhat gayer and livelier than the most without being in the least macaroni —and his homely, boyish face. A hearty, round-bellied man, he was plainly a ready sportsman. In his hand was a short double-barreled spyglass to look through with both eyes. I had never seen its like, and no fault of my being a yokel, for it was unique in the town and likely in the country. He had got it at Leyden University; and instead of a new invention it was a very old one, although fallen into disuse. It had a device for fitting both barrels to the owner's eyes.

Several men acclaimed the nomination, and any opposing it lacked the nerve to say so.

"I'll gladly give my opinion," Mr. Baker told us briskly. "True, we've never heard Indian war whoops in our races hereabouts, but our grandpas did. I reckon when they used to race for their lives, the hollering added greatly to their speed, and speed is what we're after."

Most of the men laughed. At least two did not, the piping-voiced fellow who had first protested, and another man in the same group whom I had tried to ignore. He was Samuel Starbuck, my uncle. Cunning as he held himself, he was not nearly as sharp as Dick Featherstone, who had chuckled winningly at Mr. Baker's quip.

"That's begging the question," the little man piped. "Starbuck deliberately frightened the other horse."

"We don't know 'twas deliberate," Mr. Baker answered. "Maybe he was trying to get a little more speed out of his mare. There's no rule against a rider encouraging his mount, provided he don't use profane or indecent language."

"Judge, you're all right," a sailor shouted.

"And again, any rider is apt to get excited," Mr. Baker went on. "For instance, his opponent, in trying to gain on the brook bank yonder, pressed Minx somewhat close to the edge. I saw it through my glass, and was afeared she'd have a bad fall."

This was received in complete silence, not even a scuffle of feet breaking in.

"It was a hard-run race," said Mr. Baker. "We're all obliged to Mr. Derby, Mr. Starbuck, and Mr. Featherstone. I proclaim Minx the winner."

The crowd cheered, and some hearty claps were given my back. My uncle avoided speaking to me, and Dick Featherstone gave me only a patronizing wave of his hand. But my kinsman was lost to me anyway, and it was impossible for Dick and me to be friends.

What worried me was the stand Mr. Derby would take. In spite of his generosity before the crowd, I feared bitterly that he would turn against me too.

When he finished talking to his friends he rode over to me. "It wasn't a square deal, young fellow," he said.

Wanting mightily his good opinion, I would as lief had lost the race. "I'm sorry you think that, sir."

He gave me a startled glance. "Why, blow me down, do you think I meant your frightening my nag, when the rider I'd put up tried to break your leg?"

"Thank you, kindly." I couldn't say more, out of my tight throat.

"I saw it, the same as Baker, and we spoke of it together, and he'd given you the palm, if Wilkes had come in first, with all bets off. When you beat him in after all, it did our hearts good."

"I wish I could have won you your bet on the time, but I reckon I didn't."

"No, 'twas six minutes and eleven seconds. But I hedged it with Mr. Perkins, as you were coming up to the bog. I never thought quicker in my life! Mind you, Dick would have come in six flat or better, if he'd gone around, and I had no assurance, only a sending, that you'd take to the mud and he hop in behind you. But I believed you'd see 'twas your only chance, and once I played the same trick, trying to beat Captain Cabot's brig into Boston. His was the faster vessel, but I was rigged for a sharper tack, and he all but piled her up on East Point." Mr. Derby's face shone in his joy at the recital.

"Then what did you mean, sir, that the deal wasn't fair?"

"Why, our bet. If you lost the race, you'd lose your horses, and if you won, I'd only buy 'em at a fair price, and give you a berth on the 'Hattie' that's going begging."

"You were going to let me put my capital in the venture."

"You may wish you hadn't before we're done. How much have you, if 'tis a fair question, when I've paid you for the nags?"

"Over four hundred dollars."

"You're entitled to the worth of the horses on top of that—my equal pawn in the race. If it had been horse against horse, I'd have lost a nag I'd paid two hundred for. You want to venture the full amount?"

"Yes, sir."

"That will be 4 per cent of my manifest. Insurance and freight to China and back would come to half your goods, but you pay the insurance and I'll haul 'em free. That means instead of eight barrels, I'll give you six, and all they make you will be in pocket."

30

"That's mighty neighborly, Mr. Derby." I was too flustered to pick a more fitting word than the one of such deep meaning on the frontier.

"Six barrels and insurance will cost you four hundred and two dollars, which may leave you enough for your kit and the likes of that. But the 'Hattie' sails from Boston five days hence, and you've no time to loiter."

Then I asked one more kindness of Mr. Derby: to deliver to the customhouse a letter I would write to Cap'n Dan'l Todkill, my only living kinsman to my knowledge save some married daughters of Samuel Starbuck living around Cape Cod. At Mr. Derby's request, the custom officer might find a means of dispatching it to my Uncle Dan'l's ship, the "Charity."

"I'll do better than that," Mr. Derby told me. "I'll dispatch it to our factor in Havana. Why, I'm glad to for both your sakes, for I've always held a sneaking admiration for Dan'l Todkill, and his sister was the prettiest girl in this neck of the woods."

"I thank you kindly."

"But I wouldn't want you taking up with him, Jason. He's not as bad as he's painted, but outside the law, and now we're at peace with Spain, maybe due for a swing."

Although Mr. Derby offered me transport in his sloop, he advised me to ride Minx to Boston, to make one spell of seasickness do me, instead of two. This suited me well, although for a better reason. Truly it was hard to part with my mare, all I had left now out of the old days, the nearest thing to any folks, and it would be pleasant to ride her one more time. Yet I would have gone by boat, to glean some hints on sailing, had not Mr. Derby mentioned that she would be crowded. In the upshot he himself and some other merchants with ventures on the voyage decided to go dry, there being a strong east wind despite the warm, sunny weather. So I traveled to the metropolis in their company, although riding behind with the grooms.

It was a city of twenty thousand head, with many fine sights. Only two were larger in our nation, New York with forty thousand, and Philadelphia crowding close with thirty-five. The finest sight was the "Hattie," of a hundred and fifty tons with a copper bottom. In that bottom lay six barrels of rum, put aboard from Mr. Derby's warehouse, freight and insurance paid, and belonging to me.

Dressed like a sailor now, I was paid the same respect as the other green hands, which was none worth noting. Although Mr. Derby had of course informed Captain Scott of my venture, and pointed me out to him while inspecting the ship, the stern-looking skipper did not speak to me. Indeed he looked a little grimmer than before. It seemed likely that while the officers and supercargo often stowed trading goods of their own, it was a somewhat novel thing for a man 'fore the mast. Still this was America, not Europe—it was every man's right to try to get ahead—and the sailors told me that Captain Scott was as fair and fine a master as sailed the seas. Since I was resolved to become an able seaman, doing my full stint, he would not likely long begrudge me my enterprise.

3.

There are some experiences so strange and new that we can hardly imagine ourselves undergoing them. On looking back on them, we can hardly believe that their undergoers were our common selves. So it was with me beforehand of the voyage, and with it behind me. We were not the first Yankee ship to sail to Cathay, but about the twelfth as far as we could tell; yet truly it was a magnificent adventure. Only two of our company had ever seen these waters—a couple of deckhands who had sailed with Captain Gay on the "Columbia"—and they appeared to have no end.

We did not amount to one fly on the dome of St. Paul's. A little mouse on a barren mountainside made more of a stir than we. You would think that being out on all that sea, blown upon by infinite wind, a tiny moving speck under all that sky, would have driven us daft. Instead we ate our rations, stood our watches, and took things as they came. If we were becalmed, after a while the sick sails lifted. When we were storm beaten and mightily worried about drowning, later on the wind changed and we resumed our course. We froze or baked and complained no end, meanwhile remaining the same ordinary fellows, Caleb and Tom and Jason, save for a little more strength or weakness as the case might be. Some of us talked of signing on slavers to the Guinea Coast, where were wonderful sights to see and adventures to pursue.

We rounded the Horn, an easy thing to say. We did not meet the "Flying Dutchman," but would not have been greatly amazed to do so—and after nine days would have hardly mentioned her at mess. We thought we would never get warm again, but after nine days' sailing up the coast of South America we took off our sheepskin coats and a fortnight later our shirts. Then we could not fancy ourselves cooling off, but the moon waxed and waned, the wind boxed the

32

compass, and one day we found ourselves off Monterey, where dons lived royally and rode forth to great ranchos.

"That'll all be Unitey States some day," wild-eyed Caleb Beacher told us.

We laughed at him, although I not as loud as the rest.

"Ye may laugh, but mark my words. The flag follers the ensigns of little ships like our'n. Spain's getting tired, and France and England al'ays fighting. It's one land with us, and we'll people it."

We sailed on, and one day Caleb pointed to a great inlet that he said was the mouth of a river bigger than the Hudson, perhaps as big as the St. Lawrence, which Captain Gay had named Columbia, after his ship. We sailed on, and entered Juan de Fuca Strait, behind a vast island where the sea lay still as a meadow pond, and imaged every spruce tree needle on the mountainside. Soon we anchored off an Indian village, but its people were not much like our painted devils, save for their dusky skins, flat eyes, and coarse, black hair. They wore knee-length shirts of seal or deerskin over baggy pantaloons. Before their villages stood tree-high posts, carved to represent the heads of animals, birds, and demons.

Here our supercargo, Mr. Perkins, called me into his cabin, and made me a proposal suggested by our captain. My rum, invoiced at three hundred dollars, was a fraction over 3 per cent of our total cargo. If agreeable to me, he would use it as he saw fit, trading it for pelts, or for mellowing the Indians beforehand, for it happened that our manifest was somewhat short on liquors, our main stock being ironmongery, cloth, and beads. Then when we weighed anchor, I should have 3 per cent of our haul.

I was more than agreeable to so fair a deal. After we had held what the redskins called a "potlatch" [a kind of feast, at which we gave them trifling gifts and a taste of watered rum to start them craving it] trading was brisk. My mates were somewhat appalled by these Indians' manners. I thought them admirable, compared to the Mohawks'.

Their generosity with their wives and daughters bore out Caleb's report. Truly it was not generosity as much as low valuation put upon the squaws by their menfolk, an ignoble thing—taking one nail if they could not get two, or giving them away to promote trade. Although I had intended to partake with the others—craving the sight of a woman during the long sail, and now at the age where craving turned most intense—yet I did not. It was not moral scruple that restrained me, but rather the look and fishy smell of the girls.

33

In the season we took pelts of various kinds, fifteen hundred of them a new kind to me and truly the most beautiful fur I had ever seen. Until now I could scarcely believe the tale of their selling for thirty, sometimes forty dollars apiece in China, but could better understand it now, since they made prime beaver look like cowhide. These were sea otters, much larger than the land variety, almost black with richness and depth and sheen beyond description. We got beaver too, and sables with orange-colored throats, and seals speared far offshore.

Weighing anchor then, we took off west by south toward Canton. Our next stop was at one of the Sandwich Isles, beginning to be called Hawaii, as different a region from Oregon as Cuba from Massachusetts. Here we bartered for sandalwood, mother-of-pearl and sharkskin. But here the sailors need not buy what they had bought meanly in the Nor'west, on account of it being given away in joy by the maids themselves. Moreover, to my mind there was no comparison between the two. These damsels seemed carved out of sweet-smelling sandalwood, and breathed to life by an amorous god.

After meeting a few, and being feasted and made over, I picked me the prettiest of the batch. Nor was it my lone opinion that she stood out even in that delicate bouquet. Being the youngest and greenest man aboard, I rose considerably in my mates' estimation, and perhaps somewhat in my own. Why she favored me, I did not know, unless it was for my entering into the frolicking as joyfully and almost as innocently as herself. Unlike some of our company unto their girls, I did not treat her like a harbor slut because she was, as they might put it, "of easy virtue." Perhaps because Pierre had implanted the idea in me, now strengthened by my reading, I did not condemn foreign customs because they were different from ours, and thought to respect them while visiting the country. My little sweetheart was not of easy virtue in Hawaii, but the daughter of a chief and an ardent worshiper of her god.

She cried when, after ten days, we must weigh. I went mooning about a good month thereafter, wishing I were back under the palms. Her name was Taveoa, and I would remember her gratefully and tenderly all my days.

Meanwhile my education was progressing along other lines. For instance, about this time I discovered myself a sailor. From Florida south'ard I could sing a chantey, skip to the tops, and heave at the capstan, but my zeal to prove it to my fellows was proof enough of a landlubber. After rounding the Horn they counted me one, but by then I was well enough versed in the craft to perceive my ignorance, always the beginning of wisdom. From Hawaii on, there was no longer any doubt. I was an able seaman by the standards set for men 'fore the mast. Old tars could still teach me plenty, but when Mate Milledge bawled an order I need no longer ask someone how to go about its obedience. More often than not I knew what the order would be before he opened his mouth.

This was because of using my head as well as my hands, a use greatly different from the general. I do not know why any application of mind is so tedious and trying to multitudes of men that they quickly let it slide. Perhaps disliking responsibility is partly the cause, letting their officers do the worrying, trusting all will go well. Some of my mates had wonderful manual skill, others a surprising knowledge of the world and lots of common sense, yet never bothered with the science of seamanship, only blindly obeyed orders. Seeing I did not abuse it, Mate Milledge began to put more confidence in me, and Captain Scott had me take the helm oftener than my turn, sometimes when it was most tricky business. Without my asking, he often gave me reasons for his decisions, taught me how to read a chart, and not only the use but the science of the sextant.

As to general education, my main schoolmaster had been old Pierre. In our long rides and lonely bivouacs he had imparted to me a good store of his lore. From pointing out the stars to find my way at night, it was a small step to telling me about Mars, and from thence Ares, and Venus who before Rome had been Aphrodite, and Jupiter who was Zeus. To me the Pleiades became not a cluster of misty stars but the lovely daughters of Atlas. Since the stories caught my fancy, he had spun them by the hour. So when Hamlet's actors spoke of Hecuba, she was as real and familiar to me as Molly Pitcher, my father's heroine. He had tried to orient me in space, by teaching me astronomy and geography, and in time by reciting history, from the days of the Pharaohs through Greece and Rome clean to the fall of Quebec. While at best it was only a smattering of learning, I was well grounded for my age, and certainly better posted than my mates in the fo'c'sle.

I had bought a bag of secondhand books to take aboard, and when Mr. Perkins, our supercargo, discovered that I had them, he borrowed them off me and lent me his. Since six hours of sleep did me well, I had plenty of time to devour them. Starved for good talk, he took to admitting me into his cabin, where we discussed every kind of matter regardless of our ignorance of the same. As he was only twenty-two,

I dared to argue hotly for my beliefs, and thus we became not only each other's tutor, but fast friends as well.

Canton was an eye opener to us both. Here we sold our fifteen hundred sea otter skins for an average of twenty-five dollars apiece, our whole catch for forty-five thousand, of which my share was thirteen hundred and fifty dollars. This sum I straightway put in tea and silk, as Mr. Perkins advised me.

Since we had other trade goods, we did not sail back the way we had come. Instead we drove southward through the Straits of Malacca into the Indian Sea. Off Formosa we had been chased by pirates, our trim "Hattie" giving them the slip, and now we fought a pitched battle with Malay dhows. It looked black for a time, for the yellow sails spread everywhere, but it was wonderful how our boys stood to our guns, and never loosed a ball until trained on the foe. We sank one craft, drowning every wretch aboard, and drove two others sorely wounded into port, before the rest decided we were too hot to handle. Maybe the turbaned cutthroats had never before seen the Stars and Stripes. Not many of our ships had passed that way, and likely they had never heard of our new nation. They would think twice, we reckoned, before they came out again to sack a Yankee hooker.

But one of our boys lay dead on the deck from a musket ball through the head. Another might lose his arm from a fragment of canister, and the third had been hit by a falling spar. This last was Caleb Beacher, one of our two Magellans. He was a wild-eyed man. I wondered if he had ever visioned his own end. Only about thirty, yet when he dropped overside with Joshua Brown I reckoned that he had lived three times as much as my Uncle Samuel Starbuck, and had been ten times as enviable.

Times passed, tides rose and fell as often our hearts, and on March 18, 1797, we sighted Puritan Heights. We had been gone more than a year and a half. I had passed my nineteenth birthday in Canton and would be twenty in midsummer, and the "Hattie" had logged off something over thirty-five thousand miles.

Our cargo of silk, tea, chinaware, and other eastern treasures sold for sixty-two thousand dollars, six times the worth of our invoice. Mr. Perkins and I had been skinned in Madras on a private venture, and my share was not a clean 3 per cent; yet when I took stage for Salem, in my pocket was a draft on Mr. Derby for fourteen hundred and seventy dollars, besides something like a hundred dollars pay. In my head was no great knowledge yet of the wide world, but a lively regard for its wonders, and no great reluctance to see more of it, if fortune so decreed. Though in my heart there was not near enough of something bitterly needed, deeply craved.

It felt hollow yet. When I had finished my business with Mr. Derby and had nowhere to go but a bleak room in a tavern, it would not heed my stern injunction not to ache. It should be ashamed, I thought, since God had brought me safe home with such good gain, but it seemed to know no better.

CHAPTER THREE

Love of a Maid

I.

M r. Derby had greeted me jovially. In spite of his worry and flurry, he gave me ten minutes or more of his time and a tot of rum. Moreover, he told me that since he was reorganizing his company—building more ships and opening offices in foreign cities—I could invest my gains in stock at a hundred dollars a share. This I did, receiving a handsomely enscribed paper to the amount of ten shares, reserving only my first capital and some spending money.

Also he informed me that there had been no reply to my letter to my uncle, Captain Daniel Todkill. I wrote another, more venturesome than the first, proposing that he sign me on as mate or supercargo, and undertake a trading voyage to the South Seas. I still shied at the idea of sharing his raids on Spanish commerce in the Caribbean Sea. For all my want of kinfolk, and my loneliness of heart in this port of strangers, still I had no hankering to risk my neck, while yet so young and the world wide before me.

Something else was working in me that I could not haul up and look at. It was a kind of restlessness that the sea would not serve, and had to do with Solomon's fourth and greatest wonder—the way of a man with a maid. I felt unrounded and incomplete, save in the society of young females. Tavern sluts mostly—the only kind handy to sailors—yet they were pretty and hearty, and a smooth-skinned arm about my neck was enough to thrill me.

While waiting, I thought to put my remaining capital into a boat for short coastwise hauls. The notion had been eased into my head by Andy Oats, another Salemite who had shipped with me on the "Hattie." A lean, lank man in his middle thirties, salt in the marrow of his bones, Andy had said good money could be made from such a craft, costing about six hundred dollars. He would put in two hundred. As it turned out, such a craft as he planned, for a three- or four-man crew, would cost nearer eight hundred for materials alone, and the sum he could contribute reduced with every counting until presently it was nil. The people who owed him would not pay him, he complained, and those he owed, especially his tavern-keeper who sold grog, were unreasonably prompt at collecting.

Still I could not bear to abandon the project altogether, nor yet sell some of my stock in Mr. Derby's company, which had taken a sharp drop. Andy was an excellent shipwright as well as seaman. Trimming our sails, we built a cross between a large knockabout, with a center-board, and a small sloop. She berthed three people in comfort—two in the deckhouse and one below—and stowed more cargo than the look of her revealed. Two men could sail her anywhere. Indeed she was so handy rigged, and answered her helm so lively, that by hoisting only her mains'l I could take her out alone, nose her into almost any kind of a wind, and skip her home. It took some lively stepping in a sudden blow, but I found no fault with that.

However, she proved much too small for the trade we had intended, and the best we could do was turn her into a small, efficient fishing smack and a pleasure boat for Salem people wanting a day's sail, a picnic in some pretty cove, or an afternoon's angling. While all we could make with her was a modest living, I was mighty glad to have her to fall back on, considering the present state of my other venture.

Mr. Derby's company was almost, but not quite, on the rocks. He was having more disasters than befell Antonio after he had pledged his bosom to Shylock. A Danish privateer caught one of his ships richly laden for Kronstadt, the French captured another, a third from India burned to the waterline almost in sight of Beacon Hill, and Barbary pirates looted a fourth, in spite of the tribute our President paid their Bey to pass our shipping unharmed. A Nor'west venture failed to profit because the fickle Indians wanted red cloth, instead of blue. Part of these losses had been covered by insurance, but the rates were high and getting higher, and trade languished everywhere as France and England fought each other and both raised hob with us. By the end of the year 1797, my stock would not bring fifty dollars a share. According to the wiseacres, by next spring it would not bring ten.

I could only hope that for Mr. Derby, as for Antonio, things would take a turn:

Unseal this letter soon;
There you shall find three of your argosies

39

Are richly come to harbor suddenly:
You shall not know by what strange accident,
I chanced on this letter.

And that was by a poet's pen, scratching out a happy ending, and more feebly than usual. The weather, the pirates, William Pitt, and Bonaparte might not be so kind.

For me, things took a momentous turn. Building the boat, sailing her with Andy or alone, letting him operate her while I worked a few months in Mr. Derby's countinghouse—until inkpots, pens, papers, ledgers, and indoors convinced me of what I ought to have known beforehand, that I was not cut out for a clerk—passed the time barrenly until June, 1798, with me crowding twenty-one. In the beginning of the month Mr. Derby informed me that my second letter to my Uncle Dan'l had indeed been delivered by one of his captains, and that an answer would be forthcoming in a few days or weeks. Moreover, it was rumored that his ship had been seen off Savannah, far from her usual haunts, presenting the exciting prospect of her being bound for Salem, to take me aboard.

"I hope the old rascal don't take it into his head to come on shore," Mr. Derby told me. "Those rebel dons love him, from Santiago to Caracas, but some of our merchants, consigning goods in Spanish bottoms, don't."

Still I would not miss a chance to board his ship and try my luck on persuading him to a trading venture. This was what I was living for, these early June days—the new moon to bring me wondrous luck before it waned away—my gaze turned seaward. I did not know that events could shape to push Cap'n Dan'l Todkill and his saucy jade clean out of my head.

They began with a fitting casualness—a warm, fine, airy morning, I puttering about my boat at Derby's Wharf, and three people approaching me along the quay. Then I recognized one of the three as Dick Featherstone. I could wish to be as easy of mind as before, but could not fetch it. In no way liking to pay Dick this large respect, I was curiously unable to help myself.

While I had been rounding the Horn he had been off to Harvard. Since my return, I had passed him often on the streets without his favoring me with a sign of recognition. While my stock in Mr. Derby's company had been taking a dive, grim, bespectacled Elisha Featherstone had prospered mightily, every hull and cargo turning to gold. Dick shone at the balls and apple-bobs—not caring to hear about these jollities, somehow I always did—and was patently the richest and fastest-rising young man hereabouts. Being good democrats, my water front intimates did not mean to speak of him in a different voice than when they spoke of me, but invariably did so. I doubted if he had forgotten my victory over him three years ago; I had only ceased to matter to him, he had gone so far since then. He mattered to me, though. After thinking of him awhile, I would often burst out to myself, "God damn him."

Sharply aware of him—resolved not even to glance his way unless he spoke to me—I barely noticed his two companions. One was a tall girl with very bright hair, a stranger to me, and the other a Negress whom I took for her servant. Dick was dressed in twill breeches, gaiters, a fine linen shirt, and a short buff coat of a style new to me.

"Aren't you James Starbuck?" he asked, pleasantly enough.

"No, sir."

"Maybe I've mistaken the name, but surely you're the fellow who beat me to Wilkins' pasture. I'm Dick Featherstone."

"I remember you. I'm Jason Starbuck."

"We hear you've a boat for hire, and I take it she's the one."

He pointed to my pretty girl, "Prudence Todkill," named for my mother when yet a maid. I thought to have selected it only in love and honor of her memory. Maybe it was partly in hate of stiff-necked Salem's disdain of her, a fisherman's daughter, sister of wild Dan'l. Still I had not surveyed Dick's pretty girl, although no doubt seeing her out of the side of my eye.

"Yes, sir."

"I'd like to hire her for the day, while you take a holiday on shore. The handy way she's rigged, the young lady and I can sail her."

"I never let her go out without my hands or Mr. Oats's on her helm." Andy was, theoretically, my first mate, although without a crew. I spoke of him as "Mister" when talking to Dick, although never dreaming of such a thing in speech with our tavern mates.

"Do you think I'd sink her? If I did, I reckon Featherstone Tea Company could pay the freight. My own knockabout's in the yard, getting a copper bottom."

"I still couldn't let her go."

His pallid countenance paled a little more. He had very light eyes with rather close-drawn lids and his chestnut hair made a striking contrast. I had forgotten about his marksman's gaze.

"Well, in that case—" His easy, quite winning manner did not deceive me. It was just the tone he would use to say that in that case he would look elsewhere—and put me in my place.

Plainly the tall girl standing a little to one side was alert to it too, for she spoke quickly in a warm, deep, somewhat childish tone.

"Why, Dick, don't be a zany. You promised to take me fishing, and we'll make a better catch if you don't have to mind the boat."

"I think so too," I said.

"You've bait and tackle, I reckon?" Dick asked.

"A-plenty."

"I'll look at the boat, and if she's staunch, we'll charter her."

While he looked at the boat, I looked at his companion. Her appearance did not surprise me in the least; during the conversation she had been taking shape in my mind. Perhaps there are as many levels of the mind as of the deep sea. On the surface the waves roll, the sun shines, and the rains fall, and the stars cast a dim and quickly fading glimmer. Here silver fishes leap and feed. Deeper the daylight pales, and bigger, blacker fishes roam, and sharks gaze upward, seeking prey. On the bottom, in the cold and interminable darkness, dwell misshapen monsters rarely if ever seen by the eyes of man. Yet it is all one element. I do not doubt that the surface storms and calms affect the lives of the undersea serpents, and the threshing of their tails in rage may send up eddies that make the little surface feeders scurry and leap.

I had been excited about her without knowing it. Dick did not know it either, yet she had increased the tension between him and me. It seemed incredible that she could be living in Salem without my seeing her before. She might be a visitor from Boston, I thought, or perhaps newly returned here after a long absence.

Her coloring was very rich, particularly in the marine light, the deep-blue bay rippling in the breeze, and the serene blue sky. She had eyes the color of the deep sea and hair very like the sun, when filmy clouds cut its blaze. Her skin was rather darker than you would think from this, somewhat like the ancient walrus ivory I had seen worked by Indians in the Nor'west. Her face in repose had for me a dimly sad look, somehow touching; and that was mighty strange, considering the little lines of humor at the corners of her eyes and her large, warm-looking mouth given to beaming, childish smiles. Maybe humor is bound around with quiet, thoughtful sadness. Maybe beauty itself is an alien here from some star.

There was a great deal to her. I would have goggled at her at a great ball in Brussels or Madrid, if fate would ever put me in such a spot, and wondered about her inward being. I would not have been surprised to learn that she was a great personage, or more likely a dancing master's daughter who had become the child mistress of an old king. In the codfish-smelling town of Salem she was almost unbelievable. Maybe the other Salemites were not amazed at her—at most tried to sniff at her because she smelled differently from our healthy heifers and prime pullets. I rather hoped that they did disparage her, although my motive here remained obscure. But I had sailed round the world with singularly eager eyes, had touched Canton and the Spice Isles and was not deceived. Nor was Dick Featherstone, a momentous fact. I might have known he would not be; every attempt of mine to underrate him had failed.

In a sudden, intense aliveness I saw her liven up the whole scene. The sky was seen to deepen in color near the horizon. The wet of the falling tide on some old pilings told of the twice-daily rise and fall of the world-wide sea. To these piles clung barnacles, the main of them venturing so far and no farther above low water. But a few bold fellows trusted to the highest tides to bring them food and drink, and seemed half inclined to escape from their element and dwell in the open air.

I did not think of these things, yet they were there. I was thinking, apart from reverie about the girl, that Dick would probably express doubt of the seaworthiness of my boat, and decline to take his sweetheart out on her. She would be disappointed—being quite eager to go—but he would override her protests, I thought. Then her very anger at his firmness would make her prize him more. Instead he appeared to weaken. It was an appearance only, I could be sure.

"She looks like a stout little craft," he said. "Roxana, pray get aboard."

Then it came to me that my winning the race three years before still stung him. He would just as lief let me take the two of them fishing, bait their hooks, hear their cozy talk, and, when I appeared too busy to notice, watch them kiss.

He went first down the ladder to the boat, so he could give his companion a hand. Also he looked gallantly away as she started to descend; but watching him like a cormorant, I saw him shoot a swift glance upward when she was not looking. It would be considered quite an offense in puritanical Salem; but it was no trifle to me either. It was so significant of that greedy, alert, resolute man. Doubtless she had a well-turned ankle and a fine round calf that I too would like to survey. He was human enough, and the appetizer gave him a pleasant promise of a luxurious feast not too far in the future. That one little act convinced me that the two were almost, if not quite, betrothed.

Dick took a snug seat beside his partner, and the Negress, called Eliza, huddled behind them. I cast off, made sail, and skimmed prettily out into the bay. Busy with the boat, yet I missed not one flash of expression across her face. Coming to a good drop, I threw my iron overboard, rigged their lines, and set them at one of the most absorbing pastimes on land or water. Since Dick baited both hooks—again he had been sharp, not to lord it over me in the eyes of this warm-hearted girl—I had nothing to do but look at her and try to grasp the meaning she had for me.

Her head had a lovely shape, I thought, and the bony structure of her face was delicate and fine, although rather odd looking.

Lately I had heard a good deal about "aristocrats." It was a word rarely spoken on the frontier; but in Boston, and no doubt our other great cities, the glory of our Revolutionary faith was burning low. People who had never believed it anyhow but had lain low when General Washington and coon-capped Ethan Allen had fought side by side for the same cause, now crawled out of their holes. Actually our nation had never had an aristocracy worth comparing to that of the smallest European state, only a gentry—families in comfortable circumstances over two or three generations. Precious few of England's nobility had ever touched our shores, being more comfortable at home, although some patroons in New York State had sprung from highborn Dutchmen. Mainly our settlers had been franklins, yeomen, and tradesmen. Many grandsons of our few real blue bloods had wandered west and now fed hogs in Vermont or felled trees in Ohio. But rich Boston merchants were already beginning to call themselves aristocrats, no matter if their fathers had been piddling clerks. Even little Salem had its First Families, meaning mainly those with the fattest purses, and the airs some gave themselves were all the more irksome to the rest of us, being unable to look away in the narrow town.

Yet the word aristocracy meant something, when rightly used. It was a condition not easily obtainable, often only feigned, frequently confused with ill-bred snobbishness. But when real, it permeated every vein and bone of its possessor, and set him apart from the crowd. It came to me that Roxana was a real one, regardless of whether she belonged to a First Family. Indeed I was sure that none of our merchant princes had a daughter by that name, and she did not smell of money. She was on an outing, wearing an old dress, but the garment had never been costly—I had learned a good deal about cloth from Mr. Perkins—and rich people have a way of advertising their wealth, even while catching a greased pig at a fair. Real aristocracy is a state of being, acquired by descent or by inner growth. She would fill that bill for me, whatever her parentage. Anyway I did not doubt that there was more silk purse than sow's ear in her make-up.

Her dress was becoming without her being too conscious of the fact. Her long, slim body was graceful and highly feminine—bold of breast and butt described her well. She was warm, instead of chill, sensitive to everything, and I thought compassionate, judging from a frequent lovely expression in her eyes. The best sign was her naturalness, expressed in her quick, hilarious laugh, easy talk, friendliness, and especially her excitement when she got a bite. She appeared to ripple all over, and when the fish fought on her line her eyes shone, her slim throat corded, and even her hair appeared to blaze in the bright sun. At such times she cared not at all for the primness of her skirt. Then I was not more gallant than Dick had been, and could blame him even less.

"*Le bon Dieu!*" she shrieked, when after a stout fight she boated a chicken halibut weighing about eight pounds.

It came on my tongue to ask if she spoke French. I did not do so, at first because the fact was so patent. This was not such French as our fashionable belles employed, a few phrases learned with outhanging tongues and mouthed with a Yankee accent. It had burst from her unawares with the same intonation that Pierre had used in moments of delighted surprise. Perhaps she had French blood. Thinking hard then—bent on making the most of this lucky chance —I raked over in my mind all that I knew of France, and presently I was ready to bet on the province. Most French people I had seen were dark, but at Cape Verde we had spoken and bought provision from a brigantine out of Brest, manned by tall, tawny-haired Bretons. They too had had blue eyes set wide apart and warm friendly ways.

I longed to speak with her in old Pierre's language, but could not manage it very well, as long as Dick commanded her attention. However, a way came to keep him very busy for an hour or two.

"How would you like to catch some big halibut?" I asked. "They're finer fish than cod." In fact the finest eating of any sold in Boston, firm fleshed, and tasty.

"Why, very well," Dick answered quickly.

"I know a bank that I fish for the market, but it's small, and the school limited, and I'd have to ask you to be content with one fish apiece."

"That's all right with us. If I can catch one over twenty pounds—the biggest we can make at home—I'll give him to you."

"I will too," Roxana told me, with an eager nod of her head.

Twenty-pound halibut were rarely caught this close to Salem, and Dick thought he was safe enough. Neither he nor any other Salemite knew the deep hole in the shelf that Andy and I had found while drift fishing in a dory, and Andy would be outraged at my taking anyone there. For some unknown reason huge cow halibut, large as any caught on the Grand Banks, congregated in that rockbound well —to spawn for all I knew. Andy and I had carefully conserved the school, taking one occasionally when we were lean of purse, and swearing we had caught her clean off Martha's Vineyard.

However, I did not think it likely that Dick could spot our trove and strip it later. He had no glass to find exact landmarks and did not know that bottom. Anyway, the chance was worth taking. I was after the biggest fish that swam in all my seas. Maybe I did not yet confess the fact, but my heart knew it well.

2.

Sailing near the spot, I got my bearings and looked for a white sand bed which glimmered perceptibly at a certain angle. From this submarine signpost, I anchored on the shelf upwind from the hole, so that the boat lay smack over it. Dick was furtively looking for landmarks—that Yankee trader Elisha Featherstone was patently no cuckold—but much good it would do him, I thought. Then I rigged him thirty fathom of handline stout enough to hold a porpoise and baited a small shark hook with a filet of cod.

"Why, it's not sporting to use so heavy a line," he protested.

"That's to guard against a sharp rock parting it," I explained. "Miss, if he gets a bite, I'll rig you up."

It was perfect fishing weather and tide. Old Triton was on my side that day—he too knew jealousy's pangs according to Virgil's verse—for in ten minutes there came a great tug on Dick's line. Luckily I had bent it on the bow hook, or the fish might have jerked it from his hands or yanked him overboard. If it were Roxana instead, I knew she would gladly dunk rather than let go, trusting us to bail her out—this was my immediate insight into her character. In the same pass, I would have bailed Dick out. But he did not have the same insight into my character.

His fish appeared well hooked and would keep him very busy for a while. If she weighed no more than fifty pounds, less than the run of the huge females in this abyss, there were so many projecting rocks that he could not hoist her. Roxana was greatly excited at first. She shrieked encouragement to Dick and called the fish a very coarse name in French. Of course she had no notion that either Dick or I could translate the epithet. Plainly he knew no French at all, and she could not picture a fishing guide speaking the tongue of courts.

After the fish's first powerful run, she sounded, froze her flat side behind a rock, and refused to budge. Dick could only hang on and sweat it out. Roxana became more calm. Presently she resumed her seat and asked me to rig her a line. That I must not do, I said, as the two would foul each other and Dick lose his prize. After twenty minutes' watching her sweetheart pull and perspire, she became a little bored. He was not a romantic figure now, his feet braced against the strake and his bared wrists red. The fight put up by a big cow halibut is not spectacular, merely dogged and long.

"Ma'am, I don't know how to address you, since your escort didn't favor me with your name," I began.

"Why, it's Miss Roxana Reil," she replied, friendly enough.

Knowing by now all the prime names of the town, I immediately guessed that she was the daughter of Dr. Francis Reil. Perhaps I should have surmised it before now, since he was the only blond Frenchman hereabouts, and fit to be her sire. Of leaner purse than most leading Salemites, he had the repute of being the best born. I had heard humble men so speak of him—his brother a French milord, they thought—and of his skill and humanities in physic. I had heard too—for the underlings know more about their betters than the latter dream—that he had an overfondness for the bottle and a meat ax of a wife. This handsome but grim dame appeared infrequently on the streets, and her tall, lean, prematurely gray husband was a familiar figure there. No one had ever told me that they had an entrancing daughter. Plainly she had gone so long from Salem as to drop out of the gossip, and had but recently returned.

"Reil is a French name," I said to her. "Perhaps you speak the language."

"Why, I do." Her color began to rise. Perhaps she was thinking of the name she had called the fish.

47

"Perhaps you'd like to practice," I went on, in the French tongue. "I speak it a little."

"Why, you speak it perfectly, like a—native." She had started to say "like a gentleman," I thought. I thought then she might try to gloss over her coarse invective, and somehow hoped she would not. She did not—letting it stand—and began to rattle happily away. "I'm most grateful for the chance, m'sieu. It's like sugar on my tongue! You know how one pines for its sweet sound and clear meaning."

"No doubt you learned it on your mother's knee."

"No, she can't speak a word. Even to hear it offends her—she thinks English good enough for anyone, and everything French immoral. So I did not learn much from my father, either. Poor man, he has been reproved so many times that he's all but forgotten his native speech."

"Where did you learn it, mademoiselle?"

"My uncle in Breton invited me for a year's stay at his château. That was nine years ago, and I in pigtails. It was a great fight before my mother yielded, but my father stood firm—my uncle had sent money for my passage—and I meant to return before reaching a dangerous age."

She stopped abruptly. In Salem young ladies did not confess they were ever of dangerous age. But she looked at me, happiness came into her eyes as the thought that, knowing French, I might have some of the breadth and sanity of civilized Frenchmen, and went cheerfully on.

"I had hardly arrived when the Bastille fell. When I tried to come home, there was no ship to take me. Although my uncle, a lesser noble, had joined the Third Estate, he was imprisoned and barely escaped the Terror."

The sudden pallor in her face made me ask, "You also?"

"Yes."

"Even though you were American born?"

"That was doubted. There were big and little Terrors throughout France. The worst was when—"

It was becoming hard for her to speak. "You're home now," I broke in. "You can remember the pears and the wine and cherry blossoms and lovers' laughter." Of all of these Pierre had spoken.

"*Merci, monsieur.*"

"Does your escort speak French?"

She raised her head, her countenance brightening. "He? No, and anyway he's busy with his big fish."

If that were not an invitation to frank and friendly speech, what was it? And a very busy man Dick had become, tugging wrathfully now, the fish lodged behind a rock. I think he would have cut the line save for our watching him.

"I'm greatly taken with your given name," I told her.

"My father gave it to me, when my mother wished to name me Prudence, the same as your boat. One would fit me as well as the other, I take it. In case you don't know its history—"

My brain gave a big jump, and I did know. Plainly it was excited beyond its usual powers, for such a dim and long-lost memory to return.

"Why, yes," I broke in, to display the lore. "I think that Roxana was a princess of India—perhaps of Persia or thereabouts—the wife of Alexander the Great."

Roxana was pleased with me for knowing that—perhaps quite as much as I was pleased with myself. The blue of her eyes appeared to deepen; she gave a startled and delighted little jump of her head and looked at me with a new glance.

"Do you know, you're the first man in Salem to tell me so."

"I'm glad of that."

"Are you a Republican, m'sieu?"

"Yes, but not a terrorist. More what we call a democrat."

"Where did you learn to speak French?"

"From my hunting companion, in the West."

"Oh, did you come from the frontier?" Her eyes were getting wider.

"From the Adirondack Mountains."

"Dieu! The big woods! Do your parents live here?"

"No, they're both dead."

She gave a quick nod, no other response, yet I was sure that the tidings went home to her with a great deal of meaning.

"Aren't the Starbucks a seafaring family of good repute?"

"Respectable. My mother was Prudence Todkill."

"You named your boat for her. That's good. Was she dark like you?"

"No, very fair. My father—"

"Are you self-educated?" She was firing questions at me now, hardly waiting for me to finish my replies, as though her impulse was to find out the maximum about me in a sharply limited time. It is strange how Shakespeare haunts the minds of those who pore over him, as I had done, perhaps more intently than many richer in books.

I could have thought—although I didn't—of Hamlet saying, "Very like, very like. Stayed it long?"—interrupting a fine speech of Horatio's about how amazed the Prince would be, to see his father's ghost.

"What is your given name? I didn't catch it."

"Jason."

Dick heard the confidence and turned a palely angry face.

"How about giving me a hand with this brute, Starbuck?" he called. "I think the line's got around a rock."

"I wouldn't like to spoil your sport, Mr. Featherstone. I'll shorten anchor a little—"

Meanwhile he tugged furiously at the fish and presently unfouled her. Hauling powerfully hand over hand, he shortened the line by a good ten fathoms. She fought desperately then, even jerking the boat about our anchorage, and causing her to shake when the hook brought her up short. She was either one of the largest in the school or was hooked in the tail or the back. Then she got around another projecting rock and forestalled him again.

"Put pressure on her a few more minutes, and you can bring her alongside," I advised him.

"And meanwhile, Captain Starbuck," Roxana said clearly, "I'd thank you for a little more practice in French."

"Gladly, Miss Reil."

"Are you part Indian?" she asked, resuming our conversation.

"Not that I know of."

"Your hair is too crisp looking, but you have a high nose and flat cheeks and are very dark—"

"Indian skins are mud colored. The maids of the Sandwich Isles told me ours were of a shade."

"Did they, indeed! No doubt you interposed 'em, to see."

She would never have dreamed of saying this in English. One reason that French is the tongue of courts is its power to loosen the tongue in the mouth. Almost anything can be said elegantly. Too, the language of a nation shapes as well as expresses its character. The sane, gay French love the risqué, partly because it can be so neatly put. Roxana was paying me a high compliment with her daring wit. She did not think I would misjudge her.

"How did you come to be named Jason?" she asked.

"It was my grandfather's name."

"Anyway you should pursue golden-haired girls, not dusky island maidens." She looked innocently out to sea.

"So you know its history."

"Stupid! I've been to school in France."

"I've not, but next best is to go to school to you, and take your advice." Nor could I have said this in English, at least not as adroitly. She had made me feel like a gentleman.

"How soon will you set sail?" she asked. "Anything as wonderful as the Golden Fleece must be far across the sea."

"Maybe it's right here in Salem."

That was meant for a light retort, but something happened to my voice and it did not sound so. I looked at her, not smiling now, beautiful in such a strange, new way, her face so touching in repose, and my wit played out. I was no longer fit for any trivial exchange. I was not a gay, sane Frenchman but an intense mountaineer.

3.

A thought is only a thought, stray as a cat on the stoop—anonymous, irresponsible. A thought is an egg that we may eat and savor and forget, or put under a hen to hatch. It has the germ of life in it and usually we had better let it die a-borning. If it is anything more than a series of mental images that mainly serve unlettered folk for thought, it is composed of words, but we need not own to them yet; we can shut them up until they smother in the dark closet of our skulls and no one will ever be the wiser. We may even give them voice out of everyone's hearing without interesting the Furies. But once told to a fellow human, a fact is born. Their truth or falsehood cannot reduce their having been said. That fact alone gives them a certain substance, a term of life; we must either withdraw them or be responsible for them. They have become a reality as surely as the rocks. The lower animals cannot dream of such a miracle; the apes and monkeys know of its existence but cannot work it and their faces are sad; the dogs yearn to it and worship it, and at a little glimpse of comprehension, wag their tails.

"Will you go sailing with me alone?" I asked.

"No."

"May I come to see you?"

"No, it wouldn't do any good, only harm."

"Will you meet me somewhere and talk with me some more?"

"I don't know. I think not. It would have to be clandestine. But if you want to get a note to me—"

Dick had discerned something in our tones that he did not like.

He called to me to pay out the cable, to give him a different haul on the fish. I had barely time to nod to Roxana as I obeyed him; instantly he forced the monster from her mooring and made her fight. When I raised the iron to give her freer play, she made a powerful rush that towed the boat before the wind a considerable distance out of the drop. Dick was not too busy to look again for his bearings.

As the fish tired, Dick began to recover line and soon gave us a sight of her. She was not hooked in the tail; her great fight had been the due of her weight and power. I guessed her as larger than any Andy and I had caught in this hole, comparing well with the largest taken on the Grand Banks. Amid a great splashing and savage swirls, Dick brought her alongside. When I had gaffed her, it was all I could do to heave her aboard. She weighed a good one hundred and fifty pounds, within a hundred of the lunker caught two years before and still famous in Derby Dock. No wonder Roxana shrieked.

Dick wiped his face with his hand. "There's your plagued fish," he told me.

"It's such a fine one, I want you to keep it as a reward for your fine fight." It was worth ten dollars at market, no small change to me, but my magnificence in Roxana's hearing a great deal more.

"No, when I make a deal, I stand by it. After all, your trade is fishing, and mine's not."

Making sail, we tacked prettily to port. I had not yet made a deal with myself about Roxana. Too shaken to think clearly, I would put off the decision for a little while yet. It was not one I could make and unmake. I was not a Salem merchant with many ships: it would mean to risk all in one bottom. I could not make a half-hearted fight that would not lame me if I lost.

Luck served me again when Dick paid me off—two silver dollars for my services, and two for the boat. He had left a jacket in my deckhouse: I could have provided some such occasion, with enough wit and foresight. Roxana walked a little way out of his hearing, with me hard on her heels.

"Why don't you sail, like Jason, and forget this?" she asked.

No, she did not pretend that what had happened was of no account. Perhaps nothing much had happened to her—I could not tell —but she looked me steadfastly in the eyes, her face a little sad.

"I can't forget it."

"I don't think we can meet, but if you see a way to write to me—"

"I'll get a letter to you, without anyone being the wiser."

She began talking about the dock scenes as Dick approached us.

Plainly she was not without deceit, a natural and perhaps excellent thing in women worth their salt. She thanked me gravely for a good sail, and she and Dick strolled away, followed by the Negress carrying her catch. I had hardly begun to wash the boat when Andy Oats's sun-dried form appeared on the wharf above me.

"Where did ye get that lunker?" he demanded, too surprised to spit.

"From our hole, of course."

"Ye don't mean ye took Mr. Featherstone to our trove?"

"He didn't have a glass, and can't find it again."

"I dunno. He'll try, and you can lay to that. He's Elisha's son. Ye must of lost your mind."

"Maybe I did."

"I was a-feared of that, when I see that tall, fine girl. She's the kind to set any man's wits awry."

"You're right about that, Uncle Andy." I often called him so, in lieu of real kinspeople.

I began gutting the big fish. He climbed down the ladder to watch me. "Careful with that great liver," he warned. "Don't ye know better than slash at it so? Boil out the ile, and it's the best medicine there is for colds and spindly legs in child'en. Better than cod-liver ile to my jedgment."

"I was intending to save it."

"I seen her walking with Dr. Reil, and doubt not she's his daughter."

"Yes."

"She's way beyond any Starbuck, let alone no Todkill."

"We'll see about that."

"I misdoubt but a prize crew's already aboard her, and making for port."

That night I wrote a brief letter to Roxana. I hoped to deliver it on the arrival of the Boston post, when many of our town's belles as well as sober citizens assembled at the office. She wore no bonnet and her hair was dressed in a new fashion hereabouts—one big curl worn in front of her shoulder. She was not as expensively dressed as some of the young ladies, although with more regard for her own figure and coloring. She took every eye.

She smiled and spoke to every one—as winningly to shawled old washwomen as to rich merchants' dames. In the intervals her countenance was grave. No one saw her beauty as clearly as I. Maybe some people could not see it at all, so exotic in Salem, and did not

53

even wonder why they kept looking at her. It might be a sad thing to feel beauty in one's self that others did not recognize. I was more aware of it than Dick Featherstone. That much was plain from his possessive attitude toward her. Had he perceived it fully he would have been ever startled, with wonder in his eyes. He would know he could never own her, at most only hold her by her giving, not his taking. Dick had never stood in the great dark forests of the West, or seen the ice-fields on the Horn, or the paper lanterns of Canton. He had never been very lonely, I thought.

It was not a hard maneuver to be walking behind her when she got her letters and started home. It seemed to me that she knew of it, although she gave no sign. When a little way from the crowd, passers-by saw me stoop and appear to pick up a letter from the sidewalk. Then I hastened forward and, taking off my cap, held it out to her.

"This is yours, miss."

She hesitated briefly. Only then did it occur to me that she might say, "No, it belongs to someone else," and hurry on. No, she had told me I might send a letter.

She looked at me gravely and said, "Thank you, sir." Taking my letter, she walked on.

All that day was sunny, so that I was afraid tomorrow it would rain. It did not, being again bright and fine, and all morning I busied about my boat, painting and polishing, as though her perfection would make everything perfect by sympathetic magic. I had not yet faced the possibility of her not keeping the rendezvous. My asking her to meet me at three o'clock on Gallows Hill was a different thing from her agreeing to meet me there, like one arm of a sextant. People sometimes climbed the hill for a good view of the harbor; no one would think anything of her strolling there; and beyond was a lonely, wood-grown footpath.

Among my most prized possessions was a Russian pocket-watch. I had got it from a Muscovite priest on the shores of Juan de Fuca Strait for five gallons of rum that Mr. Perkins had issued me out of my store. The clergyman had diddled me, he thought, for the piece had been tarnished and would not run; but his rum was drunk by now, its glowings gone, while the watch kept almost as good time as a ship's clock. It had needed only cleaning and small repairs, both of course as unprocurable on Vancouver Island as on the moon. After the deal was closed, he confessed that the case was not silver but a metal unknown to me called platinum with which Russian chemists had begun to experiment; but it took a high polish and now readily passed for fine silver.

I kept looking at it, forgetting my fixed resolve not to do so, remembering only when I found it in my hand with not five minutes gone by. Yet when it said three, and I was thinking I need not really look for Roxana for fifteen minutes more, there she came, sturdily climbing the hill. Although not in the least like a man in other ways, she actually thought that three o'clock meant by the clock. Even to meet a lover she wanted and was not sure of, I doubted if she would deliberately dawdle to make him anxious.

I felt a sense of the beauty of the scene, unnoticed—not even existing for me—a few minutes ago. People used to be hanged on this hill, sometimes in June, and at that last moment, when they knew there would be no reprieve, when the past could not be undone and the future appeared most uncertain, perhaps they too marked the serene blue sky, the mossy roofs below, the tender grass, the grave trees, and the sea with white sails. I had thought that Roxana might carry a parasol, so fashionable in France. Perhaps she thought it would attract too many distant eyes. She gave me a wide, childish grin.

"I was afraid you wouldn't come," I told her. For I would never get anywhere with her, trying to play little games.

"I was afraid I wouldn't too." She thought this over, and added, "That I'd obey my better judgment."

"My God, I'm glad you did."

"I am too, I guess. I had to tell Ma a whopper. I hope Mr. Featherstone isn't looking out from his cupola with his long spyglass."

"He'd be looking out to sea, in hope of spying one of his competitors' ships go down. And if you'll keep on the path a little farther—"

She did so, and then I guided her into a side path which led presently into a grove of ash. A little way back was a kind of bower, shut in by seedlings, where the grass was green and soft as a fine rug.

"What a pretty place! You must have looked a long while, to find it."

"I reconnoitered the ground yesterday."

"The way you did when you ran the horse race with Dick! I heard about that."

"Why, that was three years ago."

"It amused Pa. He had bet five dollars on you. He told me when I mentioned that you had taken Dick and me fishing. But you ought to have heard what Ma said!"

"Was it true, you think?"

"Not much that she says, is. She said your uncle is a pirate and will end on the gallows—"

"He's a privateer against the Spaniards in the Caribs, if not hung already."

"And that blood will tell!"

"Then it's a wonder you came."

"It was the last straw to make me come. No, I'd decided to already, if you were foolish enough to ask me."

There was a big mossy log on one side of the bower. I had brushed it well and without a suggestion from me, she sat down on the grass and leaned against it. I took a seat beside her.

"Maybe you shouldn't have gone to all this trouble, when I can stay only a few minutes," she went on, soberly now.

"It was no trouble. A lot of pleasure instead. Just thinking about it."

"I don't want you to be hanged, Jason, or defeated. I want you to go and win the Golden Fleece—"

"I told you what that was."

"I know, and that's why I had to come and talk to you. One reason, anyway. You must get rich and powerful and outshine all the merchants. Ma said your mother couldn't read and write—"

"She told the truth, that time."

"She said if your father hadn't married so far beneath him he could have got in with some merchant and prospered—"

"Yes—like my Uncle Samuel. Instead he had a cabin on the mountains, and hunted deer, and rode hard, and trapped fur—"

"And raised you! Jason, I wouldn't care if most boys' mothers couldn't read and write—if people told me, I'd not remember—but you're so proud. I can't stand that in you. It wouldn't matter, if you hadn't turned out as you did. Why have you turned out this way?"

"What way?"

"I'll never rest easy, until you've done all those things you have to do—got what you want."

"I told you what I want."

"You can't have me—and I can't have you. That's an unseemly thing to say in so short acquaintance—but our time's short. Almost the first thing a woman thinks when she meets a man is, 'If I want him, could I have him?' With you the answer would be 'no.' And since that's true—I couldn't bear to interfere with your voyage."

"What voyage?"

"The one you must make. I don't know anything about it, except it's awful long. It wouldn't be possible for you to find what you want in a short one."

She was speaking slowly, in low tones, not knowing what she was going to say the next sentence, then saying what struck her without considering the effect.

"Why didn't you want Mr. Featherstone to see you with me through his spyglass?" I asked.

"Oh, goodness."

"With me, or with anyone except Dick?"

"With anyone, and especially with a fisherman with no social standing. I have to be very discreet, Jason. I've got to live up to his idea of a young lady. Otherwise he'll try to break off the match."

"The match?"

"I'll have to spend my next twenty years catering to him and flattering him, so he'll do what I want."

"And that is—"

"Oh, lots of things. Let's be confidants—at least we can be that—until you go away. I want him to furnish Dick with plenty of money, and help out my Pa with some, and leave everything to us."

"Then you're engaged to Dick?"

"Yes, but he doesn't know it yet." She broke forth in a surprising girlish giggle at the oddness of that.

"I don't understand."

"Don't be formal, Jason. I know you do—understand—at least can —or I wouldn't tell you. I want to explain everything to you—so you'll put me out of your head and go about your business."

Not many girls could so trust themselves, I thought. That is what people do when they think they are trusting others with confidences. Roxana was deeply self-honest, which must arise from a faith in her own good rather than in her evil. We were talking in English because English words are harder to hide behind than French, perhaps a sign that we must get down to brass tacks.

"I'm going to marry Dick before the summer's out," she went on. "He's a very eligible young man and I can get him. He's the only one handy that can give me what I want and need. We're terribly poor. We don't know where the next meal's coming from. Pa is a gentleman and wants to live well and be clean—people can't even stay clean when they're real poor. He can't stand worry either—so he goes to his bottle. I love him awfully!"

"But do you love Dick? I'd think that ought to count."

"I wish I did. I'm afraid I never can, he's so greedy and grasping and selfish—you know that, and there's no use of us pretending. We mustn't pretend, Jason, considering what's between us. But those very qualities will make him keep the Featherstone money and make more—for me to spend. Besides that, he won't ever grow tedious. He's awfully smart, you know, and strong. I wouldn't be surprised but what he's as close to being wicked as any man I ever met."

"Good God, Roxana!"

"I wouldn't wonder, really. His father unscrupulous and money mad, and his mother hateful. The combination might produce real wickedness. But the real thing is fascinating." She paused and reflected. "I couldn't stand just a scoundrel—or an honest man that's dull—but a truly great sinner—"

"So you want me to put you out of my head?"

She turned slowly and looked into my eyes. "I'd advise you to."

"That wasn't what I asked."

Her eyes widened and grew sorrowful. "No," she said. "I take it back. I want you to remember me always."

"You said there was something between us. Do you know what it is?"

"No."

"You felt it, as soon as we met?"

"No. You started it. I didn't answer—very much—until you told me about my name—so proud of knowing. No, my heart began to race when you were looking at me so—before we got on the boat."

"How wonderful of you to tell me!"

"We haven't much time and better make the most of it. Have the most to remember." She was speaking and looking at me just as frankly as though we were discussing two other people.

"I won't let you go."

"You've got to, Jason. I wish I could put off marrying Dick awhile, but I can't."

"We'll see. Let's make the most of this time together, and then—"

"There won't be any 'then.' Make up your mind to it. What do you mean, by making the most of this?"

"I meant to pretend there isn't any Dick, if you will."

"As though we were courting, with nothing in the way? There is, though. I'd like to play that—if I can trust you."

"In what way?"

"To understand—and not take any advantage—and when you look back on it not think it was cheap—"

58

"Cheap! Don't say that."

"I know it isn't—it's a wonder—but when time passes and the things that made it all right grow dim—" Her tone dropped until she was whispering.

She did not resist when I drew down her lovely bright head and kissed her child's lips. For a second or two she did not move, then drew back and looked at me with a breathless, almost frightened question in her eyes. I knew only one way to answer—by taking her in my arms and kissing her as a lover, with all my heart. There is not the slightest doubt any more. I was drawing all the lightning like an oak tree in a storm.

Her high color—a true flame—slowly dimmed. "I have to go now," she said, wrinkling her forehead a little as though thinking of important business.

I could not answer.

"I've stayed too long already." She got quickly to her feet. "Don't come with me. Wait here a little while. It was a wonderful thing, Jason—but you know—I told you—there isn't a chance. Goodbye, Jason."

"I won't say goodbye." I was standing before her, but she would not look at me.

She began to walk away. "It's true, whether you say it or not." But when she had taken half a dozen quick steps she stopped, then slowly turned. "Goodbye, Jason," she said again, her eyes not yet meeting mine.

"I won't say goodbye."

"Oh, say it, won't you? Not saying it won't help you any."

"No."

"How can I go, unless you say it?" Her throat worked painfully.

"I'll not let you go."

She came stealing on light feet to me. She glanced into my eyes and quickly glanced away. There was a blindingly lovely sadness in her face now.

"You're so tall—and dark like an Indian and strong—and yet there are shadows in your eyes—"

"What is it, Roxana?"

"Do you love me, Jason?"

"Yes."

"Don't you think it may be—just an illusion?"

"You know better."

"It isn't reasonable, is it, when you met me only two days ago?"

"None of the great things are reasonable, I reckon."

"A girl you can't have?"

"I don't admit that."

"Then it was my fault for not making you believe me—"

"I knew you meant it."

"Maybe you think I love you? Do you?"

"Not yet, but—"

"Even if I did, there wouldn't be a chance. I'm going to do what I planned when I was a little girl—and began to think while in France might not be necessary—and when I came home found out it was. I'm strong too, Jason—maybe stronger than you. I can keep from loving anyone when it's no use."

"That's not the kind of strength I want. I'm glad I haven't got it."

"That's the trouble. That's the reason I hate this so. If it was a weak person, I wouldn't worry. But you'll love so *hard*."

"I reckon that's so."

"Give me up, Jason. All I've done is reflect back what you've felt. My heart's empty except for that. Be kind to me—more kind to yourself—and let me go."

"I never will."

"If it were some girls, you could change them, but not me."

"I won't believe that."

But maybe I did believe it a little, hating the weakness, for she put her arms about my neck and kissed me long and with such sweetness I never knew was in this world.

"I'm going home now," she whispered, her eyes bright with tears, yet smiling as to a child.

"When can I see you again?"

"I don't know. I'll walk down the dock some morning. Just as soon as I can."

"I'll be looking for you. Au revoir."

"I shouldn't have come—but good God, I'm so glad I did!"

I watched her bright head until it dimmed in the shadows of the town.

CHAPTER FOUR

The Charge

1.

Andy Oats had taken my boat and gone, and I did not see him until the morning after an almost sleepless night in a tavern. On his face was a look of mournful satisfaction.

"I knowed where ye went, yestaday afternoon," he remarked, skilfully mending a sail.

"Well?"

"Ye was out walking with Dr. Reil's daughter."

"How did you know?"

"When ye dressed so fine at high sun, and kept looking at your chronometer, and walked off with that mountain walk of your'n I knowed whar the wind."

"I hope you didn't tell anyone."

"I got that much sense. I know the folly of telling all I know, which I can't say for some others."

Patently he was leading up to something. "Where did you go?" I asked.

"Oh, a-fishing."

"I don't see your catch."

"It was a lot of bleatin' and little wool."

"You don't mean you were skunked!"

"That I was, 'cept for trash, regardless what I kept the lines wet till way arter dark, waiting for the tide."

"What bank did you fish?"

"Why, our drop, o' course."

When I did not answer, Andy spat over the gunnel.

"I hear'd a bit o' news, this morning," he went on. "Leff Atkin came by, and told me. Yestaday morning the 'Clara' and the 'Morning Star' came in to Boston loaded to the gunnels with big halibut. The run was over fifty pound apiece. They said they'd been off Martha's Vineyard, but they hadn't."

It was common knowledge that both smacks belonged to the Featherstone Tea Company. I sat down on the bait box without a word to say. Andy took a neat stitch.

"Plum busted the market in Boston for a week or more," he remarked cheerfully.

"I don't wonder."

"Night afore last was good fishing weather, the moon just right, not too fine, nor yet too dark, and a ripple on the water. Doubtless they bit lively."

"Andy, I don't see how Dick could have found that hole. He didn't have a line on it, or know the sand bed—"

"He's a sharp feller. His Pa is sharp afore him. Them two boats drifted across, soundin' and droppin', until they found it. I reckon it didn't take 'em two hours."

"I suppose that's it."

"You stole a march on Mr. Dick yestaday afternoon," Andy examined his handiwork, found it good, and spat overside. "But it looks like to me, he's still 'way ahead."

Maybe he was still 'way ahead, although not on account of poaching two boatloads of fish. That item only limned the fact that he was the kind to stay ahead.

Roxana had promised to come to the dock some morning. I could not expect her the very next one, yet loitered about till after noon, before I dared put out with Andy for an afternoon's trawl. The next morning it rained hard, but I let Andy go alone, partly from thinking it might clear up and mainly because of Roxana's unpredictability. A rainy morning might be the very kind to move her in some mysterious way. In these watches I did not feel embarrassed, or in the least belittled. They were not even especially trying. The chance of her coming was far greater than mischances I had stood watch against aboard the "Hattie." Long before that, I had learned to keep long vigils, to get a deer to bring home, or even a wild turkey. If it were the slimmest chance that she would come, I would not scorn it. In the meantime I had seen her on the street, without appearing to notice her or addressing her in any way but with my leaping heart, and was sure she had seen me.

The moon I had thought lucky waxed to full, and cut a little. A morning came up warm and fine, but the dock was not as busy as usual; at least there were fewer merchants wearing gold seals taking a look at the ladings, or clerks with their books. What business there was, slackened as the sun climbed; and the street was almost empty.

Then I recalled hearing that a famous Connecticut divine would preach that day and again that night to a huge open-air meeting at Lynn. A big megaphone had been set up to carry his voice to the multitude; and dinner and supper were to be brought in baskets. The shoemakers there—Lynn shod half of the women of the country, a matter of a quarter of a million pairs a year—would display their wares at a reduced price. It was figured that God would be mightily pleased with the fair, since while about it the customers would certainly be edified by the sermons, and certainly He had supplied perfect weather. The owners of the factories had organized the meeting and would pay the preacher, and no collections need be taken up.

I hurried back to the dock and arrived there not much too soon. There came walking along, as if looking for someone important, a tall girl with a suntrap on her head. I stood on my deckhouse which brought my head about level with her knees.

"Ma and Pa have gone to Lynn," she told me quickly.

"Then—"

"I told them I had a woeful headache. It was true, in a way. Can you get your boat into Catfish Cove, an hour from now?"

"I'll be there."

"Eliza and I are going picnicking down that way." She walked quickly on, and presently stopped one of Mr. Derby's clerks. No doubt she was asking for someone's whereabouts, or perhaps if her trunk or such like had been received from France.

Catfish Cove was the urchins' name for a slight indentation of the bay about two miles north of town, where they could go swimming jaybird naked without being seen from the houses. Before taking off I made a quick trip to a grocer's and bought a big flask of wine, the best he had in stock, and a spice cake. I could not get within twenty fathoms of the beach, but it proved in my favor, instead of against me.

Barefooted, and my breeches rolled up, I was waiting on the sand when Roxana and the Negress came over the dunes. "How wonderful," she said, apropos not of nothing but of everything—the bright bay and balmy weather and the robin-egg blue of the sky with small, pearly clouds, and the pretty boat lying off, and perhaps of getting here unseen.

"I was sorry I couldn't bring her any nearer—" I began.

"Why, Eliza's already barefoot and I'll take off my shoes and stockings—"

"I thought to carry you."

Her head gave a little jump as always when she was pleased. "That would be more proper," she told me, her eyes sparkling. "Then I wouldn't have to show my legs almost to the knee!"

So while Eliza paddled out to the boat, I lay Roxana crosswise of my arms and waded in. She made the burden light as possible for me by putting her arms about my neck, warm and close. That brought my thumping heart so close to hers and her beaming smile in such easy reach that I must stop and bend my head to find out something. She kissed me as happily and impulsively as a child might, careless whether Eliza was looking. Maybe some wooers could have taken it as their due! As for me, I was already incredulous of all this—my carrying her to my boat, the blue water and the blue sky, my arms filled with her—and now I knew real wonder. It was that solemn sort of exultation for little glimpses of which we live and look so long.

I stood there awhile, clean unconscious of her weight. Actually it was nothing to me anyway. By slinging her on my back I could have carried her for miles without getting wearied. Pierre used to say I didn't know my strength. He meant by that, partly, that none of us mountain born of the typical frontier physique—tall, limber and lean as catamounts, a little like Iroquois Indians—realized that we were one of the toughest and strongest breeds of men a-going. At sixteen I could lift one end of a wagonload of corn off the wheels—a good eight hundredweight in all—but thought nothing of it because either of the Scanlin boys could heft the other end.

I think Roxana was happy to be such an easy tote to me. Even before she kissed me, her color had risen. After that I felt her heart thumping too—a wonderfully strong heart, fit for great jubilances, and God only knew how I loved it.

I put her aboard, and she and Eliza went at once into my little deckhouse. It was a good thing they did, for before I could raise my hook two boys appeared without a stitch from behind a dune. It did not matter if Roxana saw them—she would not even bother to pretend she didn't—save for her worry that they might have seen her. I worried about it myself. While one was a mere urchin not to be interested in a town belle's going sailing with a fisherman, one was a stripling of sixteen, full of lecherous thoughts if anything like me at the same age. He was the son of Bud Williams, skipper of the smack "Morning Star" and Elisha Featherstone's creature.

I did not say anything of this to Roxana. When she looked out of the deckhouse, she did not glance back to see the boys cavorting on the beach. She had eyes for nothing but ahead, and this was a little thing significant of her character.

"How long can you stay, Roxana?" I asked in French when we were far enough out that even a spyglass could not tell her from Andy Oats.

"We've plenty of time, Jason," she answered. "I'd rather not come back till first dark."

That was eight hours or more.

"Don't look like a child with a new toy, or I can't ever go back," she went on, with that humorous, touching smile that cracked my heart.

"When will your parents return?"

"They're going to spend the night in Lynn. If people call in the daytime, I can say I'd gone to the Post Office. But if they come after dark, what can I say?"

Since I had not asked her to stay longer than first dark, this explanation seemed needless.

"I couldn't be married without seeing you one more time," she remarked after some reflection, "and that's sure." She looked at me as though expecting an argument on the point.

"Has the date been set?" I asked, busy with my helm.

"No, but Dick proposed to me night before last. He supposed he thought of it himself." She smiled with broad delight and expected me to smile with her.

"Did he?"

"Yes—and most ardently. I didn't think he could do it so well. I told him I'd give him an answer in a few days. He'll be immensely relieved to find out it's 'yes' and think it was by the narrowest of margins." But her childish joy in her wiles died quickly away as she looked at me closer.

"Oh, Jason," she cried.

"Don't worry about me."

"I don't like the idea of it so well either, in some ways—but it can't be helped—and we must laugh all we can."

"You're right, of course."

"You know I wouldn't think of marrying him if he were poor, and if I weren't poor, I'd marry you."

I tried to answer bitterly, and could not. I looked at her, so trustful of me, so honest with me, perhaps because I recognized her beauty. "You ought to know, Jason," she was saying with her eyes, "that no woman so beautiful to you as I am, could ever wrong you." It was true too, somehow. Vanity over any prime gift from God is philosophically impossible. I saw no trace of it in her. But maybe she was a latter-day Salem witch. We do not know half enough about these misunderstood, persecuted people, created to be the delight and wonder of our dull world. She was like an almost undiscovered goddess. But she never doubted it herself; and with me, its complete adorer, she could be as honest as with herself.

"I'd be so happy to marry you, Jason, if both of us weren't poor," she told me, looking dreamily out to sea. "I'd come to need you wonderfully, and then love you wonderfully. But I can't stand being poor any longer. All I could give you would fade away."

She was sitting beside me at the helm, her long legs crossed, her face pensive; and looking long into my face, she leaned and kissed me. I did not think it was a sudden burst of tenderness. She seemed to be tasting my lips, as though wondering whether her first impression of them was mistaken.

"And you know, Jason," she went on in a businesslike tone, "after Dick and I are really engaged, I can't go with you any more."

"I suppose not." But my mind was not on my words.

"If he found out about it, he might jilt me. Yes, he might, for he's a terrible temper, and he might cut off his own nose to spite his face."

"I don't think he would. He's too smart. But he'd make you sorry in some way."

"I believe you're right—and you know him as well as I do. He might refuse to give Pa enough money. Besides, it wouldn't be fair to him, don't you think so?" She turned in eager interest for my answer.

Instead I reached a long arm and drew her slanting across my breast and did not let her go until her face was incarnadined and she thrust me hard away. It was a bold address, but well I knew that only in extreme boldness lay any hope of my having her for my own. It was also a most loving one for an amateur like me, but instinct helped great longing in that respect. Eliza had her back turned and seemed to be asleep.

"Don't do that," Roxana whispered, wide eyed. "I'm going to be Dick's wife."

"He doesn't own you yet."

"He won't ever own me. No one ever will, please God. But he'll have the right to—my full attention. He's going to buy that, and I mustn't cheat him."

66

"He hasn't bought it yet."

"I can't give it all to him if—someone else—is too much in my memory." So she said, flinching only a little. She had lived many years in France, where happy carnal as well as spiritual love is frankly respected and desired as the due of marriage, not done behind God's back from the devil's tempting as in Salem.

"Anyway," she went on, "the engagement will be very short. He'll be very impetuous. If the ring isn't on my finger within a month, we'll have to sell Eliza."

My father had opposed slavery in a republic dedicated to freedom, and so had I. To make livestock out of human beings was surely a horrid thing. Eliza, although saying almost nothing on this or the other trip, was an exceedingly human being. She was young and lithe and crow black except for the palms of her hands, her heavy lips, the soles of her feet, and the gleaming white of her eyes and teeth.

"She eats more than she earns," Roxana confided, "but it would break her heart if we should sell her, and I think mine."

I came by a sunken hulk where I thought Roxana might have some lively fishing, anchored, and rigged lines for both her and Eliza. The Negress got two bites to my girl's one, the only apparent reason being that she spat on her bait. Then Roxana tried spitting on hers, although without marked effect. We could see no handy way to get the catch into the Reils' kitchen until Eliza turned her big eyes on us and spoke in her pleasant drawl.

"Why, Miss R'anna, they won't be no trouble about 'at. I know a col'ed man on a fish boat, and I'll tell Mussus how he come to the house and cay'd 'em to me."

The hours that I had thought such a great store began to depart from us. I did not know where they had gone, so stealthily their passing, but my turnip could not forbear from counting the loss and reminding me of it at every glance into its accursedly cheerful, candid face. It seemed I did most of the talking. I told Roxana no little of my boyhood in the Adirondacks, of my tutelage under Pierre, and could not forbear from giving her loving glimpses of my parents, although shunning any account of their death.

Toward evening I thought that she and Eliza needed to excuse themselves from me, and I from them. If we had been far out, I could have solved the difficulty without embarrassment to anyone. If I did not know how, staunch, forthright Roxana would have shown me. As it was, I knew a small tidal creek half an hour's sail away. We went in prettily, with Roxana able to step from my gunnel to dry land. At that she praised my seamanship so warmly that I resolved to show her some really fancy sailing on the out-trip.

As it happened, we stayed on the beach a little longer than we had intended, and the sun began tumbling down the west. All sailors know how it will give the illusion of height, and plenty of time before dark, when it is already poised for its last, swift, downward plummet. Apollo's horses were headed for the barn. My heart fell with it, and would not stop, because suddenly I perceived that my day was over. Before we tacked back to Salem, the big stars would shine.

I could hardly believe it. Somehow I had expected a miracle that had not passed. Before now I had won one great race and one little one, and a ship that I had often thought would flounder had brought me safe to shore; and so because it was strong I had trusted hope— that so often buoys us up awhile, only to desert us on the deep sea.

"I reckon this is the end."

She came quickly and sat close beside me, her arm thrown about my neck. "Jason," she murmured and made no other reply.

"You've been very generous with me. I can't keep on trying to see you, against your will."

"It wouldn't be against my will. Only it wouldn't do any good— and make trouble."

"Do you know I'll love you always?"

"In some fashion, yes. I'd be ashamed not to know it. I wish there could have been more between us. But this was all that was possible."

She expected me to take her in my arms, but I could not just now. I would sail the boat out of the creek in the difficult tack, then hold her close all the way to port.

My eyes were not as clear as usual, and I misjudged the wind a little, getting too close under the land. Yet I could have been as clumsy a score of times in this particular maneuver without accident. As it happened, there was a submerged rock that did not whiten the light ripple on the bay, and its long shadow from the low sun escaped my notice. My centerboard took the brunt of the blow and was carried clean away.

I fished it out in a hurry, then threw my hook and took stock of our situation. Eliza was big eyed, but Roxana sat watching me with a faint smile and no sign of concern.

"It's not very serious," I told her. "I can't repair it out here, and of course can't tack, but can sail and make short about five miles from Salem."

"Goodness, I don't want to walk that far, and to hire a farmer's shay would cause talk."

"You wouldn't have to. I could repair it easily in shoal water where I can keel her over. But we'd have a wet boat and a chilly time of it." The cold waters of Massachusetts Bay chilled the air quickly after sundown.

"I hate wet boats and chilly times." She was looking at me searchingly.

"Well, the wind's due to change on the high tide. It's happened every night through this spell of weather. There's not the slightest danger of rough weather and likely by midnight we could sail for Salem pretty as you please."

She considered a little while, an expression I could not read on her pensive face. She had something on her mind—a very serious matter.

"Can you fry some of those fish?" she asked, worriedly. "I'm going to be awfully hungry!"

"I tell you!" There was a little whale-oil stove in my deckhouse. "Anyway I've got some wine and cake."

She drew a delighted deep breath through an open mouth. "Jason, you don't mean it!"

"I certainly do."

"Wine and cake?"

"Good 'ns, too."

"How completely proper." I did not know quite what she meant by that. "Jason, I didn't appreciate that poetical side of you—but I might have known you had it."

"So what do you want to do?"

"Of course let's stay. It's a beautiful evening, and you've a snug cabin. Wind or no wind, will you promise to get me home before daylight? I know a girl who'll swear I spent the night with her, if I have to ask her to."

"I can get you back by two, if the breeze changes the way I know it will—by four on any account." For we could make nigh to Beverly or Marblehead in any wind that blew.

"Then I'm glad it happened. I had a feeling that it wasn't right for us to part so soon."

2.

I cut Eliza a fair third of the cake, but did not yet open the wine. When I took the wench below decks where she could make her bed,

I gave her something to suit her better—a gill of rum, poured from my jug. If it made her sleepy after happy, no fault could be found with that; and no doubt Roxana would be of this same opinion. Our hours together would count more, the more we were alone.

We had never seen so lovely a night, we thought, than the one that tacked in against the seaward breeze. Doubtless there had been a hundred finer even in our short lives, but we were full content with the no longer quite full moon, the sprinkling of big stars, the deep-purple vault of which we were the mathematical center, and the gently—it seemed lovingly—rocking sea. The nicest thing about it was, we need not look at it very long. We could go from under the open sky beneath the roof of my deckhouse where, when the door was shut and the lantern lit, we were as warm and snug as we could have been in our cabin amidst the Adirondack snows.

Indeed we could not get as far apart as in that beloved spot. When I had broached my flask of wine, we could hardly keep from clinking glasses from sheer proximity. This we did of course, and Roxana taught me a French rite connected with toasting, and I showed her one greatly favored by the youths and maidens of the Palatinate Germans, the most kindly of all. The wine was pale, sparkling champagne, kept cool enough below decks, a kind that has a peculiarly happy effect on the cockles of the heart. When she had drunk nearly a pint, she no longer worried lest our kisses somehow cheat her future husband out of his full due. Some were long and some burning, and all were sweet beyond reckoning to me, and according to all sign a great joy to her.

"Is this how young people court in the Adirondack Mountains?" she asked, glowing from our kisses as much as from the wine, and with childlike eyes.

"I reckon it's the same the country over."

"In just such little cabins?"

"Not much bigger than this, some of them."

"How do they get away from their elders?"

"The elders go to bed and to sleep. But if the courting's well along, the pa and ma don't want to waste firewood keeping the cabin warm."

"Poor things."

"They make out pretty well. It isn't fair to send the boy home early, after he's come so far, so they bundle."

"What does bundle mean?"

"Bundle themselves all up and sit propped up in the bed."

"Why, I hadn't heard about that! Is it common knowledge?"

"You've been away during the learning years. It's considered perfectly respectable among the frontier people. True, it often brings about quick marriages, but that's considered a good thing."

"I should think it would. But if it's only practiced in winter—"

"The room doesn't have to be very chilly, to bring it about."

She started to say something—decided not to—then said it anyway. "This room is plenty warm." Her color rose a little more and her voice was very low and not very steady.

"Will you bundle with me, Roxana? I'd love to have you. I'll let down the bed—"

"I'd love to, too, Jason, but I'm not going to."

"There'll never be another chance—"

"I'm thinking of that, still it would be too dangerous. You haven't enough blankets to make it safe."

"I've got a cubby full."

"There's not enough anywhere to make it safe. No, we'll forego that. I wouldn't if there was any future for us, but there isn't. Do you suppose the frontier people learned it from Indians?"

"Catch Indians inventing any custom as nice as that!"

"Did you ever go with a squaw, Jason? I've heard it's not uncommon on the frontier."

"No."

She saw something in my face that startled her. "What's the matter?"

"Nothing."

"Why did you look that way? That terribly lonely look—"

"My Ma and Pa were killed by Indians—at the same time. I didn't mean to—"

"Oh, I didn't know."

"That's all right. It's happened thousands of times on the frontier—" Yet I could hardly speak.

"How did you escape?" She had caught both my hands in hers.

"Pierre and I were hunting. They killed him too, that day."

"They were all you had?"

"Yes."

"As I have only Dad?"

"I reckon so."

"I wish we could have each other. We can't. There's not even any use wishing. How old were you, Jason?"

"Not quite seventeen."

"There's still more to it. I don't know what it is. It frightens me."

71

She was trembling and her hands turned cold in mine. She was whispering, her lips close to my ear.

"Do you want to know the rest?"

"Yes."

"Are you sure? It's mighty ugly."

"I want to know. I want to be with you in every way I can—always."

I looked at the lantern, its little flame quite still, and at the great flame, likewise still, in Roxana's face. Then I went to my cubby and got a little poke of deer hide and laid its contents on my lap.

"Oh, what are they!"

"You know, don't you?"

"It's human hair—with dried blood on it—"

"You've never seen scalps before? The Indians take ours, and we take theirs."

"But you were only a boy—"

"I grew up that morning. Two are warrior scalps. The other is a squaw's—the one who begged for sugar and then called in the war party."

"Did you—"

"Yes. Pierre took three too, before he was killed."

"Put them away, will you, Jason?"

"I shouldn't have brought them out."

Deliberately she touched all three of them, I did not know why. When they were back in their poke in the cubby, it seemed that I had laid down a crushing burden. Roxana's eyes sparkled with tears.

"I love you," burst out of me, in happiness so sharp that it hurt like intense pain. She gave me a smile at once humorous and sorrowful.

"Jason, are you sure?"

"Yes."

"Even without my loving you?"

"Yes."

"Then what if I did love you?"

"You couldn't, I reckon, this soon."

"I don't know. I've never felt so close to anyone—or so happy. If I do, I'd want to give you all I can in the little time that remains, and you give me all you can. I'd be awfully sorry later to find out that I did love you—and hadn't done it."

That was a queer way to look at it, perhaps, but it seemed entirely natural to me, we having gone so deeply into truth.

72

"I mean true love that can never die," she went on. "It doesn't come many times—it's a rare, great thing. I don't know if it's come to me, but—" She stopped, looking at me with deeply amazed eyes.

"Tell me what you're thinking—"

"Anyway that is the way you love me—true love that can never die?"

"Yes."

"Jason, you didn't know that at fifteen I was almost sure I was going to be killed."

"By the Terror?"

"Robespierre was dead—it was only three years ago—it was a little Terror in Bordeaux after a Royalist uprising. All my uncle's family—*émigrés* in Quebec—were under sentence of death—charged with conspiring with England against the Commune—and I was accused of being my cousin Térèse Reil de Pontivy, returned to France with English letters. She was two years older than I, but my name and my coloring were enough. The Committee wanted another young girl on the guillotine to inflame the mob—they were hungry and getting out of hand. I had to hide until the Directory came in, then escaped to England and finally to Quebec." All this she told me rapidly in French, her eyes burning with excitement.

When she stopped, she was in my arms, her tear-wet lips against mine.

"Jason, let's forget all that and play we're a mountain girl and boy like you said."

"We can't play, Roxana. I love you."

"I'll return it all I can."

Trembling, I pulled down my poor bed. Her face illumined and with childlike wonder she got in and wrapped a blanket about her waist and legs, tucking it in well, and making a place for me beside her. It crossed my mind that she possessed an innocence strangely like my savage maid's under the palms. That did not make sense at first, since Roxana was so knowing; it was true enough, though, and it arose somehow out of her beauty outward and within.

A half hour passed. That long we were in control of our actions, she from considerations of the future, I for her sake. Long before that I had sensed that she wanted to yield all to me for my one night's keeping and our forever memories, but had resisted still. But we had been too reckless for this to continue. She had become too vulnerable to my love. The lanternlight in the tiny, warm room, the gentle rocking of the boat, and our aloneness in the moonlit bay all arrayed against her. And her beauty felt so intensely by both of us—magical to me as desire illumined its every lineament—was never so strange and new as now.

"We might as well, now it's gone this far." The pupils of her eyes were immense and fathomless.

"Maybe you'll be sorry if we do. Will you marry me, Roxana?"

"No."

"Then I love you too much to take from you—"

"It won't be the first time, Jason."

"I'm so glad you told me!"

"There was one other time. It was a French corporal, only sixteen, who had hidden me from the Terror and risked everything for me. It was the reward he wanted, the only one I could give him. I was never sorry about that—and it wasn't a hundredth part of this. If you love me, Jason—"

"I love you."

"Then I'll always be glad."

3.

Once she too had whispered, "I love you," but the time had been no part of our common time, so the words did not apply to our common lives.

She was signally sweet and tender with me during the homeward sail, as though she had unavoidably hurt me in some way. It seemed she was seeking forgiveness instead of granting it. I did not know what this portended. But we spoke very little as she sat beside me at the helm. She sang to me a couple of French ballads and I replied with "Bobby Shaftoe," a children's song my mother had taught me and which I had always loved.

The wind shifted about midnight, and at half-past one we saw a late lantern or two on Derby Wharf. "Tell me goodbye now, Jason," Roxana murmured. "Eliza and I are going to walk home alone."

"There might be a drunken sailor on the street—"

"Come behind us, if you like. But you mustn't be seen with us. If we're seen—and we're going to take a back street—we've been staying with a sick friend. I can fix that all right."

"Good."

I was thinking how I could get our string of fish to her kitchen, but was ashamed of so mundane a thought and did not mention it.

"Have you a sack you can put the fish in?" Roxana asked after a little pause. "Eliza can carry it, and they'll be delicious for breakfast."

74

"Yes, I have a sack." While she steered I went to get it. On my return, she seemed afraid to speak.

"Goodbye Jason," she whispered.

"I can't see you again?"

"No. I'm going to do what I said."

"Don't you belong to me now?"

"No."

"I belong to you."

"No. You're going to sail and find the Golden Fleece."

"Don't talk about that now."

"I mean it, Jason. I want you to have a splendid goal—and that's a good name for it. Fortune—an honored name—wonderful experience—"

"Yes, I've got to get a lot of that to get you." It seemed such a simple and true thing to say.

"Good for you, Jason. That makes everything all right." I saw her look triumphantly at the moon.

"How much time could you give me, before you marry Dick?"

"None before, but all you need afterward."

"I don't know what that means."

"Why, you can't do all that in a day or a year. The longer it takes —in reason—the more you'll enjoy life. And I'll hope and pray for you always."

"You can't marry Dick if—"

I was stammering but she answered briskly and cheerfully.

"Oh, there's no danger of that. Look at the moon. It's started to wane."

"We can say anything now to each other."

"It's the same with a woman. An old peasant *grand'mère* in France told me so. Her month begins like a new moon, and for fourteen days it waxes, and that's the time nature provided for her to conceive. But for the next fourteen days no seed can take root. My month is nearly out."

Until now I had felt an inkling that the common miracle had come to pass. It had frightened me but exalted me too, for then she could not marry Dick and I could keep her always. But likely had the chance existed, there would never have been this much. I had better thank my lucky stars that she had sailed with me at all! Thereby she had risked her whole venture.

I went below and wakened Eliza. She came up and stood in the bow, the sack of fish clutched in her hand.

75

"How soon can I see you again?" I asked Roxana.

"When you come back with the Golden Fleece," she answered dreamily. "Anything can happen by then." Plainly the romantic notion had taken her fancy strongly.

Roxana came into my arms to kiss me goodbye. Only once before had I been so shaken, and that was with hate. The kiss was meant for a sad and tender farewell, but instead it made known what a powerful bond had been wrought between us, and how our youthful and natural strengths fought against its breach. Young love often seems pitiful to elders even as they envy it. It is so headlong, often so unwise. For the first time, I thought, Roxana was truly appalled by our impending parting. She was frightened at last. Her future was not as safe as she had proposed.

"I wish we'd stayed longer since this is goodbye," I told her.

"Oh, I wish so too!" And that was not only rewakened passion, with which she was so instinct. "But we've caused enough trouble in each other's lives."

Yet I would have dropped my anchor there, had we not been within a stone's throw of the dock. I would have headed back into the bay, if I could tack into the now stiff breeze.

"Goodbye, Jason."

"Goodbye, my sweetheart."

Then I heaved to, and we glided gently alongside the dock. When I saw that the coast was clear, Roxana and the Negress clambered up. Then I followed them at about a hundred paces through the moonlit deserted streets until they reached their door. Roxana turned and raised her arm to me.

I waited ten minutes more, until the lamp that had been lighted in an upstairs room went out. On returning to the dock, still I did not go to bed, deciding to hold vigil until dawn over something—perhaps a ghost that had walked my little deck and lain in beauty in my poor bed. During that watch I did my best to confront the almost certainty of losing Roxana for years or forever. Stubbornness is resolution carried to folly, and I could not get shed of it. In a way she would still be mine, for the sake of this night, but in no way satisfactory to me. That substance was too thin for a man like me. I must have a near, warm sweetheart, to love me and be loved, and there was none to fill her place on any land or sea.

But I could wait a long time if I had to, and fight very hard. Nor would I waste that time or forego other profit from that fight. I could live very hard, which would balm loneliness and loss, and at the same

76

time become more worthy of her—meaning no high-flown thing, but merely a man more acceptable to her. So when she had married Dick —and fate or I might somehow block it yet—I would sell my boat and put the money in another venture on the deep sea.

At present we were fighting an undeclared war with France. The President was arming our frigates, mustering men, calling General Washington from Virginia to command our forces. I did not like the notion of battling Pierre's country, our great friend aforetime, yet would gladly man a gun against its bloody governors who had sought to put Roxana's golden head in the Little Window. Perhaps I could sign on a privateer for a year or more's service. That would be patriotic and quite likely profitable too.

The stars paled, the moon hung low in the west, cocks crowed in the town, and sleepy gulls flapped over the bay. It was morning in the world, and in my life.

4.

Ten days passed without notable event. I ate and slept, and fished for the market, took some parties sailing, and caught glimpses of Roxana on Broad Street. She was likely engaged to Dick by now, I thought, but no word of it had reached me, and anyway they would observe a proper interval between betrothal and espousal. There is many a lurch 'twixt the trothplight and the church. If she longed for me one-tenth as fiercely as I for her, she might jilt him yet.

I did what I could to make her think of me. When I caught some pan fish of the same tasty kind that she had breakfasted on, I bribed a Negro cook off a fishing smack to carry them to Eliza with a careful hint, no more, of who had sent them. Quite in contrast to this, I sent Roxana, again through Eliza, a bottle of French perfume I had got from a smuggler. Also I wrote and posted her a letter in French, purportedly from an *abbé* she had met in Brest, and dropped in the Office by a passing sailor, which I thought was a marvel of *double-entendre*. To my great joy, she replied with a gay little note, delivered to me by Eliza, that a ten-year-old child could have seen through my cryptography, that she had read and burned it, that the flame had licked her heart somewhat, and when I went to sea to find the Golden Fleece to be sure and look to my centerboard, so I could return.

That message came to me on the night of the new moon, ten days since our parting. It buoyed me up of course but the deep hollow

77

under that high wave was that she still wanted me to go, and the sooner the better. After a night of unhappy dreams, I could hardly abide Andy Oats's unusual joviality, as we put out to find a school of squid he had marked down the preceding evening. If I had known what it portended—

"We ain't done so good, lately," he began.

"No."

"Ye'll hardly go out of sight o' land. But I reckon we'll do better from now on."

"Why do you reckon that?"

"Ye won't have so much on your mind, with Dr. Reil's daughter married off. I told ye she was out of reach of any Starbuck, let alone a Todkill."

"Have you heard that she's betrothed?" I asked, pride steadying my voice.

"No. I didn't hear that. But a clerk I know, at the Featherstone Tea Company, he heard the gentleman a-talking. She's marrying Mr. Dick this coming Sunday."

I sat still and watched our stem part the little waves. The impulse came to me to set my face against Andy's prying eyes. When I had won through that, I thought to go out and catch squid to sell for bait to codgers. We were already half a league from the dock. Then I remembered it was my face, my boat, and my life. The girl about to be taken from me was my love, all I had in my heart. I did not care how big a fool Andy thought me.

I yanked my helm so hard that we shipped water.

"Where you be a-going?" Andy demanded.

"To Derby Dock."

"Them squid ain't goin' to dally about all day."

"You can leave me, and go after them, but see you're back by sundown, for I might have need of the boat." So I spoke, wildly, as if planning to steal Dick's bride away in my piddling craft.

"Now, Mr. Starbuck, I advise ye not to do nothing rash."

"Thanks."

"I don't say she's too high for ye, ye being so proud minded, but your line broke, and she got away."

"Not yet."

"It looks to me like. And 'member all them halibuts she's already cost ye. No use throwing good money after bad."

I got out on the dock and then there was nowhere for me to go. I could not wait to watch Andy take off, after my frantic haste to get

78

here, so I started walking briskly in the handiest direction. Then I rushed back and had him hand me the quill and inkhorn from the cubby—we used them to tally fish—and a piece of paper. Then looking and feeling like one of Elisha Featherstone's browbeaten clerks, I made off down the dock.

Today was Thursday; Sunday but three days off. The hour was hardly seven, and the Boston post could be expected about nine. I sat on a pier and scribbled a brief note—that I would be in the Reils' woodshed at eleven tonight, and would stay there, chopping wood if necessary to pass the time, until Roxana came forth and exchanged a few words with me. The ill wind of her father's poverty blew me at least the little good that he did not keep a dog.

Roxana did not meet the post. Then I looked for someone trustworthy to deliver it privately to Eliza, but everyone about was too respectable or too disreputable. The only alternative was to roam about her neighborhood, hanging around like a homeless dog until I saw the Negress leave the yard on some household errand.

Eliza did not appear surprised when I followed her up the street and stopped to ask her the time of day.

"It's time you done quit walkin' by our house, Cap'n, suh," she answered.

"Did your young mistress see me?"

"I like to know how she could help hessef, and she had 'nuff trouble keepin' Ol' Miss from seein' you too. She say for you to tell me what you want, and please go 'way, befo' somebody call the watch."

"I want you to give her a letter."

"She didn't tell me to take no letter."

"Here's a silver dollar for you, to deliver it safely."

"Well, I reckon 'at a-same as tellin' what you want." She slipped the coin deftly into a pocket of her skirt. "But you ain't goin' make no trouble for her—" The black eyes grew wide and imploring.

"Never."

"She goin' marry Massa Dick and be a rich lady. If anything happen, I don' know what we'd do. You leave 'at letter on de gate pos' up ahead, and I'll pick it up. Somebody might be lookin' at us now."

She pretended with voluble gestures to direct me up the street, and I hurried on. Palming the letter, I laid it on the post, and waited at the corner until she retrieved it. Then I began the long wait for the rendezvous.

I walked every street and road, although wary of traversing the same one twice. I stopped and watched some men digging a well, stood by some urchins fishing from a pier, bought some sweet cakes that I had looked at too long through a window, went into the custom-house and busily read all the shipping news, legged it to Danvers and back, and talked with a little girl gathering flowers until fearful that her mother might see us and come and snatch her away. Through all of this I was aware of a progressive and painful indignity. It seemed that the day had begun with a flavor of low comedy in my conversations first with Andy, then with Eliza, and would end in unbearable farce. What could I achieve with a few words with Roxana? At best she would be sorry for me, I thought, and at worst, disgusted with me. I had nothing to say to her of any matter, no plan to propose.

God knew she had given my ill-starred love more than its due. But that was her very being—strange and new—inspiring me to try again, and never stop trying. It did not matter how big a fool I showed, if therein lay a chance to win. If I angered her, she would get over it, but I would never get over a missed opportunity. Anyway there was something working on me besides blind hope. I had a recurring sense of a turn of fortune—even of prospects brighter than before—although without seeing any reason. A motive I could not isolate was forcing this rash act—a need for something more than a farewell word or kiss. It seemed a clue to it had been given me more than once today but it had passed by unrecognized.

The sun set and the lean and lonely moon was not far behind. The stars came out and lights went out; and after a while, noiseless as an Indian, I crept into the Reils' woodshed. The last lamp in the house expired. Light feet, no louder than a cricket's chirp, pattered the boardwalk. Only Roxana could walk so light and free! Instead, it was Eliza.

"Is it you, Cap'n, suh?" she whispered.

"Yes."

"My honey come in a minute, but don't make no trouble for her, suh."

"Oh, I won't!"

Then, raising her voice a little as though talking to herself, "Bless God, I done forgot to get some kindlin' to sta't fi' in the mo'nin'."

She went away then, and then I knew why I had come. I knew what I wanted to say to Roxana. It was most momentous business after all.

Roxana came and in the darkness found my hands. "Oh, what is it, Jason?"

"Can we stay here?"

"No. Follow me." She led me past a vegetable garden to a wall where hollyhocks bloomed. "Now tell me, but you must hurry."

"Your marriage is very hasty."

"I thought you'd notice that, Jason, when you heard about it."

"Did you expect me to come?"

"I knew you'd come."

"You think the old peasant woman in France was mistaken?"

"She didn't know what she was talking about. I asked Dad—pretending to want to know for the future's sake—and he said there was nothing in it. I hadn't ought to have believed her, but it sounded so reasonable—and convenient—"

"What makes you think—? Maybe the night air on my boat—"

"It was on your boat, but it wasn't the night air." A swift delight passed through her at the ribald jest; there came a lilt in her whisper, and I knew her eyes were dancing in the dark.

"Listen. You've got to be serious. God knows it's a terribly serious matter."

"It's just an intuition, so far. But I decided to get married in a hurry."

"Roxana, you can't. If you have the least reason to suspect that, it would be dishonorable."

"I suppose so. There are times girls can't think about honor. Dad and I can't afford for me not to marry him, or have him throw me out afterward. Look at it sensibly, Jason. Granting nothing has happened, it will happen unless I marry Dick at once. We can't keep from seeing each other—if you'd tossed a pebble at my window last night, I'd have had to let you in. We'll take dreadful chances just to be together. He'll find out about it and jilt me. And if it's already happened—why, he'll never know it, and be just as pleased and proud—"

"Good God!"

"Why shouldn't he be? They say that love babies are the prettiest and the smartest. You think he's getting the best of the bargain anyway, don't you?"

"By a thousand times, but—"

"Well, I almost hope it's true, because it would make up to me—a little—for losing you."

I could not understand that kind of honesty; it was too new. I did

81

not try then, only caught a kind of glimpse of a young, oddly beautiful, bold-minded girl, in her childhood the close companion of a brilliant but tormented man, cut loose in France when new and bold ideas flashed about like lightning, and hiding in the dark from the Little Window that would darken her forever in this world. Such a girl might cut through conventional patterns of thought and discover her own mind and heart.

"No other girl would feel that way."

"Oh, I think she would, if she wasn't too bothered by what people had told her." She stopped and contemplated this in that childlike way of hers—coming forth with something on the spur of the moment and then wondering and puzzling over it. "I don't feel it's the least dishonorable," she went on thoughtfully. "Dick is such a greedy person—"

"Why do you marry him then? Marry me—tomorrow!"

"That's nice of you, Jason, but it's out of the question. Don't talk about that any more."

"No, I can't even discuss it," I said, in a sudden bitterness of anger. "Why should I be thinking about what's fair to Dick? I'd like to know what's fair to me. I'm losing my girl and for all I know losing my baby too—my only kin."

"Not for always, Jason, I swear. Some day I'll come back to you. If we've had a baby, he'll be a real son—or a beautiful daughter—to you. I've got a wonderful plan."

Roxana began to kiss me, quick, excited, jubilant kisses all over my face. She would not let me speak.

"As soon as he's able to listen, I'll tell him about Jason, searching for the Golden Fleece. He and I will have a wonderful secret—never to tell anyone—that there's a real Jason, tall and dark and strong—who came out of the mountains and has gone out on the sea. Some day he'll come back! He'll bring the magic prize. He'll be scarred from battle, but still young. Oh, Jason, don't you see—"

She stood still a few seconds; I became aware of extreme suspense. I could not see her face well in the starlight, or know what thoughts filled her starlit eyes, but it seemed possible that the same longing that was so deep in me had passed to her. Perhaps it had wakened in her, her own being. If so, I could speak—

"Roxana, before I go—"

"Oh, yes." Her hands that had been on my shoulders crept up and clasped about my neck.

"Are you sure?"

"I was never surer of anything in my life." Her murmur fell to a hushed, wonder-struck whisper. "Jason, could you let me go without—"

"Yes, if it were best for you. I love you."

"I know what it is now. *'I will not let you go unless you bless me.'*"

I did not recognize the words or know their source. It was long afterward that I came upon them and knew that Roxana, her imagination vaulting, had tried to express the mystery of love so deep and full upon her. She had expressed it well. Israel had expressed a greater mystery of love in that strange moment on the desert. Our love was only mortal, but it was not profane.

When we made our hasty bed in the summer grass, as the stars burned splendidly overhead and common hollyhocks bloomed by the wall, it came true that we blessed each other with this farewell.

CHAPTER FIVE

For Kith and Kin

1.

Perplexed by many doubts, tempted at times to extravagant designs, I managed to chart a course. I could not remain in Salem, barred from Roxana's door. It was more than a man like me could stand. But I would wait to see her wedded, crowding with the common run in the back of the church. Until then, I thought, nothing on earth could budge me from the scene, because something might yet happen to break off the match. Perhaps I would remain a month or two more, reconnoitering the ground with great care, bribing Eliza to let me know how she was getting along. Then if the marriage promised to last, I would embark on a long voyage.

It was a sensible plan, and the only one at all practical. It was fairly settled in my mind by Friday afternoon; I could decide later which of the Seven Seas to sail.

But Fate had a trick up her sleeve.

It is hard to believe in fate in the way Moslems do—it is so against reason—and yet hard to gainsay. Reason has a mighty foe in superstition. One takes thought, a painful process for most folk, the other merely credence. It had sometimes come to me that I had been fated for an unusually interesting life, as by real predestination; but out of a seed odd-dropped on a windy mountain top will grow an odd-shaped tree. My seeking such a life, and more than that, the way I moved on the spur of events, might have more to do with my obtaining it than all the looms and shears of the three weird sisters. But although I had invited some such event as occurred, one of a hundred trifles could have brought a certain sailor to Salem at some other time than the day before Roxana's wedding.

I saw the fellow at daybreak Saturday morning standing on the dock not far from my boat. Barely awake, I mistook him at first for Andy; then I saw he was a somewhat shorter, wirier man, although with something of the same sun-dried appearance. A little way up the wharf lay a sailing dingey I had not seen on going to bed. As he strolled up to me, the dim light revealed him clean shaven save for a stubby red beard, redheaded, sharp nosed, and probably sharp eyed. I thought him brown complexioned, but that proved to be a myriad of freckles.

"She's goin' to be fine," he remarked, with a gesture to all the weather.

"I reckon."

"What might your name be, if ye'll kindly tell me?"

"Jason Starbuck."

"That's what I 'lowed. Was your Pa's name Henry?"

"Why, no. It was Reuben. Why do you ask?"

" 'Tis as I figured. Would ye favor me with your Ma's maiden name?"

"I will, but don't see the sense of it. It's the same as the boat." I had an inkling of the sense of it, though.

"Then you're the one, and I can lay to that. I couldn't afford to make no mistake. I've got word for ye."

"Well, what is it?" My skin was prickling a little.

"There's no one in your boat to hear us?"

"No."

"About a year back ye wrote a letter to your uncle, Cap'n Dan'l Todkill."

"So I did."

"He got it—four months back. He's trouble readin', let alone writin', but I read it aloud to him, and he thanked ye kindly. Futhamore, he took a north'ard course, meaning to meet and talk with ye, but never got no further than South Carliney."

"How is he? Have you come from him? Have you a letter for me?"

"Nay, where he's at, it's not handy for him to get a letter written, but I'll give ye his message."

"I'd thank you for it."

"He says to tell ye he loved his sister Prue a mighty heap, and ye're the only kith and kin that's left to him, and if ye can spare the time, and have the inclination—but ye're not to do it for his sake, only if ye're bent on it yourself—he'd like to lay eyes on ye one time afore he goes up the spout."

My head swam and my eyes hurt and it was a second or two before I could answer. "Is my uncle sick unto death?"

"He ain't sick, to speak truth. I've never seen him more hale. But he's goin' up the spout a week this comin' Wednesday."

When again I could not speak, from seeing too clear a vision, he said the words for me.

"To deal plain, they're going to stretch him for piracy on the high seas."

It seemed to me that I contemplated this a very long time. Then I asked, "Who are 'they'?"

"The provosts at Charleston."

"Where is he now?"

"In the jail on Magazine Street."

This was explicit. He was a good man for this mission.

"Others of his crew too?"

"Nay, sir. He went to shore at Beaufort, and got drunk, and got nabbed."

"Is his ship taken?"

"That she ain't. She's lying less than a league from here this minute. Her name's the 'Charity,' but we've changed her to the 'Hope,' which all o' us sore need. We come to get ye, if ye was of a mind to come."

"I'll come." This did not even take thinking. "And there's no time to lose, if we run into a gale off Hatteras."

"Aye, aye, sir."

"Can you take me out in the dingey? If you can, I'll pick up my kit—"

"Aye, and I see ye ain't one to dally, in that like Cap'n Dan'l."

I took my best clothes, wherein to call on the provost-captain, and on second thought my buckskin shirt, breeches, moccasins, coonskin cap. Although there was no apparent use for them yet, they might come in handy. From a hiding place in my cubby I took the last of my hoard, one gold eagle and half a dozen silver dollars. Lastly, I brought forth both my rifle and Pierre's, mute these four years, but well oiled and finely sighted with powder horns and balls. On a bit of paper I wrote a note to Andy: that I had gone to Boston and points south and to care for the boat well until, soon or late, I returned.

There was no use looking back, as the sailor and I made out into the bay. There was no help for it though, and the Congregational Church spire began to glimmer in the rushing morning and took my eye from all other familiar scenes. The "Charity" proved to be a brig of about seventy tons, sharp and slim-waisted, and very fast from the look of her. She was heavier-gunned than a common hooker, but she was a pirate only according to the view. She simply could not get it through her head that the wars with Spain were over. I had long ago learned that at worst she was a privateer, greatly beloved by the freedom-seeking peoples of Spanish America. By the look of her crew, she had her code and conscience too.

They were by no means harbor riffraff or sea wolves. Mainly they were good salt-water sailors who liked more excitement than peaceful trading offered, and more money to spend. By and large they were restless, reckless, homeless men such as serve as mercenaries in every war, sometimes more staunch in battle than the patriots. A surprising lot were Yankees and Virginians; no few were English; and there was a sprinkling of blond Swedes and broad-faced Dutch. The ship was as clean and trig as any I ever saw.

A brawny young mate, giving his name as Dawson, shook hands with me at the head of the Jacob's ladder, and asked my companion to take me to my quarters. These proved to be captain's cabin, but I was not to sleep in the captain's bed. A cot had been placed near by, showing that I was only his guest and kinsman, and by no means his par. A couple of sailors brought my kit and guns, the dingey boat was being hoisted aboard, and presently the groaning capstan weighed the iron.

"You haven't told me your name," I said to my escort.

"It's Nicodemus, sir," he replied, saluting.

"Are you one of the officers?"

"Nay, sir, not yet 'fore the mast, in a way of speakin'. I shipped as Cap'n Todkill's cabin boy fifteen year ago, and kind of kept at it ever since."

"You must have liked the life."

"Not all of it, sir, since ye put the question. I'm a law-abidin' man, by nat're, and don't hold by runnin' rum, and takin' prizes without letter o' marque. I'd be happier as a common seaman on a sugar boat, I do vow. But Cap'n Todkill don't see his way to sign me off."

He remarked this with a long face and a doleful tone. In the white marine light I had a clear view of him now, and truly his face and form were stamped with individuality. This is true of most tars. Men cooped up on a wooden islet on the mighty main do not grow to be peas in a pod. The wide horizons and open skies invite self-expansion; in arm's reach of one another each man cherishes his own soul. Nicodemus was a fully developed personality. Something childish in his bright blue eyes and a little comic in his sharp nose set in a bewilderment of freckles emphasized the immense reliability and competence revealed by his quick, decisive movements and steady glance.

87

"Good God, Nicodemus, you don't have to stay with him unless you want to."

"I've often thought on that. But he depends on me like. Ye see—" his tone grew confidential—"Cap'n Todkill has his faults."

"I'd not doubt it."

"There's no better sailor or shipmaster. I'll say that for him. But he's stubborn no end, and ter'ble sot in his notions, and ter'ble reckless in puttin' 'em in force. He ought to knowed better than lift that cargo of Spanish wine consigned to Charleston. It set the merchants there ag'in him, and they wouldn't rest till they got their hooks on him. But a don's a don to Cap'n Todkill, whenever he comes by 'em."

"No doubt you advised him against it," I said, to keep him talking and get my bearings better.

"I did so! Cautious I be, by nat're, and long headed. He wouldn't heed me, and look what it got him!" A look of despair, at once childish and profound, passed briefly across his face. "But plenty of times he did heed me," Nicodemus went on with growing cheer, "and kept out o' trouble."

"Maybe you can get him out of this trouble."

"Nay, sir, it don't seem likely. I'm a great 'n to plot and plan, a born councilor ye might say, but not one to lead. And the mate's a born mate, not a master. If I 'vize him what to do, he still can't do it, for lack of someone orderin' him to do it. Bad times have come on the 'Charity,' I'll be blowed."

He left me, and I went out on deck for a last look at Salem. Tempted to take a hand at making sail—to show off my salt—still I refrained for vague reasons of prestige that might be useful later. Everything was vague. I could not feel quite awake. A Negro cabin boy served my midday meal in the cabin—tasty victuals on fine Limoges china—and thereafter Mate Dawson, the gunner's mate Mr. Shawe, and Nicodemus paid me a solemn call.

"Cap'n keeps his rum in yon cubby," Nicodemus told me.

"We'll have a tot, after we've talked," I answered.

"Aye, aye, sir."

Mate Dawson appeared to brighten a little. "Have you been to sea, Mr. Starbuck?"

"Yes, Mr. Dawson, to the Nor'west and China and round the world."

"You wouldn't have captained the ship, would you, though I've heard of men your age bein' in command."

"No, I didn't captain her, but I shared in her cargo, and was given responsibility."

"Advised with the cap'n, I reckon. Well, Mr. Starbuck, we'll put this matter up to you, and hear what you've got to say."

"Very well, Mr. Dawson."

"Cap'n Todkill don't merit no hangin', but it do look like he's in for it."

"You can lay to that," remarked Mr. Shawe.

"Leastwise not by an American court," Mate Dawson went on. "He's never loosed a gun 'gin an American ship, or French or Dutch, or e'en 'gin English since King George struck his colors. But he sided with Colombia in her quarrel with Spain, and he's sworn that all them southern nations ought to go free, and anyhow Spanish ships are mighty good picking, too."

"I see."

"He's due to swing ten days tomorrow, and it don't look like we can do aught to save him."

He fell silent and all three looked at me, their gazes at different angles, as though taking a bearing. These were not questioning glances exactly, merely anxious. At that instant I came out of my daze. This was a ship, and she had sailed to Salem to get me, and was taking me to Charleston to see my mother's brother get his neck stretched. She had sails and a helm and a keel and cabins and she held men's hearts and occupied men's hands. This was where I was, not in Salem waiting for my sweetheart to be married. I had gone into another business.

"Why does it look so, Mr. Dawson?" I asked.

"Well, sir, he's in a stout jail. One of the seamen, Nat Brown, was in it one time, and he says 'tis a regular fort."

"Does Nat Brown know Charleston well—and the country there-abouts?"

"I reckon he do. He come from Edisto Island."

"They'll have to bring my uncle out to hang him, won't they?"

"They usually hang 'em in the prison yard, Nat says."

"There'll be a big crowd to watch it. Couldn't a number of the crew mix with it?"

"I reckon some could."

"I'd not want any man who can't keep his head. There mustn't be any killing of our countrymen. My uncle's being hanged by a United States court for offenses against the law."

"Ye know," Nicodemus remarked with a suddenly flushed face, "them's Cap'n's very words."

"The spittin' same," said Mr. Shawe, "or ye can blow me down."

"He got word to us, you see," Mate Dawson explained. "He knowed we'd hang off James Island, and a prisoner new let out signaled and spoke to us, and we gave him twenty dollars as Cap'n promised. Cap'n says there was to be no killing of the guards and such like, for they was not to blame, and he didn't want murder on his soul. He says we was to get word to you, and fetch you to see him if you'd care to come, and sooner than kill any countrymen of his, go back to the Caribs."

"Some of our men might be killed," I ventured. "If there's a rumpus, it will be the guard's duty to shoot."

"That won't stop our boys, I'll be blowed. To speak plain, Mr. Starbuck, they'd go there with empty guns—if there was somebody to lead 'em. We can sail the ship without him, you mind, but can't take her nowhere. It 'pears like there's nowhere to go with Cap'n gone."

"And ye can lay to that," said Mr. Shawe.

"I don't know how to say it no better."

"You've said it well enough. Mr. Dawson, if you'll sail the ship, I'll lead the men."

I had said that too well. The instant the words were out of my mouth I wanted to take them back, so boastful, so presuming—

"Jesus bless you!"

2.

I would have been easy to rebuff at this critical time but, since no one did so, became a thruster. Taking immediate command of the rescue party, within two days I was captaining the ship as well. Mate Dawson, hardly older than me, did not like responsibility and was given to worry. I did like it—at least was excited by it—and was more inclined to trust myself than anyone about me. He was always in doubt whether to skirt a shoal or try to skim it, to take in a little sail or to put more on. Still he would never have trusted me if I had sailed under him; it was being Cap'n Todkill's nephew that turned the trick. But I think all would have resented my sleeping in their skipper's bed; and if I had piled the pretty hussy on a rock all hands would have been so furious with themselves for obeying me as to want to hang me.

I had heard the bells all Sunday morning, and when they struck eight, my heart reverberated with every one. This was noon, the moment that my love, in a long veil, walked queenly to the altar to plight her troth to Dick. The church was hushed and the summer sunshine through the windows lusted for her hair; Dick stood tall and proud, flushed with a triumph that he need not try to understand. She was "a rich lady" now, as Eliza had dreamed. Tonight or more likely this afternoon he would make first use of his purchase. I did not shrink from the vision—he was in his rights; and her quick body would enjoy such a vital lover no matter the state of her heart. My only consolation was, she would see that he paid in full. I did not doubt that he found himself making certain promises, believing them his own offering. His new filly, so my perverse thoughts ran, must be fed before ridden.

Meanwhile I cooked a plot for my uncle's rescue, as simple as I could shape it, although necessarily difficult and dangerous. Nicodemus, whose boast of wiliness was not in vain, helped me with it, and so did crafty old Pierre, four years in his grave. I heard him telling me to overlook no detail, to check and recheck, and on all account to survey the ground.

We would have been in a bad fix without Nat Brown, born and raised about Charleston. He drew me a map of the region in less than an hour. By my keeping him at it, after two days' sweating and hanging out his tongue, he had completed eleven, the last two on the back of big charts, one of which showed the streets and alleys of the city, and the other the roads, creeks, fords, ferries, swamps and forests, even many of the plantations of part of the countryside. My ordnance and supply officers could furnish the troops with plenty of pistols for their pants' legs and there was no end of money—I reckon several thousand dollars in various pokes—at our disposal.

Dropping our hook in Chesapeake Bay I made overland to Norfolk with Nicodemus in stout attendance. There I bought some ready-made clothes fit for landlubbers of common station, a groom's outfit for our Negro mess boy, and the finest gentleman's riding suit that the tailors had on hand. There was a gale making off Hatteras as we came by Albemarle Sound. We could either run to shelter or try to cut between the storm and the perilous shores. Since our time was short, I decided on the latter, not without a cold lump in my heart. The weather hesitated, uncertain where to strike; we did not hesitate willy-nilly. We fairly skipped around the bulge and then flew before a smacking wind clean by Charleston Harbor. Not putting in there, in respect to its bristling forts, we pushed into the mouth of North Edisto River some twenty miles beyond.

Here was sailing of a new sort to me, up the estuary and into Stono Creek. For our skins' sake, we made the cruise at night on a rising tide, occasionally grating on sandbars and scaring the 'gators, and flushing great flocks of sea birds that croaked eerily in the gloom. Nat had told me that well up Stono Creek, about sixteen miles from Charleston, there was a heavy palm growth on either bank that would conceal our vessel. He was right, and here we put her, trusting to luck that no fowler or fisherman would spot her between Monday morning and Wednesday noon, the latter our appointed time to weigh. If we missed it very far, the price of hemp might rise in Charleston, and the hangman buy a manor with his fees.

Nat Brown, Nicodemus, Jehu the Negro steward, and I were rowed to shore in our longboat and put on landlubber clothes. I dressed finely as a country gentleman, Jehu as my groom, Nat and Nicodemus like sober countrymen. While my companions hung out of sight, I entered the gate of the first plantation house we came to, inquired for the master, and told him a well-rehearsed tale. I was Mr. Reuben Jennings, a newcomer to Charleston from Norfolk, had started for Edisto Island with the hope of buying Brickhouse, an ancient manor there, but my horse had gone lame a mile or two down the road. It was a fixed rule of mine never to borrow a horse—this gentlemanly stand the Carolinian approved—but I would rent one, or better yet buy one saddled and bridled, provided his stable was overstocked.

The planter was a Scotchman named Ferguson, and straightway sold me a gelding at half again the nag's worth. A little later he spared me a mare, having liked the way I skimmed her over the fence. Riding the mare with Jehu astride the gelding, a few miles farther on I entered the iron gates of another manor—this time a very fine one, owned by a Ravenal, with a mansion fit for an English barony. But horse-lovers are incorrigible horse-traders, blue-blooded or red.

Mr. Ravenal sold me a pretty beast, then directed me to a horse-breeder close by on Ashley River. At his paddock I selected five, making eight in all, which would afford a raiding party of six—about as large as could foregather without awakening suspicion—and two with empty saddles.

Nat and Nicodemus went about their duties with six of the beasts; Jehu and I rode into Charleston in some state. The sun had gone down when I stopped at the prison gate on Magazine Street and asked to speak to the jailor. Deeming me a somebody, the turnkey admitted me, admitted a silver dollar into his pocket, and presently showed me into the worthy's presence. He was, indeed, Mr. Silvester, in charge of the jail; and what could he do for me?

My tale was as simple and credible as I could make it. I was a Jennings of Virginia, thinking of settling in Charleston, and a blacksheep cousin of mine had once sailed with a prisoner in the jail, Captain Daniel Todkill. The youth had never returned, there was a pretty legacy awaiting him at Norfolk, and might I have a few words in private with his captain? The matter, involving the good name of the family, was one I would not care to have noised abroad.

Mr. Silvester was instantly sympathetic. While it was against the rules for the condemned prisoner to receive any visitors but men of the cloth, an exception would be made in my case. He himself escorted me through a strongly locked passage and admitted me into my uncle's cell. "Here's a gentleman to see you, Captain," the jailor told him in a friendly and quite respectful tone.

The day was dim and the cell almost dark. I could have kept my countenance anyway, and no doubt the old privateer was a good hand at it too. The jailor saw not even a sharp glance pass between us, and immediately went about his own affairs. However a turnkey with a lantern loitered in the corridor, and we must carefully guard our words and voices.

My uncle was not nearly as old as I had expected. "About fifty" had sounded venerable to a youth of twenty-one, but his sunburned face was young, his eyes alive and shining even in this dusk, and his compact figure sturdy. His hair, ungrizzled, was quite fair. It was the same ripe-straw hue of my mother's. When he spoke, his voice was hearty, the kind I liked in a kinsman.

"Are you Cap'n Dan'l Todkill?"

"Ye can lay to that."

"I regret to find you in such deep trouble."

"I thank ye kindly."

"I want to ask about a gentleman adventurer—though some would call him a scoundrel—by name Boots Jennings—who sailed with you. My name is Reuben Jennings." "Boots" was my mother's pet name for her brother Daniel.

"Why, I remember him well. A rogue tall as ye, who liked his glass, but fairer complexioned. He repented his ways and took the air. In that he showed good sense, or he might be in this same pickle

93

with me." My uncle was quick on the trigger, glowing my heart.

"Is that all you can tell me about him? There's a legacy for him, at Norfolk."

"I had a letter from him, which one of the lads read me, but I misremember what's in it. It's in my chest on the 'Charity.'"

"I'm afraid that won't do me any good."

"I reckon not. Even the key's hidden in my sea boots."

"I reckon you've quite a treasure in your chest."

"Mainly old clothes, and a little Spanish coin. Burned the candle at both ends, I did, and only an inch to go. But if ye ever go aboard the 'Charity' ye can try to get that letter. On second thought, my old mate, Joshua Radcliffe, heard from him too."

Plainly my uncle was trying to tell me something of great moment, but I could not grasp it yet.

"Perhaps Joshua Radcliffe would have information for me as to my cousin," I suggested. "Where would I find him?"

"Now that's the question. The last I heard of him, he was captain of a slaver, the 'Saint Agatha,' 'twixt Havana and the Guinea Coast. But your cousin now—I'm glad he's not about here. The rash young fool might be tempted to interfere on Wednesday morning."

"Why, he'd have too much sense for that."

"He'd only be shot for his pains. Why, if I could get word to him, same as my other lads, I'd bless him for his faithfulness, and order him off to sea."

I was glad, then, ten times more than before, that I had come.

"Well, I thank you for the information, and—" Then I stepped to the barred window of the cell door and addressed the big-eared turnkey in the corridor. "Get me a glass or a cup, please. I'm going to give this poor man a drink out of my flask."

"I ain't supposed to leave a minute, when visitors are here," the fellow answered. "For their own pertection, ye see. Can't you let him drink out of the bottle?"

"No, I cannot."

Somewhat abashed by this lordliness, the turnkey hastened a short distance down the corridor. Before he could return in hearing, I had whispered to my uncle all he need know of our plans.

"Don't give up hope. When I yell 'Look out,' run for the nearest gate. We'll take no lives and take care of our own."

He wanted to protest, but could not, because of the eavesdropper's quick return with a metal cup. I gave my uncle half the contents of my small flask, and salved the turnkey with the other half.

"Goodbye to you, Captain, and good luck on the other shore."

"That's kindly of ye, and I thank ye."

"And I thank *ye* for the drink," the turnkey told me as he let me into the corridor. This saved me the trouble of breaking some ice.

"Why, you're courteous," I answered. "That's not readily seen these days. And I'm much obliged to you for treating that man kindly. Otherwise he'd been surly, and my time with him thrown away." For I was excited enough, and had enough at stake to play my part comparatively well.

"I'm kind to all of 'em, if they deserve it, but little thanks I get for it."

There had been no way to tell until now whether it would be safe to offer him money. He had now assured me it would be quite safe.

"Here's five dollars for you. You deserve it, and I can well afford it. I hope they're not going to give you the ugly job of hanging him."

"Oh, no, sir. I wouldn't do it for no 'mount of money. The reg'lar hangman bucked at it too, since Cap'n Todkill's popular in some quarters. So they got an old tosspot out at Tavey's Tavern." This last was a water-front resort well known to the crew.

"You don't say! Who is the fellow?"

"Now that I ain't allowed to tell. He wears a mask, ye know, when he jerks out the stool, so no one can disfame him or seek revenge ag'in him."

"I beg your pardon. I didn't know it was a secret."

"I know ye didn't, and since ye're but a visitor here, there'd be no harm in my telling ye. I can't straight out, but if ye'd drop into Tavey's—young gentlemen like ye roister there sometimes—and ye'd see an old soak, all but bald, with a snag tooth and a big nose, ye'd not be far off the track."

"If I pass that way, I'll look in at him, but not say a word."

Most of the next day Nat and I scouted our path of flight, from the gate of the jail to the waiting longboat on Stono Creek. At sundown Tuesday we were as well outfitted and organized for the morrow's stroke as our cunning and care could provide. The five raiders under me were cool-headed, quick-thinking, young, and agile men, besides being good riders. Nat Brown and Nicodemus were to be my two lieutenants, the others, carefully chosen from our whole company, vying for a place. I had been hard put to it to exclude both mates, neither of whom knew withers from rump, but at last I had ordered them to stay to maneuver and sail the ship in any duress.

Well after dark, I made for Tavey's Tavern. It had the look and smell of a thousand dives facing the Seven Seas. My entrance caused no flurry—two other richly-dressed young men sat at a corner table with harbor girls on their laps. It was child's play to identify tomorrow's hangman seeking Dutch courage for tomorrow's trying task. There was a vacant place beside him at the busy bar, since to stand near him was no doubt deemed unlucky. The regular inmates did not know him for a hangman but knew him for a deadhead taking every treat but giving none.

I called for uncut San Diego rum. He leaned toward me confidentially, his throat working.

"Now I've never tried that brand, but it must be extra fine, for a fine gentleman like ye to order it," he began, deep-dyed sot that he was.

"I heard this mughouse carried it. Will you try a glass?"

"Why, I don't care if I do."

When he had downed and praised the drink, he signaled to the tapster.

"Two more of the same." He spoke quite lordly, now.

"Orderin' drinks is one thing, payin' for 'em another," the tapster remarked sourly.

"You'll get your money midday tomorrow, sure as sunrise."

"I've heard that 'n before, Jud Bailey."

"I'll buy another round," I said quickly. "I'm sure this gentleman is only temporarily embarrassed."

Some one guffawed farther up the bar, at which my new friend turned to him with a lofty expression, delightfully characteristic of a boozer, and impossible to anyone else. I was going to enjoy this present phase of the project.

"Ye may laugh, for 'tis the right of fools, but ye'll see."

I winked at the laughers, somewhat against my heart, but it was necessary to account for one of my dress associating at length with such a barfly. The ready explanation was I could afford to buy him a few drinks for amusement's sake.

"If you can give me some proof that you'll be in funds tomorrow, I might make you a small loan," I told him.

"Now that's what I call a gentleman. It ain't exactly proof, but if ye knew the ins and outs of it, ye'd never doubt it."

I suggested that we take a table, well out of hearing of the crowd. Still he was not willing to confide in me the source of tomorrow's wealth, pretending at first that it was the expected payment of a debt;

and when this did not loosen my purse, hinting that it was to be his reward for a difficult public service.

"Have you already performed the service?" I asked.

"Well, no, but—"

"You will, however, before noon tomorrow. Why, then, if I'm right in my guess, I'll gladly lend you ten dollars."

"I ain't allowed to say—"

"I'm allowed to guess! The court needs a good steady man for a job to do—a public-spirited man who knows the law must be enforced. Why, I admire your courage!"

"Well, it do take a lot, and I'm the man to have it. But ye'd be surprised how many of them sots there would hate me for it."

"They don't know any better, Mr. Bailey."

"My very words. Why, a man ought to be proud to be picked for such a delicate, nerve-takin' job."

"It takes skill, and I'll hazard you've got it."

"Well, I did it only once before, and it shook me. 'Twas the sheriff what caught him, and the judge what sentenced him, but 'twas me what launched him into 'ternity. The mighty power and vengeance of the law was sitiated in my person!"

How often the angels must weep, while the devil holds his sides! One might wonder what God Almighty thinks of His handiwork when well soaked in rum. Yet the sots only overact on natural impulses, such as showing off with a tragicomic grandeur. It came to me I might make use of this. Certainly our original plan, to offer the hangman a thousand dollars to play a comparatively simple trick, had gone by the boards. Jud Bailey would sell out for one bottle of rum, but I would not dream of trusting the bibulous, garrulous fool.

"Do you have to bind his hands and feet, as well as tie the knot?" I asked.

"His hands is already bound, when he comes out o' the jail. I bind his feet so he can't do no kickin', which some of the vulgar admires to see, but which them with fine feelings, such as your'n and mine, can't hardly abide."

"Which do you tie first, his feet or his neck?"

"Sometimes one, sometimes t'other, 'cordin' to my fancy." You would have thought he was Jack Ketch.

"It's more merciful to put on the noose the last thing, and looks better." I bought him another glass.

"Why, I've come to the same opinion."

"You should order one of the guards to bind his feet, while you stand erect behind him at attention. That's the way it's done in England by the King's hangman—always a noble personage—and in Philadelphia and New York." That ought to appeal to a drunk.

"Now, I'd heard that, but my aim was to git it over—"

"It's beneath the hangman's dignity to stoop. You must remember that. It's very impressive to stand your full height and look straight ahead."

"That's the way I'm goin' to do it, from now on."

"Well, here's ten dollars for you, on two conditions. First, that you'll take it straight home to your wife and family."

"That was my aim, arter I'd treated you." In his brightening eyes were visions of another boozing-ken just around the corner.

"I don't want you to spend it on these ruffians, or for them to know you have it, so I'll slip it to you under the table. But the other condition is that you perform your duty tomorrow with all the solemnity it calls for. Let it come as a surprise to the spectators. Let them go on thinking you're an ordinary bungler—even the jailor and the captain of the guard—then show them how you know your duty."

"That's my very notion."

"I'll be looking through the gate. If you do a first-class job, you needn't pay back the money. I'll contribute that much to public good."

"Now that's gentlemanly of ye. To have the guard tie his feet—while I stand mighty proud and fine—and put the noose on last."

"You've got it, and I know you won't forget."

Maybe it was a mistake to give him the money. Actually I thought he would be more likely to remember my instructions if he continued to drink than if he sobered up. A few hours' sleep between bouts would do him if he were like most drunks; I would be surprised if he were not able after a stirrup cup in the gray dawn to execute, unsteadily but pompously, his gruesome task.

3.

My greatest worry was that the gate to the prison yard would be closed and locked. Since there had been popular clamor for a completely public hanging, likely the officials would keep their promise to leave it open, although strongly guarded. To my great joy—for our hope of forcing the barricade or getting my uncle over the wall was crow thin and chicken frail—it was opened well before time, two musketeers each with a fixed bayonet to hold back the crowd. In the front rank of the throng were three of my five comrades, they having taken their places as soon as it began to gather, before a glimmer of dawn. They were dressed like honest countrymen come to town for the show, and apparently had never laid eyes on one another until then.

Their nags were hitched across the street with the chevalier's knot that Pierre had taught me. At a post a little to one side of the gate, Nicodemus tied his horse. He was dressed in my buckskins, passing himself off as a long hunter from Cherokee, no rare sight in the sybaritic city. His costume thus accounted for my two rifles, pricked and primed in saddle scabbards. They might be very useful, I thought, in holding off pursuers armed only with short-range pistols. The mare I had bought from Mr. Ferguson stood about ten paces off, with the gelding's bridle strap fast to my saddle and his reins hooked handy. Jehu, a first-rate rider and a cool, brave man, held his horse near by.

The sun had barely cleared the rim of the bay—big and round and red gold—when the sudden quiet of the crowd before the gate told my trembling heart that the hanging was starting. My mother's brother, Cap'n Dan'l Todkill, was being marched out of the jail to the waiting gallows. Beside him were two soldiers with fixed bayonets. If there had been more than two—the usual number—Nicodemus would be signaling that fact to me by waving his cap. I figured my uncle walked well, with his head up and his eyes bold. He had commanded men all his grownup years, and before he could do that, he must have learned to command himself. Anyhow he was the captain of his own ship, the peer of anyone here.

A man's pride is a fine thing. It might be he was not even sick to his stomach, its heavings cured by magic medicine of will. He must be wondering and worrying about what we, his crew, were up to. He did not like the idea of his not being able to give us orders in this business; he did not altogether trust us not to bitch it. Skippers are like that.

Thinking of that, I was no longer sick to my stomach. I was high pitched but not unsteady, not even very afraid since what we were about to do could not be helped.

My maneuver needed careful timing. I must be in front of the gate at a certain point in the ceremony. While it would be most awkward to arrive more than a few seconds too soon, one second too late might cook our goose. Jehu mounted his horse and I mine. Haughtily— and no one on earth can appear as haughty as the Negro servant to a vainglorious master—he pushed his nag bluntly into the pack before the gate.

"Make way for Mr. Jennings!" he intoned, without a trace of nervousness. "Make way! Make way!"

It did not seem possible that the close-knit throng would part to make room for him, but it did. Those directly in his path scowled and cursed at him, but seeing they would be trampled if they did not give ground, they turned their scowlings and cursings on their fellows resisting their shovings. Such is human nature that they became our partisans. "Make way for the big gun," they were saying in effect. "Can't ye gawkers make more room? Mr. Jennings has got to get through."

"Make way, make way for Mr. Jennings!" Jehu commanded with a fine ceremoniousness, playing his part to perfection.

We aimed for a point about fifteen feet in front of the open gate. Greatly impressed by Mr. Jennings, the guards did not let on that they had never heard of him before, and were completely indifferent to the throng's annoyance and discomfort at giving us way. Meanwhile I glanced as though idly over the people's heads into the prison yard. The ceremony had progressed further than I had reckoned and there was not a second's leeway.

My uncle was standing with his hands bound behind his back on a stool beside a dangling noose. Beside him stood a chaplain, and farther off a dignitary that I took for the captain of the guard. Before him loomed two guardsmen with fixed bayonets. Behind him, wearing a black mask, swayed my old friend Jud Bailey.

"Tie the prisoner's legs," came Jud's bleary but pompous voice. He was holding out a thong to one of the guards.

"What ye say?" the startled soldier asked.

"Tie his legs, I tell ye. 'Tis the proper way."

The guard was torn between inclinations. He took the extended rope, awkwardly holding his weapon in one hand, and at the same time glanced at his captain for instructions. The other guard, sympathetic with his fellow's dilemma, also took his eyes from the prisoner. Jud Bailey, master of the situation, drew himself to his full height and with his arms rigid at his side, stared straight ahead. He rocked a little; otherwise he was indubitably an impressive figure.

But his moment of grandeur was cut woefully short. I dared not wait for a better chance. Both guards and their captain were disconcerted and the two soldiers at the gate gaping at the proceedings. Wheeling my mare toward the gate, I set my spurs hard and gave her a brutal lash with the whip. Terrified, she sprang forward into the press of people heedless of how many she ran over. Some would have been knocked down had there been room for them to fall, and no few were struck by her flying hooves and bruised and battered by her surging shoulders.

"Now!" I shouted at the top of my voice as I gained the gate.

At that instant two of our party had at the sentries. Both drove for their fellows' knees, as I had told them, spilling them and then ramming the crowns of their heads against their victims' chins—old and effective tactics in frontier fights. To my glory, Cap'n Dan'l Todkill sprang off his stool full on to the breast of his more alert guard and bore him down. In spite of his bound hands my uncle surged to his feet and legged it toward me.

I caught him by the collar of his coat. He was a heavy man, and I needed all the strength that the West had bred in my muscle and bone to heave him up in front of me. As I wheeled the mare, out of the side of my eyes I saw the second guard raise his piece. If he kept cool and took good aim, he could hardly miss my back. Those seconds of waiting for his shot—we riding fast, but woeful slow compared to a bullet's dart—seemed never to end. But instead of a musket's roar, we heard only the crack of a pistol. I thought that the guard had been afraid to fire lest he hit one of the throng at the gate. Later I learned that my black Jehu had followed me into the yard and in spite of the brandished musket had run down and over the musketeer. The pistol ball fired by the captain did no worse than sing by our ears.

We gained the gate, and the crowd parted prettily to let us through. As we turned down Magazine Street, our men were already darting for their horses, and presently we heard their drumming hooves. Only one of the sentries had been able to fire his piece at them because of the crowd. Later my coonskin cap worn by Nicodemus proved minus its ringed tail. Whether the chance bullet had clipped it off we never knew.

My mare could not long bear this double load, so I made haste to draw my knife—it still felt at home in my hand—and cut Cap'n Dan'l's bonds. After shaking his arms a few seconds to restore circulation, he loosed the gelding's hitching strap from my saddle thong and drew him alongside. I could hardly believe he could gain his seat without accident, but 'fore God here was a sailor—from young manhood used to skipping to the tops and hanging on by his fingernails in heavy blows. That nimbleness—at least the good balance and the good fight —abided in him yet. The maneuver was incredibly awkward, an outrage to fancy riding, and only my own agility in the saddle gave him enough play.

My mare drove forward as though with a new set of legs.

It was only the beginning of the race. We had some fourteen miles to ride to Stono Creek, and if our pursuers brought enough spare horses for fresh remount they could likely overtake us. For the present only three horsemen made chase—not very resolute fellows, for a few pistol shots at hopeless range discouraged them. A stouter party was no doubt assembling, but we had turned the first trick handily, and got away with a long head start.

When we gained the Ashley, we did not wait for the ferry, then on the far side of the river. Every manjack swam his horse, hanging on to the saddle to spare the beast. On the frontier it was our only bridge, miserable enough in wintry weather, but a new thing to these tars; and it did my heart good how they took to it, shouting bawdy jokes while the horses snorted. On the other side Nat Brown took time to free the ferry barge and let it drift down river, while we galloped on. It was almost certain to beach itself on swampy ground where our pursuers could not readily launch it. The bolder wights would swim their horses too, but many would not care that much about three inches' stretch to my uncle's neck.

On the road who should I meet but Mr. Ferguson, the planter, on an after-breakfast amble! He recognized me and waved, and was no doubt puzzled that I only waved back above flying hooves instead of stopping for a chat. More puzzling still was the company I kept, and where we might be going in such haste. Maybe he thought we were fox hunters, although he had not heard or seen our hounds, and would be greatly astonished to discover that we were the foxes instead, with the hounds baying far behind us.

We had, I believe, one close shave. Once or twice I had heard a hard-riding horseman a furlong or so behind us, and when we were crossing some swampy country on a causeway, I caught sight of him emerging from some woods a hundred and fifty fathoms on our stern quarter. That is, he was three hundred paces, as we count on the frontier, for it came upon me to turn quickly from part sailor to all mountain man. The fellow knew the short cuts. He was taking one now—an old corduroy road through the swamp that our maps had not revealed. Probably, he carried word to some military post hereabouts, or to a swift frigate in the mouth of the Edisto. If he got where he was going, we might never be where we were bound.

There was use for my rifle now, and for a mountaineer. Snatching the piece from Nicodemus' saddle scabbard, I spurred my mare to the best she was good for, cut her through the thickets within a hundred yards of our foe, then pulled her up so hard that she almost fell. The piece was already swinging in my right hand as I dropped the reins. I had killed running deer at this range scores of times, but that was a different thing from shooting down a horse without hitting its rider. It looked like murderous recklessness on my part. It was not, because like any real rifleman I knew my gun and what I could do with it in an extremity—my last-ditch, top-flight shot which only now and then could I drive myself to make. A good rifle is a mathematical instrument. Granted a trained marksman, the rest is will-power. I appeared to loose quickly, with careless aim; actually I had thrown a day's work into that brief interplay of eye and hand. My bullet was well molded, my calculations of time and distance perforce correct. Aiming a quartering shot at the point of the horse's chest forward of the saddle, from the way he dropped I did not miss it far.

It was a great joy to me when the rider clambered up from the dust patently unhurt. He had even fallen like a real horseman, used to tumbles in sport and war. The tribute he paid me as we dashed on— a hand raised in a slow, ceremonious wave—I would put away and treasure among my trophies.

4.

We gained the longboat, and then the ship. No cannons blazed at us as we took down river on the tide. At midnight Cap'n Dan'l Todkill, high on his quarter-deck instead of low in his grave, ordered the first double ration of grog to the men off watch to celebrate our victory.

We drove northward, with a brisk, quartering wind—a fine piece of cunning, the men reckoned, since our pursuers would expect us to run for the Caribs. There was more to it than that, though, as I discovered when we were off Hatteras, and my uncle and I sat alone late at night, over a bowl of grog.

"The main reason I'm taking this north'ard course," he told me, "is to take ye home."

My uncle did not say much that he did not mean. The vision of a noble voyage in search of Golden Fleece—this trim "Charity," our Argo, my uncle a piece of Dodonean oak, and his crew heroic timber —turned into cold mist.

"I didn't say I wanted to go home."

"Ye may not want to, now, but if ye stayed with me, later ye'd wish you had. I'd not hear of it, Jason. It would be the poorest kindness to ye, my nephew by blood, and my deliverer." For good captains of the sea, such as my uncle, can speak nobly when they choose. A kind of nobility grows in them—if not, instead, a deep iniquity—from fighting the sea and from holding men's lives in their hands.

"I thought you might go on a trading venture, as I wrote you."

"We've no bent for it, Jason—either me or my men. My ship's a lean fighter, not a fat merchant."

There was no more to say about that. "If you wanted me with you, in the Caribs, I reckon I'd go."

"I don't want ye with me, Jason, in that work. We've chosen it, and will stick to it, but I won't have ye—born a captain of greater ventures—risk a hanging under my command. Men defile themselves as they jerk and kick, and make mockery of God."

He took a deep drink and wiped his mouth. "I could never bear to mock God," he told me with unconscious, simple dignity.

It was strange how the words bit into me, spoken by this sunburned man famed as a pirate. I would think of them always in keeping with this little cabin, rocking on the sea, the lantern swinging from its bracket, and star-spangled darkness. I could tell him anything now.

"Why did ye save me, Jason, when you'd never laid eyes on me?" he asked.

"If you don't know, I reckon I can't tell you. Why did you want to see me, before you passed on?"

"The tie of the blood that small men don't understand. So I'm making ye my heir, such as it is."

"I'd thank you kindly."

"Not to my ship. She'll go to the lads, for sailing her, and fighting for her. I'll take her back to the Caribs, and put her in the service of the Revolution party in Colombia, and then if we're caught, we may be shot like men instead of hanged like dogs. What I have to leave ye, I'll give ye now. But first—are ye going back to Salem?"

"Yes, sir, I've business there."

"Charleston's a long way, and there's little chance of the Salem people hearing of the break, and if they did, they'd hardly figure ye were in it—yet it's possible."

"I've thought about that. The danger's too slight to regard." Perhaps not a dozen letters from Charleston had been received in Salem in the past dozen months. Our ships called there occasionally, and their hands might hear a garbled tale of Cap'n Dan'l's escape, but hardly connect the lordly Mr. Jennings with a codger docking at Derby Wharf.

"Here's the key to my chest. Open it, and look in its larboard bow on the lower deck, and ye'll find a sealed paper and a letter."

I did so and handed him the documents. He broke the seal and handed them back. "Before they'll make sense to ye, mind that Joshua Radcliffe and I were first and second mates of the 'Happy Chance,' of Salem. Cap'n Barnaby was her skipper and owner. There was bad blood 'twixt Joshua and me, and Barnaby played one of us against tother. Yankee born, he was, but Tory, and in '76 he laid his course to arm her under the King ag'in his own people. Joshua, black as he was, wouldn't stand for it, nor of course would I. We quit the ship, and Cap'n Barnaby flew into a towering rage."

"Aye, sir," I said when he paused.

"'Twas worse at me than at Joshua, for I was the hottest rebel. I thought he'd never forgive me, but laying sick in Havana, far from Salem and soon to die, he did. Now read the papers."

The sealed paper was a will, dated Christmas Day, 1793, leaving the "Happy Chance" to his old friend and second mate, Daniel Todkill of Medford. The other was a rambling letter of repentance of his sins on land and sea, asking forgiveness for his cursings and enmity when my uncle had quit the ship.

"What happened to the 'Happy Chance'?" I asked.

"I never got my sea boots on her quarter-deck. I went to Havana for her, but she'd changed her name to the 'Saint Agatha' and sailed for Africa. And who, do ye reckon, had claimed and captained her? None but Joshua Radcliffe."

My uncle expected no comment from me, and I made none.

"He had some papers, it seemed, which some scoundrel forged, and money to victual her and lade her with sugar. He wasn't alone in the steal, and ye can lay to that. Off and on since then, I've looked and waited for her, to engage and board her, but I can't berth in Cuban waters or go ashore, 'cause the dons itch to hang me; and busy fighting the dons besides, it's a well-nigh hopeless watch. But it wouldn't be for ye. I'll write ye a deed for her to go with these papers, and by ye going to Havana, and greasing the right palms—two hundred pesos might do the trick—and making the right friends, I doubt not ye can turn the tables on Joshua Radcliffe, and keep her for your own."

"Then that's the course I'll chart." For it would be a splendid thing to own and captain a tall ship.

"She's a worthy vessel, Yankee built, fast and yare. It sickens me to think of her as a stinking slaver. I'd want ye to put her into honest trade. I'll give ye a catalogue I've kept, which Elisha Featherstone would pay a pretty for. It lists the ports of the world, what they'll buy and sell at what season for the likeliest price, who can be greased with profit, who to beware of, and many a good tip. But let her home port be Salem, where she was built and berthed."

"Why did you mention Elisha Featherstone, Uncle Dan'l?"

"The skinflint flint-hearted bastard! But that leads me to speak a word ye'll not like to hear. The only soul I told about Cap'n Barnaby's will was my kinsman by marriage—but blood kin to ye. I wish I'd cut my tongue off first, for I reckon it was he who hatched the scheme to skin me. I'd forgot that Radcliffe had had dealings afore with his Company. I mean your father's brother, Samuel Starbuck."

"I hope he was the one. He tried to skin me too, and I'd like to sand his prat." But that prospect was not what made my neck prickle so fiercely. "But he'd not have the money or the power to put the scheme through and victual and lade the ship. So you reckon Elisha Featherstone was behind him?"

"It was a Salem affair from start to finish, and Mr. Derby sails a straight course. Who does that leave but Elisha Featherstone and his creature, Sam'l Starbuck?"

Well, it left Dick, Elisha's son and heir. Some of the fine clothes he wore could well have been bought by money made in a dirty trade by my Uncle Dan'l's—now my own—tall ship. So our feud had begun before I ever knew it! It was fated, I thought, that when I made off with Roxana, she and I would berth in the captain's cabin of the "Happy Chance"!

"Why can't we go after this together, Uncle Dan'l?" I asked.

"I've my own work to do, Jason, and my happiness to find, and no need of another vessel. But I want you to have it, in due course, for risking your neck for mine."

"I didn't do it in hope of—"

"That I know. Jason, your Pa gave up a lot when he wedded my sister Prue, a poor fisherman's daughter, and he was good to her, and you're their son. 'Twould please me to have ye live in a fine house in Salem—a prosperous shipowner and revered gentleman. I can think of little else that would please me as much."

"Then I'll make the 'Happy Chance' my Golden Fleece."

"'Twill be a long, hard sail at best. And Jason, when ye've won her, I'd want ye to marry a fine lady—the best in Salem none too good—and have children by her to bear your name in the great days to come."

"I've one picked out already." It was odd to feel my heart glowing, with a cold, frozen lump in the middle—a little like a meteorite, perhaps, which is hot as brimstone on the outside, and colder than polar ice within.

"I want ye to have housemaids, but not slaves, and a manservant of your own. Ye don't know how I liked the look of Jehu riding behind ye." I had not known this side of my uncle until now. His weathered face had lighted.

"I will, and a coach-and-four."

"Jehu's a good cook, and good cooking's half the strength of a crew, or ye could have him straight off."

"I've no money to pay him, till I capture the ship. Anyway if I had my pick—"

When I hesitated, my uncle cried, "Speak on."

"I'd choose Nicodemus."

My uncle's eyes grew slowly bigger, half with incredulity, half with joy. "Why, 'tis a providence," he cried, "for all three o' us!"

"I don't ken you, sir."

"Well, he's a joy to me, in a way, which I'll gladly lose for the trial he is to me, too. He's ever cautioning me to keep out of trouble, which is good for a young and reckless man, but now I'm too timid for my own good, and the crew's. 'Tis the way of advancing years."

I almost laughed aloud at my uncle's timidity.

"Don't ye know that a gaffer, with only a little weak grog left in his glass, and but little time to swig it, is ten times as wary as a young 'n, with a whole hogshead of uncut rum, and fifty years afore him? 'Tis the oddest paradox in life."

"I'd never thought of it."

"Nicodemus was born cautious—and yet brave no end in heavy weather. He'll be glad of a lawful life, in reason, and if he's taken to ye—but for that, he must speak for himself."

My uncle stepped up on the quarter-deck. He was a man of quick and positive decisions. Alarmed at what I might be getting into—quite certain I could not afford a follower and doubtful of wanting the responsibility—I started to call him back. This I could not do. It would disappoint my uncle, and be an anticlimax. Going ahead with it was a kind of bravado, perhaps, not of my own inclination but forced on me by the expectations of others.

"Aye, aye, sir," said Nicodemus, saluting his captain.

"Mr. Starbuck has something to say to ye, Nic," my uncle responded. Then he sat down, waiting for me to speak.

I had to live up to that. Sitting at ease, I looked Nicodemus over for a long ten seconds, whereat he flushed a little and in some inward fashion put his best foot forward.

"Nicodemus, I've been looking for a stout fellow to take service under me on some enterprises, and it strikes me you might be the very one."

"Aye, sir." That did not mean "Aye, aye, sir—" that he would do it. It meant only respectful interest in the proposal.

"How you'd fare in the way of money, I don't know. I've very little to go on. I've a small sea-going boat, and a large venture. I'd say a sixth share to you of all prizes."

"Would that venture be within the law, so to speak? I make bold to ask, 'cause I'm a law-abidin' man, by nat're."

"Yes, it would, by and large."

"Would it be by land or sea? I'm a salt-water man."

"It would be by sea, with turns on land. I've need not only of your hand, but of your counsel. There'll be risk of life and limb, and risk of failure. What do you say, Nicodemus?"

"Well, sir, I'm taken with the notion, but misdoubt if Cap'n Todkill ought to sign me off. He'll tell ye he's needed me sore up to now, or I took it he did."

"I did indeed, Nicodemus," my uncle said. "I still need ye, but can get along without ye now, since I've learned my lesson. On the contrary, my nephew, Mr. Starbuck, is of a rash and I fear reckless nature. I'll sign ye off, and by your leave, sign ye on to him."

" 'Twill be a heavy haul to leave ye, sir, and the lads."

Nicodemus had turned white, his freckles standing out like specks of golden dust. All three of us were solemn.

"That I don't doubt, and a heavy haul for me."

"Well, then, since ye wish it, and Cap'n Starbuck wishes it too, and since I'm agreeable to follering him, why, I will."

"Spoken like a man, Nicodemus!" my uncle cried.

"Nicodemus, I'll be very pleased to have you follow me," I said.

We shook hands all round, and Captain Starbuck poured out three tots of uncut rum. The ceremony was a very simple one, considering its import in all our lives, yet meaningful.

I had a good and likely venture, and a worthy henchman to help me succeed. While I could no longer picture it as a quest of Golden Fleece, the fancy had been most extravagant even for young love. My seeming intuition that I had been fated for a greater and more breathless pursuit was no doubt the fault of a summer dream.

CHAPTER SIX

Salem Witches

I.

Cap'n Dan'l Todkill dawdled all the way to Nantucket Sound to lengthen our time together I was in no hurry to return to Salem, for I had a kinsman to be proud of now, who taught me lore of ships and the sea. He told me what it meant to be a captain —the privilege and the responsibility of command. My heart was wide open to him—and no man can learn much of value with his head alone. Almost without my knowing it, he was substituting for both my father and my mother. It was a wonderful thing to have someone of my own blood close to me again, whose advice might be mistaken but never colored by self-interest, and who would never break faith with me.

On my last night at sea, I told him all that I myself knew of my love affair with Roxana.

"It's stormy weather, Jason," he said. A poetically minded man, he was wont to speak attuned to dashing waves.

"Yes."

"No clearing anywhere that I can see. I know what I'd wish for ye. To meet some other lass who'd take her place in your life—near enough, that is, so ye'd give her up."

"She'll never be happy with Dick."

"Ye can't tell. He's a strong man, and women cling to strength. He's rich, and that's oil to smooth the waters—women set much store on riches. Ye'd be surprised how many ill-matched couples do make out, taking the rough with the smooth. It's not the wedding ceremony that counts, or what's happened before; it's the years together. If she becomes his mate in life, no man of honor can take her from him."

"That wouldn't stop me," I said.

"I think ye love her mightily," Captain Todkill went on. "Young men are often mistaken on that score, but your heart was mighty empty and by nature, strong. But maybe ye only swept her off her feet for a little while. In her it could be a reflection, not a joining."

"She said as much, but why do you say so?"

"Because she let ye go to marry Dick."

"I told you she had to, when her father was going to the dogs from poverty and drink."

"Those are strong motives, but I doubt if strong enough to keep a girl from the man she deeply loves."

"She'd lived through the Terror in France—"

"That might account for the bluff way she sails. Ye say ye saw her beauty hidden from most, and she gave it to ye. 'Tis the same if you admire something a Chinaman owns, but he expects ye to give it back."

"Many a woman has given up the man she loved," I told him.

"Yes, when she had her babes to think of, and the happiness of some man who'd done his best by her. Sometimes a woman does it for her lover's good. That's a strange, wonderful thing—I've seen it in common whores. Well, maybe she does love ye, full sail. Maybe the combination, care for her father—and many daughters love 'em out of the world—and some feeling about ye such as topgallant women know, made her chart this course."

He thought this over—reading entries in the log of his long years.

"Women are queer, that way," he went on. "The real ones can see deep into a man—they're all half witch, when ye come down to it. Even my sailors say ye are a born captain. Maybe she saw ye've got the chartings of a great life—a rowdy, full-reef-gale sort she'd like to live herself if she were a man—and settling down with a wife would cheat ye out of it. Some men seem fated to such lives. The world is their oyster. Cap'n John Smith was like that. But for one who won fame, there's a hundred who get only a foreign grave and some yarns told in a fo'c'sle. They look for trouble and it looks for them. Mind ye, I'm just plumbing an unknown bottom—but if Roxana saw what comes to me like the shape of a ship in fog—"

My uncle's voice died away. "What advice do you give me, Uncle Dan'l?" I asked.

"Why, that's easy." We were meandering along off Monomoy Island, well out of sight of land, one dot of life in a vast salty death. Cap'n Todkill had been looking away, but now he turned his gleaming eyes to me. "Live!" he said. "Sail your ship to the last spread of her canvas. Go hunt your fortune. Man your guns for what ye love and stand for. I take back what I said about giving up that girl—that would do for some men, not for ye. Think of her as your home port. Look out for the rocks, but sail close to 'em at your call."

The next night we anchored off Marblehead and put overside the sailing dingey. Into it went my gear and a kitbag that contained all of Nicodemus' worldly goods. He had talked to his captain alone in the cabin, no man knowing what passed between them; then he spent the remainder of our time aboard with his old friends. The men appeared to regard me as a new but firm friend. They gave me a golden candlestick and sachet box, part of their spoil from an affluent Spaniard, to the weight of twenty eagles. I was not in command now, and they felt free to tell me that I had served them well, and if ever the chance came, they would serve me well.

"Snatching our skipper from the jaws o' death was as pretty as a pi'ture," Mr. Shawe told me, "or you can blow me down!"

When all was ready, my uncle and I stood at the windward rail, looking out on the silver path made to our eyes by the rising moon.

"We'll lay here till morning, Jason, or until ye signal with the lantern I'm putting in your boat," he told me. "Maybe something's come up that ye'll want to go to Boston or such like. Wave the lantern crosswise if everything's all right. Wave it up and down if ye want us to bring back the boat."

"I'll do it. Goodbye, Uncle Dan'l."

"Goodbye—and a fair wind—and a good port at last."

We shook hands and I went down the Jacob's ladder to the sailing dingey. Nicodemus had already gone down, and Nat Brown to bring back the boat. The breeze filled our small sail. Nat sat at the tiller, smoking a corncob pipe—the tobacco smell came strongly to my nostrils in all this freshness. The lanterns on the deck of the "Charity" burned dimmer, colder.

So did my heart. It seemed that I was breaking with my only brightness and warmth. The nearer we drew to Salem, the farther Roxana drew away. I could hardly bear to look at Nicodemus, sitting in the bow with his kitbag at his feet, gazing toward the sparse, scattered lights. I had swindled him. I had nothing but a two-man boat and an unratified deed to a ship and a Castle in Spain. A chill mist blew over the bay. The moon looked icy and the stars obscure. It was midnight—the sun long gone, long ere it rose again—when the darkness fills every nook and cranny and men's hearts. The wharf we touched was dank and slippery.

"Goodbye to you, sir," Nat Brown told me, when he had helped Nicodemus discharge our little cargo. "Nicodemus, we'll miss you on the old brig, but I know you'll have a good life with Cap'n Starbuck."

"'Tis a gamble, but so's everything," Nicodemus answered with perfect truth, but rather startling frankness.

To keep Nicodemus from gazing seaward, I bade him help look for my boat. Perhaps Andy had her out fishing. In that case we would go to bed in a tavern. However, we found her without trouble, moored in a little backwater out of the way of the ships. She looked far larger than life, like all close-by things on the water at night, but when we had boarded her from a handy fisherman's skiff, I had never seen such a piddling craft.

She seemed not only small but abandoned. Her deckhouse door had swollen stuck; gulls had dirtied the roof; she smelled of loneliness and idleness and soon decay.

"She ain't no ship o' the line," Nicodemus remarked, after a studious survey, "but handy rigged."

"She is that." I was taking down a paper tacked to the wall.

"She can't stow no big passel, but staunch," he went on, throwing his light on the paper.

"It's from Andy, who worked with me," I explained. "He's signed on the 'Morning Star' and fishing off Cape Sable and won't be back till Saturday."

That was five days from now. The "Morning Star" was owned by Elisha Featherstone, but I did not believe that staunch, honest Andy would gossip about his former shipmate's love affair. Probably he had quit me because his feelings had been hurt by my sudden, unexplained departure.

"A letter came for you the Tuesday after you left," he concluded. "I was afraid to leave it on your boat for some loafer to pick up so I'm keeping it for you."

It would be a farewell letter from a new bride, asking me on no account to try to see her or even to speak to her on the street. Yet when the letter reached me, I would still hold fast to our real farewell:

"*I will not let you go unless you bless me.*"

"Like as not this here Andy owns a share in the boat," Nicodemus was saying.

"Not a board or nail of her."

"Well, she ain't the 'Charity,' but looks like a good sailer. We'd better go get our gear in the skiff, and stow it aboard her."

We boarded the skiff and Nicodemus bent to the oars. Men look small in a rowboat among tall ships, and feel small; the mere wharf loomed over us like a mountain cliff.

"Rest on your oars a minute, Nicodemus," I said, when we had gone a short distance.

"Aye, aye, sir." We lay rocking on a little swell.

"The 'Charity' won't set sail till we signal all's well—a lantern waved to and fro. A lantern waved up and down will bring back the dingey. Anyway she's not halfway out to the ship, as yet."

"A fair halfway to my judgment."

"Well, I've something to tell you. I've got a good venture in mind, but it's only the means to an end. That end is to get a girl. She married another man and is living here in Salem. I won't ever be able to get her off my mind."

"Sink me."

I could tell from his tone that he believed me. It was not a scene for lying, or even for being badly mistaken—the patch of lantern light in the big dark.

"So you see, Nicodemus, I'm not free to come and go as I please. I might leave any other business to come back here. I should have told you so in the first place."

"Well, sir, it do cut out our work for us—like Cap'n Todkill helping them Spanish rebels."

"What do you mean, Nicodemus?"

"None of our crew gave a damn about 'em. What we was after—though I didn't hold by it—was lifting them rich cargoes off the Spanish ships. But oft he'd run right up to a sloop o' war and we'd have to fight her tooth and nail to stay afloat. He was that hot in it."

"Why didn't they quit him and turn pirate?"

"They couldn't do naught without him. Ye have to take the bitter with the sweet. Then, ag'in, hating Spain so, made him keep after and catch a prize that a pirate would give o'er, for lack of vim. I reckon it gave spice to our lives, when all was said and done."

"Harken to me, Nicodemus. That was a big and noble cause. This of mine is to win one girl away from her lawful husband."

"E'en though I don't hold by it, 'twill be my place to help ye. Ye'll be surprised how much I can help ye, being a student of women and their ways, from the crow's-nest like. Every man's got his faults."

"Well, I've warned you. The lantern's there at your feet. All you have to do is wave it up and down, and the dingey will take you back to the ship. Use your best judgment."

"If I listened to my best judgment, I'd ne'er gone to sea. I didn't reckon this here was a bed o' roses."

"Well, then, since the 'Charity' will be safer on the open sea—and there's nothing more we want aboard her—you can give her the signal."

Nicodemus stood up and waved the lantern staunchly to and fro.

2.

Nicodemus and I slept aboard the "Prudence Todkill." In the early morning I told him about the "Happy Chance," now the "Saint Agatha." In a few days we would set out for Cuba, to begin our salvage operations. Meanwhile there was no sense in paying tavern prices when we could live so handily and cheaply aboard my boat. Buying and cooking victual would help occupy his time while I saw to my Salem affairs.

After breakfast I noticed Luff Padget, a 'longshoreman of my acquaintance, repairing a lobster trap on the dock. Luff was not much of a talker—if he had died while I was away I would never have thought of him again—but I had nothing better to do just now than visit with him.

"I missed ye, around the dock," he said pleasantly. "What had become of ye?"

"I had a little business south of Boston."

"More'n I've had here. The shipping's been uncommon scant. I thought ye'd been to sea by the weathered look o' ye." He went on mending the trap.

"Just off and on the boats." Starting to turn away, I saw no harm, although little gain, in asking a few haphazard questions. "Any doings in town since I went away?"

"Squire Baker's barn caught fire and burned to the ground, but they saved the hosses and the shay."

"Let's see. There was a fashionable marriage to come off, just before I left. I thought to be invited to the feast, having once run a horse race against the groom, but I wasn't."

Luff finished filing a piece of wire, then to my amazement, put his work aside, and squatting on his hams, folded his arms.

"Queer how you'd mention 'at 'ere," he remarked. "The whole town's agog."

"How's that?" My heart stood painfully still.

"It's nothin' to me. I don't hardly know the people by sight. I'm not one to gossip about fashionable folk. But since you brought it up—" He paused and shut his lips tight, as though holding in a mouthful of tobacco juice.

114

"I know Dick Featherstone fairly well."

"Do ye, now? Then I'll tell ye that marriage was a mighty queer one. Leastwise I'd think it queer, if 'twas mine."

"I thought the pair well matched."

"So did the town. I know only what I hear. But she was married on a Sunday, and I seen her and her Pa and the nigger girl takin' a ship for France on a Wednesday. Maybe they got along fine, and some kinfolk over there was sick or something. *I* can't say."

I turned my back on Luff. He saw me looking in the direction of my boat, but didn't see it swimming as though in summer heat. He heard me say, "I wonder what's keeping Nic," but maybe he did not notice how my voice shook. "Nic's a man I brought with me from below on some business."

"Do tell!"

"Excuse me—you were telling me about Dick's wedding."

"That's all I know about it. 'Tis no business o' mine."

"Do you reckon they've gone for good? The town would miss Dr. Reil."

"They say Bonaparte hisself sent for him to doctor them French people. But they say too that his daughter slept at home even Sunday night, and Mr. Featherstone slept at *his* home. If it's true—*I* don't know—it's a mighty queer way of doin' for a bride and groom."

"I'd say so myself, Luff."

"Are ye well, Mr. Starbuck? Ye didn't catch the fever in Boston, did ye? Ye look mighty white in the face."

"No, I've not got the fever—just ate too much fresh flounder for breakfast. I'll take some sulphur and molasses, and see you later."

I got aboard my boat and sat in the stern in the sun. At first I could feel nothing but fury at myself for letting the "Charity" leave so soon. The slim-waisted brig could have taken me to France in jig time, and sacked a Spaniard or two on the voyage to grease the men. But there was no way under heaven to catch her now.

When my head cleared a little, I tried to figure out what had happened. The most ready explanation was the most unwelcome—that Dick had been a gentleman of sorts, and had given Roxana a chance to get out before he threw her out. He could have discovered within a few hours an excuse for breaking the bargain. Then her father had taken her to France to save her sitting in the stocks of Salem contumely.

The letter might have been an appeal to take her away from the scene of her disgrace—and I had not been here to receive it. It was

115

hard to imagine my tall, valiant girl writing such a letter, but perhaps she had bowed beneath that stunning blow. Only then had she appealed to her father. Plainly she had loved him with full cause.

What was I to do now? I could not set out for France until I knew where in that great populous country to look for her. The only person in Salem that might know—provided she too had not fled from the babble of wagging tongues—was Roxana's mother. Crawling into a she-bear's den without a gun or knife would be a small chore compared with facing that grim Puritan in her parlor.

Yet it came to me, in a little while, that I must do that very thing. She was Roxana's mother and I Roxana's lover; no matter what she felt about me, it could not change that relationship. I felt its moment, even its dignity, welling through me, steadying me. This time I would not hang outside the door or hide in the woodshed.

After a bath at a tavern, I returned to the boat to dress. It was a great temptation to wear the costly clothes I had bought at Norfolk —clothes fitting to Mr. Jennings of Virginia—but in the end I put on the good but plain garments that had been my Sunday best before. These were fitting to my station and it would be long before the others would become me, but more than ever I was resolved that time would come. Walking up Broad Street, speaking to acquaintances now and then, I tried to think out what I would say to Dame Reil. No wonder the sweat came out on me.

Had Roxana told her I was the wrecker of her marriage? Who could say what had passed between her and her parents in those desperate hours? If so, my task would be no heavier—perhaps lighter. Had she chosen to leave me out of it—a common fisherman, son of Prudence Todkill—and attributed her disaster to an experience in France? Quite likely she had made up a story that would sound less shocking than either of these. If so, it was my lot to expose it. Then the truth came to me that any story Roxana could invent would not help her in the long run—it could not grapple with heavy trouble. But there was no doubt of my grappling with any trouble of hers I could get my hands on.

My walk changed a little then—became more like the mile-devouring mountain walk—lazy looking, as though to topple forward. Old Pierre, looking down from heaven, knew that was a good sign. My belly no longer felt cold. Honesty may not be the best policy, but it calms a man's nerves. What difference how I said it, as long as it was said? The blinds of the windows of the Reil house were down and some of the shutters closed. These told the passers-by not to gawk, visitors not to come. Someone was here, though; the kitchen chimney breathed out pale smoke hardly more palpable in the summer air than a man's frosty breath in winter.

I rapped with the brass knocker and thought of my first night in Salem, calling on Samuel Starbuck. When no one came to the door, I knocked louder. A window upstairs opened and a woman's head leaned down. It was not Dame Reil's; it belonged to a younger, fatter, more affable woman, perhaps a country cousin.

"What do you want, young man?"

"I want to see Mistress Reil."

"She's not at home to callers. She's not well."

"It's very important that I see her—to her and to me."

"Well, I'll ask her. What's your name?"

"Jason Starbuck."

The window closed. There was a long wait, the only sound a humming of bees in some morning-glories growing by the door. I thought of hollyhocks by the garden wall, and did not become troubled or rebuffed by the delay. The door opened narrowly.

"Come in, young man," the same voice reached me from the dimness within. "Mrs. Reil will see you."

I was given a seat in a very formal, very shabby parlor. Here was genteel poverty at its most carking. The carpet was walked thin, the tapestry on the high back of a sofa worn past mending, the spinnet was closed and no doubt out of tune long years ago; the room smelled of dejection and endless soap and water. Cabins on the frontier with a deal table and bed and two iron pots appeared splendid compared to this, because Hope sat laughing by the fireplace. I understood better why Roxana had gone to the church with Dick Featherstone.

An inner door opened and I rose. Indeed I had never fully sat down, fearing that the rickety, fragile chair would give way. A medium-tall woman on the slender side, entered with firm steps. This was Dame Reil—I had seen her on the street, once or twice—and now I tried to see into her to find something of Roxana. She was dressed in black but that was her native color. It appeared all but incredible that she had ever been pretty or young. However, she was a strong character. No doubt Roxana had inherited some of that strength only to have it take what her mother considered a strange and godless form. That was Dame Reil's most bitter defeat.

"I am Mistress Reil," she told me. "Are you Jason Starbuck?"

"Yes, ma'am."

"The son of Reuben Starbuck, who wedded Prudence Todkill of Medford?"

"Yes, madam."

"What is your business with me?"

"I wish to ask the whereabouts of your daughter Roxana."

"I'm aware that you took her and her escort Mr. Featherstone fishing in your boat. I know of no further acquaintance between you that would make her whereabouts of any concern to you." The words came as smoothly and as formally as though she had written them on a paper and was reading them.

"They are of deep concern to me, ma'am."

"Then pray be seated."

We both took chairs, facing each other across the dimly lighted room. She waited for me to speak.

"My concern is that I love your daughter," I told her.

She sat perfectly still. After a long time she asked, "Merely from seeing her on the fishing trip?"

"No, I saw her several times alone."

Her countenance changed a little. She did not look shocked or even amazed; only as though some bitter inkling had been proven true.

"So you are the one," she murmured.

"Yes'm."

"There had to be someone, and after all, what does it matter who? I don't blame you. My daughter led you on."

"No, I wooed her with all my might and main."

"You are a fool. She led you on even as Eve led Adam into breaking God's ordinance. She could make any man love her."

"To that, I agree, but this was my doing. She warned me again and again it was no use."

"That was the French blood coming out. Well, she was caught in her own net. But if I had had my way, I would have whipped her back to Dick's house and bade him whip her until he tamed her. Instead, her weak, degenerate father opened his arms to her."

I opened my mouth and only by the narrowest of margins kept from putting my foot in it. I was about to say, "Oh, good God, did she leave him by her own will?" Then Dame Reil would ask what had happened between her and me, in our secret meetings, to make Dick throw her out. I could leap to my feet and holler, but a quiver started at the base of my neck, spread swiftly across my shoulder blades, and raised gooseflesh on the calves of my legs.

"What's come over you, Mr. Starbuck?" the lady asked in a colorless tone. "Do you rejoice over breaking up her marriage?"

"Yes, ma'am. Greatly."

"It's a pity you couldn't have persuaded her not to undertake it. But it's her scandal, not mine. I've washed my hands of it."

"She was bent on marrying Dick to help her father. I did my best to dissuade her. I thank God she changed her mind, even so late."

"You'd better thank the devil. It was his work."

"Will you tell me where in France I may find her?"

"A fool should be answered according to his folly. I would tell you without a qualm, if I remembered the name of the port."

"Was it Brest?"

"I haven't the least notion. I didn't pay any attention. I washed my hands of the whole matter."

"Will you tell me the name of the ship she sailed on?"

"I didn't see them off."

I could find that out at the customhouse, as well as her ports of call.

"Do you think she and her father will have means of support in France? I implore you to tell me."

"I'll tell you what I know—it's nothing to me. Dr. Reil received a letter from his brother—whom that rascal Talleyrand had invited back to France from Quebec—a good week before the marriage. He was offered some sort of a medical position in the government. Because Roxana had never hinted to him that she was marrying Dick for his sake he said nothing about the offer—which he was scheming to accept the instant she was happily married. When Sunday evening she told him she couldn't go through with it, of course he proposed that she and Eliza accompany him."

"Then they'll get along well, at least for the present—"

"You should have seen the three of 'em as they started out! Happy as children going on a picnic. But they didn't ask me to go with them. They knew better."

"I've but one more question to ask. Roxana told me that her father was very poor. If you are in need—"

"I'll get along much better now. All the money we lived on came from my father—my husband spent the little he made on drink. I thank you for your consideration."

"Then, ma'am, I'll take my leave, and if I may serve you in any way—"

"I won't call on you. I call on no one but the Lord, who takes care of His own, while the devil takes care of his own. I have atoned for my sin of marrying for love instead of for duty, by driving away both my husband and my child. I did not mean to drive them, but the Lord put the whip in my hand and taught me how to use it. I am redeemed."

"Good day to you, Mistress Reil."

"Reil. Reel with drunkenness, reel with dancing!"

She closed the door and I went out into the sunlight. I had never seen it such a pure and fluid gold. The bees were busy, the flowers effused sweet scent, the birds twittered in the tall, grave elms. There was no lovelier place than Salem by the sea, a natural spawning ground for witches. I loved the most beautiful of the batch and knew that in her witchy fashion, she loved me.

3.

If I went to France at once, I would have to raise money for passage by selling either my boat or my golden prizes, the first very useful for trading along the Cuban coast; and the gifts for victuals and cargo for the venture. Indeed if Nicodemus and I were so rash as to start out now for France in the dinky craft, we would arrive, if at all, too poor for any use.

But we need not fear striking out this summer weather for the islands, there to seek the "Agatha," my legacy. The sale of one of my two presents would lade us well, and the voyage log no more than two thousand miles. I figured we would be laden and ready to weigh on the hour that Andy returned and delivered me my letter. Meanwhile it was no trouble to learn the name of Roxana's ship—the "Caroline"—and that her first port of call would be Brest.

My golden candlestick brought two hundred silver dollars and a quizzical look from the buyer. We put aboard salt and smoked beef, salt cod, sealed tubs of biscuits, sacks of potatoes, a tub of butter, baskets of dried beans and other long-lived vegetables, casks of water, jugs of rum to lift our spirits, and green limes to ward off scurvy. We had decided to break the journey at Bermuda; and on consulting Captain Dan'l's catalogue, we shipped for trading half a ton of first-grade Haverhill leather. Because those were stormy seas—"Still vexed Bermoothes" I remembered from my reading—we stowed spare canvas, cordage, and such like gear.

While dickering with Mr. Derby for the goods, I asked him how my investment in his company had thrived. He shook his head wearily. "You might get ten cents on the dollar, but I wouldn't give that, myself. Young Pitt and young Bonaparte together with the devil have ruined Derby and comp'ny."

Busy as Adirondack bears before the freeze up, Nicodemus and I were ready to sail by Friday supper time. Just before sundown I was sitting on the edge of the wharf, smoking one of my companion's clay pipes, when it all but fell out of my mouth during a sudden intake of breath. I seemed to be aware of danger before knowing its source. It was like the cold breath of a fog-shrouded iceberg in the path of my ship. A tall man was walking toward me. My heart knew who he was before my eyes fixed on him. *Look out,* it was beating—*Look out! Look out! Look out!*—plain as the clang of a fire bell from a tower.

Dick sauntered toward me, swinging a walking stick of cane. He was dressed more dandyish than I had ever seen him—in a plush coat and breeches, a three-cornered hat, a bright blue stock, and high, glossy boots. A fine figure of a man, Dick, carrying well his heavy bone and brawn; a very handsome man too, pallid of countenance, light of eye, ruddy of hair. He smiled faintly as he came up to me.

"Mr. Starbuck, I'd heard you were back."

"Yes, sir," I answered. "Here I am."

"The intelligence was slow to reach me, or I'd been here sooner. Will you favor me with a few minutes of your time? I'd like to talk to you in closet."

"No closet is as safe as this open place, and no time better than now. Shall we sit down?" For my skin's sake I had got on my feet.

"As you please."

He picked a dry spot, dusted it with a handkerchief, and sat with his feet over the edge. I chose a place about five feet away. The light of the low-down sun slanted in over the roofs behind us and threw our immense long shadows across the water to meet and merge far out in ominous marriage and consumption—like an evil soothsaying. A solitary gull caught the pale-gold light on his wings and a small fish, maimed by a hook or by some voracious hunter of his element, flopped in feeble circles on the surface, causing a rather bright and pretty ripple.

"You're quite a fellow, Mr. Starbuck," Dick began in a low, good-humored-sounding voice. "I didn't give you enough credit at first."

"Thank you, Mr. Featherstone."

"By your leave, I'll call you Jason. I invite you to call me Dick. We know each other quite well by now, and 'll know each other even better before we're done."

"I agree gladly."

"You recall our horse race. Probably not as clearly as I do—since you won—but clear enough. I failed to realize at the time what a notable and telling victory it was—wilful blindness, of course. I told myself it was mainly low cunning—your scouting the course with such care, and decoying me into the bog. Instead, of course, it was unusual wits."

"Since you are so generous, I was practically raised on a horse."

"I might have known that, you being a mountaineer. Instead I was led into another error, human enough, but preposterous. Since the defeat stung me more than anyone knew, I struck a pose of superiority over you—a gentleman outsmarted by a low-born backwoodsman. I managed to believe it in a fashion—I had been to Harvard, had plenty of money, moved in the best Salem society. But I've had cause to examine that, Jason. I've been forced—for my own good—to appraise you honestly. True, my mother was better born than yours. But my father was not nearly as well born as yours—his father an illiterate sailor and he a trifling clerk until sharp practice got him ahead. In some fashion you have become as well educated as I, and as cultivated. I can't lord it over you—it would be silly as well as disastrous. I recognize you as an equal."

Dick was speaking slowly and evenly, the words falling from faintly smiling lips. There was no contempt in that smile, only a dreadful humor. Meanwhile the sun had knocked off—with no more fuss than a sailor going off watch—yet our joined shadows on the water were still discernible from the fading glare in the west. My imagination was strongly moved. It seemed to foretell that Dick and I were linked in life, and linked in death.

"I recognize you as an equal," I replied, when he had paused.

"I'm glad of that. I don't want any gulfs between us. I want it man to man."

"That suits me, too."

"Well, then, I'll speak freely. When I became engaged to Roxana, she told me she didn't love me. That didn't matter to me as much as you might think. I didn't want to be loved, I suppose. It would get in my way. Do you follow me?"

"I think so."

"But I wanted her at any price. She didn't tell me then that she was in love with someone else—if she had, it would have made no difference to me. I'd perceived she was very eager to marry me—rather to marry my money. She played, very cleverly, a game of being hard to get, which I saw through from the first. She was not the first one who has underestimated my powers. But I don't want you to, Jason."

When he paused, I spoke courteously. "I'll try not to. I think it would be very dangerous."

"What is before us will be far more interesting to me if you are fully on your guard," he went on, in a pleasant tone. "At the same time you see I'm liable to grave mistakes—that will make it more interesting to both of us. My plans were for Roxana and me to spend the first night in our house and then take a fortnight's voyage on one of my father's ships. Mid-afternoon after the ceremony I brought her home and soon had her to myself in our bedroom. I hadn't locked the door yet. Have you ever broken a horse?"

"Plenty of them."

"You have to begin easy, you know. Roxana is a very proud, high-spirited girl. What I should have done at the very first was to divert her attention, lock the door, and put the key in my pocket."

He was looking out to sea and I stole a glance at his face. It had turned very white and there was an agony of self-fury in his eyes. My mouth felt dry and my heart very cold.

"We'd had very few kisses, but that hadn't worried me much either—my time was coming. Well, I didn't control myself properly. She sprang back from me and said, 'Dick, I'm sorry, but I can't go through with it.'

" 'It's too late now,' I answered.

" 'You're wrong about that.' Those were her very words—as though I could ever forget. Then she told me she couldn't be my wife—that she'd known it for several days but wouldn't believe it. If I were like most men, she said, she'd feel awfully sorry and ashamed. She'd try to break it more gently, so not to hurt my feelings. But that didn't seem necessary in my case—and of course she was right.

"I intended to let her talk a few minutes, then pick her up, and carry her to the bed. It didn't make any difference to me how she fought—I would have conquered her. If she'd yelled, I'd 've stopped her mouth. Before we were through, she would have known that she belonged to me. She would never have got it out of her head again. But I waited too long, and she guessed my intention. I underestimated her mind and resources."

"I'm glad of that," I told him, after a long silence. I found myself very alert to any move he might make.

"I thought you would be. That's one reason I'm telling you about

123

it. She maneuvered to get me farther from the door than she was, and suddenly darted toward it. I never saw anything so fast. Her hand swept it open in one movement and she was down the stairs and into the street before I could catch her. There were some people going by and she fell in close behind them. If I took hold of her there, she would have fought me like a wildcat and made me the laughingstock of the town.

"So I fell in beside her and said we'd talk it over. She said that would be useless—she'd never live with me—and when I asked her if she were in love with another man, she admitted that she was. She told me it was a Frenchman." Dick gave a brief laugh. "She's a very skillful liar but I'd learned to see through her."

The glimmer in the west had died. In the deepening twilight Dick's face appeared even more pale than before, his big body relaxed, ominously graceful.

"Now we're getting to it," I said.

"I dare say. Her father met her at the door and asked me to go until he could talk to her. They're very close, you know. Mistress Reil began some sort of tirade but the doctor told her to shut up. When I called again, he refused to let me see her and told me he would have the marriage annulled. I knew that would take a long time but did not know he had a chance to go to France. I'd bide my time."

He was biding it now very patiently, I thought.

"It turned out that Mr. Derby advanced him the passage money on one of his ships. I found out about it a day ahead but there was no practical way to stop them. Anyway—the affair had begun to take another shape in my mind."

His tone grew even more impersonal. "I would get Roxana in the end, but there was no hurry about it. There was something I must attend to first—not only to clear the road to her but for my own enjoyment and satisfaction. My deepest need."

Until now I had thought likely he intended only to fight me hand to hand. Now it came to me strongly that only by the utmost care would I live to the full flood of this tide.

"I see," I said.

"Not yet, I think, clearly. Looking back over my affair with Roxana, I could pick almost the moment that she began to struggle against marrying me. It was the day you took us fishing, of course. I thought her best chance to have seen you alone was when her parents spent the day and night in Lynn. Also I soon got the idea that the crew of the 'Morning Star,' which we own, knew something about it—they looked so wise. A little inquiry brought out the fact that Henry Williams, the skipper's son, had seen you carrying her out to your boat at Catfish Cove. Watching the house, I saw Eliza carry a letter to the wharf and give it to Andy. I could have taken it from her or got it off him but that was piddling. I wanted you to know the full extent of your victory over me."

"That was considerate of you."

"That's why I'm telling you the whole story. It was a very great victory. From little signs that I've lined up and looked at, I know that you bedded her that night and, quite likely, put her with child. That won't make any difference to me, you understand, when I get her back. In fact it will make *my* victory all the more complete."

He turned his face to me now, his eyes glimmering in the dusk, his lips twisted a little in a smile.

"It's going to be very complete, Jason," he said quietly. "My whole life is bent on it. It wouldn't be complete if I did not warn you—if I didn't let you live a good while in dread of it. I want you to know at once how much you've won so you'll know how much you lose. There's no doubt in my mind that she loves you almost as much as I hate you."

"I'm glad that a man of your intelligence is of that opinion."

"It would be small satisfaction to me if you were a piddling man. But even now, you're underestimating me. You think I intend to kill you here on the dock—tonight. In the first place, we've likely been seen talking here. Why, Jason—I mean you to live several years! I want you to get along fine—everything rosy, except for my shadow hanging over you. I expect you to have many more victories, including many nights in Roxana's arms. Then I shall break you—your heart and pride. Finally when I do kill you—as I certainly will at last—you'll almost thank me." He paused, smiling at me.

"Is that all?" I asked.

He started to rise. This was the moment I had been preparing for—my preparations not in the least reduced by his plausible excuses for not attempting my murder tonight. I had looked for a weapon and perceived one in his cane. Its balance in his hands indicated a heavy weighted head. One quick blow would knock me out, and one thrust as I fell, shove me over the edge of the dock. The wound on my corpse could easily have been made by my striking a piling. He knew what he would do with the stick afterward: I guessed it would disappear and a light, unweighted cane take its place. People would suspect he had killed me and know the reason, but he would not mind—he would rather enjoy it, especially if he brought Roxana back to Salem as mistress of his house.

It was as though I must make now, a difficult, crucial shot, with a quick, steady aim of staying alive. My left hand was flat against the dock, with the muscles of my arm flexing. There came an exploding rush of event. Dick's motion, leisurely to start with, turned into an upward spring. It was as though he had rehearsed the action, so smooth it was, and so inhumanly fast. As his left arm shot him upward his right was swinging the stick. But my left arm shot me upward too, and not attempting to dodge—swinging my feet up on the far side of him instead of the near side—I rammed my head and shoulders with all available strength against his body. He was hurled back off the dock.

He struck clear but for the moment was too stunned to do more than grab a piling. I snatched up the cane he had dropped and, crouching on the boards, leaned over the edge to give him his own medicine. Again one well-aimed blow would do.

The big splash he had made had attracted no one's attention. We were still alone in the heavy dusk, but just thinking of that made me listen for running feet. My luck had been good so far but how long would it last? Presently he would shout for help or swim out from the dock.

He did neither, because he knew, before I did, that he was safe. My hand had been seized in the vice-like grip of caution. The shadow of the gallows cools many a passion to kill.

Dick released the piling and swam jauntily to the nearest ladder. I did not move from my place. He came up, streaming water, and walked a short distance toward me.

"This adds to it, doesn't it, Jason?" he asked.

"I reckon so, Dick."

"Why didn't you knock me on the head, when you had the chance? You'll regret it all your short life."

"I was afraid of the hangman, if you want the truth. I want to live and get Roxana."

"You'll have her for a while, I reckon. I'm reasonably well satisfied. You're a less resolute man than I thought, but more alert, long headed, and nimble. I'm rather glad you got away. I'd 've regretted cutting the game so short."

"Well, you'll have to buy some new clothes."

"No, I think these will wash and be good as new. But I've lost my hat."

"You've also lost your walking stick. I'll keep it as a memento of the skirmish."

"You've every right to it. Well—I'll see you later."

"I'll look forward to it. Good night."

4.

Nicodemus had been on an errand in town. When he returned, I sat with him in the lantern-lighted deckhouse and told him of my whole affair with Roxana and Dick, trying to win his sympathy and full help. He listened solemnly, his nose appearing to sharpen, the color growing in his freckled face.

"'Tis a good thing I shipped with ye," he said, "or ye can blow me down."

"I need your counsel, that's certain."

"Ye ought to of had more sense than try to steal a girl from a man like him. But I knowed by the way you drove the 'Charity' ye was foolhardy."

"I may improve with age."

"A little, maybe. But if ye can salvage the 'Saint Agatha' and make a fortune, ye'll have a strong arm ag'in him. Money makes the mare go, the saying is. Now it's like ye was a sloop o' war engaging a frigate. He'll outgun ye, and outsail ye, and weather storms that would sink ye."

"You're right about that, Nicodemus."

"I wish we could put out in this fair wind for Bermuda." His blue eyes gleamed like a terrier's playing ball.

"We've got to wait for my letter from Roxana. Andy's due in to-morrow."

Tomorrow, the "Morning Star's" day to dock, began at midnight tonight. Twice I rose to look for lanterns gathered on the quay. At dawn I felt almost certain she was in port, and made the round of the docks seeking her. There was no smell of her, and nothing for me to do all morning but look to sea; although Nicodemus, a great believer in a stitch in time, took many a thrifty one to make our gear shipshape. Shortly after our noonday meal Mr. Derby came puffing down the dock and stopped to speak to me.

"So you're not off yet," he remarked.

"No, sir."

"Did you tell me you were taking her to Halifax, to work in the fisheries?"

I had told him no such thing. "We may touch there, before we're through."

"I reckon you could go 'most anywhere in that tight little hooker. Well, I've brought you the *Boston Post*." He handed me the paper he held under his arm.

"Thank you kindly. I'll keep it to read at sea."

"Why not read it now? It's the first copy in Salem—my agent in Boston gets it to me by special dispatch—and you'll be four hours ahead of the town on the latest news."

Instead of walking on, he waited for me to look at the paper. "There's some interesting news on the inside page, larboard side," he remarked.

I opened to the page and read:

DARING ESCAPE

Our correspondent in Charleston writes us about an event of interest to the people of the Bay Section.

The notorious pirate, Captain Daniel Todkill, native to Medford, is loose on the seas again. Caught in Beaufort, South Carolina, while on a drunken orgy, and sentenced to hang, he escaped from the Charleston jail on the very morning the sentence was to have been executed.

Members of his crew, in various disguise, mingled with the throng, and by attacking the guards, effected his escape. This would not have been possible save that an unknown rogue, captain of the rescue party, had disguised as a gentleman and hoodwinked the jailor into letting him conspire with the prisoner. Also he had plied the hangman with liquor, inducing him to vary the usual procedure, thus diverting the guards' attention. Well-known planters hereabouts with whom the villain made free could hardly believe that the affable, well-dressed "Mr. Jennings" was in reality the chief conspirator. Mr. Ravenal, of Rosemont, still maintains that he is a gentleman of quality who has taken to crime.

The merchants here are more incensed with this modern Morgan than with Captain Todkill himself. However, certain irresponsible elements of our populace are openly jubilant at the trick played on the authorities. A good description of the knave has been obtained to be posted in customhouses throughout the coast. He is under twenty-four, tall, dark as an Indian, an excellent rider and rifle shot. A former member of the crew, now re-formed, declares him a newcomer to the ship.

The rescue was effected without bloodshed, save that Colonel Stono had an excellent horse shot from under him while riding full-tilt at a distance of a hundred paces.

I handed the paper back to Mr. Derby. His countenance was grave—almost lugubrious—but his eyes sparkled.

"You've done me a favor, sir, letting me know of my uncle's narrow escape," I told him.

"I reckon I've done you a favor that evens us up for my selling you a thousand dollars worth of stock now not worth an hundred."

"Well, that could very well be. How long did you say before the paper's current?"

"About five o'clock. Mind you, not many would ask where Dan'l's nephew was, during the hanging. People see the name of your boat and never think of it again. But if you have an enemy—"

"It's possible. If any one asks for me, will you say we sailed for Martha's Vineyard—" I looked at my watch—"at one-fifteen o'clock?"

"That's five minutes from now."

"We might beat it by a minute. And I thank you kindly."

"You're welcome, Jason, and see my factor at Baltimore for the latest news. It will blow over, some day—or maybe you'll blow it over. Goodbye, and a good sail."

"Hoist the mains'l," I called to Nicodemus.

"Aye, aye, sir," the stout fellow replied.

The breeze so useless to us a moment ago—thin stuff of which one oxen would seem to outpull a skyful—swelled our sail and easy as winking sped our heavy-laden boat into the bay. The dock drew away as though drawn by a thousand oxen. Exhilaration swelled out my heart.

"There must of been some 'portant news in that there paper, that we got off so lively," Nicodemus remarked in the first breathing spell.

"Why, yes," I answered, easy at the tiller. "It was an account of our lifting Cap'n Todkill off the gallows. There was a good description of me in it, and I'm known here as his nephew."

He was silent awhile, thinking this over. "I don't reckon my name was in the paper," he said wistfully.

"No, nor mine as yet, luckily."

"But it do look like we might be gone from this coast a good while."

"You're right about that, Nicodemus."

"'Tis a pity we've got to sail without that letter."

"I don't propose to. We'll lay behind Eastern Point till dark, keeping a sharp lookout for the 'Morning Star.' Out of Casco Bay she's almost sure to beat in close, the wind where it is."

"Cap'n Todkill couldn't of figured it no better," he remarked after a pause. "Ye've a good head, when ye'll use it."

"If we miss her, we'll have to go to shore in the still of night."

"Well, I reckon we could assay it without great hazard. They won't be lookin' for us back to Salem soon, and we can lay to that. But we better not tarry long, and slip away fast in the dark."

As it happened, we did miss the "Morning Star" too wide to speak her. After a long but not too weary watch, Nicodemus' gull eyes picked her up nearly two leagues south'ard of the Point, tacking in to Salem on a westward course. The wind had changed a little, and no doubt her captain's plans had changed during the voyage on account of the way the fish bit or did not bite. We could not catch her short of the dock. We could only wait till twilight, then slip in behind her.

The dark stood heavy and the house lamps lit when we slid alongside the wharf about a hundred fathoms from the fishing smack. The town lay very quiet; I could scarcely believe that the report of my knavery was as yet on people's tongues. However, I hoped fervently that my search for Andy need not be long. The harbor master might be searching for him too, to inquire of my whereabouts at present and for some weeks past. With him might be the constable, and in his wake or even on his bow such people as sought my downfall by the handiest weapon. Nicodemus tied our boat as lightly as he had tied his horse outside the jail in Charleston. I slipped his pistol into my belt under my coat.

The smack's ports were open, and it was immediately apparent that a good part of her crew was yet aboard, although not started to discharge her load of fish and wash her down. Presently the silence had a salty flavor, which was Andy's unmistakable twang. He was speaking respectfully to someone, and yet with a certain stubbornness.

"There's no charge ag'in him yet, that I know of, sir, and I don't see my way to give it to ye."

Good for Andy! He might be done with me, but not with his New

England conscience. I sprang lightly down on the deck, no longer feeling half a fool for bringing the pistol. I might have to draw it, and conceivably fire it at someone's leg. But turning back without the letter was inconceivable; so much that was dear to me might hang on its little thread of ink.

A short ladder led to the cabin. I stopped to locate Andy in the group of men, and another whose position in the room was of equal moment. I could not find this second one for the simple reason he was not there. The gentleman whom Andy had addressed as "sir" was not Dick—only a flurried mind had boggled that it could be Dick. My great antagonist would not stoop to business of this kind. He did not want the help of the admiralty; his war would be waged in silence and alone. Nor was it an officer duty bound to catch and hang pirates. It was a measly man with a foxy face—my Uncle Samuel Starbuck.

On a less urgent errand I would have enjoyed watching the faces of the men as at various degrees of quickness they grasped my presence among them. They would not have been greatly astonished to have a town dignitary appear on their high-smelling hooker, but did not expect to see me. One or two gaped as though their visitor closely resembled Jason Starbuck but could not possibly be him. Samuel Starbuck, his villainy against his own blood brought home to him, turned white.

There was no sound until I spoke. "Andy, I'll thank you to deliver my letter."

"Well, I don't say I ain't got it," he replied, scratching his head. "But I must say, I wasn't looking for ye to come back for it."

"He came back because it's a very important letter," Samuel Starbuck broke in. "I advise you not to give it to him, but to turn it over to the law."

"I advise you to keep your mouth shut, Samuel Starbuck, or piddling as you are, I'll put my fist in it."

"Don't be hasty, Jason. You can't possibly escape. As your uncle, I advise you to surrender and throw yourself upon the mercy of the court. It's for your own good, Jason. As a public-spirited man—"

He continued talking as I walked toward Andy but stopped suddenly when that movement brought me unexpectedly close to himself.

"There's no charge against me," I was saying to Andy. "If there were, you'd still have to give me my letter."

" 'Tis what I just told Mr. Starbuck. I've kept it for you, and here it is."

"Thanks. I'll be going, now. But it would be well if you'd all stay here a few minutes longer. The crew of the 'Charity' are waiting outside, and I can't answer for their behavior."

No one made a movement or a sound as I climbed up the ladder on to the dock. A shrill whistle to Nicodemus set him to casting off, and he stepped almost too lively, for there was a water gap of six feet as I sprang aboard. Still there was no sign of pursuit. By themselves these weathered fishermen of the "Morning Star" might have poked their inquisitive noses out to sniff the wind. They would take with a grain of their own salt my yarn of blood-thirsty pirates waiting to knife them. But that respected citizen Samuel Starbuck stood among them—or perhaps sat wilted on the nearest bench—and timorousness is more catching than pinkeye.

The darkness consumed us. Already we could give the slip to a fleet of provost boats.

"Will ye take the tiller, sir?" Nicodemus asked, when we were well out of hearing of shore.

"No, I'll just take it easy."

"What's the course, if ye've set one?"

"In the general direction of Bermuda."

"Then I reckon ye got the letter."

"Thank you, I did."

The dead lights of my ports needed calking. I waited until we were two leagues from shore before going into the deckhouse, shutting the door, and lighting a lantern. Then I sat on my bed with the sealed page in my hand.

My name was written on it in capitals. Within this enclosure was charted my life's course—at least my bearings and seamarks for many a voyage. My hand shook like a wench's as I broke the seal.

My darling oaf—

That's what you are, to fall in love with a cockatrice like me.

But I must have fallen in love with you too or in some fashion lost my wits. Although a very nice-looking bride—so the beaux all told me—I took pity on Dick the last minute and backed out of the bargain. Ma was greatly upset but Pa mighty pleased, and since it turned out he had been offered a medical post in France, he and Eliza and I are sailing tomorrow. We are good company for him and he is safe from Ma's righteousness so I think he will work hard and stay reasonably sober.

Jason, do you love me? If you do, don't you dare come to see me for at least a year. If by then you haven't found the Golden Fleece you must only kiss me and get on with your voyage. We can forget all about Dick [she was wrong there!] and I'll have a wonderfully good time in France, with lots of beaux.

However, I do insist that you put into Brest when the cherries are ripe. Maybe I will go with you for the rest of the journey. Inquire of the prefect for Dr. Francis Reil.

Shall we say July? It's a lovely month in France. If you are so impetuous as to come the first day of July, you won't surprise or disappoint

Your own

Roxana Reil.

P.S. It was a false alarm.

CHAPTER SEVEN

"I Will Not Let You Go!"

I.

The year had turned, and cherry time in France only a few months away. Nicodemus and I were putting into Cape Haiten, that island Paris, jewel set under mighty mountains. We had spent the fall and winter in Cuba, without a glimpse of Captain Radcliffe or a smell of his dirty slaver. Now we were seeking the best route to Brest.

In other ways we had prospered, trading up and down the coasts, for the island had been left high and dry by the storms of war, and all the freight we could stow sold at a fancy price. Spanish stuck well on my two-edged tongue. My manners had been smoothed and bettered in the company of sugar-planting dons, and their dark-eyed, duenna-guarded daughters. True, we had left in unseemly haste, without one *"Adios,"* and heaven only knew when we could return. Despite changing our names and the name of my boat, we had finally been recognized as two pirates wanted in Charleston for delivering from the gallows an arch enemy of Spain. Save for the warning of a Spain-hating rebel, we would now lie rotting in the dark of Morro Castle, chains on our legs soon to turn to ropes on our necks, instead of bespanking along in the sparkling air before a cheerful breeze.

A harbor boat full of French marines ran pop eyed to meet us at sight of our high-flaunted American flag, but they grinned when they looked us over, and welcomed our half-cargo of Spanish sherry we had been about to run to Antilla. Among the many ships in the harbor, tailor-made to fit us was a Brest-bound brig getting her wounds dressed. Eight of her hands including her first mate had been killed by a bursting gun.

I found her captain, a broad-beamed Breton, in his favorite cafe, and with Nicodemus solid behind me, gave him my best bow.

"Captain Barteau, have you filled the berth vacated by the loss of your first officer?"

"Since you ask, I expect to put my second officer in that berth, and promote my bosun to the other."

"Instead, I propose you let me fill it, and give my man Nick a berth before the mast."

"Pray take a seat, and have a glass of wine with me." Then when we had performed the pleasant rite, "Granted that good officers are scarce these days, with English and Yankee frigates blazing at us, what French ships have you sailed on, with officer rank?"

"None, sir. I'm Captain Jacques de Stael of Louisiana, of old French family, but born since the Spanish occupation. My request is for first officer, not second."

"You've captained American clippers?"

"Yes, sir, the 'Hope,' a brigantine of a hundred and fifty tons."

"Of course you've testaments to that."

"Not in the way of papers, which would be awkward to have on me, the 'Hope' being a privateer of no small fame, but in ten minutes on your ship at sea I could show you my credentials."

Captain Barteau had not heard of the "Hope." However, he invited me to inspect his ship, and was greatly taken with my proposal for rerigging her topsails to add a good half-knot to her clip—perhaps enough to outrun a sloop of war and get home safe to *la belle France*. However, if this notion got me the berth, Nicodemus should get the credit and the pay, since it had hatched in his brain.

It happened that Captain Barteau was going around to L'Hôpital to lade sugar. He had hardly mustered the crew, when he bade me take the quarter-deck, and I took the hooker at full sail through the strait into Windward Passage, then spanked her clear under the lea of the land in La Gonaíye Gulf, eighty leagues in twenty-eight hours. If that did not land me my berth as first officer, I was a lubber.

But the good captain had been bitten once or twice by flashy strangers. In the upshot, I could have the berth of second mate with Nicodemus—Nicholas Diego—as carpenter, or stay on shore. For a moment or two I came close to staying on shore for my injured dignity's sake—this in spite of my resolve to ship before the mast rather than be late a day in meeting Roxana. Presently my common sense prevailed, and in the end my reward was greater than a little extra pay and glory, being a lesson never to cut off my nose to spite my face, and if first prize is not in reach, to be glad of second, and there is more than one way to skin a cat.

Meanwhile we had been trying to sell the "Prudence Todkill," a difficult as well as doleful chore. The best offer we had got in Le Cap amounted to two hundred dollars, hardly a third of her value, so Nicodemus had sailed her alone to L'Hôpital in the tall ship's wake. Here she went a-begging, save for a slave-trader's bid of a hundred francs more. After he told me of the use he would put her to, delivering new-caught slaves from the baracones here to plantations along the coast—twenty or more packed in my deckhouse where Roxana and I had made love and Nicodemus and I had made free—I swore I would sink her first. My mother, whose maiden name she bore, would turn over in her Adirondack grave. Then suddenly I discovered a noble disposal of her.

While we were lading sugar, two shabbily dressed Frenchmen came to look at her. They were making off with sad faces when I accosted them, for these were fine faces, similar enough that I thought the two men must be brothers. By their bows and their accents, I knew they were gentlemen.

"Didn't you like the look of her?" I asked.

"Very much. She's just what we want, the two of us able to sail her," one of them replied, "but we've no money to charter her, let alone buy her."

"Where did you want to take her?"

"To Quebec, where our families have newly come from France. Once there, we could pay for her well."

"Would it help you any to get as far as Boston?"

"The good God! I know the Dutch consul there."

"My boat is victualled for a week's cruise, and I'll gladly furnish her for the whole journey, and you can leave her and the money I'm out, with the Derby Shipping Company."

But I was half-paid already by the joy in their faces. Moreover, they had enough to buy stores, and promised to deposit a hundred dollars with Mr. Derby for the boat's hire. Within an hour they had written me a promissory note that they said their families would honor, were they lost at sea; and I gave them a letter to my old friend, asking him to use or sell the boat in any way that he deemed to our mutual profit. The notion that these two French gentlemen would cheat me could hardly enter my head.

Nicodemus and I saw off the little hooker, both of us green in the gills. We had already put our kits aboard the "St. Almo," and shortly thereafter, ourselves. The voyage was a very happy one, blessed by good weather, and cursed by no fights with frigates, for if we were caught by a Yankee, Nicodemus and I might have been thrown to the sharks.

We were soon in Brest, pleased with every prospect, our good luck holding wonderfully. Mr. De Fosse, the first officer, still grateful for his berth after my fine sailing around Haiti, had influence here, and obtained me immediate entree to the prefect, ahead of a hundred who had been waiting days. The blood of the French Revolution had hardly dried, but the millennium of equality and fraternity was still a long way off.

"Francis Reil," he echoed with pursed lips, when I asked the doctor's whereabouts. "I vaguely remember clearing a physician of that name for Lyons."

"Citizen," a worshipful clerk spoke up, "it was Marseilles you're thinking of—you issued him a pass to go there at the end of the year. But he returned to Brest about three months ago and is now head physician to the naval station at Lorient."

"There you are," the great man told me. "I'm robbing the Republic of my salary as prefect—Monsieur Garat runs the department." Then he scribbled passes for Nicodemus and me to travel about France and was in great haste to get shed of me.

Nicodemus and I sailed to Lorient in an oyster boat, chilled and begloomed by fog. Walking the dank streets of the town, I could not now be sure that Roxana was waiting for me, with lips to kiss and arms to enfold me. She might have gone to Quebec, or back to Salem, or into the ground. No, that was only the bad weather oozing into my heart. She might not be in Lorient but she was waiting for me still, and I would go to her. I listened to my heart and it told me she was warm and alive.

Nicodemus and I drew near the naval station. I felt a little faint—not at all the nonchalant fellow I showed my companion—lest Dr. Reil not approve of my suit of his daughter. The more he knew about me, the less he might welcome me. We came to a large, bleak building, where a rugged peasant with one leg, a clerkish fellow with a file, and a sad little man with one arm gave us confusing and somewhat contrary directions.

An orderly told me to go into an anteroom. He himself would seek *monsieur le docteur* but he was very busy and—"*merci, m'sieu!*" Nicodemus waited in the hall for me; I waited with a cramped heart for Roxana's father.

He appeared presently, holding a little bloody knife in a red hand. Then I forgot myself for a brief time, wondering at him. He was dressed better than I had ever seen him, yet his journey to France had not prospered him. He appeared very thin and frail, and his hair had silvered a good deal. I thought that he had entered the room with a bent head although it straightened at sight of me.

"I'm Dr. Francis Reil," he told me in French. "How may I serve you?"

"Do you know me, sir?"

He looked at me more keenly. "I'm sure I've seen you somewhere before. Perhaps one of Admiral de Bruey's officers—"

"No, sir," I said in English out of a corded throat. "I'm Jason Starbuck, of Salem."

His expression seemed to be one of moderate pleasure and surprise. There was another beneath it, covered up, but I could not make it out. He pronounced a long, good Yankee "Well!" and walking briskly toward me, held out his hand.

"I'm glad to see you. Don't mind the blood—it's from the wound of a heroic French sailor. Forgive my not recognizing you—it's been more than a year—you've changed—all for the good—and to meet you across the sea—"

"I never had the honor of knowing you well, Dr. Reil." Then, getting down to it, "Is your daughter well?"

He had to get down to it too, I thought. Until now he had put it behind him, as civilized people learn how to do with awkward or painful situations. It came to me that this situation was, for yet unknown reasons, extremely awkward; he was not succeeding in hiding it very well. For such an urbane Frenchman it was a poor showing. I felt the first stir of anger, believing that he was going to put difficulties in the way of my seeing Roxana.

Yet his first question startled and baffled me. "Did you know my daughter?" he asked in a dry voice.

"Yes, sir."

"You knew her well?" I thought he spoke with a terrific effort.

"Yes, very well."

"May I ask if—pardon me—has she anything to do with your coming to France?"

"She has everything to do with it. I came here to see her."

He passed his hand across his forehead. "There was a young man in her life who had something to do with her not going through with a marriage to Dick Featherstone. She did not tell me so, yet I suspected it. Are you the one?"

"Yes, sir."

"Jason Starbuck, you said."

"Yes, sir."

"Am I to understand—I beg you, pardon my way of speaking—that you're in love with my daughter?"

"Yes, and she's in love with me."

"Follow me, please."

He turned and went out the door and I followed him through a door into his living quarters. Throughout that little walk, my mind and heart were like a clock that had run down, and were waiting for someone to turn a key. He shut the door, then turned to me with a deathly white face.

"Will you sit down?"

"No, sir. I'll hear what you have to tell me about Roxana."

"My boy, I've no reason to think Roxana is alive."

2.

Dr. Reil turned away from me to hide his twisted face and streaming eyes. I stood over him, my eyes sharp and dry, waiting for him to recover. He had not told me my girl was dead and turned out all the lights. He had said he had no reason to think she was alive.

"Can you tell me now, Dr. Reil?" I asked, when his eyes wheeled back to mine. "I pray you not to spare me, and tell me the worst, no matter how hard it is for you."

"It won't be hard, since you love Roxana." He controlled himself well.

"Sit down, please, sir."

He did so, his throat working. I sat in the chair he had offered me.

"There's really very little to tell." He spoke in a low, clear tone. "In January I was ordered to a naval post in Marseilles. Roxana and Eliza sailed with me, on the 'Leghorn.' In the Mediterranean, off Barcelona, our ship was fired on—at night by an unseen enemy. The ball pierced the hull at the water line and the vessel began to sink rapidly. There was no room for Roxana on the first boat that got off, but she made room for Eliza. She forced her into it in spite of her own protests and the clamor of the others."

"That would be just like her," I said with a great surge of my heart, when Dr. Reil paused to rally strength.

"Roxana got off in the second boat, a small one, with an elderly woman, a baby, a one-armed man, another man who rushed the boat ahead of the women and children, and four sailors." He paused again, to see if he had forgotten anything. "In the morning," he went on, "that boat was found stove in, and upside down."

He fell silent, and I could go now, if I pleased. We could go our ways and each of us attend to his own mourning. He did not ask me to hear another word. He had told me the essential facts that would be required by a crown officer—a coroner, we called him in America.

"Were the other boats saved?"

"Yes, in the morning—when the light broke. A Spanish frigate spied us and picked us up."

"What time of night was the ship struck?"

"About nine. We hadn't gone to bed."

"Was there a heavy sea running?"

"No, it was quite calm."

"Did you hear or see anything more of Roxana's boat after it put off?"

"No. I was in the last boat that got off, with the captain. I tried to call her, but he forbade me, saying that the enemy ship might still be lying about, and I would endanger the lives of all. We lay still and didn't make a sound."

"How would it endanger the peoples' lives? They might be taken prisoner, but surely not killed. Well, I see that sinking the ship without warning indicated a cruel and ruthless enemy. You don't think it was an Englishman."

"I thought at first it might be—mistaking us in the dim moonlight for a French war vessel. One of the men in my boat thought it might be an American privateer—he'd heard that the Yankees were barbarians—but I told him I'd lived many years in America and they wouldn't do that way. Most of the men thought we'd been attacked by a Turk—the Sultan had declared war on France."

"Surely even they wouldn't murder helpless people in boats."

"They'd murder those they didn't want for slaves, the captain said. Not the regular Turkic navy, responsible to the Sultan, but Turkic privateers, many of them pirates and fanatics."

It came to me then where the chance lay that Roxana might yet live. It lay where Dr. Reil could hardly bring himself to gaze. But I could gaze there, presently, and would treat with it full well.

"Were any bodies found?" I asked.

"Yes, the old woman's with the baby's still clutched in her arms. They had been drowned. Two men's bodies were found, washed up on shore.

"Were they men in their prime?"

His eyes met mine briefly. "One was the one-armed man. He'd

been drowned. The other, a French sailor in his prime, had wounds that could easily have been made by rocks or sharks."

"Were there any rocks near by the wreck that could have stove the boat?"

"No, there were not. It was an old boat and perhaps some one started to fall and put his foot through the bottom. Perhaps the ship that fired on us ran into it, or our ship drifted onto it just before she sank."

Plainly he had considered all these possibilities with sore care. But he had something else to say in this regard; I saw it in his eyes.

"However," he went on, in a dry, cold voice, "one of our sailors who saw the boat—he examined it carefully—told me that he thought it had been deliberately stoved."

"Why did he think that?" I asked, holding Dr. Reil's eyes with mine.

"I didn't ask him why. I was too stunned. But I did say to him, 'Are you sure?' And he said, 'No, I can't be sure.'"

I could picture that scene clearly, but my imagination yet balked at the great scenes.

"Did you find out if any Turkic ship was in those waters?"

"Marquis Talleyrand himself made inquiries. No regular ship of the Turkic navy was anywhere about. But a Turk pirate, the 'Zainab,' had been spied not far away. She had been making for Tunis on the Barbary Coast. Through the French consul there, Talleyrand demanded that the Bey discover if she had attacked our ship or brought any prisoners into port. He declared positively that she had not."

"That makes it all the more likely." My brain was lurching, but I made it work. "It would account for the Turkic pirate's firing in the dark and sinking the French merchantman instead of capturing her. She could lay off and catch a few slaves that she could smuggle into port and sell—she couldn't handle many without showing her bloody hand. One sailor who resisted was killed, those not worth selling were thrown overboard. If they kept only three of four it would pay them for the powder and one cannon ball."

He had thought of that; I saw it in his face. "It's possible, but more likely—nine chances out of ten—Roxana is—" He stopped, very white.

"Has the suspicion crossed your mind that Dick Featherstone made the attack and has taken Roxana prisoner? As you may know, he's a resolute and utterly ruthless man."

"It did cross my mind, only to be dismissed as impossible. He was still in Salem hardly a month before. My daughter and I boarded the

'Leghorn' because of a last-minute change of plans. If he schemed to abduct her he would never choose such an uncertain, dangerous, and clumsy method."

"That's true, of course." I had only to think of Dick to know it. "Have you any more to tell me, Doctor Reil?"

He stopped and considered. "No, there's nothing more."

"To find out what my rights are, in this—" that was the best I could put it—"I've got to ask a personal question. Was Roxana still legally married to Dick Featherstone?"

"No. I instituted proceedings before we left America to have the marriage annulled on the ground that it wasn't consummated. I've since heard through Quebec that the Featherstones consented and our plea was granted."

"Well, I'm glad of that. Roxana and I are betrothed, and I stand next to you in the affair."

"To mourn her, yes. That's all that's left."

"I didn't mean that."

"What else can you mean? Jason, what you mean is, Roxana and you *were* betrothed. She was lost at sea on the 'Leghorn.' In a short time she'll be officially declared deceased."

"Officially, perhaps; I've nothing to do with that. I love her, and won't give her up."

"Listen to me, Jason." Dr. Reil paused to rally strength for a great effort. "There's only a ghost of a chance that she's still alive. In all probability she met the—not—too—terrible death of drowning. In my soul that's what I believe. Jason, do you know anything about Islam? If you do, do you even want to *hope* that she's still alive?"

"Yes. It's my dearest, greatest hope."

"Even though she's better off dead than a slave in Islam?" His eyes did not falter now but burned into mine.

"I don't admit that could be true of Roxana—I won't even consider it. She's young and strong. Anyway if she still lives—"

"She *is* dead, to me. I've been forced to that conclusion, as though I'd seen her laid in her grave. Jason, there are things in life that we can't help and can't fight. There's no use hoping against hope—all men find that out—people have to go on living, making out the best they can. Islam's gates are locked to Christians. If you knew she was in any one Islamic city—say Tunis—yet you could never find her. In that city alone there are hundreds of prisons—one in every rich man's house. In Islam there are a hundred cities."

I heard him while thinking of something else. The things he was telling about Islam I could find out later. I waited until he had finished, then told him my thoughts.

"Roxana had a lively imagination. When I was with her, we played with a lot of romantic ideas. She made quite a lot of my name being Jason—although it was just my grandfather's name. She knew I wanted to see the world—have adventures—make a fortune—and that was one reason she had me wait a year before coming here. She liked to imagine me searching for the Golden Fleece. Well, it looks like there was more truth in it than we knew. I told her once she was my Golden Fleece—and now fate has decreed—"

"That's foolish talk, my boy," Dr. Reil broke in. "Of course any imaginative girl like Roxana would make something of your name—especially since you're a natural rover—and she had golden hair. Don't mistake a minor coincidence of that kind for fate. Fate is a dreadful thing. It means something inevitable."

I started to speak but he raised his hand. "You're a young man, with name and fortune to make. These are the best years of your life. You mustn't throw them away—maybe your life too—on a hopeless quest. Don't be fooled by a romantic conception of fate."

"Anything I do will be practical."

"I'm afraid of what a young man may consider practical."

"I'm going now, to think it over. It'll take a whole lot of thought. But I'm certain to see a good deal of the world, if I live, and if Roxana is alive—"

"I've failed my duty toward you, Jason, if I haven't made it clear that Roxana—as far as our living world is concerned—died at sea."

"Why, she may even get word to you somehow. If she does—or if you get final proof of her death—will you have the French government notify the American consul in every large city in Islam?"

"I will, but I don't like the sound of it. I don't like what I see in your face. If I'm responsible—"

"It was your duty to tell me all you knew. What I decide to do about it is on my own head."

"That's true, and I know now you love Roxana greatly. My temptation—I confess it—is to employ your youth and strength to serve my terror and despair. But it would be a poor kindness to my lost girl. I've no doubt she loved you as you love her. So I say for her—as she would say in heaven or on earth—'Let the dead past bury its dead!'"

My heart leaped strangely at sight of Nicodemus, waiting patiently for me. We went into the windy road and tramped in silence to our tavern. I thought to take him to my room to tell him what had happened, but on second thought, I led him to a table in the warm taproom. We could look at the matter more sanely and sensibly here.

"If I was ye, I'd order me a brandy," Nicodemus told me.

"I don't need it."

"Your face says ye need it mighty bad, and so do your eyes. I don't know what's happened, but it's no trifle."

"I'll order brandy for us both."

When we had downed the fiery drinks, I told him what had happened. The freckles stood out on his weathered face.

"Well, I feel for ye, if that's worth saying," he told me at the close.

"It's worth saying, and worth knowing."

"What would be in your mind to do about it, if anything?"

"My mind's still a blank."

"I wouldn't be playing square with ye, unless I told ye that what the doctor said about them Mohammedan countries ain't half of it. There was a Dane on the 'Charity' who'd once been a slave in Tripoli. He told us about the harems, and such as that. Not even another heathen can look at their women, let alone a Christian. The only Christians that can get along at all are them that join their religion for good, and become one of 'em."

"Did he tell you anything that might throw light on what happened?"

"Well, yes. It struck me while you was a-talking, but it won't be no comfort to ye. Slave catching is a regular business. In the open they do it on the excuse of war, but a lot of it's done on the sly, on land and sea. Not just black people, either. Them bashi-bazouks go into Greece and other Christian countries and run off with the prettiest girls they can find and sell them all over the Orient. A real pretty blond girl will bring a couple of thousand dollars. And no one ever hears of 'em in this world again."

I did not want to say something that would sound silly. "What would you do in my place, Nicodemus?"

"Now that I can't say. I wouldn't know where to start to figure, 'cept it might pay to go into the Mediterranean ports handy to where she was lost—and smell around. 'Twill be no trick to earn bread."

He lighted his pipe and for the first time I noticed that his hands were shaking.

"I'd thought to start out for Malta—that's at the door of the Turkic empire," I told him. "Our business with Captain Radcliffe must be laid aside for now."

"It's a long watch, and ye can lay to that. Granting she's alive somewhere—it would take years to find her and get her back."

I heard him say "years" but could not bring myself to heed him, yet. I should have pretended to heed him, meanwhile holding my own foolish hopes; as it was, he saw denial in my face.

"Mark me well, Cap'n Starbuck, and don't let yourself be misled," he told me with solemn dignity. "At best, if ever, it will take years."

"I know it."

"Now 'tis for ye to speak."

"We'll take ship for Malta, and then try to decide what to do."

It was the merest makeshift of a course but we followed it for want of a better. Presently we were in Brest, looking for a ship eastward bound. As far as my actions went, I appeared resolute and practical. Actually I was moving in a queer, inward daze, somewhat the same as in the last summer I had worked the mountain farm, after the events at Eagle Pass. This fellow busying about the harbor did not interest me: I was still traveling toward France on the "St. Almo" to meet Roxana, full of memories of my farewell scenes with her. In my nightly dreams I got to the door of the room where Dr. Reil told me of her loss, but never passed its threshold.

When I saw her in fancy, that forlorn look on her face, I could not keep from crying; but I was careful not to look at it when anyone was near. There were some other memories that I did not let occur to me even when alone.

Among the ships thronging the harbor was one so patently American that Nicodemus ventured that our little war with France was likely over. A wharf rat had pointed her out as soon bound for Naples and by the cut of her jib I recognized her as the "Molly Stark," a staunch, fairly fast Bridgeport schooner that had frequently put into Salem. I looked at her, and saw Derby Dock on a June day, pilings left wet with the falling tide, and a tall girl walking with long strides beside Dick Featherstone.

But a bustling clerk soon set us straight. The war with France was worsening, if anything; the "Molly Stark" had been captured by a French frigate and renamed the "Félice Céleste" . . . and that tall girl on Derby Dock had not been waiting for me in France. . . . "I *will not let you go unless you bless me"* . . .

The American schooner would do as well as any, I told Nicodemus. Her berths yet free from vermin in the Yankee way, she would have a homey smell, and Yankee tackle on Yankee trees. It did not matter to me if a French captain stood on her quarter-deck and the Tricolor flew where the Stars and Stripes belonged. In this waking dream nothing appeared to matter; I could not feel anything deeper than the skin. I was much farther from any great decision than when I had left Dr. Reil's door. I seemed to be waiting for sealed orders.

It happened that we almost did not get aboard her—not that I cared. Captain Raynal did not take kindly to our having no passports, only the travel permits of the prefect. Only the scarcity of able seamen—every ship short handed, sailors picking and choosing berths, many pressed for the ever growing fleets of war—made him accept a plausible story and sign me to the bosun's berth and Nicodemus— Nick Diego—as man 'fore the mast. Lest we were English or Yankee spies, he locked my two rifles and Nicodemus' pistol in his armory.

We sailed first to Granville on the Normandy coast to lade salt fish. Evidently I did my work well, making the men step lively, satisfied to be Jacques de Stael from Louisiana with nothing behind or before. But Nicodemus was worrying about the war. It struck him as mighty queer, he said, to be one of a prize crew on a Yankee ship. It looked like he was going back on his own kind.

"If ye say the word, we'll desert and get on an American ship o' war," he told me the third day out. "It would give ye something to do that's lively, where ye'd have friends and comrades of your own sort, and take your mind off what's happened."

"Taking my mind off it, won't change it."

"Nothing will change it, and it don't stand to reason anything can be done about it."

"That's the trouble. I can't fly in the face of reason. But give me a little more time, Nicodemus. I'll decide what I have to do, then you can do as you see fit."

But we were to get into the war without our asking—briefly, up to our necks.

4.

On the return sail from Granville, off Port Sall, we were hailed by a French sloop of war and ordered to heave to. All that I thought at first was that the Turkic ship "Zainab," seen near the scene of the

"Leghorn's" sinking, had been a sloop. But Nicodemus raised his eyebrows at me. He was always nervous when a provost was in sight, afraid with little reason that the affair in Charleston had found us out. Then I felt a stir of living more quick than any since leaving Lorient. It was at least possible that our lack of passports had been uncovered by some piddling clerk in the admiralty and we would be taken off. I did not know where I was going or what I had to do, but one sure thing was, I did not want to go back to Brest.

The sloop's captain was piped aboard. Straightway he talked with Captain Raynal in the latter's cabin; then the first officer mustered our whole crew amidships.

"*Mes hommes,*" he said in French, "any of you who speak English, step forward."

It was as though a cabin boy was shaking me to wake up and go on watch. I was sure now that this business was not aimed at Nicodemus and me, but almost certain it had to do with France's war against one of the two English-speaking nations. One of those nations was my own, of Salem and Derby Dock. When a small, swarthy man called Jules stepped out from the line I was close behind him. Nicodemus did not step out because we had agreed that he should conceal his knowledge of English while traveling as an illiterate native of Louisiana of Spanish descent.

Jules and I were sent to the cabin, where we saluted the two captains. The visitor revealed that he was Captain Montfort of the sloop of war "St. Jerome." My mind seemed by now completely alert and turning over fast.

"Where did you learn English, Monsieur de Stael?" he asked in that tongue with a strong French accent. As a petty officer I was entitled to the "Mister."

"In my native country, Louisiana, sir."

"Is your accent more that of England or United States?"

"United States, sir. The people had come down river, settling on the East Bank."

Captain Montfort turned to Jules. "Where did you learn English, my man."

"I larn it en Angland, my capitan."

"You may return to duty."

When he had gone, Captain Montfort asked our captain if he might invite me to sit down. After this courtesy, he addressed me in French.

"The duty I have for you is a delicate one, but I'm sure not beyond your powers."

"I'll be glad to attempt it, Captain Montfort."

"You speak French like a gentleman."

"I'm a scion of an ancient family of Lorraine."

"If you succeed, one-quarter of the worth of a good ship and cargo will be awarded this vessel, and the admiralty will declare your share equal to your captain's."

"I thank you kindly."

"The American brig 'Trenton' is at present lying off the north shore of Ouessant Island, two hours' sail from here. She's waiting for a convoy to escort her up the channel to London. She's very fast and in her present position we can't get close enough to her, without being seen, to bring her under our guns."

"Yes, sir." I think my voice betrayed eager interest, nothing more.

"You'll run up the American flag and come alongside her. Since this vessel is Yankee built with Yankee lines the deception should be easy. You, in the guise of the captain, are to speak to her. You're to tell her captain you've just spied a French frigate on the south shore, making along eastward under the land to round the north cape and capture his ship. In this wind he won't feel it necessary to skip across the Plymouth—his clipper can outrun any warship in the French fleet—but to stay clean out of range of the mythical frigate he'll no doubt move farther westward along the shore. I intend to lie just behind the more westward cape, until my spy on the island signals her approach. With good way, I can pounce out with my guns blazing."

"Very good, sir."

"You start westward too as soon as you've spoke her, to encourage her to take the same course. I don't think she'll try to run once we're in likely range. Those Yankees don't like to risk their skins."

"Captain Raynal's coat will be a little tight on me." It was such a jest as a devil-may-care fellow may make with his superior officers. "But I'll try to wear it well."

"I've some English-speaking fellows on the 'St. Jerome,' but they can't imitate the American accent. I'm in the same boat, or I'd turn my command over to my first officer and play the trick myself."

"They won't question that I'm a Yankee."

"I remind you again, Captain Montfort," our captain interposed, "that Monsieur de Stael has no French passport."

"Ah, but he has! His command of our language! What Yankee yahoo could obtain that?"

Captain Montfort returned to his heavy-gunned sloop. I did not go back into the lethargy that had becalmed me lately. When Captain Raynal mustered all hands to explain the stratagem, I was not only excited but greatly frightened about the outcome—both good signs. It would be perfectly easy to give my show away and be hanged on the yardarm as a Yankee spy.

Still I could not possibly have refused the post—fate had provided that. Had I confessed American loyalties Captain Raynal would have put me in chains and some other English-speaking Frenchman would attempt—perhaps successfully—to trap the American ship. Nicodemus would leave my service, and the Roxana of old—Roxana of the bright dreams and highborn creed—could not believe it of me if I flinched.

Without trying I put by all remembrance of my loss; Roxana stayed in my heart but now she was alive, loving me, demanding the best in me, waiting for me somewhere. Pierre and the forest had taught me guile in a few tight fixes. An old Indian fighter, I was out to make a good showing.

My head had never worked faster or better than in composing my opening address to the "Trenton's" captain and preparing answers to his likely questions. In two hours' sail we raised her, waiting with outspread wings for her convoy on the north shore of the island. What a beautiful ship she was, standing into the wind! I would have known her for a Yankee far as I could see her—foreign shipbuilders had not yet learned the trick of her flaring hull, low freeboard, tall, tapering sail plan, and canted masts.

We had painted out our false name and now we too ran up the Stars and Stripes. It meant Nicodemus and I were serving now not under the French flag but our own.

The "Trenton" had her long glasses on us now. She had heaved to, but one hard-over of her helm would let her run. The man in her crow's-nest was counting our guns—their weight not enough to worry her—and singing out to her master. I had taken my place on our quarter-deck in Captain Raynal's coat and cap. He crouched in the companionway to give me orders. Jules, who might understand English a great deal better than he spoke it, had a post just forward. This was not happenstance, or I missed my guess.

"We'd better avoid bringing our guns to bear, or she'll get suspicious," I told the master. For if he uncovered my trick, he might fire on the Yankee, hoping to cripple her for the sloop's easy kill.

"Very well."

"Have I your permission to give orders?"

"Aye."

So I brought the "Molly Stark" across the "Trenton's" stern and heaved to at a cable's length. A broad-beamed skipper who made me think of Captain Scott bawled in the broadest Yankee across the blue.

"Who are you, and what do you want?"

"The 'Benedict Arnold' from West Point," I shouted my lines in reply, speaking rapidly as possible. "We've a cargo of fish."

There fell the briefest silence while he caught his breath.

"What can we do for you—friend?"

"You know a humbug when you see one. A French frigate coming from behind the island." Here I pointed as though in great excitement to the east.

"Aye, aye! Where had we better sail?"

"Make a play westward to save my bacon, then light out."

"What's your name, Cap'n, if you'll give it?"

"Jason Starbuck of Salem." For my trouble in Charleston would blow over in time, Mr. Derby had told me, *or I could blow it over*.

"Thanks, thanks. I'm Captain Ethan West." Then he called to the hands on his decks. "Boys, give three cheers for Yankee Doodle!"

Lusty shouts resounded across the water and raised gooseflesh all over me. We moved westward, apparently setting a good example to the "Trenton," and keeping faith with me, she fell into our wake.

"It looks like you've done it," Captain Raynal told me in a low voice, his greedy eyes on the prey. "What do you think, Jules?"

"It was American talk truly, not English," the man answered with a curled lip. "Monsieur de Stael speaks American remarkably well! I'll praise him more when the prize money's in our pockets."

"No doubt you could've done better," I said, "with your bastard English." For the more I antagonized him, the less weight his testimony against me would carry.

"We'll wait and see, my friend."

"Captain Raynal, if the ruse fails it will be because of one mistake I didn't notice in time. Our topgallants are not rigged in the Yankee fashion. When he asked my name, I thought he was a little suspicious."

"Whatever the cause—*Sacré bleu*—he's changing his course!"

"By the good God—"

"Look at her, putting out to sea! A thousand devils! Cabbage head, you bungled it! And if you cheated us, you'll wish you'd never been born."

Flushed with fury, he and the crew watched the "Trenton" catch the wind in her wings and skip toward Plymouth. The sloop of war's spy on the island had evidently signaled her flight, for soon we saw the warship rush from her ambush with bow guns roaring. But the range was long and growing longer, as the slim-waisted clipper skinned the waves. Only a devil-guided shot could halt her now.

"My captain, shall we give chase?" our first mate stopped swearing to ask.

"And have Captain Montfort turn his guns on us, as he is angry enough to do?" Raynal roared in reply. "I'm ashamed to look him in the face! His curses would shrivel my ears! Set your course for Naples."

With an ominous glance at me, Captain Raynal beckoned Jules to follow him to his cabin. They were gone a good twenty minutes, wherein I dared not appear to notice the glowering faces of my mates. Not one of them cursed me, though, knowing I would answer with my fists; anyway I was still chief petty officer of the ship. Jules appeared and told me with sinister politeness that the captain had sent for me.

I had prepared for this trial as well as within my power. But there was something else working on me now, grappling with my terror of his hemp and yardarm. All men have resources greater than they know, and I had taken new bearings in the last hour. I had great goals.

Captain Raynal's face appeared more grim than angry, and I knew he could be as vindictive as an Indian. But I was an Indian fighter; old Pierre had taught me how. Saluting, I stood at attention. Jules hung like a squaw at his side.

"I've decided to give you a chance to defend yourself," Captain Raynal began.

Perhaps he did not mean to trick me with that, but I could have been tricked regardless. I did not show any guilty gratitude.

"As far as I know, sir, I've done nothing that needs defense."

"Why do you think the Yankee took alarm?"

"From the rig of our topgallants, sir, as I mentioned. The merest suspicion would cause her to stand to sea instead of waiting for the convoy. Besides, my answers to his questions might not have satisfied him. It was a difficult feat to gull him, and it didn't come off." This reply had been carefully prepared.

"What name did you give for this ship?"

"The 'Betsy Arno,' the name of a Creole girl from Acadia I knew in Attakapas."

"Jules, did you understand him to say the 'Betsy Arno'?"

"He may've said that, although it sounded slightly different. And from West Point."

"No, my captain, from Westport. That's a shipbuilding town in Massachusetts."

"Then you said it through your nose, like a Yankee," Jules retorted spitefully, without waiting for the captain to answer. "By what name did you call yourself?"

"Sir, have I your permission to answer Jules directly?" I had not prepared for this chance to show respect for him and the rules of the sea in contrast with Jules's breach. Perceiving and seizing it was worthy of a more subtle, cool, capable fighter than I.

"Yes, you may, Monsieur de Stael. Jules, I'll do my own questioning, from henceforth."

"I gave the name of Jason Starbuck, a good New England name."

"Well, I suppose your using American terms with which Jules is unacquainted isn't proof of treachery. I won't hang you or put you in chains, but for bungling the job you're reduced to man 'fore the mast."

It was hard to put on a long face and not an amazed one.

5.

Trouble with the hands did not seem very likely, after their heads had cooled. Poor men learn not to cry over milk forever being spilled; and while they bring few riches from the past, they also bear few grudges. I had bungled, been punished, and that ended it. A few were sullen with me for a day or two, but soon listened with the rest to my tales of Indians, bears, painters, and tall-horned stags in the Louisiana forests. Was it true that lowborn men could hunt in those forests the same as the landlords? By the good God, they would go there, when Bonaparte had beaten the English.

Meanwhile I was checking my new bearings again and again. Alone on the deck I shot the sun and the moon and the polar star; I tried not to let a wish be father to a thought; I was hammering out on the anvil of common sense the decision conceived in inspiration. Nicodemus waited patiently and asked no questions. We had cut across the Bay of Biscay and were off Cape Finisterre—the End of the

Land that every nation marks—on the clear, fine, moonlit night that I had him follow me to the fo'c'slehead. We were alone there, save for dolphins that precoursed the ship; and even these seemed partners in my business, their forever-quest up and down the seas significant of mine. My heart felt exalted but my head cool.

"Nicodemus, my sweetheart was lost at sea," I told my companion. "Common sense tells me she was drowned. Sometimes I have a feeling—like an intuition—that's she's alive, but that's not enough to build on. It's hard to believe she could die—she was so beautiful and intensely alive—but that won't stand in court."

"No, the most beautiful and the best go away and leave us," he answered in simple dignity.

"The evidence that she was taken captive is very real, but too slight to keep a man hunting for her year after year on that alone. If she's held captive, he still might search all his life without finding a trace of her. She might be anywhere from Tangier to the China Sea. She would be in a secret, forbidden prison."

"That's looking at it straight," said Nicodemus.

"Most lovers couldn't undertake such an almost hopeless search. They have too many other affairs—people dependent on them, people they love and must stay with, money to make, ambitions to pursue. This is the world of the living and the now; the dead past must bury its dead. Dr. Reil said so, and it's true."

"Aye." Nicodemus glanced once into my face, then looked at the waves being parted by our stem.

"Now it happens I'm not in the same boat with those other men. My parents were killed by Indians—so was another old man I loved—I've no real kinfolk except my uncle Dan'l Todkill. I've no home and there's no one dependent on me. For instance there's nothing to stop me from joining the war against the French, but I've decided not to. It's an unpopular war that will soon be settled and there's something else I want to do and feel I must do."

"I'm fearful of what you're about to say."

"No, you needn't be. It will affect you only as far as you let it—you needn't be sorry or afraid for me. You see, I too have got my life to live. I've got ambitions—big ones. I want to make money to live well—an honored name within my limited field—a broadened mind—a full development of my powers—ultimately a wife and children to be proud of. Much more than some men, I want rich and exciting experience. I think I'm willing to risk more for it than most men, either because I want it so much more—I don't know why—or because

I'm more free than most. I don't have to stop and remember that if I'm killed, people I love will come to disaster."

"It's a combination of both, I reckon," Nicodemus ventured thoughtfully.

"So it would be a foolish thing for me to drop everything else and devote my life to the search. I was tempted to do just that, at first, before I'd thought it through. If I could believe I was helping her, I wouldn't mind what it cost—I'd find a kind of solemn happiness. But I'd always be beset with doubts that it was all in vain. That would slow my hands and dull my heart and slowly destroy my spirit. What if after ten years—when my youth and strength began to go—I'd find out she had drowned that night at sea? Could I ever start again? I'd hate myself for my folly and maybe hate her memory. I'd rather be dead."

"Ye've figured it well, I allow."

"Excuse me for using what you may think is a fanciful comparison. Roxana was greatly taken with the idea of Jason searching for the Golden Fleece. But once she said to me that even if the Argonauts hadn't found it, they'd had wonderful adventures all the way. They heard the gods speaking through oracles, visited strange islands, fought lively battles with men and weird beings, saw many wonders, and yoked a bull that snorted fire and had bronze hooves. The essential story is true. Nobody knows what the Fleece was—maybe the discovery and use of metals—but the dangers and the triumphs were real."

"I reckon I see what you're getting at, Cap'n Starbuck." But I could see nothing yet in his face.

"Many an adventurer has turned renegade in Constantinople or the Barbary States just for the exciting life there, and the prizes to win. It's as fine a field of adventure as Mexico when the Spaniards came. I might have fetched up there anyway."

I wasn't speaking as quietly as at first, and Nicodemus gave me another quick, wondering glance.

"This is the decision I've come to, Nicodemus. I'm going to keep on loving Roxana, whether she's alive on the earth or lying dead under the sea. I'll believe she's alive—and know she lives in my heart. I'm going to live the life she visioned for me—the all-sails-spread life Cap'n Todkill wanted me to live—but it's going to have more meaning for me than any of us ever foresaw—more excitement—more riches—because it will have a goal. I'll have nothing to lose but my life—it would be a hazard wherever I sailed—and everything to gain. I'll be doing what she wanted me to do—with the glorious chance that in the end it may bring her back to me."

"Your life will be at heavier hazard in them Mohammedan countries, than on any sea of the seven."

"The only use I've got for it, Nicodemus, is to live it hard. I've got no other appointments I can't break. I'm going hunting, Nicodemus, and I may never find the quarry I'm seeking, but I'll enjoy looking for spoor, and every new sight and experience along the way. I'll make camp to get meat and see the country. Maybe it will last one year, maybe five. I'm sure I can give five years to it without loss or even regret. Wherever the trail seems to lead me, I'll go. In five years I'll either come to the end of it—provided it ever existed—or it will be too cold to follow any more."

There was no sound now but the swish of the waves on our bows and the creaks in the rigging. Nicodemus glanced at the moon and the weather, then wheeled his eyes to mine. "I reckon it was bound to be so, ye being the sort of man you are," he remarked.

"I reckon so."

"Ye've got it laid out pretty, but it won't pan out that pretty."

"No, I guess not."

"Ye always carry too much sail for a sensible man. What happened to them Indians what killed your folks?"

"The old man and I hunted them, until he was killed. Then I hunted them alone."

"Ye killed 'em all out, I reckon, before ye was through."

"Yes."

"And ye was only a boy then, but the boy's father to the man. Ye go too far with everything, Cap'n Starbuck, and too headlong. Ye're able, but not temperate."

"You're right about that, Nicodemus."

"I might of knowed ye'd kill them Indians all alone. What about that fine, tall ship, the 'Happy Chance'?"

"I couldn't use her for this hunt. It'll be by land, not sea. But you're a sailor born, and I won't ask you to go with me, Nicodemus. It's too much to ask."

"Well, ye said lots of men go to Constantinople for the life. And the loot too, I reckon."

"That's true."

"Do ye want me to go wi' ye? Speak plain, Cap'n Starbuck."

"Yes, sir, I do."

"Well, there's no reason I shouldn't. I've got no kinfolk neither.

155

My mother was a harbor woman and I never knew my Pa. I've got no other 'pointments, as ye said. I'm not able to get nowhere by myself, or do anything o' note—God didn't see fit to give me the brains or the spirit—and the only way I can live good and lively is follering a man like ye. What ye're going for and where ye go don't really make much difference to me—I couldn't think noways of what to do or where to go myself. And the life ye've given me so far has been first-rate."

"Well?"

"I'll foller ye, and help ye all I can."

"God bless you, Nicodemus."

"I hope He blesses ye, in your endeavors. And I can't say no more."

Neither could I, thinking that though I had blessed him, he still would not let me go. Roxana and I had blessed each other by a wall where hollyhocks bloomed, but still I could not let her go in life or death. I could not loose the silver cord of love. I would not break the golden bowl of troth.

Roxana, you are too beautiful to die! I will keep you alive with my love, as I saw you last under the moon. I will live for us both, if need be—life on the flood tide and not the ebb—life without respite.

But as the moon ventures the sea of heaven in full sail and the stem of the "Molly Stark" boldly clefts the waves below, there comes to me the same intuition that I felt in the fog of Lorient—that somewhere in the mists you are warm and breathing, alive in earthly loveliness, and wait for me.

END OF BOOK ONE

BOOK II

CHAPTER EIGHT

Rifleman to the Dey

I.

That Roxana had been captured and sold into slavery was not such an improbable chance as Dr. Reil had thought, or as my innocence of the violence of the times had led me to believe. These were war times. No ship a week out of port knew what ensign marked friend from foe, so swiftly were treaties made and broken. At present the Mediterranean was one great battlefield in the war between England and France; Napoleon had conquered Egypt only to have the Turk declare war against him; of late his fleet had been largely destroyed at Aboukir. And while the tigers fought, the jackals had rich feeding. They lay off a little way, in their lairs or hidden by the sea mists, then tore down the weak or wounded. They were growing bolder every day.

These were the Barbary pirates, sailing under the flags of Morocco, Algeria, Tunis, and Tripoli. They did not pretend to be anything else; the business of their states was the looting of ships and the enslavement of all hands for sale or ransom. The greatest kings of Christendom paid them tribute that their merchantmen might be allowed to sail unsacked—so did the President of a little western nation—but they demanded more and more. The corsairs grew restless, lying in their sun-drenched harbors fronting the blazing Sahara, and often broke the truce that the *giaours* bought.

At the gates of Hercules my shipmates had quailed from the English. Save by convoy by their Spanish allies, we would not have dared enter the straits. Now they constantly scanned the horizon in fear of a lateen sail. True, France was presumed to be at peace with the Barbary kings—she had laid her tribute at their haughty feet—but the Turkic Sultan had declared war against her, and the Dey of Algiers was his sworn vassal. His pirate den lay due south of us now.

If captured and sold in Tunis instead of Algiers, Nicodemus and I might find a measure of consolation. I had not forgotten that the

Turkic pirate "Zainab" had been bound for there; it might be the likeliest place to begin our quest. But although we did not know how or where to enter Islam, we could ill-afford, in time and peril, the usual route of Christians. My vague plan was to go to Malta, now under French control, and get into the service of some Jewish merchant or renegade Christian with establishments in Constantinople.

But it was not well considered, and kismet had laid another.

On a misty morning we were off Majorca in the Balearic Islands. This was the very sea, wide open between here and Barcelona, that had swallowed up the ill-fated vessel; the actual scene might be within one day's sail. I had been thinking of Roxana only a few minutes before when the lookout raised a cry of "Sail on our starboard bow!" Down on us out of a rainstorm bore a lean warship flying a Moslem flag.

It was instantly apparent that we could not run and hide from her in the mists without first standing her off with a broadside. The warlike act might be tantamount to suicide—that would be Captain Raynal's thought, as mine in his place on the quarter-deck. The Mussulman was revealed as a middle-sized frigate, no doubt of thirty guns or more. On her decks and hanging from her rigging thronged two hundred cutthroats in Turkic or Moorish dress. My shipmates watched in the silence of deep dread. I had never seen so many men so pale.

"That's not the flag of Algiers," a sailor beside me exclaimed. It leaped in my heart that the man would proclaim her a Tunisian. He did not, though.

"By God," he went on, turning to the mate, "she's a Moor."

"But we're at peace with Morocco," some one bleated.

"Her cursed Amir may have changed his mind since we set sail, and every Jacques Bonhomme of us will wear chains."

But the shout across the water was in English! I could hardly believe my ears at the "Heave to, or we'll trim your sails with fire," in a harsh imperious voice and with an oddly unalien accent. Evidently he took us for a Yankee ship flying the French flag; but America too had been at peace with Morocco the last I had heard. Perhaps English was the only European tongue that the Moorish chieftain knew.

Captain Raynal pointed frantically to the Tricolor flying from our main. Quickly he signaled to Jules to stand beside him and act as interpreter to the English-speaking corsair.

"We are French!" Jules shouted. "She French ship, vairy good friend! Do not fire!"

"We'll come aboard and look at your papers," the corsair captain bawled.

At once a large boat was heaved overboard from the frigate's boat deck, and at least forty riffraff dropped into her, agile as monkeys. They were a wild, fierce-looking lot, their belts stuffed with pistols and knives, every man with a long saber at his fore; and it was hard to believe that they would not run amuck and murder half of us, ere they sacked the ship and led off the rest in chains. I half expected our captain to seize a momentary chance, its substance thin but real, to fight and fly. We were not under her broadside guns; in his contempt for us the Moor had not so maneuvered. One roared command from our quarter-deck could rally the stunned crew, bring the foe briefly under our light guns, and stand us ready to run for a nearby rain-squall. Instead Captain Raynal forbade any man to raise a hand against the corsairs, no matter what they did.

My companions were brave fellows at heart, furious fighters for that they held by. Now their hands hung flaccid and their faces looked like blobs of paste. There was no accounting for it save by the legend of the pirates' ferocity and invincibility. Yet I would bet my skin that the last was legend only. Half of their fearsomeness had been no doubt earned in berserk battle; the rest was a show of arrogance, wild costumes, bristling weapons, and outlandish howls.

They were shouting with every pull of their oars. Yet when they drew within a stone's throw of our rail they suddenly fell silent at one dog-like bark from their captain. I had a good look at him now. Although black-bearded and sun-browned and dressed in Turkic costume, he had western lineaments and there was no reason to doubt that English was his native tongue. Actually a surprisingly large number of Barbary pirates had European captains.

He was surveying us with his oddly brilliant eyes. His ruffians rowed as sedately as a cutter's crew bringing a customs officer to look at our manifest. I reckoned that he was becoming persuaded that we were French, sailing under French passport and protection—and it might be he was cursing in his beard. Our captain appeared to quit quaking and my shipmates showed signs of life.

The corsair chief came aboard with about twenty of his men, and returned our master's salute. "I am Hamet *Reis*," he said. "Can you speak English?"

"*Non,* Hamet *Reis, pardon. Je suis francais.*"

"I don't understand that lingo. *Habla Espanol?*"

"*Non, mon capitaine.*" Then Captain Raynal bade Jules speak for him.

"Fellow, tell your captain to command his hands to keep their posts—not a man to move—and show me his passport," Hamet *Reis* demanded.

Jules asked him to repeat the order, and then with some difficulty translated it into French. Captain Raynal obeyed like a cabin boy. While the pirate waited to be shown our papers he stood with arms akimbo, grinning at us in contempt. Here was a true renegade, I thought, of the school of Simon Gurty, who pranced and danced around his countrymen roasting on redskin stakes. I feared him the same as the rest, but had a peculiar interest in him that tended to steady my heart and cool my head. He had entered into Islam and prospered there. He knew by now what went on within the sun-baked walls; if he wished to learn the fate of a certain captive, he might readily succeed. He had paid a high price, perhaps; I wondered if he had been born with that shark mouth and those coldly brilliant eyes. In fact the whole episode had a different and deeper meaning for me than for my shipmates.

The corsair glanced at our papers and returned them. "Tell Cap'n What's-his-name they're in order," he directed Jules imperiously. "But I'm not done with you yet. My Amir's royal kinsman, the Dey of Algiers, has a finger in this pie."

"I do—I don't understand," Jules stammered.

"By God, can't you understand plain English? Maybe this will teach you!" At that he struck Jules a blow in the face that almost knocked him down.

"If you weel speck slower, sir," Jules entreated, almost weeping. "I know vairy leetle Anglais—"

"Then get me someone who does, damn your eyes!"

Jules spoke rapidly in French to Captain Raynal. The latter, stammering with fear, made the reply I was waiting for.

"Tell him if he wishes I'll call De Stael, who speaks English well, but I don't trust him not to twist his words—"

"Get him up here," Hamet *Reis* replied when this had been translated. "If he tries any monkey-tricks on me, he'll hang on yon yard-arm."

Captain Reynal beckoned to me. For the second time on this short cruise I had got neck-deep into big and perilous business. That had come about naturally enough, since I was the only man aboard known to speak fluent English, yet there came to me the strange and thrilling surmise that my search for my lost one had auspiciously begun. I mounted the quarter-deck, stood at attention before our captain instead of Hamet *Reis,* and gave him my first salute.

"Your name's De Stael?" Hamet *Reis* asked.

"Aye, sir."

"It's not the one you were born with, I'll lay to that. You might be a Canuck, but I'll bet you're a Yank—like me."

A wild hope struck me, only to dim quickly. "If so, we're both under wrong flags, Captain."

"I'm not. I meant I was born in what is now United States, but that was my cursed luck instead of being born to the Faith. *Allah, Allah ursul el Allah.* [God, there is no God but God.]"

"Yet you seemed disappointed, Hamet *Reis,* that this wasn't a Yankee ship!"

"A bold'n, I see—like the rest of the cursed breed. Well, how do you know I didn't crave to sink her?"

"Maybe you did, sir, but it would be no shame on Allah or you if you wanted only to ask news of Boston—and sniff Boston beans a-cooking."

"You speak too free, for a man 'fore the mast. Why aren't you an officer?"

"The ups and downs of Kismet, Hamet *Reis.*"

"It was Baltimore, not Boston—and hot, buttered biscuits." He stood still an instant, sneering at himself. "But the infirmity's cured, and we'll get to business. Tell your captain I'll put a prize crew aboard his ship and take her to Algiers—as a neighborly kindness."

"Since when has France been at war with Algiers, Admiral?"

"Don't you know the Sultan of Turkey has declared war on France, and the Dey is his vassal? Whether Mustapha will draw his scimitar is his business, not mine. If not, he'll let your ship go."

All this save for the corsair's personal remarks to me I translated for Captain Raynal. Somewhat to my surprise, Hamet *Reis* waited patiently throughout, finding some cruel kind of amusement in watching the Frenchman's face.

"Jules, did you understand the same?" Captain Raynal asked.

"Yes, my captain."

"Did De Stael say anything to arouse your suspicions?"

"No, my captain."

"Then, De Stael, inform Hamet *Reis* that I submit under protest to his seizure of my vessel." He stood like a man now and spoke with dignity.

When I had translated this, Hamet called to the quarter-deck a villainous looking Turk whose raiment and jeweled weapons indicated that he was an officer. Speaking fluent French, he would captain our ship to Algiers. Greatly to our hands' surprise and relief, they were not put in chains or even imprisoned below decks, Captain Raynal continuing to give them orders under the Turk's command. About fifteen of the pirates were left as guards; the remainder with their insolent commander returned to the frigate.

My French shipmates showed signs of increasing cheer when they had talked among themselves. This talk neither Nicodemus nor I were permitted to hear, they falling silent with sullen looks when we drew near. I had appeared too prominently at the present misfortune and in the escape of the "Trenton." However, one bold, knowing fellow came to our defense.

"Monsieur de Stael may be a Yankee and tipped off his countrymen, but he and his man aren't in league with dirty pirates," he told his mates. Then he made some shrewd guesses as to our present fix. He did not think that the Algerian Dey would break with France, and by forcing the issue Hamet *Reis* hoped for a rupture between the Dey and the Turkic Grand Seignior. Probably he had seized us by his Amir's orders on the excuse of some antedated alliance of Morocco and Algiers, in spite of its being a violation of Moroccan neutrality. It was a political move, our sage explained, although its ultimate purpose was yet invisible.

"But if the bloody Dey does set free the vessel and all the Frenchmen, what will he do with ye and me?" Nicodemus asked, when we had a chance to discuss the affair. "We haven't got no French passports."

"If we were being brought to Tunis instead of Algiers, it might come in handy to have no passports. We could be stranded in the pirate nest but not in the chains of slavery. But if we don't say anything about it, I reckon it will be overlooked."

"It won't be your fault if it ain't, seeing how much notoriety ye've got. I know ye couldn't get out of warning the 'Trenton.' I was proud ye did, and so would be Cap'n Todkill. But ye needn't have spoke so bold and showed off so fine, talking to Hamet *Reis*."

"I suppose not."

"Or did ye do it a-purpose?" he asked, his eyes getting sharp. "Would ye be figuring on playing him some ways? It's not Algiers ye want to get to, or yet Fez, but Tunis."

"I don't know any way to play him. He'd lean backward to spite a Yankee. We just have to wait and play the cards as they turn up."

Running before the wind, we made the harbor of Algiers on the afternoon of the second day. At least a score of boats manned by a thousand yelling Moors put out to meet us, but it was a wonder how they quieted at one bark from Hamet *Reis*. When our ship was tied up to the royal dock, not one of the wharf rats was permitted aboard, for our purses would fly from our pockets to his as by Ali-din's Lamp. These magicians of theft could steal our mainmast if we turned our backs, the sailors said. And the fact that we were not at once marched to the Dey's palace they took as a favorable sign.

Before long, an Algerian provost guard replaced Hamet *Reis's* Moroccans. When he and a resplendent court official had talked in Raynal's cabin, the Yankee corsair strutted down our gangplank with a sneer on his bearded lips. One thing was certain: I was not going to play him in any fashion. At once he boarded his frigate and set sail.

Our next visitor was a Frenchman, elegantly dressed and perfumed, with a portfolio under his arm. And now for Nicodemus and me a momentous hour was striking. Captain Raynal mustered the whole ship's company and bade every man produce his passport. When Nicodemus and I could produce nothing but the prefect's permit, we were ordered to the cabin. There the French consul listened coldly to my well-practiced tale of Louisiana nativity, while Captain Raynal's angry countenance boded no good.

"All I can do is relate the circumstances to the Prime Minister of Algiers," the official told us. "I can't anticipate the action he'll take." There was no doubt whatever that Captain Raynal had voiced his suspicions of my conduct in the "Trenton" affair.

"Ye don't look worried," Nicodemus remarked when we had gained the deck. "Maybe ye wanted this to happen."

"No, I didn't want it, and maybe I ought to be a lot more worried than I am. We may be allowed to sail, but if we're not—well, we've got into Islam through the front door."

He thought this over. "Maybe the luck's breaking for ye good. But luck's all it is, good *or* bad."

When hours passed without the consul's returning with their passports, I could feel enmity against us thickening like fog on the foredeck. It was a brutally hot night. The men had tired of dropping sous to the tireless native boys swimming around our hull. They thrust closer to us—Yankee spies who in some fashion had brought about the ship's capture. We stayed close to each other, our backs to the rail.

There was plenty of powder for an explosion; the chance spark of a curse or a blow would set it off. Nicodemus and I would be set upon by a French mob, many of whom had red hands in the Terror. Still I did not think that would be our suddenly ardent kismet—my feeling was that we were being paid off a little, in fright, for a potentially magnificent break. It was a sailor's feeling—men of the sea cannot help but personify fortune. I still believed that Hamet *Reis's* capture of our vessel marked the beginning of the flow of a long, high, and auspicious tide. I thought we were on our way.

2.

The cabin boy brought word for Nicodemus and me to present ourselves to the captain. Once more our shipmates suspended judgment. Raynal was seated at a table, the consul beside him, and his expression was grave now, rather than angry. What he was about to say hurt his conscience a little, if that was any comfort.

"I regret, Monsieur de Stael, that the Dey of Algiers refused to let you and your man leave his dominions without passports."

But he did not regret it. He was only too glad to get shed of us. No doubt he had hinted to the French consul not to plead for us, and that a strict enforcement of the Dey's rules would be quite satisfactory.

"Then what are your orders, sir?" I asked.

"You're no longer under my orders. My paymaster will hand both of you your wages, and you may remove your kits and belongings including your weapons. We must set sail at once."

"Louisiana is under the Spanish flag," the French consul broke in. "If you can convince the Spanish consul that you're native there, he may be able to send you home."

"That would be very difficult, considering we have no proof, and I don't speak Spanish well." I could make out with it though, thank God; for a corrupt Spanish was a lingua franca throughout North Africa.

"It seems to me more likely—although of course I'm not party to any deception—that you could more easily convince the United States consul that you're both American citizens. Your captain tells me that your English has a decidedly Yankee flavor. I'm not aware whether your man speaks English—"

"There'd be no difficulty about that—"

"I didn't think so, after a good look at him. Sailors frequently lose their passports and Mr. Richard O'Brien is a reasonable and very able consular officer."

"How soon do you think we may see him?"

"You'll both be taken to the Bagnio Belique to spend the night, and the Prime Minister has consented for you to visit your consul tomorrow morning."

"You've been good sailors," Captain Raynal broke in. "I've no fault to find with you in that respect. Consider how much worse your position would be, if you were charged with aiding and abetting an enemy of France while sailing under French names on a French ship. To be frank with you, I've no longer the least doubt but that you warned the 'Trenton' and brought about her escape."

"If you hold that opinion, sir, I thank you for your leniency."

"I'd have done the same thing in your boots, monsieur," the French consul told me.

I bowed to him, and Captain Raynal returned, quite smartly, my salute. One of the hands was told to help us get our gear onto the dock. When my shipmates saw that we would delay the sailing no longer, their rage at us quickly cooled, and some of them waved and called bawdy jests as we descended the gangplank under Algerian guard. Although cold comfort, it was the last we had that night.

America was not at war with Algeria, but this did not save us from the enmity of the heat-racked city. We had hardly set foot on shore when a score or more evil-visaged wharf rats gathered clamoring about us. Save for the corporal of the guard they would have instantly snatched up our gear and vanished in the darkness. But I trusted this yellow-eyed brute no more than the rest. When he picked out three of the pack to carry my belongings—Nicodemus had shouldered his own—it was perfectly patent that he did not intend for me to see them again. At that instant I started fighting, with Nicodemus staunch behind me. That too, this soon, was in the cards; and the last one must turn up before I could stop. My baggage bearers hurried past us to disappear in the narrow streets.

"Tell those men to wait," I said to the corporal in Spanish.

"*No comprende.*"

"*Para!*" I shouted at the thieves, then dashed forward, caught the foremost by the neck, and forced him to lay down his load. The two others stopped, snarling like pariah dogs.

"Señor, I've orders to take you at once to the Bagnio Belique," the corporal protested.

"While those dogs make off with my gear?" In the excitement the Spanish words fairly leaped to my tongue, and the Moors understood it perfectly well. Then I halted an old man with a donkey.

"How much will you charge to take this baggage to the Bagnio Belique?" I asked.

"One peso, señor," he answered, his eyes gleaming in the lights of the Moorish lanterns.

At once I began to lash the bags to his packsaddle. "Note there are six, counting the two guns, and there will be six when we arrive, you keeping in my sight all the way."

"Si, si, señor." Meanwhile the corporal was gobbling and gesticulating.

"Nicolas, your Spanish is better than mine. Tell this corporal what we expect of him."

"Be mighty careful, soldier, how you treat the Señor," my companion instantly complied with great vigor. "He's no common sailor. Don't judge him by his dress, or by him being put on shore in your dirty, thieving town—it's business too big for you to understand. If one centime's worth of our gear is stolen, you'll be crow meat before tomorrow night."

The corporal muttered sullenly in Moorish, but when I had given the three Arabs a few sous each, we resumed our march with something like dignity. We passed through roasting-hot streets almost too narrow for the loaded donkey, climbing steadily and steeply, to gain at last a three-storied building with a terraced roof. It proved to be a hollow square, the lower floor of which fulfilled my idea of a bagnio, truly the vilest appearing den I had ever seen. It was occupied by grog shops and brothels, dimly lighted by dirty lanterns, and thronged with riffraff clamoring in the tongues of Babel. With the guards carrying our luggage, we climbed to a balcony surrounding the third story, then were led through a dark passage into a foul-smelling room where twenty or more naked men, some of them wearing chains, slept in four-deep tiers of bunks. Ignoring the corporal's noisy protests, I at once retreated to the balcony.

"We'll sleep on the terrace," I told the rogue.

"Señor, you're ordered—"

"Tell your captain that I'll answer to the Dey of Algiers."

The very name silenced him and our goods were brought to the terrace without further fuss. Then the guards quit being any sort of soldiers and turned beggars. I detested greasing the wretches, but could hardly afford not to—five pesos to the corporal, and one to each of his men. Actually this show of opulence put us in less danger of robbery than if we had passed out centimes. It appeared to bear witness to Nicodemus' making me out an effendi of some influence.

The guards withdrew. Nicodemus and I heaped our baggage against the wall, and fixed one piece to fall and clatter at the lightest touch; then we prepared to sleep in front of it. Not that our sleep would be very deep or long, in the merciless heat of the sun-baked stone, and the hour already the second after midnight.

"Cheer up, old sailor," I told my friend. "We've made port without a scratch on our paint."

"Aye, but what port? Not Constantinople."

"No, and we may have to stay here a while, before we can get there. But we'll be learning our way about, and we've agreed from the first to take our time in this venture."

"We may learn how to break rock in the Dey's quarries, with a bloody chain on our legs. Well, I trust ye to keep us clear o' it. Only trim your sails a little, when ye go to speak to His Majesty."

"I'll talk to the consul first and he'll advise us well. There's something else that occurs to me—maybe our luck is better than we ever dreamed. If Turkic pirates bound for Tunis sank a French merchant-man without warning, they wouldn't want to carry their captives to Constantinople. It's a long way, and they might be hanged by their Sultan's admirals."

"Yes, for he's pretending to be civilized."

"Would they sell them in Tunis? The Bey is friendly to France, and slaves are harder to smuggle in than gold or jewels. I think more likely the 'Zainab' would sneak at night into some other port—the bigger the better—sell her captives to a 'fence' and run."

"Leastways she'd want to get shed of 'em straight off."

"Well, Algiers is the biggest port on this coast, and the nearest in all Islam to Barcelona."

3.

In my finest raiment, carrying the walking stick won from Dick, followed by the henchman won from Captain Todkill, I waited on the American consul soon after sunrise. If the show would not impress him, at least it impressed the lone Algerian soldier appointed to guard us. This fellow was put in wonderful humor by our seeming prosperity, ran about, pointed out the sights, drove off beggars and hucksters with angry cries, and became my dragoman more than warder. Our goods I had left safely in the care of a Venetian brothel-keeper at the bagnio.

While the two escorts hung outside, Mr. Richard O'Brien received me in his private office. He was a pleasant-appearing man, and his bright, Irish-blue eyes evinced lively curiosity as to who in the devil I might be. The only ship of late arrival from Europe had been the "Félice Céleste," yet I had sent in—my own—an English or Yankee name.

"I regret having to come so early and perhaps interrupting your breakfast," I told him.

He was listening to my accent as much as to the words. He replied in a friendly manner that he had had his coffee, pancakes, and eggs in the relative cool of sunrise, but missed his beloved rashers of bacon, the stock he had imported giving out, and the heavens would fall before the Algerian butchers would touch a hog. These homely tidings did not strike me as trivial. They indicated that he accepted me as a gentleman and had plenty of time for me. Then I remarked on the pleasant surroundings compared to my lodgings of last night, the Bagnio Belique.

"Good God!" He burst out. "How did you happen to spend the night there, instead of in one of the fendukes?"

"It's a long story, but I'll make it short." I related that after adventuring in Havana, Nicodemus and I had sailed for France, took ship for Naples, and had ended up here sans passports.

"If you've come to apply to me for passports, the situation is an awkward one, on account of your traveling on enemy ships under French names," he told me. "You must speak French."

"I do. My man doesn't."

"As the consul here, I'd have to have assurances that you're not Frenchmen wishing to get on an American ship, but loyal Americans."

"I think I proved my loyalty on the voyage." Then I related fully, not hesitating to give myself all credit due, the saving of the "Trenton" from the French guns. Mr. O'Brien had me repeat the names of the ships and the captains involved, checking them against a marine record. His eyes were again warmly bright instead of coldly bright.

"If Cap'n West will substantiate the story I wouldn't hesitate to send you to Washington with a personal letter to Mr. Adams," he told me. "But that will take a long time."

"As it happens, I'm in no hurry to return to Washington. I didn't come here to apply for passports; I'm on much graver business. It may take me to Constantinople shortly, but might keep me here."

"It's next to impossible to stay here without passports. I can give you temporary protection—" He stopped, eyeing me with growing interest. "I believe you're a loyal citizen, Mr. Starbuck. Your arriving here in this fashion is odd, to say the least—but I think you'd better tell me what business you hope to do here."

"Do you remember the sinking of the 'Leghorn'?"

"Yes, I heard about it from the French consul."

"Did you hear that some of the passengers were believed to have been taken captive?"

"Yes, the consul had orders from Talleyrand to try to find out if they were sold in Algiers. However, the general opinion was they were drowned at sea." But he was thinking of something he did not say; I saw it in his eyes.

"Is that your opinion, Mr. O'Brien?"

"I'm hardly entitled to an opinion, knowing so little about the matter. One circumstance came to my attention that I thought might have bearing on the affair, and I reported it to the French consul, but he thought there was nothing to it. Probably there wasn't. However, perhaps he was a little nearsighted in his eagerness to avoid trouble with the Dey."

"Will you tell me what it was?" I had trouble steadying my voice. "I'm betrothed to the young lady, Roxana Reil, who was in the missing boat."

"Gladly—but don't make too much of it. A Moorish spy in my employ reported to me that four people from Frankistan—as they call the West—had been landed here about a month after the disaster. He understood there were three men and one woman. But it was only a rumor he'd heard on the water front."

Mr. O'Brien had advised me not to make too much of it! He had as well tell the weather not to make a gale. I need never again fear that my voyage was in vain. It was a long but wonderful voyage to my happy port. I could hand-reef and steer!

Mr. O'Brien waited patiently and kindly for me to recover my self-possession. In a short while I asked, "Is the Moorish spy still in reach?"

"No, he was suspected of dealing with the consulates, and strangled. This is a violent country."

"Did he give you the source of the rumor?"

"No. It was a dangerous one."

"Did he say they were brought here by a Turkic pirate or have any idea what became of them?"

"No. I questioned him carefully, but that was all he knew or would tell." He expected my face to fall, but it did not.

"Could she be in Algiers—now?"

"You know that without my telling you. There are five hundred or more prisons in which she could have vanished, never to be seen again. Only a few Mohammedans would ever hear of her. She'd never speak to a living soul outside of the eunuchs and attendants and other women of the haremlik—unless her master trusted her to go to the baths. No alien could hope to find her."

"No alien could—more than hope, I mean. That's not what I'm here for—just a lot of hoping. I'm going to stay here awhile, Mr. O'Brien."

"She may never have come here. If she did, she could have been sent to Constantinople—the best market for white female slaves—or to any city in Islam."

There were pictures in my mind, and looking at them I spoke. "I'm sure she was brought here. If I'd been the Turkic pirates—frightened at having sunk the ship without warning—frightened by their very prize—her beauty that everyone would remember and the highborn grace—I'd have brought her straight here, to the biggest city and the nearest. I've underrated the evidence until now—afraid of being too optimistic—doubting what my heart told me. This clinches it. She may have been taken anywhere in Islam, as you say, but this is the place to start looking for her."

Mr. O'Brien rose, opened the door suddenly, closed, and locked it. "I've Algerian servants with large ears," he told me, smiling. It was a nervous smile and his face was quite red.

"The trouble with all that is," he went on, sitting down with a show of calm and leisure, "it would take you a year before you'd know how to begin."

"I expected that."

"You never will know how, if you stay on this side of the wall."

"I'm going on the other side as soon as I can."

"How are you going to get there? I can't help you. You can't stay in Algiers except as an employe of the consulate or under some powerful Algerian's protection—in bondage to him. There are no free Christians in the city except credited officials from Christian governments. You see—"

At that moment someone knocked on the door. It proved to be his secretary, announcing a caller, Boni Abdulla. Bidding me wait on him, Mr. O'Brien received the visitor in an anteroom.

In his absence my mind began to work very strangely. It seemed that I did not think directly on what in the devil to do, somewhat the same as not looking directly to find a dim, distant light on a dark night at sea, rather letting its faint glimmer steal into the side of my eyes that appeared more sensitive than the front. Certain facts were arrayed before me, but they were like buoys along a difficult channel. The channel existed though, if I could find it.

A dim glowworm of a plan kept capturing my thoughts. One part of my mind protested that it was the wildest folly, but so would be any other I might conceive, short of giving up and going home—that abysmal folly of defeat that often parades as wise expedience, and panders to men's fears in the name of common sense. I had no home. If I did have on my native shore, I could not go there until the Charleston business was settled. Thank God I did not need these little props. My girl had been brought here as a slave. She had escaped from the Terror in France only to fall into the toils of Turkic pirates, as bloody-handed and godless as Teach and his rovers on the Spanish Main. Tell me no more not to believe in fate: what do the gods care for our reasonableness, our nice rules of probability, when they find someone like Roxana? I could have seen in her face, in that sad look when it was in repose, that fate had dealt and would deal grandly with her. I might have told it from her beauty that ever attracts the lightning—itself the lightning for all I knew. I had loved her for it, and thus fate dealt grandly with me.

Mr. O'Brien returned with a deeply troubled countenance. "That's the opening gun," he burst out, when the door was closed. "The Grand Vizier sent his cat's-paw to find out if I'm harboring two sailors without proper passports. I could only tell him I'm investigating the case, with the idea of giving you passports and sending you home."

I leaned forward a little but appeared calm as possible. "He's very zealous in his duties? Why?"

"The possibility of making something out of you, of course."

"What would happen if you reported to him that for some reason you couldn't send us home?"

"I'd either have to employ you under consulate protection, or turn you over to the authorities as vagrants." He paused, his eyes narrowing. "By the way, Mr. Starbuck, does that happen to be true?"

"In a sense, yes. You'd certainly put us in a fix by sending us home. We haven't committed any serious crime—"

"What's your servant's name?" he broke in.

"He's called Nicodemus. He has never told me, and I've never asked, his last name."

Mr. O'Brien drew a portfolio from his desk and began to skim through its pages. "Thank God," he told me, "I haven't received any official notice of two men of your names being wanted."

"But you've no doubt heard of Cap'n Dan'l Todkill."

A very strange expression came into his eyes. "I knew him well, when we both fought England. Were you two men members of his crew?"

"Nicodemus was. I'm Cap'n Todkill's nephew."

"Bless my soul." That he said quietly, but the expression was more telling than if he had barked an oath.

"I don't suppose you heard of his recent rescue from the gallows at Charleston?"

"No."

I gave him a brief account of the episode, without fear that this gallant American of Irish blood would send Nicodemus and me to Charleston in irons. He listened in frank enjoyment.

"I'm glad you got the old bucko out," he said. "If Captain West lives to tell what you did at Ouessant you'll get out of it too, with nothing more said about it. Mark you, I want to help you in this affair. That's my job, to help out Americans—"

"Roxana Reil is an American too."

"What!"

"She was born in Salem of a French father and New England mother. That's where I met and fell in love with her. Now she's the harem slave of some Moor or Turk."

He sat still a moment. "Do you remember the tall elms there?" He drew a deep breath. "What scheme were you about to propose?"

"Can't you tell the Dey we've been exiled from America, and you'll put us to his use until the President permits us to return? He won't know but it's fully in your power as the American consul-general."

"He'd believe it in a minute, but that's voluntary slavery. For your man it's out of the question—he'd be sent to the quarries—but I can employ him in the consulate. If the Dey takes to you and thinks he'll profit by it he may give you a pleasant post—one where you could learn the language and hear many secrets of the court. If not, he won't hesitate to make you a quarry slave, to be half-starved and beaten with the bastinado."

"I'll have to take a chance on that."

"You're a gentleman. That will impress him more than he'd let on. But unless you can speak Spanish or Moorish—"

"I can make out with Spanish."

"He might use you as an account-keeper or secretary or even a personal attendant. But if you knew some tricks to amuse him—card or gambling game—anything he'd find novel—"

"Is he interested in hunting? I can teach him some frontier methods he doesn't know and show him some shooting in the frontier style."

"Good God! His son Ali is an avid hunter—it's the main sport here. The Algerians have the repute of being deadly shots, but compared to American frontiersmen—" He stopped and looked at me with a searching glance.

"It seems to me a wonderful opportunity to get into his court."

"Would he be suspicious? No, I don't think so. A good many of his *reis* are European fugitives turned renegade. He'll think I'm taking advantage of your hard luck and lending you to him to curry favor. The brute has no respect for my integrity or patriotism, only for the cunning with which I get ahead. That's the way his filthy mind works."

"Then—"

"Giving slaves to nabobs is an old Oriental custom, but I never thought I'd practice it." He thought over the proposal and his Irish face shone. "You bet I'll do it. It's the best and only way to go about getting track of your sweetheart. You may hear something of value to your country, too. If you do, report it to me."

"I'll go to any lengths to get information for you," I told him, my heart burning.

"Just pick up what comes your way. You mustn't make him suspicious. It's a great enterprise, but never forget it's at great hazard."

Everything depended on the first impression I made on His Highness, Mustapha, Dey of Algiers. I wore my best clothes, with Nicodemus marching behind me, carrying my rifle, powder horn, and bullet pouch. At the appointed time we marched through the narrow, stinking streets to the courtyard of the palace, thronging with resplendent Moors and Turks, black slaves, blond Mamelukes in silks and satins, and numberless guards and attendants. Here we bared our heads, entered a hall whose gaudy glories I was too excited to observe, and climbed five flights of winding stairs. Then we were guided through a maze of ornate, dimly lighted rooms to a small audience chamber.

This sacred precinct, which we must enter barefoot, was unlighted save for gaps between the iron gratings of the small, cell-like windows. I saw first the jewels, then the raiment; and, as my eyes grew accustomed to the gloom, at last the face of the pirate king.

He was a fat beast of a man, with a long beard and cruel eyes, squatted like a tailor on a richly upholstered sofa. Three daggers adorned his broad, golden belt, their hilts a rainbow blaze in the dim room from solid-set diamonds, rubies, and emeralds. His turban, very large, appeared to be muslin, bearing a jeweled crescent and plume, and encircled by a blue sash, the gold fringes of which hung in front of his shoulders. The jeweled hilt of his scimitar rose from a scabbard of gold, marvelously worked with jewels. He wore various jackets and gowns, each slashed in such a way as to reveal the decoration of the one beneath. His pantaloons, ankle long, were rose-colored silk.

Mr. O'Brien bowed low and kissed his extended hand. This honor was not yet granted me.

I was able to follow fairly well the consul's elegant Spanish. He told the Dey that Nicodemus and I were indeed Americans, that the latter was my servant, and that I was a person of some prominence in my own country. However, I had incurred the displeasure of our President and been banished overseas. Nicodemus could become a servant of the consulate, but would the illustrious Dey make any use of me that he saw fit, until the President authorized the issue of a passport for my return from exile. Mr. O'Brien had no doubt that I would prove a very useful servant to His Highness.

With the Dey's consent I was presented and permitted to kiss his greasy paw of a hand.

"What's your name?" he asked in Spanish.

"Jason, Your Highness."

"You're young and look strong. What kind of service can you do me?"

"I hope to be allowed to make your son Ali Pasha the best marksman in Barbary."

The Dey did not appear to have comprehended this. He sat more like a bearded Buddha now, with a look of bovine stupidity on his face. I was about to be deceived when old Pierre, or someone or something in my past, warned me too look out. He was not in the least stupid. He could not remain monarch of a pirate state, rule a wild court full of conspirators and poisoners, unless he had a foxy, powerful mind. No pack of fools could turn the trick that the kings of Barbary had worked for three hundred years—with a desert domain, mouse poor in natural wealth, they had ravaged the Mediterranean and forced the proudest nations of Europe to pay them tribute.

Actually I had made an alluring proposal to the royal corsair. The consul had told me that the youth was the apple of his father's eye, favored and shown off to the best advantage at every divan. Good riding and shooting marked a man throughout Islam; long before Tamerlane, great kings must be great nimrods. To shoot well from the back of a running horse or camel was a prized attainment. These barbs dwelt between the desert and the sea, and harried both.

"Many can vaunt but few can vanquish." This was the gist of the Spanish proverb the Dey finally pronounced.

"Señor Jason brought his own rifle," Mr. O'Brien answered for me. "Will Your Highness send to the courtyard for it?"

The Dey nodded, and dispatched a servant. When the piece was brought, he tried its balance, and then examined it closely. It came to me he was a good rifleman himself; nor was his coarse, hog body as inert and awkward as it looked.

"I've seen many more costly guns—mounted in gold and silver, and adorned with precious jewels—but none of better fitting and workmanship," he told me quietly. Indeed the quietness of his voice and manner almost hid from me the wonder of this statement from a king; and every inch a king in his vile way he surely was.

He ordered an iron grating over one of the windows to be opened. Then he rose—indeed a more active man than I had supposed—and looked out.

"Mark the topmost cocoanut on yon palm tree. Can you hit it from here?"

"I think so, Mustapha Dey."

"Let me see you do it."

I loaded my piece, primed the pan, and let go. It was an easy target and the nut fell to the ground.

"It must be a magic gun," the Dey told me gravely, "for you didn't aim."

"By your pardon, sir, I did."

"You flung up and touched trigger before it came to rest. It was a piece of luck."

"Will you choose another target, of like difficulty?"

He did not answer for a moment and instead gazed long out the window. Taller than he, I looked over his head to a horrid sight. Half a cable's length distant, along a narrow road of cobblestones, about two hundred beasts of burden tugged at a great rope at the end of which was a cart bed of square-cut logs supported by low, iron wheels. On the cart was a block of stone that could easily weigh twenty tons. The slaves were naked save for a few rags and iron bands

177

around waist and ankle connected with a chain. Two overseers with kurbash [rhinoceros-hide whips] paced up and down the line. In the white tropic sunlight flooding from the luminous sky and beating off the white-washed buildings, I could make out stripes on no few bowed backs, dark red or black against flesh as white as mine. No Mohammedans can be slaves in Islam: these were unransomed captives off European ships and the haul of the slave-catchers raiding the lands of Greek and Coptic Christians.

Roxana too was a white slave in Islam.

One of the quarry gang had fallen and the file of his fellows plunged on. The overseers were too busy to lash him to his feet and by the time he had struggled up the cart had passed him. He tried to run after it, reeling like a drunken man. His long hair and beard were almost white.

The Dey's coarse lips curled in his beard. "There's a moving target for you," he said. I caught the words plainly, my scalp creeping.

"No, Your Majesty, he's fallen again."

"Now he's getting up. He's old and worn out and good for nothing better than for trying your aim."

My sickened brain worked well; or the words came out of my heart without the burden of thought.

"Mustapha Dey, it is forbidden by our God, and besides the target is too easy."

It was either inspiration or instinct, one as mysterious as the other, that caused me to employ an easy, conversational tone, as though it had not occurred to me that my thwarting of his will would enrage him. Meanwhile I peered out the window as though in search of a likelier target, on no account glancing into his face. The warning had been perfectly distinct, but its source unknown. There had come upon me the same alertness, an enhanced power of perception, that had stood by me on the ship. The need was so unthinkably great.

Mr. O'Brien sucked in his breath—I heard him in the silent room. I did not glance at him either but his face was a pale blur at the edge of my vision and he was standing rigid.

"So the target's too easy for you," the Dey murmured, breaking that long and terrifying silence.

"The newest recruit among your janissaries, Mustapha Dey, couldn't miss it."

"Then I'll choose you one somewhat harder, and this time we'll lay a wager."

"At your pleasure, Your Majesty, if within my means."

"If you hit, you shall become my son Ali Pasha's tutor in marksmanship. If you miss, you'll be given a place on the rope."

"We couldn't call that a wager in my country, Mustapha Dey. It's only a chance at two posts, both to your profit."

It seemed a desperately bold answer but the pass was desperate too. I had no feeling that it would anger him and it might mitigate the ordeal. In the latter respect it failed.

"That's good wit, but I've spoken, and I don't often speak twice to Christian dogs. I spy a bird—a pigeon, I believe—on yonder roof. There's your mark, and this time I advise you to take good aim."

"Mustapha Dey," the consul-general broke in, "that's an impossible target."

"The American aspires to teach marksmanship to my son Ali Pasha. I wish to discover if he's worthy of the post."

"I remind you that he's an American subject. Rather than have him made a quarry slave I'll—"

"All Americans are my slaves," the Dey interrupted with an evil smile, "else why do they pay me tribute?" He turned to me, and spoke tauntingly. "Will you try the shot, for a post of honor, or be sent to the quarries at once?"

Actually Mr. O'Brien was mistaken in thinking the mark impossible. The bird was not much more than a hundred paces distant and in excellent light; an expert frontier sharpshooter with a perfectly bored barrel and aligned sights could hit it three or four times out of five from a dead rest. My trouble was that even if the Dey permitted a dead rest, I had almost never used one. Learning to shoot freehand the instant my bead covered the target, I could not stand the strain of prolonged aiming. I shot with the same violence, by the same kind of nervous process, that an angry man hits another with his fist.

"I'll try for the post of honor, Your Majesty," I said.

His eyes gleamed. For a quick, freehand shooter the mark did not miss impossibility very far. I had often placed a bullet finely enough to kill a pigeon at this range, but would never dream of trying such a shot except in an emergency. This was an extreme emergency. I rammed a rag through my barrel to remove burned powder and slivers of lead from the preceding bullet. Then I loaded the piece with utmost care, measuring the powder, choosing the most perfectly molded bullet and likeliest patch in my pouch. My sights were set at a hundred yards. I had tried them out the day before. My hammer was instrumented by an unusually powerful spring, to fire the charge the instant I touched trigger and save long leads at running game. I cleaned the rear sight, and blackened with charcoal dust the front one, to remove its glare in the blinding light. Finally I inserted a new flint.

"Will you call my shot, Mustapha Dey?" I asked.

"Any time you're ready."

I held my gun down until the pigeon, strutting on the edge of the roof, showed me his profile. Then as the gun leaped up like a live thing, there leaped in me a thing hard to describe, like a ferocity but yet cold, more like my whole life force suddenly rushing to my eyes and hands, by the truly dreadful drive and travail of my will. These being true, the result was a kind of mathematical inevitability. All I did was look at the bird through my sights, and so heightened for this instant were my powers that it loomed big as a wild turkey. It was as though that look had killed.

Even so, I had come near enough missing. If hit squarely, the bird would have been blown to pieces by the heavy ball; barely clipped, it flapped its wings for two or three seconds before it died. There was not a sound in the room and I felt too spent to speak. Then the Dey swore by Allah in his native tongue.

"I've won the wager, Your Majesty," I told him.

"Yes, by the beard of the Prophet! There is no majesty and no might save in Allah! But if it wasn't by witchcraft—" He fell silent and spat on the floor.

The consul saw his chance to make a little hay for his country. "American riflemen are famed the world over," he said, "but I grant you Señor Jason is one of our best."

"But he didn't aim! I've had a marksman among my Janissaries who could hit that target one or two times out of three with long, careful aiming from dead rest, but this gun flew up and went bang!"

"The prince's gun will fly up and go bang, Mustapha Dey, if he'll learn the American style of shooting," I told him. At least this was the frontier style, developed by the long hunters.

"O'Brien Emir, I'll accept with pleasure the services of this rifleman, and be loath to return him to my pasha in America. In case of war between Algiers and the United States, I hope he fights on my side."

"*Salem alicum*, Mustapha Dey." [Let there be peace between us.]

When the Dey had given us leave from his august presence, the consul broke out, "Damn his insolent soul to hell! But war would be less likely, if he'd see a few more Yankees behind their guns."

This was the consul's business, not mine. I was leaving the settlements to go forth on the long hunt; I would presently vanish in the forest and have no thought or care of their affairs. I had found a pass over the mountains.

CHAPTER NINE

The Crossing

I.

I was given decent quarters in the thousand-roomed castle, the equal of those provided for the Dey's *hampers* [bodyguards below the rank of Mamelukes]. Furnished by Mr. O'Brien with an American passport, a boat, and a net, Nicodemus fished on shares for the market to their mutual profit. Both of us began our education in Orientalism, he in the school of the streets and the docks, I in its very cloister.

The barrier of language was the first I meant to tear down. In a sense I was born bilingual—English and French—and perhaps that made me more apt in foreign tongues. I had picked up passable Spanish but now I must learn not only Moorish, which to all intents and purposes was Arabic, but Turkic with the same alphabet and thousands of Arabic words. All classes in Barbary spoke Moorish. But the slave-traders throughout Islam were mainly Turks; since Constantinople was still the heart of Islam all well-educated Moors spoke Turkic fluently and it was frequently employed at court functions and in fashionable private life. I could not pass as a gentleman of Islam without knowing it, and anyway the search for Roxana would likely take me to the great capital as soon as I was equipped and able to go there.

To learn two new, allied languages did not strike me as a formidable task. It would be only a steppingstone to where my heavy tasks began. Merely to get ahead in business, money-changers and rug merchants learned all the main Islamic tongues as a matter of course, and from two to half a dozen European. My first move was to install in my quarters a down-at-heels *munshi* [teacher] recommended by a Neapolitan renegade of the court, to talk with me every waking idle hour. It was simply a case of buckling down.

For the first months of my bondage I saw almost nothing of the Dey, although I was a regular attendant of his son Ali. He was a rather engaging youth, born to one of the Dey's slave girls, and an apt pupil in marksmanship. In his company I was thrown with many of the court officials, courtiers, and his own flatterers, and other attendants; in his *gulphor* [an entertainment parlor to which the women of the household were forbidden] I met and listened to the talk of the city's great, including the *agas* and *reis* [captains of his majesty's army and navy]. Straining for the meaning of every Moorish or Turkic phrase, in a few weeks I began to catch the drift of the conversation.

Ali furnished me with garments suitable to wear in his train. They were of the style, although had nothing of the richness, of those worn by the Mamelukes, blue-eyed, fair-haired Caucasians captured or bought in early childhood and raised in the courts and the most prized of Christian slaves. This attire differentiated me from the Faithful—I wore a headband and shawl instead of a turban—yet concealed my alienhood. While the Moslems did not fraternize with me as with the renegades with which the court was rife—I was yet a Christian dog—they made as free with me as with their Negro slaves. As the desert sun leaned and browned me and I grew a black beard, my appearance ceased to be strange in any company of highbred, pale-colored Moors.

I spent many hours on camel or horseback in the desert, hunting with Ali. I had found him a fair marksman to start with, considering that his piece was nothing more than a richly jeweled and ornamented smooth-bore musket. Straightway I prevailed upon Mr. O'Brien to order him a fine Kentucky rifle—it appeared there was a ready fund for greasing the Dey and his family—meanwhile schooling him in quick leveling and aiming. These brought so much more game to his bag, especially when he shot from a running horse, that he swore by me and appeared to regard me as his favorite attendant. When he was ready to attempt long-range and fine shooting, I lent him Pierre's rifle, somewhat against my heart. But not often had it been put to as noble use as raising me in Ali's esteem.

From this steady practice, I gained skill at shooting running game from horseback, an extremely difficult but favorite sport of the Moors. In old days with Pierre we had raced with deer in open forest, drawn alongside, and rolled them over at twenty or thirty yards. Some of Ali's smooth-gaited horses had been especially trained to cut in on and flank running antelope and gazelles. I think it was a survival from the days when the kings and noblemen of the East rode after game with spears. Anyway, I had an immense advantage in my swing-

and-blaze style of shooting, for no man can hold aim on a racing horse.

Once when we were homeward bound from some lively and close shooting, Ali gave me a chance to fire the first gun in my great hunt.

"*Sahabti* [friend], you love riding and shooting, both favored sports in Islam, but there's another sport of good repute among us, in which you don't indulge."

"What could it be, Ali Pasha?"

"The sort played in the haremlik, with beautiful Caucasian or Numidian female slaves."

I had waited a long time for this opening. Old Pierre would praise me for my patience, the first requisite in a hunter, lest he alarm the game. Until now I had not dared breathe the peril-fraught words so long shaped on my tongue: the better I knew Islam, the more strident the warning to bide my time.

"I was once betrayed by a Spanish woman, and hate all woman-kind," I answered.

"Why, you don't have to love them to enjoy them. That's the notion of Frankistan [the Islamic term for Western Europe] that makes us laugh. I'll buy and present you, as a token of my esteem, a beautiful Numidian or Ethiopian girl, virginal, rounded, and when aroused, ardent beyond your dreams. Their skins are very warm, their limbs exceeding strong, and their breasts—but you know the beautiful passage in the Song of Suleiman."

"She'd yet remind me of the dusky Spanish wench."

"Then what do you say to a Circassian, with eyes blue as the sky, hair like spun gold, and rose-tipped breasts of warm snow?" The Moors, only less than the Turks, were given to extravagant speech when describing beautiful women. Lust stole into his face, and my thoughts sickened me, and I could not wait any longer.

"No, Ali Pasha, I've seen but one Circassian that could make me forget the Spaniard and my shame, and she's as unobtainable as the moon."

"No woman is unobtainable, *sahabti*, if the coveter is more powerful than he who stands between him and the coveted." He was a prince and uttered this with a proud smile.

"That may be, but I don't know who she is, or where she is, or even her name."

"Where did you see her, if you'll confide in me?"

"Aboard a ship that had put into Cadiz. She may not have been a Greek, but she certainly wasn't a swarthy Spaniard. She was tall,

184

and rather slim—the slut that betrayed me was short and fat—and very fair. I'd have given a hundred sequins to bed her for one night. She looked proud, and I ached to tame her. But the fortune fell to another—some rich pasha in Tunis, I believe—and I never saw her again."

"What makes you think she's in Tunis?"

"Only a tale told on the water front. The ship was sunk by a Turkic pirate bound for Tunis, and she and a few more made captive. I've forgotten the name of the vessel—"

"The 'Leghorn,' I believe. Some inquiry was made not only in Tunis but to our *Chiah* [viceroy]."

"Why should any questions be asked here? I think that was the name, but perhaps not. No matter, anyway." The drumming of the horses' feet hid the thumping of my heart.

"It was thought that the bashi-bazouks might have sold their catch here. The ship sunk was French, and the Bey of Tunis is friendly to France. Actually the *reis* of the 'Zainab' denied he had ever seen the 'Leghorn.' "

"Isn't that a bustard?" I pointed excitedly across the desert. "No, it's a stone—or a shadow."

"You're an avid hunter, *sahabti*."

"It's better sport than the other."

"That I question. Well, I'll inquire of the Tunisian minister if the girl was ever brought there. He may know, but it's unlikely."

"Pray do not, master. I want no one but you to know I'm such a fool as to lust for a girl I saw but once. She's lost her maidenhead months ago, although that wouldn't—" He grinned at me and I spoke in a more earnest tone. "Ali Pasha, I'm an exile from my own country and you're my only protection. Why, if she should be in Algiers— you've suggested the possibility—and her master should hear that a Frankistan slave dared covet her—"

"I'll make my inquiries as though I coveted her myself."

"Pray don't concern yourself with such a trifle."

"Not unless it falls in my way. Truly the chance that she'll ever be put on sale again is most unlikely—in all probability she was drowned at sea—yet I'm pleased with you, Jason, and if I learn anything of her history, I'll tell you. You'd not have remembered her this long, save for a strong desire for her enchantments."

I told him a bawdy joke that this seemed to suggest, then let him beat me in a close race. Thereafter I tried to give the impression that the matter was too trivial for his royal attention. When he felt especially friendly toward me, I often amused him with fo'c'sle tales, never shrinking from any vulgarity now that I knew him well, and invented amorous passages with the fictitious Spanish girl, but pointedly avoided mention of the pretty blond on the "Leghorn." I caught him smiling to himself sometimes, for having surprised the secret of my lingering lust—or again smiling fondly upon me for the amiable weakness I was seeking to control. Occasionally he would sing the praises of tall, beautiful blond girls, watching me out of the corner of his eye.

The impression I had received that day, in ways beyond my sense, became strengthened with the passing months by his very reticence. I could not doubt that he had heard of the smuggling into Algiers of three male and one female slave from a Turkic pirate ship, and when he could trust an alien such as I with the dangerous secret, he would tell me.

In the spring, the armed brig "Sophia" put into Algiers with the rifle that Mr. O'Brien had ordered for Ali Pasha—a superbly tooled piece of about .70 caliber, firing a ball of about 350 grains with three drams of powder. Itself reminded me of a frontiersman—lank, brown, plain, and with good balance. Ali appeared a little disappointed at first—he could hardly believe that the mountings would not be gold or silver, and jewels not set in the stock—but felt better after he had swung it to his shoulder. It seemed to sight itself.

We sped to the desert, and the first mark we saw was an antelope grazing in thorn scrub at a good two hundred paces. I told him to hold about twelve inches over the animal's shoulder. He wanted to lie down and take a dead rest—he pined for it before every hard shot like a reformed drunkard for a dram—but I made him stand up and swing. At the roar of the piece the antelope dropped as though poleaxed.

Sighted at a hundred yards and shot from a vise, the piece would put four bullets out of five in a three-inch ring. Indeed it was every bit as good as Pierre's or mine, which I had thought the ultimate of the gunmaker's art. Ali would not have traded it for the most voluptuous maid of Numidia; but he did not express his gratitude until we were taking refreshment—dates and the perfumed juice of pomegranates—in a cool oasis.

Waving his other attendants out of earshot, he held out his hand for me to kiss. When I had done so, without the least reluctance— indeed pleased with the sign of favor so vital to me, and perfectly willing to kiss his dusty feet if it would carry my own feet one step forward on my way—he clapped his hand from his breast to his forehead and back again in a pledge of friendship.

"Jason, why were you exiled from your native land?" he asked.

"For piracy on the high seas." This should appeal to the son of a royal pirate.

"Do you wish to return there?"

"I'm done with the stinking country, where a man can't measure his strength without fear of the noose."

"Then, by your leave, I'll entreat my father, Mustapha Dey, Defender of the Faith in Algiers, to invite you to embrace Islam." Ali's voice shook with emotion.

I too appeared all but overcome. When he had first dismissed the others, my heart had stood still in the hope that he was about to tell me news of my lost love. That hope had failed, as I might have known. The sinking of a friendly nation's ship without warning remained a closely guarded secret in the Barbary courts.

Yet I had made a notable advance. Apostates were given every privilege afforded those born to the Faith; I could never be enslaved and might aspire to any office in Islam short of a few religious and hereditary ones. The road to success would be wide open, no matter how steep, perilous, and long.

"Allah upon you, Ali Pasha!" I cried. "You ride with green spurs!" This last was the highest compliment that could be paid a desert Mussulman, given rarely save to princes, and seemed to mean that green grass sprang up wherever his horse set foot.

"Consider well, my friend. There's no retreat from this path."

He meant that renegades were never permitted to recant. If they tried to leave Islam and were caught, they were hung alive on iron hooks on the city walls.

"I've considered well, and followed my heart. There's no majesty and no might save in Allah."

That very day I underwent the ceremony. It consisted of two rites, one of them the mere declaration before a mufti of *Allah, Allah ursul el Allah*. The forswearing did not prick my conscience in the least. The other rite was painful and I would have got out of it if I could; that being impossible, I made the best of it. If the humor that saved me was of a rowdy sort, it was at least human: I did not think my beautiful bride would mind.

In divorcing himself from all former ties and cleansing his soul of the *giaour* taint, a convert to Islam invariably took a Mohammedan name. I cheated in the business, taking the name Selim because it reminded me of Salem. Thereafter I put on Moorish custom with a muslin turban and was considered a full member of the court.

The Dey himself noticed me occasionally and more frequently admitted me into his perfumed, stinking presence. Now that I was seen more often in the royal train, the court adventurers began to flatter me and frequently grease me with gifts, sometimes gold or jewels to the amount of a hundred sequins. These fattened my purse for trying days to come. Until now I had hardly begun to pay my debt to Mr. O'Brien—smuggling out to him through Nicodemus only the piddling gossip of the palace, but now I began to hear of the higher politics of the court. I could see no profit to my country in reporting the rumors, but taken together perhaps they formed a riddle that Mr. O'Brien could read.

A riddle that I could not read was how well I seemed to fit into the flamboyant life. I still did not want any female slaves, and when I accepted Ali's invitation for a carousal with public dancing girls, it was with the fine excuse of furthering my quest. All this was valid enough, but so was my share in the debauch—one that would have raised the eyebrows of a cockney sailor.

I was living high, with more excitement than I could well digest. But it was all bound 'round my undertaking. Every day Ali trusted me more. Once he hinted of something to tell me, when my turban would cease to be new. The least intelligence forbade me to throw away my best and probably only chance by impatience. Those who did not know Islam might think I could steal down into the docks and alleys, listen and peep, and by some wonderful stroke of cunning unearth the secret. Actually nine out of ten secrets come to light through someone's imparting a confidence.

It came September and Ali and I were going to ride far into the desert and be gone from Algiers several days. To show his progress in marksmanship, nothing would do but that he shoot a lion. I had tried to dissuade him—he was a long way yet from the nimrod he fancied himself, inclined to blow up in excitement; and if he were torn to pieces by the ravening beast, I would no doubt be fed to the lions in the Dey's dens. But the youth persisted in the undertaking and indeed persuaded the Dey to join the safari. He loved the royal brute, and wanted him to behold his triumph.

So I made the best of a risky business and wangled a place for Nicodemus among the camel-tenders. He hardly knew one end of a camel from the other, while I was almost as much at home aboard these desert ships as a ship at sea. Neither would ever equal in my heart a plucky horse, yet I had learned to revere even the ill-tempered, foul-smelling, baggage camels, let alone the wonderful, slim-legged Umaniyan riding beasts that clipped off fifty miles in half a day. On these the prince and I had made many a jaunt into the desert, to hunt leopards and gazelles. The royal expedition would take us into the foothills of the Atlas Mountains, where ranged the king of beasts.

Our caravan contained at least two hundred camels, including the Dey's priceless mare Charatsa and other fleet Umaniyans for Ali, our scores of attendants and me; and our first camp, which we pitched eighty miles from Algiers at an emerald-green oasis, would have bunged out the eyes of the long hunters bivouacked in the American West. No venison steak broiled on a ramrod, but sybaritic feasts in bright-hued pavilions—ensigns, majesty, and might. Our second camp was in lion country; and before dawn the Dey, Ali, and I, attended by Nicodemus and two other trusties, rode eight miles to a desert of aloes and thorn scrub where the scouts had seen a dozen or more of the big-maned kings of beasts.

Before sunrise the second morning we flushed from his kill a huge lion with a heavy, black mane. He disappeared in a thorn-grown ravine that led to his lair in the craggy hills. Yet when Ali began beating up one side of the narrow gully I took the other. It seemed to me a useless procedure, since any beast I knew would certainly use the cover to beat a safe retreat; and in all conscience I was glad to have him run, since black-maned lions are famed for ferocity, and we had only one shot each to stop his charge.

The Dey had dismounted from his camel and was standing watching us at the mouth of the ravine. The still desert air carried his command to an attendant to fetch him a cup of water from the bags, and the clear, pure desert light just before the glare of sunrise showed him small but unbelievably sharp as I glanced back, the bejeweled hilts of his dagger and scimitar like little suns.

Suddenly there came a shocking noise behind us. It was the angry roar of the lion as he burst from the ravine to attack the Dey. The king had picked a king for his prey, and the scene was scored on my memory like the picture of a pharaoh battling a lion on an Egyptian obelisk. But the corsair king held no spear and shield. He was snatching out his scimitar, but it did not seem possible he could bare and wield it in time to deal one stroke, and what a reed it was compared to the might of his foe! The huge beast ran low to the ground in a terrier-like scuttle, his tail rammed out behind—an incredibly fast and fearsome advance.

It was death to the Dey, I thought, and I would be glad. But before I knew it, I had flung up and blazed. Perhaps it was against nature to stand by while a beast tore down a human being. At the roar of the piece—before the smoke cloud half blinded me—I saw the lion shatter down as though struck by a cannon ball. It seemed impossible that the ferocious fountain of life lay stopped and still.

By one of the best shots of my life—at a rapidly moving target a good hundred paces distant—I had saved a bloody tyrant's life! But such is shifty human nature that I felt triumphant instead of sorry, from thinking of the rich reward he would give me. He might make me a pasha of one horsetail—he boasted three—and grant me a high office to which would come the secrets of Islam. Meanwhile I was reloading my piece—a chore of fifteen seconds, instead of sixty needed by his musketeers.

"The brute's mate may be about," I warned Ali. "Perhaps that's why he stole down the ravine to attack, instead of running away."

"A black-maned lion never runs away. And you, my comrade, laid him low with the best shot I've ever seen. Truly there is *baraka* [magic powers] in your eye and hand."

We found the Dey in good color, apparently unshaken by his cobweb-breadth escape. I had never until now appreciated his nerve, either to conquer terror or to conceal it. His attendant's hand shook as he handed him a silver cup, and some of the water spilled on the desert. The Dey laughed at him, drank the remainder, and carefully wiped his beard.

"It's a magnificent lion," he said. "I've never seen a finer. Which of you two bravos killed him?"

"I did, royal father," Ali answered quickly.

"Didn't you shoot, Jason Effendi?"

"He shot, my lord, but was behind a thorn bush and missed," Ali answered in my place.

"Let him speak for himself, Ali Pasha," the Dey said coldly.

"Ali Pasha speaks truth, Mustapha Dey. The thorns caught my sleeve and I could not find my aim."

For I could not believe that Ali had lied for his own vainglory. If he had shot at all, the two reports had sounded as one, and only one bullet hole showed in the tawny side. While I did not fully grasp his motives, plainly a great deal depended on my falling in with anything he said.

The Dey looked at us with cruelly gleaming eyes. "All I know is, the one that killed him made a shot worthy to be recorded with the wonders of Suleiman," he told us. "But I mean to know more."

"I assure you, royal father—"

"Sidi Osman, unsheathe your knife and search for the bullet."

Trembling, the attendant obeyed. Ali waited with a pale face; the Dey sat him down at ease on a cushion of cloth-of-gold. Deep drove the knife into the heart chamber ere Sidi Osman's probing fingers found the bullet and brought it forth. He handed it to the Dey.

"Each of you, Ali Pasha, and Jason Effendi, give me a bullet from your pouch."

I could not have deceived him, if I had dared try. It was the same with Ali. But as the Dey compared the fatal ball with the other two the grim expression passed from his face, his cruel lips curled a little, and there came an exultant shine in his eyes.

"Ali Pasha, my son, you've spoken truth," he said. "The bullet is from your gun."

For all my hard-to-conceal incredility, the Dey was right. Ali's gun was of .70 bore, mine .65, and there was no possibility of mistaking the heavier ball.

"Plainly you missed clean, Jason Effendi," the nabob went on. "I choose to believe that a thorn brush got in your way, or more likely, the target was too difficult for you—not that you secretly desired to feed my brother, the lion."

"I thank you kindly, Mustapha Dey!"

"In any case, you have fulfilled your word to me, given in the presence of O'Brien Emir more than a year gone. There is no majesty and no might save in Allah! My son Ali is the best marksman in Barbary."

So I was not to receive high honors in the court, or even a great jewel worth a thousand sequins! But Ali gave me an exultant glance and I was more excited than before. All men know that fate—kismet, we renegades called her, turning her into a male spirit—has a queer, sardonic sense of humor. My miss might turn out the best hit I had ever made.

On the return journey Ali was flattered and feted by the courtiers and nabobs like the heir to the throne. The Dey bade him ride on his right hand, and sent a fleet camel to summon the *bubor* [royal band] to escort them with sounding brass into the city. My fellow attendants paid me no more than courteous respect: while the Dey might smile on my good tutoring, again he might cast me off now that the job was done to his satisfaction, or even cast me down for missing the lion. Ali hardly mentioned the event on the few occasions we were alone. However, his manner toward me was one of princely patronage that thrilled my heart.

On the second evening of our return he invited me into his *gulphor* to have coffee. After dismissing all his attendants and making sure that the doors were locked, he bade me light his houka for him.

"Selim, through your good teaching I saved the life and won the gratitude of my royal father," he told me, puffing lazily.

"It rejoices me, Ali Pasha."

"I'd like to give you some token of my thanks. For instance—a beautiful Circassian virgin."

"Master, long ago when you would so honor me, I made bold to tell you there was only one female slave that I desired—folly I cannot help—and if I can't have her, I'd rather have none." And I controlled my voice well.

"You haven't forgotten her in all these months?"

"Nay, and it must be she wakened love in my heart, even as the first glimpse of the king's daughter in the heart of Ali-din." The tales of *Arabian Nights* were constantly quoted by all well-educated Moors.

"*Keif, keif.* [It is so.] And could it be that Allah felt for you, even though you were then a Christian, and ordained that you should be landed here and become one of the Faithful?"

"Unfold your wisdom to me, Ali Pasha."

"Was it His will, that if you proved worthy, you should see the maiden's face again? It doesn't seem possible, but He's the Omnipotent One. And here in Algiers you've walked where her feet have trod!"

It was not necessary for me to speak or to make any show. Ali no longer puffed lazily; the bowl bubbled fast. He had flushed at the cheekbones and his eyes glistened.

"I've waited long to tell you so," he went on, "because the secret is a very dangerous one. The Grand Vizier of Frankistan—Talleyrand by name—made great trouble for the Bey of Tunis, and would have made more for my royal father, had it become known that the four captives were landed and sold in Algiers. Only by great cunning did the Bey persuade him that all the people drowned. I confess too that my fondness for you could not suffer you to leave me until our joined fate was fulfilled."

"I had not thought to leave you, Ali Pasha, but truly Allah saw fit to waken great love—"

"If it's Allah's will for you to seek this woman—*Alicum salem!* [There is peace between us.]"

"By my head, then, you must know the road to take!"

"That, and little more. The four captives were sold to a Turkic slave-trader named Kemal, hidden here for some months, and then three—the girl and two French sailors—were taken by him on the sloop 'Salome' to Stamboul."

3.

Stamboul was Constantinople, one of the greatest cities in the world. Its traders bought and sold slaves from Tangier to China. A score of ships carrying the chained cargo had docked at the Golden Horn every month of the year. But I would go there, and pick up the spoor. I had never let myself hope that the trail would be smooth and the search short. It was the long hunt, like those made by the Kentucky woodsmen, in which the forest swallowed them, not to give a glimpse of them for many moons. In my case, it might be several years.

"When did the 'Salome' sail?" I asked, after a long pause.

"In the fast of Ramadan, last year."

So Roxana had not yet gone from Algiers when I had talked to Dr. Reil at Lorient!

"I long for her beauty as for the moon of Ramadan." This was a favorite expression of longing in Islam, since the cruel fast ended, and the feast began, on the new moon. "Did you hear, Ali Pasha, of what happened to her in Stamboul?"

"Not a word, Selim *Sahabti.*"

"Has Kemal ever returned here?"

"No."

"What happened to the other captive?"

"He was a Spanish felon, escaped from prison. A noble Moor bought him, and made him his master gardener, on his sworn oath that he would never breathe a word of the affair."

193

"Could I talk with him?"

"It would be difficult, but not impossible."

"Will you believe that love has so ingressed my heart that I wish to go to Stamboul?"

"Readily, my friend. I've seen you fight against it in vain."

"Anyway I wish to travel throughout Islam, amass riches, and in time make a pilgrimage to Mecca. Will you, in your great kindness to your servant, help me to get there?"

"Selim, it would have been impossible even a week ago. My royal father had resolved that you'd either make me a great nimrod, or yourself make food for worms. That's another reason I didn't confide in you—you'd have tugged at the leash in vain. He'll let you go now, I believe, but whether to Stamboul I can't tell you. It happens that our relations with the Ottoman Sultan are delicate just now."

I could not shilly-shally: I had to know everything. "Why is that, Ali Pasha?"

"The Sultan is enraged with my royal father for maintaining friendly relations with France, when he's at war with her. France pays us rich tribute which we are loath to lose. Perhaps my father can placate the Sultan with gifts."

"I see no reason why that should interfere with my going."

"Nor I, although one may exist. It may be that kismet means you to find her—if so, you'll be guided to her in Allah's good time."

"You've spoken wisely, Ali Pasha, and with great mercy to your servant."

Still needing his help, I kissed the hem of his garment in the ancient Oriental expression of humility and gratitude. But because he had been a true friend to me, I wanted to shake his hand.

On the following evening he arranged a brief meeting between me and the Spanish captive. It was held in the garden of one of his country houses and in great stealth; I never saw the man's face in the darkness or he mine. His name was Pedro and his voice indicated that he was badly frightened. Not until the prince assured him that we would keep the matter secret—and of course he must also, lest he be garroted—did he admit having ever been aboard the "Leghorn."

"What was the girl's name?" I asked, the back of my neck prickling.

"She told me it was Reil. I don't remember her first name. I'd never heard it before."

"She spoke to you in French?"

"Yes, effendi."

"Describe her appearance."

"She was tall, and very fair. I thought her beautiful." He did not say "*bonita*" but "*bella*," and Latin love of beauty rang in his voice.

"That's the one. When did you see her last?"

"About a week before she was taken to Constantinople."

"Was she well?"

"Yes, but greatly worried about her father."

I took a deep breath and went on. "When you found out that you were to stay in Algiers, did she tell you anything?"

"What might she tell me, effendi?"

"She might have thought that her father would try to search for her. Perhaps she left some message for him."

"She prayed that he would not attempt such a great task, as he was no longer young, and frail."

"Yet she gave you some message for anyone who might question you about her? What was it?"

"I remember now. She said to tell anyone searching for her to be careful, and not try to hurry, and thus die."

"Is that all?"

"Let me think. It was more than a year now. Yes, and she said for him not to be afraid for her. She too would be careful and get along all right."

I could hear her whispering it and see her eyes like jewels in the dim prison.

"Think again, Pedro. That's not all she said. She would seek to guide him to her." This was dangerous ground, because Ali was listening to our talk, but she was far too wary, and loved me too well, to have mentioned my name.

"Why, she gave me the impression that she found no fault with becoming a favorite of some great pasha even though she was a Christian." This was for Ali's benefit. Yet she might have been resourceful enough to say just that.

"That would be unnatural, if love had been wakened in her heart for this effendi, as I believe," Ali said. "Speak freely, Pedro."

"*Allah barik*, Ali Pasha! Effendi, she didn't know where she was going, and could leave no directions. Even so, it comes to me now that she did say something more. She asked me if it was the custom in Islam for ladies to have boxes of growing flowers beneath their windows. I told her it was not."

"And then?" Then my heart stood still.

"She said that when she was sold, she would have such a box beneath her window to mark the house."

"If that's all," I heard myself saying after a long silence, "I'll give you fifty sequins and be ever in your debt."

"It's all, by Mary Mother of God."

"By my beard," Ali burst out, "that Christian maid deserves her freedom!"

"Aye, but will she ever gain it, Ali Pasha?" Pedro asked. "She is too beautiful."

CHAPTER TEN

Good Hunting

I.

For my audience with the Dey, I prepared with extreme care. Strong cards were in my hand: the passage between us required no great guile but a considerable Oriental *savoir-faire*. He would look for hidden motives in my proposal and I had only to let him uncover the one a Moor best understood—the pursuit of riches and power in the Golconda of the modern world.

"Mustapha Dey, I've taught Ali Pasha all I know, and the pupil excels the teacher," I told him when he had permitted me to kiss his hand.

"Allah is witness that you speak truth." The Dey helped himself to figs from a golden platter. "But you've been a good learner as well as teacher, to speak so well the language of the Sublime Porte."

It was the first time I had employed Turkic in his hearing. There was a good reason for showing it off today.

"On first resolving to embrace Islam, I sought to prepare myself to serve Your Majesty well."

"You shoot straight, Selim Effendi."

"Now it's come to me that Your Majesty is sending gifts to your brother, the Sultan. Perhaps if you sent me in the train of your ambassador, as one fit to teach princes the sport of kings, he'll not take it amiss. I've heard that he keeps many game parks."

"He also maintains great armies of horse and foot. Two centuries ago it was the master swordsman who could roam the world, sure of a welcome in any court that pleased his fancy. Now it's the expert rifleman."

"Do you think, Mustapha Dey, there are princes or favorites in the Sultan's courts that might be interested in the style of shooting I taught Ali Pasha—instant aim, and reloading in fifteen seconds?"

"Any lover of hunting might be—and any Serdar of *Spahis* [cavalry general]." He was watching me closely.

"Is it in your heart that I'm worthy to be sent, under your firman [letter], for such service as I may do him in the field of sport or war?"

"It would do no harm. His *Reis* Effendi might have use for you."

"If I may be furnished well, as befitting the least of your envoys—" For this too was expected of me, now that the Dey was showing himself agreeable.

"By Allah, you learn fast! You wish to go not as a poor *munshi* but a great effendi and sportsman, worthy of high office and rich baksheesh."

"My first thought was to represent you well—"

"Yet you'll not hold your hand from the gold of the Golden Horn!" The Dey's lips curled in a smile of friendly contempt. "How many of my good sequins would furnish you suitably?"

"Only a thousand, great king."

"A thousand! So you would outshine Mohammet Wadi, my ambassador. You shall have four hundred, and one black slave. And let my ambassador hear good reports of you!"

I kissed the hem of his garment. "Allah upon you, Mustapha Dey."

"The Grand *Chiah* will give you the firman. The ship will likely be an English man-of-war, lent me to honor my throne."

He held out his hand for me to kiss, then dismissed me. I could hardly believe what he had told me last, although it was in accord with rumor current in the palace. Surely the king of England would not turn one of his ships into a packet boat for a Barbary pirate. Actually the upshot was hardly less credible, and of far greater import to me.

On the following morning a tall ship I had not seen before lay at anchor in the harbor. She looked like a Yankee frigate, and to my amazement, was soon revealed as the "George Washington" of twenty-four guns. She was the first American man-of-war ever to enter the Mediterranean, and had come in shame to deliver our yearly tribute to the Dey. God knew I rejoiced in her clean rigging and trig lines and stern gunports, but if I had had my way, Captain Bainbridge would never have anchored her under the Dey's forts, where he could blow her out of the water at his whim. I did not trust his infidel soul, and feared what might be brewing in his mind.

I longed to go aboard her, to hear Yankee accents and stuff Yankee food, and perchance speak with men who knew Derby Dock—an utterly hopeless longing in a seeming Yankee renegade who must never waken suspicion of his embrace of Islam. The best I could do was look at her through a glass and see Yankee specks on her deck. Even a glimpse of Captain Bainbridge on the street made my spine tingle—a full-faced, big-nosed man, with a curly topknot and side whiskers, resplendent in his blue coat with white facings and gold epaulets.

Little he knew what he was in for! Then and there the Dey ceased badgering the English consul and sent his *hampers* to bid Richard O'Brien appear before him. Seated in his divan, in the presence of the princes, the *Reis* Effendi, several other ministers and their attendants, he made a "request" that his arrogant manner and contemptuous smile turned into a *dahir* [decree from the throne].

"It's my desire to send an ambassador with certain tokens of fealty to my master in Stamboul, the Sublime Porte," he pronounced. "For his journey thither, I ask the use of the American frigate 'George Washington' and her crew."

Our consul's ruddy countenance turned gray. "I'm sensible to the honor," he replied after a brief pause, "but Captain Bainbridge has no orders for such a long journey."

"You're the consul-general of the Barbary States. It's my wish that you give him the necessary orders."

"The President of the United States is the commander-in-chief of our navy, and can alone order the disposition of the ships. I've no authority."

The lids drooped over the Dey's eyes, which the whole court knew was a sign of his anger. "The President of the United States is my vassal, paying me tribute," he said. "My ambassador will be ready to sail on October 15."

In vain did Mr. O'Brien protest that we could not protect the Algerian ambassador from the fleets of Portugal and Naples, with whom the Dey was at present at war. He left the divan white with anger but that very night found out that he must yield—partly by some tidings I was able to deliver to him through a most faithful messenger! If he refused the "honor" the Dey would seize the "George Washington!" He would like nothing better than an excuse to add a new frigate to his fleet, and take one hundred and forty captives worth great ransom: he had not the least fear of a backwoods nation beyond the Atlantic Ocean. Moreover, he would not pay one peso of the ship's expenses on the trip and would insist that the flag of Algiers fly from her main.

The *Reis* Effendi had given me this information in great glee—without a thought that I might still be loyal to my native land. He had forgotten, if he ever knew, that I was of American birth; it meant nothing to him or anyone in the court; I was simply another apostate from Frankistan. Anyway the renegades in Barbary almost always hated their own countries and rarely had been known to turn back. But the messenger I had employed remembered well! He was Nicodemus, still in Consul O'Brien's employ, and enjoying life in Algiers. He and I had met hardly once a month since I had donned a turban but our bond stood firm.

Only a few nights later he smuggled me into an arbor in the consulate garden to bid me goodbye. I could not see his face well; his voice was the same—a little petulant sounding, low, and strong.

"It don't seem to worry you none, Cap'n Starbuck—this here humiliation to our country."

This surprised me. "Well, I thought it did, because it ought to—but I reckon it don't," I replied.

"Yet wearing that turban hasn't changed ye none, in your heart," he went on, a little anxiously. He knew a good deal about renegades by now.

"I'm getting to Constantinople at least a month sooner than I hoped. Why, the English vessel the Dey intended to use isn't due to put in here till nearly Thanksgiving."

"I reckon it's only human."

"Humiliation isn't going to hurt us any. America's just what she was before. And it's a great piece of luck for me, traveling on an American ship. I wish we could go together."

"'Twould gratify me too, but it's no way possible. I couldn't pass for no kind of infidel, and for a Yankee turncoat to have a Yankee slave would look too fishy. I'll miss out on a heap of novelty and change." His tone had grown wistful but now he spoke with increasing cheer. "Spying for the consulate ain't no sinecure, though, and far from te'jous. I'll fare well till ye came back, and fu'thamore I'll like enough buy me a slave girl to help clean fish and fan me on hot nights."

"Good for you, Nicodemus."

He fell silent and I knew his freckled face was reddening a little and looking solemn.

"War's a-coming some day 'twixt us and them Barbary kings," he went on. "A real war—not just a scuffle like we had with France. Humiliation is one thing, but sinking our ships unless we pay 'em tribute is another. Well, if it breaks out, are ye going to take hand in it?"

"No. I'll not be able to leave what I'm doing. But it brings me to a matter I've been thinking about lately. You can do it or not, at your will."

I could see by the lift of his head in the dimness that the tone I had used, or something, had riveted his attention. He waited.

"Mr. O'Brien has given you a passport. You could sign on any Christian vessel that puts in here, now that the war with France is over, and make your way to the Caribbean."

"That I could—and easy."

"Tell my uncle and his crew what's happening out here—Christian ships being sunk and Americans sold into slavery. They'll want to do something about it on general principle."

"Well, it would be a heap more satisfying, right now, than looting Spaniards."

"Tell my uncle privately what happened to my girl. His crew will have to be told she was drowned in the attack. Tell him I'd like to have him hunt down the Turkic pirate 'Zainab' and sink her without warning."

Nicodemus drew one deep breath. "Aye, aye, sir," he said quietly.

"He needn't pick up any of the people that get off in boats. And he might as well sink any Barbary ship of war he comes on, that he's able. He needn't worry about how many go down. They're all cut from the same cloth. As to Barbary merchantmen, he can sack them and let them go."

"Them Indians what killed your Pa and Ma and the old man," Nicodemus remarked after a thoughtful pause, "they didn't have no chance."

"This is a lot harder. When you start the hunt, write me a letter in care of our consul at Malta, giving me a clue how to find the 'Hope' when I return from Constantinople. I might need her help mighty bad. There'll be some little port on the northern coast where she can revictual safely. If you decide not to make the trip now—"

"Oh, I'm already resolved on it. I thought ye knew it." Then, when I could not speak in wonder of him, he went on in his honest, cheerful way. "We'll be in these waters in a year easy, and maybe six months. Cap'n Todkill'll take to the scheme—I'll guarantee that—

and the lads will be pleased no end. The 'Hope's' so fast them heathen hookers can't catch her. The pickings ought to be mighty fine, the treasures of the Orient, ye might say, and the cause, noble."

"A one-ship war against infidel pirates is a fine thing. You'll be under no nation's flag, so you can run up your own. The old Pennsylvania flag of 'Don't Tread on Me' would be a good one."

"Real fitten, I'd say. Well, I reckon ye'll be going now."

"Yes. We've both got a long journey ahead of us."

"I'll bid ye farewell till we meet again. I'll not be able to counsel ye, while out East, so I ask ye to heed me now."

"Why, I will."

"Don't try to shine too bright. That's your main fault. Ye got too much show-off in ye, to deal plain, and won't let well enough alone."

"You're right about that, Nicodemus."

"Don't carry too much sail, if ye foller me."

"I'll not, and here are my claims to the 'Happy Chance.' Give them back to my uncle to keep for me. If I'm not back in five years, go get her by law or force, and if you can't take her, sink her. She's a Featherstone ship—at least they've got their hooks on her—and I don't want Dick to have her."

"I'll explain that to the other lads, and they'll be glad to do what ye say."

2.

Nicodemus went on his way; and the once-proud "George Washington" laded for her ignominious voyage. The ambassador's suite alone numbered a hundred. The Dey's gifts to the Sultan included one hundred Negro women and children, one hundred and fifty sheep, twenty-five wild-eyed cattle, four horses, regalia and gold worth a million dollars and, to cap the climax, a regular zoo containing four lions, four tigers, four antelope, and a dozen parrots!

"Things have come to a pretty pass," a Boston sailor remarked in my hearing. "I signed on a man-o'-war, not the traveling menagerie of a bloody pirate pasha."

"If that pirate standing there could understand English, he'd have you signed off on the yardarm," his fellow replied.

A more fantastic voyage than ours up the Mediterranean into the Aegean Sea was never made. A muezzin called to prayers from a Yankee masthead; and one of the crew must gesticulate directions, lest the Faithful on their prayer rugs make a mistake and turn their rumps toward Mecca. The lions and tigers roared, keeping the whole ship in a dither lest they break out of their cages. The Moslems cared naught for the growing piles of manure, so the men of the United States Navy shoveled tons of it into the sea—horse, cow, sheep, cat, antelope, and a sprinkling of parrot. Even so, when the vessel passed up wind from Lemnos, the very goats must have swooned. Two hundred Turks and Arabs and one hundred well-oiled blackamoors combined their effluvium with that of a stockyard plus a zoo, seasoned with frankincense and myrrh.

Yet Captain Bainbridge hauled down the Algerian flag from our main and flew her from our fore, and ran up the Stars and Stripes. I suppose he did so to save us attack from the Dey's enemies rather than from national pride.

A sailor I had known on the "Hattie," wild-eyed Caleb Beacher, had prophesied that our nation would some day stretch from sea to sea, one of the greatest and most powerful on the globe. If so—if France or England did not gobble us up—I wondered what our multitudinous posterity would think of this first voyage of an American warship, bearing the name of our first president, through the Mediterranean to the Golden Horn!

We anchored in Constantinople twenty days out from Algiers, and were presently visited by an Ottoman officer. It was inevitable that Captain Bainbridge would ask Mohammet Wadi to supply an interpreter from his suite, and almost inevitable that the Wadi should come to me, the only "renegade" aboard the ship. I did not confess to knowing English, but one of the American officers spoke fluent French. According to all signs neither the Turk or the Americans doubted that I was a well-educated Algerian, speaking both French and Turkic. Sun-browned to the shade of upper-caste Moors, with a passable black beard, I punctuated with a finger in my palm and flaunted my bejeweled scimitar like any son of the Prophet.

After reporting our name and business to the Sultan, the Turk at once returned with word that his master had never heard of our nation and would we identify ourselves a little more explicitly. The French-speaking officer had me explain that his country was on the continent of North America, discovered by Columbus, and that his President—the emperor of a free, sovereign people—desired peace with the Grand Seignior. "And it's true that the *giaour* dogs have sharp teeth and wolf hearts," I added on my own hook. A few hours later the envoy reappeared with a lamb and a bouquet of flowers, tokens of peace from his lord, and invited our ship into the inner harbor.

Every Yankee aboard save me stood bemazed in the beauty and

splendor of the scene. Hardened guttersnipes gaped like farm boys, hardly believing in such a city outside of a fairy tale. Palaces and gardens lined the shore; a thousand fountains played, craft of many-colored sail festooned the harbor. What a miserable, shabby, dirty den was Algiers compared to ancient Byzantium! Here was heaped the pillage and lootings of half Eurasia, and the tribute-treasure of vassal kings from the Adriatic to Afghanistan—from the Gulf of Aden to the River Don.

On a promontory where the busy Bosporus met the shining stream of the Golden Horn, stood the Seraglio, the fabulous seat of the Sultan. The sailors fancied him watching from a window, wondering at the stars in our flag since his own bore a crescent moon, perhaps peering from a cranny in a cloistered garden wall, where frolicked his two thousand concubines and slave girls picked by connoisseurs of beauty from the Adriatic to the China Sea. The hands sprang nimbly to our guns, when Captain Bainbridge ordered a salute to the Sublime Porte. Twenty-one of them thundered their awe of his luck and fortitude.

But I did not join in the cheers, and the blue devils had their way with me. It might be that Roxana was behind those massive, turreted walls—if the Sultan's slave-buying connoisseurs had looked her over, it was a likely chance. I could vision Kemal removing her veil for their knowing eyes. Yes, they were interested—but they must have some notion of her other charms. Then a woman slave had arrayed her in an almost transparent *baracan*—yet protecting the Sultan's honor if the deal went through—and loopholes to her chamber permitted a first survey. If it was satisfactory, an old woman from the Seraglio, knowing well her master's tastes, had given her a thorough inspection. The delicate question would then arise as to whether she was a virgin. That could not be guaranteed—although still in her first bloom, she was of about twenty summers, and the maidens of Frankistan were not guarded like the daughters of Islam. The Sultan knew this and was of unusually broad mind. She was of high birth and station—possessed of many graces—beautiful ladies from Frankistan were no drug on the market in Stamboul.

All that was nothing to me. It did not cause the least crawling of my scalp. In one respect, I could wish her owned by the Sultan before any of his subjects—she would probably receive better protection and care. But one measure of her protection—even from an intruder's admiring glance—was the Sultan's ordinance that if any man by accident or design entered the harem gardens his head be immediately struck off and brought before him. Lord Elgin himself, the Ambassador of the British Crown, would not dream of raising the question of a Yankee girl imprisoned in the Seraglio on such slight evidence as I could present. As for rescuing her by force or stratagem, I could not stomach such an absurdity. Of the countless windows of the palace, I could see only a few hundred; thank God that under none of these hung a flower box.

The ambassador's suite went ashore to be presented at the imperial divan. On the strength of the Dey's firman I demanded and took the second place in the line, attended by my sullen, useless slave Na'od. The parade we made, trooping in our finery, the black slaves carrying chests of gold, jewels, and precious stuffs, reminded me of a scene from *Arabian Nights* read to Pa and Ma and me by old Pierre. Even so, the vast, vaulted room dwarfed us, and the jewels in the Sultan's belt were worth twice our tribute.

Mohammet Wadi quaked and his voice trembled as he made his flowery speech of presentation. He had submitted it to me beforehand, in respect to my speaking better Turkic than he, and it was so typical of Oriental lavishness as to be worthy of chronicle:

"To our Sovereign, the asylum of the world, powerful and great monarch, transactor of all good actions, the best of men, the Shadow of God, director of the good order, king of kings, supreme ruler of the world, emperor of the earth, emulator of Alexander the Great, possessor of great forces, sovereign of the two worlds and of the seas, King of Arabia and Persia, Emperor of Islam, to whom these paltry presents shall come, from his humble and obedient servant, submitted forever to the orders of His Imperial Majesty's noble throne, Mustapha, governor and chief of Algiers—greeting!"

"There is no majesty and no might save in Allah," the business-like sovereign replied. Then permitting the ambassador to kiss his hand, he got shed of us. I too might have been lost in the shuffle, had I not perceived the essential fact behind Stamboul's existence. At first sight, the great city seemed dedicated to luxury. Visiting the khans and markets, seeing the caravans from a hundred vassal cities and watching the countless ships at the quays, a merchant from Bagdad might regard it as a monument to commerce. But behind the palaces and the bazaars, Constantinople stood an armed camp. The Sultan's business was war and his very title meant a military chief.

I did not glance again at the "George Washington" at anchor in the harbor. My anchor was weighed and my sails spread: my first move was to get into Turkic dress and my next to advertise myself as a gentleman drillmaster in marksmanship and rapid fire, as well as a famed nimrod. Mohammet knew nothing of my history save my Christian origin, and to put his best foot forward repeated the boast to the *Reis* Effendi. Since the Sultan was having his usual trouble with the murderous, power-greedy Janissaries—he was building up a rival force, known as the artillery corps, to defend his throne against them— it stood to reason I would not be neglected very long.

The first notice taken of me was in no way flattering—a brief visit from a junior officer of the new artillery corps. But I meant it to lead to great things.

"Selim Effendi, you're quick to take our ways," he told me, looking at my costume after we had both praised Allah.

"When in Rome, Capudan! Anyway my mother was a Turkish lady, and I feel I've come home."

"Why, I'd received the impression that you were born outside the Faith."

"Perhaps I was. I don't remember. If so, all who love me have forgotten."

"I pray your padon. We be brothers in Allah. And patently you learned Turkic on your mother's breast."

"Aye, and sucked the milk of the true Faith."

"The Algerian ambassador declares you a famous marksman, and an experienced drillmaster in the art."

"Doubtless he overpraised me, but I know one end of a rifle from the other."

"Then report at once to Ismael Capudan at the *Spahis* Barracks of the Seraskierat. He admires good shooting."

I did so, Na'od carrying my rifle, powder horn, and pouch. At this great military post, no few European mercenaries taught Occidental warfare to the Sultan's troops, and the competition might be keen. However, I saw no lank American frontiersman or Kentucky rifles. Ismael Capudan, a pleasant-faced youth of twenty, took me to a rifle range where about a dozen soldiers were having desultory practice at ringed paper targets about a hundred paces distant. Ismael beckoned to a big, bearded fellow called Kabul—later I learned that he was an Afghan—and bade him show me what he could do.

Kabul took a prone position by the earthworks, rested his elbow on the ground, aimed carefully and long, and squeezed off the trigger of his Brown Bess type of flintlock musket. Reloading with mechanical stiff motions, never learned on the desert but rather on a drill field—wasting enough time for Indians to rush in between volleys and set a stockade on fire—he fired five rounds in all. When Ismael had the target brought, it showed all five bullets in the black ring of two hand's breadth.

"This is the kind of shooting we do for the Sultan," Ismael told me. "Perhaps you've brought silks to sell in Samarkand."

"Kabul Effendi is an excellent marksman. Is he among the best in the Sultan's forces?"

"He'd be quick to tell you he's a child compared to Omar-id-din, of the Janissaries. But take his position, and show me some good hits."

I could easily duplicate Kabul's feat, from what was for me his awkward position. The run of American soldiers could do as well, and these were counted tyros by the frontiersmen, for all that they had amazed the British regulars in our war for freedom. Like other mountain men I had learned to shoot on my two feet, the full swing of the piece in my arms seeming to put the target magically into my sights, touching off almost without knowing it—the only way to make sure of a deer, a wild turkey, or a redskin glimpsed on the run in thick country. But the prone position was the mainstay of desert warfare, where men must hug the sand or stop a bullet. I did not cavil at it, when another paper target was set up on the backstop, and fired five shots in about half the time Kabul had taken.

"I've never seen quicker aim or handier reloading," Ismael remarked. "But it's where the bullets go that wins battles."

The target was brought to show all five bullets in the bull's-eye, closer grouped than Kabul's.

"By Allah, that's a good showing," Ismael cried. "I'll recommend you for a puny-captain's commission, to teach rapid fire to recruits."

But I must do better than this, or I should be lost sight of in the Moslem horde as a mere instructor or even man-at-arms.

"Will you put up another target, Ismael Capudan?"

"Do you think you can improve on this one? You made a good score—"

"I'll show you the style of shooting of my own tribe."

The target was erected, and I swung my piece and fired.

"You pulled off that time, my friend," remarked a bejewelled officer who had strolled up to watch. "If a French hussar had been bearing down on you with a brandished saber, you'd find yourself in paradise with a houri on your knees."

Three or four other officers who had quickly followed him laughed loudly. They were not laughing at me—I stood only in a corner of their busied minds—or hardly at their chief's jest. Rather they laughed to be heard by him, every one making sure that his tribute would not be missed in the general acclaim. Plainly this was quite an important person. I had heard our own junior officers laugh the same when their colonel cracked a joke at the encampment at Plattsburg.

"Perchance it would not have been my hour," I answered, ramming home the ball for another shot.

"For an Algerian, you speak good Turkic. If your shooting is as fine—but by Allah, you're quick at reloading."

"I've never seen a faster, Hassan Serdar," Ismael remarked complacently.

By now I had primed my pan, and instantly flung up and fired.

"Hold!" cried the Turkic general. "Do you mock us for the sport of it? Granted you're a gentleman, we're not troopers of the rank. Or is it an exhibition of rapid fire into the wind?"

"No, Hassan Serdar. I'm showing the style of shooting I was schooled in."

"Go on with it, for you may kill an afrit, flying unseen in the air, even as the merchant with the date seed."

I fired three more times as rapidly as possible. There was no laughter now; and Hassan Serdar had the target brought for his inspection. No one dared look over his shoulder at it, but all could see the holes not widely spaced in the center of the sheet. I would have been dumfounded not to see them there, since the mark would be relatively easy to ten thousand American riflemen of the frontier. In a pinch, I could have put four shots out of five in a three-inch ring.

"Ismael Capudan, was this a new target?"

"Verily it was, Hassan Serdar."

"Then this is a rifleman second only to Omar-id-din."

"Is he greatly my superior?"

"He's not so quick to load, and shooting at long range not nearly so quick to aim, but had he fired your five shots with careful aim, you could have covered them with a coffee cup. At ten paces he can hit a perched sparrow shooting from the hip."

"Peace be upon him," I said, bowing.

"He's also a great *spahis* [cavalry officer]," the pasha went on thoughtfully. "Can you shoot from a running horse?"

"I can't hit a sparrow at ten paces, but can discharge my piece."

"Such feats are in high esteem among the nomads, and if you would care to try—"

At my bow he called up a trooper on a shaggy pony. The chair-like saddle did not fit me, restricting my movements, but after trying all the beast's gaits. I discovered that his canter was fairly smooth. Riding straight toward the target, I was sure of having placed the ball in the black at thirty yards. In an easier saddle on a very smooth-running horse I could have reloaded with no great waste of powder—my best feat of horsemanship, which Pierre had laboriously taught me and in which I had practiced while shooting with Ali. As it was, I stopped to reload but did not dismount. Then I tried the more difficult shot while riding across the target at twenty yards. This ball missed the bull's-eye, but entered the white ring not far off.

"What is your name, Effendi?" Hassan Serdar asked when I rode back to him and saluted.

"Selim-ul-Reuben, Serdar." My father's name was not rare in Islam, and designated a town in Syria.

"Have you practiced at shooting from a running horse at a running target—say a French hussar?"

"Not at a trooper, Hassan Serdar, but at game on our deserts."

"By Fatima's teats!" After this startling invocation, he became briefly silent. "Well, I'm Serdar of *Spahis* of the artillery corps," he went on, "and will have you commissioned a full captain, in charge of training recruits in rapid fire."

"Allah upon you, Hassan Serdar."

"You're at home on a horse and, with a better beast, you'd be worth a wager in a meet with Omar, but only one dinar against ten."

"My eyes yearn for the sight of this great *spahis*."

"I doubt not they'll get their wish, before you're done," he replied with a rather grim smile. Then he turned on his heel, perhaps to forget me in nine days, but perhaps to make my fortune.

3.

For about a week I accomplished nothing but a first survey of the city. Then a plainly dressed but good-mannered and considerable Ottoman named Bayezid called for me at the barracks, and bade me come with him on orders of the Serdar-i-ikram [commander-in-chief] of artillery. He took me to what seemed a paddock of His Majesty's cavalry. There, grooms led forth from elaborate stone stables five of the finest horses I had ever seen. Two were Arabs, two Barbs, and the fifth a Kazak pony from the steppes. They were slim-legged, trim-headed, high-spirited beasts with liquid, friendly eyes.

"My master wishes to know how well you can judge a horse," Bayezid told me. "Try all of these, and choose the one you would rather ride all day in battle or the chase, never setting your feet on the ground."

"How long may I take to make my choice?"

"Let us say till the sundown prayers tomorrow. If you can't make up your mind by then, you're a hair-splitter of no use to my master."

Before departing he provided me with quarters and a hard-riding groom. By sundown my choice lay between a black Barbary stallion and a piebald Arab mare, the others' gaits too rough for saddle shooting, or their heads not cool enough, or too hard for quick maneuver in a pinch. By noon the next day I had picked the stud as the best war horse, being taller and fiercer, but for hunting deer in forest or antelope on the desert, leaned to the mare. Like the stud, she ran almost as smoothly as ducks fly, and in addition she could cut in and draw alongside the groom's horse more nimbly and, I thought, with a better estimate of the other's distance and gait. Patently both had been superbly trained as hunters in the Arab rather than the English sense of the term—not to follow hounds but to bring their furious riders on to the flank of furiously running game. The maneuver was in harmony with the wild horses' instinct to herd up when excited or frightened, and had come to be second nature. After taking them both on a kind of steeplechase through the roughest country that the groom could show me in these parts, I was still in doubt which to choose, for lack of knowing whether they were to be ridden in sport or war.

A little more thinking and less rushing about brought me to my decision. Such mounts as these would not be furnished mere captains in the Imperial Cavalry. All might be pashas' gifts to the Sultan, and the mare Amine seemed fit to become his favorite hunter. Shooting from the saddle in running battle was a rare practice anyhow and it was my tutorship of Ali in the hunting field that had won me my little fame. Almost certain that I would be given a similar post to some princeling of the court, I chose Amine.

Bayezid seemed pleased with the choice, when he returned to the paddock the following morning. That big game was afoot became crystal clear when he led me into a building—it would be lese majesty to call it a barn—to choose a saddle. Perhaps my eyes would never bung so far again. There were at least twenty here, some with solid gold and the rest with silver stirrups, all marvelously worked, with gold and ivory inlay and green-and-gold saddle clothes; and, to cap the climax, each reposed on the back of an expertly-carved, life-size wooden horse.

"There is no majesty and no might save in Allah," I told Bayezid. "Do these belong to the Sultan?"

"The whole world belongs to the Sultan. But this stable, with its horses and accouterment, being a trifling one among his minor hunting stables, he has given to one of his viziers. And my friend—as has been said since time out of mind—if you'll ask no questions, you'll be told no lies."

After trying half a dozen of the saddles most likely to fit me, I chose the plainest and lightest that glued well to my buttocks, fashioned in Hungary in more the Western style, instead of a sedan chair on a horse. Its peaks were a little too high for my comfort, but I could turn and swing in it with great ease.

"The *Reis* Effendi, being fond of venison, may send you hunting in a few days," Bayezid told me. "You'll need a spare musket, carried by the groom. There's an armory near by where you may choose one."

"I have a spare rifle, Bayezid Effendi."

"It is well. The groom Zimil, who, you see by now, knows one end of a horse from the other, will continue to accompany you, instead of your misbegotten black. Tomorrow you may teach him how to reload your piece swiftly, with the best charge for heavy stags at close range."

Zimil proved a horseman before Allah and the best of fellows. A Macedonian Christian belonging to the *Reis* Effendi, he casually mentioned one day that he was a eunuch. It was hard to believe, in this lean, hard rider; perhaps the mutilation having occurred when he was a grown man—Bayezid told me later that he had cast amorous eyes on a slave girl of a previous owner—it had wounded but not killed his inner manhood. He reminded me more of a plucky gelding than a fat capon.

Daily I drilled him in loading my piece until he was quick and handy. The trick of reloading on a running horse would be beyond him, short of months of practice, so we wasted no time on this. Meanwhile he either did not know, or would not tell, the affair's rhyme or reason.

One morning Amine and Zimil's mount were mysteriously gone from the stables. We idled all that day and the next; on the following morning we received orders to go aboard one of the Emperor's ships, with our rifles and accouterment. Zimil looked wise, but it would be bad Ottoman manners for me to ask why.

The vessel proved a fine sloop of war, although with dismantled guns, and my fellow passengers, junior officers of the Sultan's artillery corps and minor officials of the court. None of these gave me openly more than "Peace be with you" and observations on the weather, although many covert glances and an impression that I was the main subject of their conversation. Truly I felt something of a personage for the here and now, berthed in a cabin finer than the captain's and with a bearer at my beck and call.

We sailed into the westward narrows of the Sea of Marmora, a distance of perhaps sixty miles, and anchored there until daylight. After the dawn prayer, Zimil brought me a *spahis* habit suitable for a minor nabob, explaining it was a gift from the *Reis* Effendi. This I was to put on at once.

Going ashore, we found a hundred head of Kurdistan ponies, hardy, shaggy little beasts, bridled and saddled in charge of nearly as many *sice*. The likeliest-looking of the lot, and certainly the best leathered, was for me. On these we rode into the thickly wooded hills a matter of fifty miles—the tireless nags loping all the way. Then we came to a long earthworks, a good twelve feet high, that appeared to enclose heaven knows how many square miles of ground. We followed it a good league before we came to a great log gate, and from thence it ran on out of sight. When some slaves opened the gate, I saw that the inner side was a sheer, mud-plastered wall unclimbable for man or beast. But there was no sign of a city within—only wooded hills and natural parks and a cluster of distant towers.

We had not gone a furlong when a red deer with a big spread of antlers bounded across the road.

"The hunting ground of the Sultan, peace be upon him, must be alive with game," I remarked to Zimil.

"Among the many game parks of Allah's shadow on earth this one, though smaller than most, is fairly well stocked," Zimil replied. "And the game has been driven by beaters into this area."

About a mile from the gate we came to the box, as a snorting English lord might call his hunting lodge. The main structure, the quarters of the Sultan when perhaps once a year he journeyed here, loomed nobly over the trees, a many-towered palace fine as any on the Golden Horn save the Seraglio itself. Behind it stood guest mansions, equal to the finest manor houses of Carolina, huge stables and kennels and other outbuildings, all enclosed within a high stone wall. Some richly dressed pashas strolled about the gardens, and every mother's son of them gave me a sharp look as our cavalcade swung by.

Quarters in the second-best guest house had been provided for me, and these in the rear instead of overlooking the fish pools and playing fountains. Plainly I was in company that greatly outranked me. But my meal was served on massive silver dishes, and later I joined a dozen high-ranking officers and medium-high court officials in watching a small company of dancing girls perform in the great hall.

"On some other night, one of them could be sent to your chamber, as a gift from the seneschal," Zimil, attending me, whispered over my shoulder.

"Why not tonight?"

"The least of them is such a moon of beauty that the head eunuch would fear lest you not rise for prayers, and might be tired of riding before you mounted Amine."

"Is it tomorrow that we ride?"

"Yea, Selim Capudan—and if kismet smiles, ride well!"

"Are these maidens the equal of those who dance before the Sultan?"

"It is well that only my ears, your slave's, hear effendi's jest."

Early to bed and not given to worry, I slept well. Soon after the morning meal, a *sice* appeared with Amine, beautifully groomed, and there passed a pleasant tingle down my spine as I got her between my knees, my rifle across the pommel. Zimil mounted his fast gelding —the two paired off well, I thought—carrying my extra piece. As we took a bridle path behind a file of richly dressed nabobs, half a dozen or more mounted men, each with a bundle of long canes topped with white pennants, fell in behind us. They all appeared to be grooms or minor gamekeepers, but their captain's apparel indicated a considerable official of the park. He carried a silver trumpet that no doubt served as a hunting horn.

We rode to a natural amphitheater amid the hills, to find a breathtaking assembly. Its central and most radiant figure, a pasha of three horsetails, turned out to be Timor-id-Osman, the Sultan's half-brother. There were at least a dozen pashas of one horsetail, bejeweled and bedizened, with their grooms and attendants, as many generals of the artillery, including Hassan Serdar, some of their Janissary rivals in the company of the very chief of the corps *Yenicheri Agassi,* and a motley crowd of courtiers, minor officials, and *spahis.* By now I would not have been surprised to see the Grand Seignior himself outshining the sun. He did not appear, and I took it that Timor would be his viceroy at this affair. My old friend Bayezid, plainly dressed as ever but as plainly somebody in the Ottoman hierarchy, gave me a sly smile.

He stood back while Hassan Serdar rode to my side.

"Have you the same talisman you wore the day I saw you ride and shoot, Selim Capudan?" he asked.

"Yea, my general." I had no lock of Roxana's hair, only some coarse black tresses stuck together.

"Are you sure its *baraka* has not been dissipated?"

"I think not, Hassan Serdar."

"There is no majesty or might save in Allah, the great, the glorious! But for God's love ride hard and shoot straight, or I'm reduced to a private in the rank if not to food for worms."

"Allah Akbar!"

He withdrew; and waiting for the next development, I began to get faint whiffs of some big brewing. While the artillery officers and court officials gave me friendly or at least hopeful glances, the Janissaries looked at me disdainfully or wrathfully, according to their rank. Long before coming to Constantinople I had learned of the bitter hatred between the two corps. They were not merely rivals for the Sultan's favor: one was his staunch defender and the other his most powerful antagonist. For the past two centuries the lords of the Golden Horn had been so in name only—actually no more than cat's-paws of the Janissaries. Selim III had thrown off their yoke and was trying to modernize the Empire. My best guess was that this was a sort of gymkhana or field day, I representing the artillery to ride and shoot against the champion of the enemy corps. That this champion would be Omar-id-din, I had little doubt.

That best guess proved only half-right, as Bayezid revealed to me a few minutes later.

"The *Reis* Effendi is most hungry for venison," he told me, smiling faintly in his wont.

"I'll try to get him some, if he gives me leave."

"You have leave to shoot for him all you can, between the start of the race and the midday call to prayer. There are many mouths to feed in his court and among the poor, and no bone will go ungnawed, so don't save your powder."

"To hear is to obey."

"Do not dismount to admire your trophy, but change your empty gun for the loaded one, and ride hard to lay low another. The grooms will plant staffs by the fallen, and their captain's trumpet will blow to tally the kill. It must be a great kill, and not only of red deer and fallow. The hides of wolves and bears, if you should meet any, make warm robes for cold nights. Any beast larger than a fawn is fair game."

"Effendi speaks of a race. I take it the other runner will be Omar-id-din."

"You take it wrongly. Omar will be here to watch, and be sure he'll gnash his teeth every time your trumpet sounds, and rejoice whenever your rifle roars in vain. You'll ride against the guest of the Sultan. Omar expected to have the post—by the Beard of the Prophet he was sure of it, since no other in the Empire was his peer—but the *Reis* Effendi dared appoint you."

"Even though I'm worthy of only one dinar against ten in a match with him?"

"You're of the loyal corps, while he's a Janissary. You're the best we could find in our lists. It will be a blow to their pride and prestige, if you make a good showing. But if you make a bad one—you may only be sent in disgrace back to the Dey, but half a dozen of us who recommended you—mainly on the reports of a mere slave, your groom —Allah have mercy upon us."

"Is the guest of the Sultan such an Esau?"

"You can't hope to beat him and anyway it would be inhospitable. Even Omar's swift hand and deadly eye would be sorely tried. But if you take a bag half as heavy as your opponent's, the *Reis* Effendi will be content."

Just then all eyes turned to a new arrival. Plainly he was not my adversary—he carried no rifle or powder horn and his rich garb did not fit him for riding through brier and bush—but certainly a pasha of importance. Tall as I and hardly older, he rode with extraordinary grace. A swarthy black-bearded man on a tar-black stallion, he loomed a somber figure save for his jeweled raiment, small jewel-bright eyes, and his big teeth like misshapen pearls. I did not doubt the identity of this *haut,* dangerous Janissary.

"Speak of an afrit, and you hear the whip of his pinions," Bayezid murmured.

Some of the wardens and slaves attached to the park stared hard at his groom. Well they might, for if his intimates in Constantinople were accustomed to the sight, it shocked devout country people. Instead of a typical bearded *sice,* his attendant was a young, fair-haired, unveiled slave girl. I instantly identified her as a Circassian out of the Caucasian Mountains, and of course some manner of Christian. Even so, it took a bold bashaw to display her in public dressed in groom's attire and with bared face.

"The lady rides well in my opinion," I remarked to Bayezid.

"Better than does Omar in her opinion," he answered with Oriental love of bawdry. "Anyway she told him she would rather be his groom than his filly—and he took her at her word."

The incident had been the passing sensation and scandal of Constantinople two months before, Bayezid told me. Bets had been placed as to how long she would undergo the humiliation—many of them already paid. I caught myself rejoicing that she still rode behind him with such savage grace and pride. Yet God knew I would not want my Christian maid to defy her master—not only the studied judgment of my mind but my true heart's desire, it seemed, prevailing over base, jealous instinct.

As every Christian slave girl stirred thoughts of Roxana, so did every brutal owner. Omar was that sort, and was already inimical to my fate. His very flaunting of his defeat to all the sybaritic city displayed his arrogance, vindictiveness, and power. Discerning from my weapons that I was his supplanter in the day's race, he looked me up and down, then brought his charger across my fore, blocking my path. This itself was a deliberate affront. When as the lower in rank I saluted him—he appeared a colonel of *Spahis*—his gesture in reply was more an insult than a salute. Your Turk can be subtle when he tries. In expressing contempt for underlings, he does not try.

"So this is the great Bairam." He spoke loudly enough for many of the company to hear him.

I did not know then that this name was synonymous with nimrod. "I'm Selim Capudan, at your command."

"I'm sure the *Reis* Effendi chose well, when he appointed you to the race, instead of me. I'm Omar-id-din."

"Truly he did, Omar Pasha. He knew you'd not only lay barren the Sultan's park, but shame his guest with your great slaughterings. Why, your fame is so great that he could not sit in saddle."

"Your opponent rides without a saddle, even as my groom. You did not know that, Selim Capudan? You must be a stranger in these parts."

"I'm new to Stamboul, surely."

"Could it be that I smell a Christian?" He sniffed, his bold nostrils flaring.

"It's a wonder to me, Omar, that you can smell anything, the same mercy Allah has on a polecat."

The vituperation was not excessive, according to Algerian standards. The only remarkable thing about it was that it passed from a mere captain to a colonel. But even if he were a pasha as he was commonly addressed—perhaps he had once been a military governor, for he displayed no horsetail—today I was the envoy of the Sultan. That meant I could reply to him, as Shakespeare put it, from a full-flowing stomach. Indeed I was done for if I did not, in the hearing of my chiefs; and I gloried in it.

"That will be seen to in due course," he remarked, smoothing his beard. "Yea, I'm persuaded that you mock your turban, and are of the same faith as my groom." He spat on the ground.

"At least your groom is of good wit, and doesn't mistake a fellah's donkey for a king's charger." This expression was commonly used to denote a knowledge of horses.

"A dog, a hog, and a Christian sat at meat together," Omar replied with another proverb, "but the dog sickened, and Allah sent the hog to Eblis for shaming his tribe." That won a loud laugh from the other Janissaries.

"That Christian yonder will never sit with a hog—or lie in his sty. Moon of beauty, have I spoken truth?"

"Why, I would rather lie with even you," she answered instantly with a twisted mouth, without even a glance in my direction.

Omar-id-din clapped hand to the hilt of his scimitar. He quickly raised it, for any warlike gesture toward me would count as lese majesty while I was on the immediate business of the Sultan. None the less I had made a serious mistake. If not against the law, it was at least a shocking breach of propriety for me to address one of his female slaves without his consent. That he had employed her in the low office of groom ameliorated the offense somewhat in just men's thinking, and he could ignore it without loss of face. However, there was nothing to stop him from making an issue of it if it prospered his interests or if his savage heart desired.

There was no laughter now, and Bayezid looked shaken. I was careful not to glance again at the Circassian girl, but her image lingered awhile on my inner eyes, wonderfully vivid, her shadow long and sharp across my fate. Her strange, wild appearance denoted a strange, wild nature. By the same token Omar desired her mightily unless I missed my guess. He would be far less likely to overlook my offense, especially since she had made such a stinging reply.

Luckily our audience suddenly forgot us. Into the amphitheater rode my opponent of the day's race.

I had expected a mighty emir of some sort, entering with all the pomp of power. Instead there came an old, little, skinny man in a coarse woolen robe and jodhpur-type breeches on a shaggy pony, followed by about a dozen savages clad in sheepskins. His saddle was a padded cloth fastened by a cinch, and with plain, steel stirrups. He wore only one ornament in his white turban—a blood-red stone that blazed up in the winter sunlight. But his bony, yellow face with its slanted eyes and thin, long, down-curved, grizzled mustache and the scantiest wisp of beard marked him as a mogul. Next to the Sultan he might well be the mightiest I had yet seen.

Timor-id-Osman, half-brother of the Emperor, greeted the new-comer with a deep salaam.

"Greeting and good fortune, from the Sublime Porte to his illus-trious friend and most honored royal guest—my lord the Cham of Tartary."

4.

My head swam, yet soon was able to grasp the essential situation. The old Cham loved hunting, was still a mighty hunter, and greatly proud of his prowess in a luxuriant age. This he wished to display to the princes and pashas of Osmanli, in competition with some other famed nimrod of officer rank; and he would have been insulted to run against a tyro, no matter how noble. Doubtless a subject emir, he was yet greatly powerful, perhaps a lineal descendant of Tamerlane, and surely entitled to the best entertainment the Sultan could afford him. Bold indeed showed the *Reis* Effendi in choosing me for his royal guest's competitor, so that the Janissary corps would lose face.

I hauled up Amine on her hind legs and saluted the Cham. He continued to peer like an old eagle over the woodland, and his only reply was a slight lifting of his bridle hand.

"Have I the Presence's leave to speak?" I asked.

He nodded gravely.

"I am Selim-ul-Reuben, Captain of *Spahis* of artillery, and have the honor of hunting with Your Majesty today, and beg your royal indulgence of my little skill."

When his trumpeter had translated this into the Tartar tongue, a faint shadow of what I thought was disappointment flicked across his still countenance. No doubt he had hoped to ride against the famed Omar-id-din. Now I would give him a good race if I broke my neck.

"What if I ride Amine to death?" I asked Bayezid.

"Better that, than return with a paltry bag," the stout fellow an-swered. "If she falls under you, take Zimil's horse, while he rides the best of the staff-bearers."

The Cham gestured to the leader of his followers. The latter blew a shrill note on an ivory horn with a flaring silver mouth. At once he made a guttural sound to his pony and touched him with his heel. The beast bounded forward as though struck deep with a spur.

Amine and I were not far behind, with Zimil's gelding thundering at her heels. The captain of my staff-bearers blew a hoarser blast and followed with his band at a slower pace. We had not gone a furlong when we flushed our first stag, too far for a sure shot. Trying to cut off the quarry, I rode Amine fast as she could fly, but not fast enough to score against my adversary. About two hundred paces on our flank, he instantly surmised the path of the stag's flight and rode like a demon for a shot at him at close range. I saw the swing of his piece and heard its full-throated roar. An instant later his huntsman blew a shrill of triumph with his hunting horn.

Here was a Tartar worthy of the name. The glimpses that I caught of him through the trees showed him taking the most desperate chances, bursting through thickets, leaping brooks and huge fallen logs, holding his rifle by the breach in his right hand, mastering his pony with the lightest touch of his left. Yet my need of giving him a close race was greater than Bayezid had warned me. It was not enough to take a bag half as heavy. That might suit the *Reis* Effendi, but it would gladden the fierce eyes of Omar-id-din. I knew only one way to keep out of a rifle duel with that deadly marksman, and that was to prove so near his peer as to give him pause.

I heard the Cham's rifle roar again—and again the sound of his horn. But it was my turn now. A young roe cantered through the woods half a cable's length distant. As Amine cut in on his flank, I was appalled to hear my opponent fire his third shot. It would stampede my quarry, I thought, and even that disappointment would not sting like his trumpet's shriek which seemed to hover on the tongue of the forest. It did not come. There rose no sound but the beating of horses' hooves and the crackle of thickets of the now hard-running deer. So the Cham had missed and was only human after all! With that piece of luck, the roe changed his course to a little nearer mine.

Putting spur to Amine, I drew within thirty paces of the young stag before he discovered me. Then we ran almost abreast for a brief but long enough time for me to swing my piece; and so nearly equal were our speeds, it was almost like a standing shot at a standing target. Hard on the gun's roar burst the triumphant blast of my horn.

"How do you like the sound of that, you black-bearded bastard?" I heard myself exult in good American. For he was my real adversary in the race—the kills he could have made when I missed, the greatest threat to my cause.

Before long I flushed a gray wolf, larger than any I had seen in the Adirondacks, that ran off into heavy cover out of my reach. I ached for him to pass wide of the Cham's gun, only to hear its roar resound through the woods. Its echoes died away. Maybe he had missed again. Then my rush of exultation died in one fall, for shrill blared his trumpet, blasting my ears. Probably the hard-living beast had run a distance, heart shot, before he dropped.

In contrast to such noble game, I came on a hind—a pretty, graceful thing, standing in a glade. She was looking off, her ears erect, one foot lifted nervously, and I did not give her a race for her life, but pulled up Amine even as my piece swung up, and potshot her. Instantly, I snatched the extra gun from Zimil's hand, tossed him mine, and rode on. It seemed likely that something alive had so engrossed the doe's attention that she had not heard my approach— possibly her playmate or her lover. It was neither of these that broke from the covert, but a brown bear.

He loomed larger than any bear I had ever seen—higher in the shoulders and no doubt of a different species. As I overtook the brute for a close, sure shot, he turned to fight. It took a wrench of my will to loose at him with only one loaded piece, and the brave beast, mortally wounded, still plunged toward me with a furious, rumbling roar. I kept out of his way until his warrior spirit was overwhelmed. Meanwhile the Cham had scored again.

Now my bag stood one head under his. Before long a standing shot at a browsing fallow deer two hundred paces distant gave me a chance to even the score. Amine shifted her feet a little, but this could not have disturbed my aim had I swung and sighted fiercely enough. The miss vexed me all the more when, a few minutes later, a long vista of an open park showed the Cham roll over a wild boar at nearly half that distance, both the beast and the pony running full-tilt—quite possibly the finest shot I had ever seen made. The sow flushed a moment afterward, almost ran under his pony's feet, and when he had fired at her and missed, seemed determined to run under mine. I missed her at twenty feet, then snatched the empty gun, chased her squealing through the woods, and finished her.

So again I hauled within one of my competitor. We both missed a shot at the same running stag, then I rode in pursuit of an animal glimpsed briefly in some tall grass. It had looked to me like a leopard and could well be so, either native to the country or planted here from the Sultan's wilder domains. The beast eluded me, and I wasted time beating through the thickets. What seemed a likely stretch of ground, a wide valley with scattered groves, turned out a "hungry hollow" as our large-speaking Westerners would say, affording but one long shot that did not win. Meanwhile the Cham's guns roared five times in hardly half an hour, and thrice his hunting horn raised its triumphant peal.

I stood four down now—a lead I could hardly hope to cut, if it did not increase. The sun climbed high, perhaps within an hour of zenith. Yet I took time to climb a steep hill to a wooded spur—a woeful waste of my numbered minutes if the venture failed—spurred by no more than a memory from old days in the Adirondacks.

This was the kind of place Pierre would have bade me scour, a natural retreat for animals at midday, especially when frightened by gunfire. The risk paid off with two noble red-deer stags, one of them a giant, both brought to bag within the same minute; and I could have had two does besides, if the guns had been loaded. Topping the hill I shot a lean wolf that ran out of a rock pile, and it must have been that the roar of my piece drowned out the distant, simultaneous report of the Cham's, for a few seconds later we heard, thin in the distance, his trumpet sound.

But his lead had been cut to two, and then there stole upon us the most thrilling episode of the chase. Zimil saw the leaves tremble in a rank thicket, so I burst into it full-tilt, hoping for a close, sure shot at a laired stag. But Amine suddenly whirled, snorting. And then sprang into the open not a stag, not a wolf or a bear, but surely the most beautiful and dangerous beast I had ever seen in the woods. A leopard is both beautiful and deadly, but this sultan of the wild would make three of the spotted cats. He was likewise gaudy in gold and black, but with stripes instead of rosettes. Bayezid had not warned me that among the royal game I might encounter a royal tiger.

Big as the biggest tiger the Dey of Algiers had sent the Sultan on the "George Washington," he could well be the same beast, freed of his cage to play havoc among the deer of the park, and give sport to the Cham. His great yellow eyes looked into mine and instantly blazed with fury—his red mouth opened showing his big fangs. Amine started to rear as I dropped my reins and shot quick for my dear life—the rifle ramming out and blazing.

My frantic bullet missed his huge, flat head at ten paces, striking him in the breast. It did not knock him down, but as he rushed forth I think his aim was to fly more than fight, since he did not veer from his course. Amine had veered from it as she had never run from a stud, scooting as never did Eclipse to win the King's Plate. She needed no encouragement from me.

The beast took cover in a thicket half a cable's length away. I waited until Zimil had loaded the empty gun, his hands quick and steady, and then advanced cautiously down wind so my mare would not catch the rank scent. Even so I had to rowel her with my spurs to make her advance. But if she thought she had a cruel master, so had I. I was being whipped with a stinging lash of will that somehow had no mercy on my fears. Suddenly these became real terrors, as the raging tiger began to roar.

It was a crashing, resounding, almost continuous thunder, stunning amid the silence of the forest. It could be heard a mile. The staff-bearers, stopped by my last kill, listened, looking into one another's eyes. Now the foe had compelled the battle to go on. There was no good of my cold ache to leave the field. I did not notice when it was drowned in a great surge of excitement and passion to win.

"Zimil, draw off about a hundred yards, but if I ride toward you, stand till you can hand me the gun."

"Nay, I'll stay at your heels."

"You'll have no defense if I fail to stop him. Then pick up a stone and be ready to throw it into the thicket."

It was a trick I had employed a hundred times to flush deer and turkey. Zimil sprang down nimbly, seized a stone as big as his fist, and regained his seat. One glance at our path of retreat showed the Cham racing toward me across open ground about three furlongs distant, his wild Tartars behind him. He had heard the tiger's roars and craved to put him in his bag. That fierce old man would ride into his jaws, rather than miss such hunting!

"Throw the stone."

Its crash in the thicket tripped the trigger of the beast's nerves. Jet-black and bright gold in the winter sunlight, he cleared the thickets in one bound and opened his charge. It was a magnificent attack, his head down, mouth open and roaring, tail stiff as a broomstick. But my rifle leaped and leveled at the first glimpse of his gaudy pelt, and I touched trigger before my horse could wheel.

Still the beast came on in great bounds. I could not possibly snatch the gun that Zimil tried to hold out to me in time to send home another bullet. Since I had dropped my reins over the pommel in order to shoot, my life went into Amine's keeping. She had her head now, and on how good it was, and on how fast her slim legs, hung both our fates.

She did not take time for a full turn before she got her feet under her to fly. She was wheeling and darting at the same climactic instant. Even so, the beast would have been on our backs save for his crippling wounds. His bounds became shorter, with a longer interval between them. He ceased to gain on us, and then to keep pace with us. I took the rifle Zimil handed me, guided Amine in a long turn, dropped the reins, and gave the now faltering tiger the *coup de grâce*.

He had hardly hit the ground when the Cham, half a cable's length away and riding fast, put his panting pony on another course. As he turned to re-enter the woods he raised his hand

The call to prayers would sound in a few minutes more. Amine and Zimil's gelding seemed both about to drop, and I thought to take two of the staff-bearers' horses for the remnant of the race. In the end I did not, perhaps because I threatened to fall off my mare's back, and took it that we might as well reel home together. If I were in her shoes, I would like to finish what I had begun—for my head was swimming from fatigue as from fig brandy. Not for any sensible reason, only from my pride in Amine and her well-earned pride in herself, I stuck to her.

I was now only one trophy down on the Cham of Tartary. Sick at the thought of killing any more deer, I rode hard as before to the broken rock where I had flushed the gaunt wolf, thinking that her mate might be thereabouts, sniffing at her spilled blood. If so I might preserve more deer than the Cham and I had slain, our kill atoned for before another spring. Up flushed a huge wolf, gray and savage, the slayer of a hundred fawns and scores of hinds and horned stags, and when I cut off his flight he turned snarling to give battle. I checked my horse as I had once checked Minx when an Indian rushed me with a raised tomahawk; then what had been a running target became a flying one—leaping clear of the round to tear out Amine's throat. My faster-leaping bullet shattered him to earth.

Neck to neck with my opponent now, suddenly I beheld the dazzling vista of victory. He had started a stag that came bounding up hill toward me. I caught glimpses of him between the trees, his horns, it seemed, tall like the trees, a stag to feast the multitude, descended from one that had led parched Mohamet to the desert well! Trying to cut off his flight, wildly rode the Cham with his mad Tartars behind him. Out of my head, all mercy dead, careless how much innocent blood I shed, wildly rode I—a Turk, almost a dervish, caught up in some ecstatic rhythm of beating hooves and slaughter.

I took a more cunning path than my foe. I knew that the quarry would labor up the steep of the hill, striving to gain the thickets there, instead of following its easy-sloping shoulder. And no matter how fast he or my horse ran, or whether the range was short or long, within human limitations I would not miss. It seemed I had run amuck and could not miss, for there was no God but Allah, and Mohamet was His Prophet!

The stag plunged up the steep as I had known he would. I sped my maddened mare down the abrupt slope and turned her loose. The stag saw me, checked, and tried to wheel as my butt plate hit my shoulder.

But as he dropped into my sights, I swung the barrel past him and pulled off.

The sudden mysterious wrench of my will to miss when my whole being was centered on the death stroke left me blind and faint. I could not yet lift a hand to check Amine's headlong runaway down hill and kept my seat only as a sleepwalker might traverse a parapet, from deeply-ingrained balance. But as the stag fled from me in mighty bounds into the death trap below, it came to me that I had had a narrow escape from disaster. As far as reason went, I had only a remark of Bayezid's to go on—"Even if you could win, it would be inhospitable."

The Cham's rifle leveled and blazed. The stag pitched down, turned a somerset, and lay still. And before his trumpet could sound, the Lord of Tartary raised a great cry.

"*Allah Akbar!*"

He had turned his horse to seek other quarry when a noonday gun roared from the palace battlements. On the highest tower, a muezzin called to prayers. I hit the ground with my face toward Mecca.

5.

Perhaps the old Cham and his shaggy pony were tired too. They ambled to the starting post barely in the van of Amine and me. Without a glance at the waiting nabobs, he stopped his horse and again like an eagle, though well-fed now, gazed out over the hills.

"My lord, did you have good sport?" asked Timor-id-Osman, the Sultan's half-brother.

The Cham made some guttural sounds to his bugler. The latter replied in the same tongue. They spoke gravely together, as though far from anyone.

"His Majesty the Cham of Tartary bids me tell you that the sport was fair."

"It would rejoice this company to know the measure of his bag."

"Ten head in all—five stags, two wolves, a bear, one boar, and a leopard."

"There's no majesty or no might save in Allah. He blessed your arms, my lord of Tartary, and we, your servants, rejoice."

When this was translated, the Cham raised his hand slightly.

"Selim Effendi, this company of lords and gentlemen will take pleasure in hearing that you too have done well."

"Not as well as my lord of Tartary," I answered. "But I'm satisfied and honored to have ridden with such a hunter, verily the son of Bairam, peace be upon him." For the name had stuck in my memory, and now I appeared to remember it from *Arabian Nights*.

This was translated by the trumpeter to the Cham. I could see no trace of writing on the ancient yellow parchment of his countenance. Anyway he had no doubt counted the blasts of my horn and knew he had beaten me. But there was good and easy reading on the face of Timor-id-Osman. Its look of strain and the tension of his body instantly passed away and I could almost hear him sigh with relief. No doubt he too had listened for our peals, but had not been sure of the sum. Now he leaned forward in his saddle, flushed as with triumph.

"Will you tell my lords your score, Selim-ul-Reuben?"

"At your pleasure, my lord. Four deer, one of them a hind, a bear, a sow, two wolves, and a tiger—nine head in all."

"Allah has blessed your arms, to have done so well against so great a hunter." His voice rang.

To the amazement of us all, the Cham of Tartary spoke without being addressed, guttural sounds that only his mad followers understood.

"My lord Timor-id-Osman, my master the great Cham declares that if by the will of Allah he and his honorable adversary should again come hither, it is his wish that they may again hunt together," his trumpeter told us.

At that I yanked Amine on to her hind legs and saluted my royal victor. He replied with a slight lifting of his hand, then wheeled his pony and cantered away toward the palace, his nomads behind him.

"The meet is over," Timor-id-Osman declared, when the sound of the Cham's cavalcade had died away. "Be there peace between us, my lords and gentlemen—and farewell."

"There be peace between us, Timor-id-Osman," all of us replied.

He too rode off with his train. The next highest in rank stood the Agazzi of the Janissaries, but he did not at once take his leave. Plainly there was some unfinished business here, which he wished to see transacted. It concerned one of his high-ranking officers.

Until now I had not even glanced at Omar-id-din. Out of the side of my eyes I had seen him lolling in the saddle, occasionally spitting in the way of even lordly Turks, stroking his black beard. Now I could not ignore him any longer. While the company stood still, even the horses seeming statuesque, he rode slowly to my fore.

"It has come to me that I've underestimated Christians hitherto this day," he remarked in a lazy voice. "My Christian has proven an excellent groom—and lo, you've killed within one head of the Cham of Tartary."

"There's no majesty or might save in Allah," I replied.

"My lord has even expressed the wish to hunt with you again, Selim-ul-Reuben. But only if 'tis the will of Allah, in whom all might and glory repose."

"Do you think, Omar Pasha, that I may never meet him again?" For in the hearing of these lords—in my own too, it seemed in that proud moment—I was forced to meet him halfway.

"Who knows what kismet holds in store? The Cham may fall from his horse and break his neck, God forbid, before he gains the palace. But mark you, he didn't command you to meet him. You're no longer in the personal service of the Sultan, Allah upon him. No one is bound to sacrifice his own honor or to fight his own kismet that you may ride with royal Tartary again."

Very little doubt remained as to what he was getting at. I had figured wrong on Omar-id-din. My good shooting had not scared him out, only made the issue between us unsettleable save by combat. If I had made a poor showing in his fellows' sight he might have held his nose, spat, and ridden out of my fate. Now the prestige of his corps and his own fierce Moslem pride had taken a fall. Perhaps too he knew himself for a far greater marksman than the Cham or than his fame declared him. It might be vain conceit, but I was not sure. Anyway he was a Son of the Faithful, fearless as his kind, living by and for battle, and in passionate love with it.

"I agree with you heartily, Omar Pasha," I said.

"Before the race you chose, in spite of your lower rank, to bandy words with me. That might be excused by the conceit born of the honor paid you by the Sultan. But no conceit will excuse your casting your eye on my female slave."

"Why, from her attire and unveiled face I took it, Omar-id-din, any pariah dog in the street may cast his eye on her."

As I spoke, my now-restless mare turned more abreast his huge black stallion, and moved a little nearer. I did not think he saw the slight tightening of my rein that accomplished it. He would be expecting me to edge off, rather than closer.

"You've presumed to a higher station than a pariah dog's," he told me slowly, showing his big, gleaming teeth through his black beard. "Otherwise my slaves would give you the bastinado and let you go. As it is—"

With a quick flip of his wrist he struck me across the face with his riding whip.

It was a light blow, and by Ottoman chivalry I should call Allah to witness the insult, then ask one of my friends to deliver to him through one of his friends my challenge to a duel. But the challenger to deadly combat is not only at a moral disadvantage. What counted far more with me was the right of his opponent to choose the weapons and stipulate in some cases certain rules of the engagement. That loss would be one I couldn't afford. My dizzy head had cleared wonderfully during the talk with my enemy—it had worked as hard as ever in my days—and I was not unprepared for the blow.

My rifle lay across my pommel, the reins lightly hanging in my left hand. It was the hand nearest him, and my arm had been poised at my side for some time now. I could not use all its power from this position, but the leather had hardly hit my mare's neck before my fist swung sideways like a hammer, catching him on the side of the head and almost knocking him out of the saddle. Surely he would have toppled were he not a horseman before Allah. As it was, the lurch of his body from the blow threw his horse off balance and caused him to wheel away from me. Rallying with terrifying power and swiftness, Omar regained his seat, tightened his rein to control the stallion, and started to draw his scimitar.

"Put down your steel, Omar-id-din!" roared a great voice. It was *Yenicheri Agazzi's*. "The captain is unarmed!"

But he was wrong about that. I had exchanged my empty piece for Pierre's loaded one before Zimil and I left the field. I would have had its muzzle on Omar's breast before he could deliver his stroke—shoot him off his horse and be shed of him. But he controlled his fury well. Maybe my hands dropping to my stock had made him think twice. They had gone there too soon—maybe the little and last mistake that many a soldier makes.

Omar resheathed his scimitar with a hissing sound. "Your pardon, Agazzi," he said quietly, his eyes gleaming. "I'm not used to having swine's flesh touch mine, and became heated."

"The Koran bids us beware of the fires of rage," his chief answered, "but, by Allah, you were mightily provoked."

"Perhaps Selim-ul-Reuben isn't used to horse leather touching his flesh," remarked Hassan Serdar.

"Next time it will be a donkey whip, unless he gives me satisfaction," Omar went on. "Agazzi, will you honor me by delivering to the one appointed by Selim-ul-Reuben my sworn word that despite his turban he's a dog of a Christian, the son of a pariah bitch by a Barbary ape, nurtured on swine flesh, and a worshipper of Eblis, and unless he's a coward as well, to be flayed by my kurbash and flung into a cesspool, I'll prove the charge upon him in single combat to the death?"

"How many hours may he have to reply, Omar-id-din?" the Agazzi asked.

"If he is one tittle more than I've declared him, he'll answer here and now. But he may take refreshment before we meet in battle, for the Koran bids us have mercy on the weak and weary, even if they're but curs."

"Hassan Serdar, will you deliver my answer to my lord the Agazzi?" I asked.

"Yea, verily," Hassan Serdar answered in classical Osmanli.

"I call Allah to witness that Omar-id-din is a liar black as Eblis, a spotted traitor to my lord the Sultan, that his mother was a whore and his father a donkey-driver without a nose, and this I'll prove on pawn of my life, after sunrise tomorrow."

It had not occurred to me to set a later date, affording time for us to return to Constantinople and the possibility of the *Reis* Effendi stopping the fight. If I failed to meet him on any excuse my prestige would be lost and my quest all but hopeless. If he killed me in the duel, that quest had ended, but while alive I had to live, that mysterious compulsion to something more than breath. Pride was a weak word for it. Legions of men had been driven by it into peril; they could not help themselves. It was not a case now of carrying too much sail, against which Nicodemus had warned me; I was sure of his support and of old Pierre's.

In Aleppo once
When a malignant and turban'd Turk
Beat a Venetian . . .
I seized by the throat the circumcized dog,
And smote him thus!

"It's your right to choose the weapons," Hassan Serdar told me gravely.

"Rifles, one each, shot freehand at four hundred pics."

"Why not throw pillows at fifty paces?" one of the Janissaries asked.

"Omar-id-din is a most famous marksman," Hassan Serdar answered quickly. "My principal, in honor and chivalry pleasing unto Allah, gives him a chance to employ his prowess in the duel. Obviously they'll continue firing until one or both are satisfied."

But my honor and chivalry in the matter were instantly transparent to all. Truly I would have set a range longer than four hundred pics —just under three hundred yards—if it would not have sounded too chickenhearted. Presumably we would fire our first rounds at a signal. If the mark was so difficult that both of us missed, my faster reloading would stand me in good stead.

"The blows were passed from horseback," said Omar's second. "They should be avenged the same."

"Why, if one gentleman surprises another in his wife's bed, must the duel be fought there?" my second replied.

"It's our custom for *spahis* to settle their affairs of honor astride their steeds, in the knightly tradition."

Even some of my party nodded approval of this. After all, I was only a captain of horse, of new and not great fame, and with no great likelihood in their opinion of being alive at this hour tomorrow. They did not care to offend the Agazzi by taking too solid sides with me. Tomorrow he might have the Sublime Porte murdered and put a new Sultan on the throne.

"We'll bow to Selim Effendi's choice of rifles instead of scimitars, although it's a new thing," the chief went on, encouraged by the acclaim of his last proposal. "We take it that he's not skilled in the use of the ancient arm of Islam. But the range is far too long. The opponents may take their posts at that distance, and at the signal, be free to shoot, then if one wishes to risk holding his fire while he advances upon the other, he may do so. If both fire without obtaining satisfaction, truce is to be declared while they return to the starting posts to reload."

"By Allah, I'll never agree to that," cried Hassan Serdar. "Swift reloading is a feat of arms, the pride of every *spahis*, part of the game of war. The field shall be not four hundred pics, but a thousand. The contestants may ride and shoot at will within that field, but if they miss their shots, they must reload the best they can. And that will give a show worth seeing!"

"You've spoken wisely, Hassan Serdar," burst out a one-tailed pasha who until now had straddled the fence.

"It is meet, it is meet," others murmured.

"Omar-id-din, do those rules of the joust suit you?" the Agazzi asked.

"Any rules my lords agree on, will suit me well," the arrogant Janissary replied.

"Selim-ul-Reuben, do you agree?" my second asked.

"Yes, my general."

"Then if there's nothing more to be decided but the issue of battle—"

There was something, though. It rose, it seemed, out of the deep gulf of loneliness in which I was going down. Around me ranged bejeweled pashas with proud black beards. Of my advocates, only Zimil, Bayezid, and perhaps Hassan Serdar cared whether I lived or died save to prosper their designs. But of the witnesses there was one whose prayers might follow me tomorow—not for any care of me but for hate of my foe. She sat still on her horse, gazing into the distance and apparently oblivious to our quarrel, but I thought she was my ardent ally. Then since I must fight him anyhow, against odds which every man here considered heavy, why not bid for more than my naked life?

"In olden days, when two soldiers met in single combat, the winner could claim the loser's armor," I said, my voice trembling, the best I could do.

"Even so, Selim-ul-Reuben," Hassan Serdar answered.

"We wear no armor these latter days, but we have rifles and accouterment to put in pawn."

"The point's well taken, Capudan."

"My opponent owns a noble horse. I'm sorry I've not one to wager against him."

"I'll give you for your own one of my horses, the best in my stable, if Omar-id-din will pawn Rustum."

"Selim is mistaken, Hassan Serdar," Bayezid said quickly without his usual faint smile. "The *Reis* Effendi has presented Amine to him as a prize for his good hunting, and he has no need to accept your generous offer."

"Peace be unto him, for his charity, and Allah upon you both," I said. "In that case, I'll pledge Amine against Rustum on the fortunes of battle, if my opponent agrees."

"By Allah, I'll pledge the Christian head for head, to be stuck on a lance, or any other prize without counting the cost." Thus kismet, in whom I did not always believe, gave me a smile.

"He has spoken, Hassan Serdar. With a good horse, goes a good groom. I've a black slave of a groom—Zimil was only lent me by the *Reis* Effendi—and I'll pledge him against the white slave that is Omar's groom."

A long silence fell. Black Turkic eyes gleamed everywhere about me. I did not glance at the Circassian girl, but knew that she did not turn her head, and that her face remained still.

"It is meet," cried a horsetailed pasha. "The white slave doubtless cost the more—but Omar doesn't count costs—and since we've heard so much of her in this affair, it's meet that she be a prize of battle."

"Yea, it is meet," said half a dozen voices. All but the Circassian girl looked at Omar.

"Allah be praised," he said, with a strange light in his eyes and sweat on his pale face. "If kismet frowns and I fall in tomorrow's fray, I freely bestow the white slave on my victor. For then—even in death —I'll be avenged."

CHAPTER ELEVEN

The Prize Fight

I.

That night I was quite a fellow in the Sultan's guest house. The pashas appeared pleased with me, for representing the artillery corps so well on the hunting ground, and for affording them the prospect of a good show tomorrow. My jests won almost as loud laughter as Hassan Serdar's. Horsetailed bashaws repeated in great joy some of my retorts to Omar, being especially taken with the description of his father as a donkey-driver without a nose—an insult current in Algerian invective but new to Byzantium. I had shown the true Moslem spirit in defense of my honor! Have another cup of fig syrup! On this concoction, supposedly permitted by the Koran, I could have got as drunk as on white corn whiskey. My fellows became flushed, glistening eyed, and loud, but I fought shy of the sickly-sweet beverage, lest it dull my eyes tomorrow.

Arguing hotly over matters not my concern, they forgot me soon after supper, and hardly noticed my departure to my chambers. Greatly wearied, I went swiftly to sleep, only to waken three hours after midnight—too soon to get up without a heavy head, almost too late to return to my dreams.

Omar could kill a sparrow from the hip at ten paces. He was probably a trick shot, and I a silly rabbit at his hands. The slave girl might be sorry to see me topple from my horse, but that night she would yield to her unconquerable master. . . . But it was not in me to worry very long—a matter of native optimism. I got to thinking of the fame and influence to be won tomorrow if Omar, not I, bit the dust. There was also a bejeweled rifle, a black Karadagh stallion of great price, and—an exciting thought—a beautiful Circassian slave of unbroken spirit. Roxana need never know about her; she might not understand. I would have sold her by then to some trustworthy Turkic friend and the matter would be a closed book. But it would furnish good reading for the here and now.

A little tingle started down my spine.

The next I knew Zimil was softly repeating my name, gently to summon back my soul from its far wanderings, for if he wakened me too suddenly it might be lost and never find its way home. The dawn had cracked, he said, and he had fixed some strong coffee for me. The day would be fine for shooting—cool, with filmy clouds to cut the glare of sunrise. I wished for my buckskins to put on for the biggest hunt of my days, but the Ottoman habit would do me very well.

Amine appeared in excellent spirits. She did not know that if the shooting became wild, she might stop a bullet herself. Indeed she knew nothing of the affair, other than my weight on her back again, and a thing in her mouth that was not a corncob which in some fashion caused her to stop, go, and turn, and a pain in her side which eased when she ran like mad. The sun was straining to rise when I boarded her.

In the short ride from the stables to the bridle path, we came on a grotesque figure squatting by the paling. It sprang up as we approached, but not to man's height, and yet it had not the pretty shape of a child. It was a Negro dwarf, richly though horridly dressed in a semblance of a pasha's habit. He began waving his arms and rocking sideways rapidly on his stunted legs in a fantastic dance.

"Eblis, Belial, Ahriman, Samael, Abaddon," he was gobbling hoarsely. "Light on *giaour*, light on *giaour*."

"Don't look at him," Zimil whispered sharply. "It's Omar's magus, and he'll give you the evil eye!"

While Zimil turned away his face, I risked a glance; and if the desperate look that the dwarf returned me was the evil eye, I had lost the fight. Instead my heart began to leap in excited hope. No few Dutchmen and Scots on the frontier had a lively belief in hex, but my well-read father and even my illiterate mother had laughed at it. Anyway the dwarf made a gesture that did not appear to fit in with the casting of a malign spell. With a quick movement he touched his finger to his thick, simian lips.

"Ride on and don't look back," I ordered Zimil. "A greater sorcerer than he taught me how to fend off enchantments."

"Light on *giaour*, light on *giaour*," the dwarf continued to gobble. But he stopped instantly when Zimil had ridden out of hearing and I spoke to him in low tones.

"What is it, little man? Speak quickly."

Still in his grotesque dance, the dwarf spoke quickly and well. "Selim Effendi, tell your second to insist that both you and my master

Omar remain dismounted until the starting gun. Say 'tis the custom of your country, lest one of the horses break across the line aforetime. Do you understand?"

"Yes, but why?"

"Heed me, lord, and ride on."

"It may be a trick—"

"Yes, it's a trick that you may live. Ride on."

Zimil awaited me with an ashen face.

"Have no fear of that sorcerer," I told him. "I gave his evil eye back to him."

"Would that a *malla* would teach me the same wisdom!"

"The curse was on me alone, not on you. Is the dwarf a famed magus?"

"All dwarfs have strong *baraka*, it's well known. If they're kindly disposed, to touch them on the back gives good luck. True, I'd never heard that Giafar was more than a buffoon to divert Omar's guests. He's full of monkey tricks for their delight. But certainly he was invoking great devils against you."

I could picture Giafar's monkey tricks, while the bearded Janissaries bellowed with laughter. If he failed to make them laugh, his back was touched in another manner than to borrow good luck. He did not then speak with the good words and accents of a wise, learned man. I decided to follow his instructions.

"What horse does Omar ride today?" I asked Zimil. For he would have heard all the gossip of the stables.

"Why, he'll ride Rustum, his great war horse, although he rode an Arab mare to the field."

"Why didn't he ride Rustum to the field?"

"His Negro *sice*, the only one of his attendants whom the stud will let curry him, had done himself too well last night on the juice of bitter cherries of Kandra, stored too long. When Omar came at dawn and found Rustum with a rough and dirty coat, he was thrown into great fury. He mounted the Arab, for he wished to survey the field, but roared his orders that Rustum be cleaned and led there before sunrise."

"Not ridden there, by one of his attendants?"

"Rustum will allow no one on his back but Omar-id-din."

I wondered if a little opium of Tokat had been mixed with the juice of the bitter cherries of Kandra. "Perhaps he had his Circassian groom curry Rustum, since the black *sice* was begrogged," I suggested.

"She doesn't dare venture in reach of his teeth! I told you, lord, that only the *sice* may curry him, although 'tis said that Giafar may walk under his black belly without harm! Truly Allah takes care of idiots even as drunkards. The Circassian slave girl does nothing more than clean his empty stable, barefoot and ankle deep in mire, and ride behind him in show for Omar's sport."

I was to meet my second, Hassan Serdar, at the amphitheater. I could not make haste on the bridle path because of Timor-id-Osman and his train riding ahead, but I caught sight of Bayezid in a company of court officials behind me, and waved to him to join me.

"A pleasant morning, Selim-ul-Reuben," he remarked, with his mocking grin. "Allah has smiled on the meet."

"And surely it stands to reason he'll smile on Omar by bearing him swiftly to paradise. Knowing I was once a Christian—but pray you, keep my guilty secret—he'll let me remain on the sorry earth."

"Alas, there's no logic in the Lord. Ride and shoot as you never rode and shot before!"

"Bayezid, you've honored me with your friendship, or at least with your good company. I charge you, in its name, to tell me the worst and not the best of the pass I'm in."

"Would you'd spared me the task! Selim, you're pitted against the best marksman and best rider in the Ottoman Empire! Unless kismet befriends you with a great stroke, you'll not taste meat again."

"That I know. What's his best range and tactics?"

"He's only your equal at shooting from a running horse at medium or long range. Yesterday I watched you with a strong glass from a high hill, and 'tis an even wager. But he has taught Rustum to stop as he drops his reins over the pommel and cries the command. It's as though the black devil had run into a stone wall. By raising his stirrups and bracing against them, Omar saves himself from being thrown. Then he follows his target for one beat of his heart, and no matter how fast it flies, at any distance short of two hundred pics, it falls."

"Then I must fire before he does." But anything like two hundred pics would present an impossible shot from the back of a running horse.

"God help you if you miss!"

I asked Bayezid to speak up for my proposal that both Omar and I be dismounted at the starting gun, races being so conducted in my country, and it might bring me luck. He looked at me curiously.

"Superstition is the bane of Mussulman existence," he told me, "but I'd seen no signs of it in you until this moment."

"I need all the help I can get, *sahabti*."

We came to the amphitheater to find even a larger company than had attended yesterday's hunt. Most of the pashas could hardly conceal their excitement, but not so Omar! Sate he well on his Arab mare, stroking his beard, occasionally drawing on the long stem of a houka carried by a footman, and his only notice of me was to spit on the ground. Behind him his Circassian groom straddled a skinny gelding. I kept looking at her until her eyes crossed mine. Her voluptuous mouth twisted a little in the furthest from a smile; it appeared an expression of heartfelt repugnance and disdain. Perhaps she wanted Omar to win. Maybe his harsh treatment of her appealed to her savage soul. Her resistance to him might be only a little game she was playing.

I put her out of my mind. Now that Timor-id-Osman had arrived, the whole company rode to the field, hardly ten furlongs beyond. It had no features of which I could take advantage save, perhaps, one broad, bushy tree toward the farther side. Otherwise it was a grassy park between wooded hills, big enough for a farm, sloping gently toward a brook, and almost as smooth as a table top. A thrall had plowed a furrow enclosing a square a thousand pics broad—approximately a hundred acres.

"Will the adversaries draw straws for choice of sides?" Timor-id-Osman asked, glancing at the already risen sun.

"By your leave, my lord, I don't wish to get that close to the Christian, in respect to my nose," Omar answered. "His second may draw against mine."

"Hassan Serdar, will you draw for me?" I asked. "I too don't want to get near him in respect to his nose. Being large and red like his mother the whore's—not eaten away like his donkey-driver father's—I might be tempted to flatten it."

The company seemed to consider this a fair exchange. Timor-id-Osman fixed two grass blades in his hand.

"The longer straw wins, and the defender's second will have first draw."

Hassan Serdar did not draw the winning straw, and Omar chose the far side. "By your leave, my lord, I'll wait here for my nag," he said.

"But it's the appointed time for the meet. Unless your opponent consents to the delay—"

"By Allah, Timor-id-Osman, I'll not accept favors from a *giaour* dog. I'll take my place, and unless Rustum arrives before the starting gun, I'll ride the mare."

It might be that Giafar had overdone the business of delaying Rustum's arrival at the field. I made a diversion by dismounting Amine and signing for Zimil to get down from his gelding.

"Why do you dismount, Selim-ul-Reuben?" Timor asked gravely.

"Why, my lord, to await the starting gun."

"You may be in your saddle and ready to ride."

"I call Allah to witness that a fair meet demands we both be down at the gun, the same as *spahis* before the fife is blown. One horse or the other may break into the field before time."

"A cur whines at sight of the whip," mocked one of the Janissaries.

"Peace, thou reviler," Bayezid cried. "Of Christian birth or no, Selim hasn't flinched from a foe of far greater name. It seems to me a fair proposal."

"Anyway it's a trifle," replied the Agazzi, Omar's second. But it was no trifle to me, remembering the look on the dwarf's face, and might not be so to Omar in the upshot. I kept listening with growing anxiety for the great hooves of Rustum on the bridle path.

"Methinks he's caviling in hope of stopping the meet," Omar said, his finger beside his nose. "But I'll agree to the great innovation. Perhaps I'm as swift at mounting as a trained pig at a fair!"

"It's true you can mount your black stallion more easily than your white filly," I replied.

The company waited for Timor-id-Osman to laugh before they would dare. He did not—only his eyes sparkled. In spite of their tension I thought my advocates relished the jest, and the wolfish gleamings under the heavy brows of the Janissaries was momentarily less cruel. The Circassian girl put her hand on her belly and appeared to retch.

"Enough of this gabble, I say," cried Hassan Serdar worriedly. "My lord, the sun's up, and the time for the meet long struck." I had been unable to warn him not to speed the affair.

"By Allah, here comes Rustum now," a junior officer exclaimed.

"You fool," Bayezid murmured in my ear. "While you've won your silly point, Omar's won time to get the stallion under him, instead of the mare."

"I'll not wait for the black jinni," Omar cried. "I'm in haste to stop a cur's bark, and I'll ride the bay."

"By Allah, he won't," I shouted. "My lord, pardon me, but the winner of this fight takes both steeds, and he pawned Rustum, not a mare I'd never seen. I entreat you, see that the terms are kept."

"You fool, you cursed fool," Bayezid told me in deep dismay. "If he'd ridden the mare, you'd have had a shadow of a chance!"

"Omar-id-din, it's meet that you ride Rustum, the horse you pawned, now that he's here," Timor pronounced.

"Gladly, my lord. I thought the company might see a slightly better fight, but since my opponent is so bent on being sent to his father's gods—" Omar shrugged, and turned to the black groom leading the stallion. "Follow me to my post. I'll mount Rustum at the starting gun."

Omar rode the mare across the field beyond the distant starting line, got down, a small, black figure, and stood beside his black stud to mount. The spectators dismounted likewise, to be less likely to stop a stray bullet, and a few of the more wary lay on the ground. But not one took refuge behind distant trees, as I would expect of my own countrymen. They were believers in kismet in a way unthinkable to self-willed Yankees. Also they liked to flaunt their courage and perhaps believed even more staunchly in Omar's marksmanship. My first bullet would certainly fly in the other direction. They firmly counted on Omar's flying straight to me.

The Osman rode into the middle of the field. "Are you ready, Omar-id-din?" he shouted.

So strong was Omar's voice that I heard it thin but clear at more than a third of a mile.

"I'm ready, my lord."

"Are you ready, Selim-ul-Reuben?"

"Yes, my lord, and may Allah preserve me."

Someone laughed behind me, a laugh of some bitter music, and I thought it was the Circassian girl.

2.

Timor-id-Osman drew his pistol to signal the start of the race, and in those long-drawn seconds of waiting I got my bearings. It was as though I had been gale driven of late, with only fleeting glimpses of the sun, but now the golden beacon burst from the black rack and I had shot it.

I need no longer regret the fix I had blundered into. This and others almost as bad had been unavoidable for a man like me, in an undertaking such as mine. There was poor glory to be won today and likely but crass profit save life alone, but I was neither very wise nor good, and could not always sail a true course. Many a night I would lie drunk on shore, and seek many a sorry pleasure, and worship many a strange god. If I did not gain my port, it would be because of evil fortune or the faults of my own nature, over which my best heart could not prevail. But there had never been any doubt what port it was. The way had been nobly charted and the journey illustriously starred.

Timor aimed his pistol in the air. A small, black cloud engulfed its muzzle, and a little thunderclap rolled tardily down the field. I sprang on Amine, my rifle across the pommel, and at my spur, she leaped across the starting line. Far across the field I saw Rustum racing toward me in great bounds, as though a bunch of firecrackers had been fastened to his tail. Omar's hard-drawn rein looked like to break his jaw, without checking his furious rush. Whatever magic a black dwarf had made against him, certainly it had not slowed his hooves.

In a very few seconds my foe and I would approach within two hundred pics. There Omar meant to stop his horse for a sure shot. My mare had not been trained to stop nearly as quickly, so I pulled up to wait for him, meaning to fire the instant he checked his horse. The first trouble with that was, he might check him at a range in which he could hit but I would miss. I did not trust myself beyond two hundred yards—holding more than a foot high—while he might be deadly at three hundred or even more.

The second trouble with it was, he had swung to get the tree between him and me. There was nothing to stop him from riding to its very trunk and potshooting me in safety. When I rode forward and to the side, he swerved enough to stay in its shelter. So again I spurred Amine and dashed toward him.

But as the huge black stallion bounded nearer, he did not seem in Omar's good control. It came to me with a rush of exultation that he might not be able to stop his furious sweep down the field. If he did start to pull up I meant to charge on, shortening the range at every hoofbeat, meanwhile swinging my piece. We drew within a furlong of each other, but still the pincers closed. Omar's beast appeared crazed. I heard him shouting unheeded commands and saw him saw the reins.

With thrilling swiftness the range bettered for me. If he could check the beast now, I could swing and fire before he could find his aim—still a long shot from a running horse but one I did not fear. Instead he dropped his reins and his gun barrel winked in the pale sunlight. Still I dared wait a little longer before swinging up my piece, for I did not think he could hit me from the back of the bounding monster. But I must not wait too long. If he could shoot a sparrow from the hip at ten paces on the ground, he could surely down a hard-riding man when riding hard at twenty.

Suddenly I divined the swift and deadly change of his strategy. That bold and ready soldier would waste no more time struggling with a maddened horse, but meant to sweep on until I started to raise my piece, then blast me without bringing his gun to his shoulder.

I had counted him in my bag. To know that he could fire first and at short range, kill, threw me into panic. The shot offered me now was easier than I had counted on. Amine was running smoothly, with Omar coming straight into me, and I forgot he could not hit me yet save by a whim of fate. But because I was coming straight toward him as well, I let go an advantage for which a moment ago I would have thanked my lucky stars. So dims the mind when it turns tail. Instead of dropping my reins, swinging my piece, and firing, I swung Amine from the course to widen the range.

Almost instantly I perceived what might well be my fatal mistake. It did not cool my head, only made me lose it altogether. To win the fight I should again have taken the offensive, closing in boldly, running at Rustum's flank or head-on toward him. Instead I flung up to fire. It was a far more difficult shot than had been offered me a second before, and as my hammer fell, Rustum changed his course. He meant to intercept my mare, for he too had been trained to flank running game. As the smoke cloud streamed by, I saw him and his rider charging on.

"*Allah Akbar!*" howled Omar-id-din as the bullet whistled harmlessly by his ear. From the watching Janissaries rose an exultant roar, "*Allah Akbar!*"

I was done for, they thought. If I thought so too, it would be true. Truly though I was a long way from it, for no reason other than the sudden welling of my heart with passion to win and live. Without knowing it, I had stood on the defensive until now. Now I was launching an attack upon him, no less real because for the moment I was flying out of range of his murderous hip shot. It was in the fury of attack that I spurred the peerless mare, guided her lightly with my left hand, and thrust my rifle, muzzle up, under my left leg to begin the terrible task of reloading.

I could not ride off the field to be pistoled by the Janissaries. Not yet could I drop my reins to employ both hands. I had learned the trick only as a feat of equestrianship, because old Pierre could do it, but had never dreamed of performing it under close pursuit of a killer—that dream would have been a nightmare. That Omar could not control his horse well gave me half of a fighting chance. The other half was Amine's wonderful wits and dazzling speed. She seemed to know that the game was to stay far from Rustum, as though in her first race to save her maidenhead, when a desert filly. Yet she ran smoothly as she had been trained, obeying the lightest tightening of her rein.

Waiting until she was well away, I gave her her head while I poured powder directly into the barrel, roughly guessing at three drams. By instinct Rustum tried to intercept our course, but Omar was unable to turn him from coming up on our left side, from which no right-handed marksman can swing and shoot. When we drew away again I spat into my palm the patched bullet I had carried in my mouth, again dropped my reins, and rammed it home. Omar managed a short cut that brought him within fifty yards of us on his left and shooting side, but he did not risk a shot. We raced on, for the most delicate task of priming the pan was still before me.

But now Omar made a mistake. Perhaps the steady progress of my loading when he had thought me done for, made him lose his head as I had lost mine. While my heart fainted he almost cornered us, then instead of firing, he tried to stop his horse for a sure shot. With wonderful horsemanship and great strength he managed to check Rustum's furious run, but the raging beast would not stand, plunged and reared, and his raving, cursing, sweating rider could not drop his reins to fire. In this respite I sped Amine to the far end of the field, stopped her, and began to prime my pan.

Rustum appeared in full revolt, thundering back and forth across the field. It seemed the climax of the battle between him and his terrible master: a few seconds later he began to yield to the punishing rein and spurs. But now the sound of my hammer cocking came sweet to my ears. At once I rode straight toward the stallion, my heart on fire, and Omar must needs loose him, before I drew within half a furlong for a standing pot shot. His horsemanship showed superb, now that he had largely mastered the black brute, although still unable to quiet him. Riding full-tilt to keep me at impossible range when I was on his right hand, circling and weaving as I approached in any kind of gunshot, he closed fiercely when he had me on his left. He was no terrified deer, instinct driven, unable to foresee my maneuvers, but a *spahis* before Allah. He meant to blast me out of the saddle without shouldering his piece.

More than once I had to turn tail to get from under his bristling muzzle. Rustum had yielded his head to that hand of tempered steel. In position I could shoulder-shoot him at forty paces almost sure, while he in position must draw in nearly half that distance to hip-shoot me, but the advantage seemed very slight, so boldly he rode. The thundering stallion strove ever to close with us, while my mare tried to fly.

No sound rose from the watchers. Each of us rode not only to live but to kill, lost to all else as two Arabs met in blood feud on the desert, and the pashas of Islam would not see such riding soon again. But not horse or horseman could stand the pace much longer. Omar hauled his beast around in an incredibly fast turn, then ran in at a sharp angle on my right side, my finish if the scheme worked. I was too near the edge of the field to wheel off, so must likewise haul around.

Omar did not believe I could make it. Otherwise he would not have held his fire for the sure shot he craved in a second more. But roweling Amine to a great, twisted leap, I did make it, kept my seat, and saw the huge black stallion with his demon rider almost over her low-hung, driving head. He was hauling his right rein to keep me on his left, even as I dropped my reins. I did not take time to hang them over the pommel. I would have no more need of them after these rushing seconds, unless I shot quick and straight. If these seconds sped with Omar still horsed, he would have me under his gun at twenty paces.

My piece swung up with my enemy riding hard into my sights. Through them he would pass in the twinkling of an eye, but for that immediate instant I became part of a tube of steel. I smote to kill my foe at forty yards. Even of this, I was hardly aware—it seemed that I need not take aim or pull a trigger, only decree his fall. I did not know when the hammer fell, only realized I had made an effort like the hurling of an almost unliftable stone.

The roar of the rifle did not quite eclipse a sharp crack as of an ax on board. Before my barrel's belch of smoke could spread, I saw Omar's rifle hurl from his hand and what looked like a chip fly high. The pall streamed behind me. Omar hung out of his saddle, striving in an agony of effort to regain his seat. But his right arm flopped helpless. Unable to hang on, he jerked his feet from the stirrups like the horseman he was and fell clear of the flying hooves. With a last contortion of his powerful, agile body he landed on his left shoulder, slid for twice his length, and lay still.

Omar opened his eyes, gazed into mine, and waited in dark, fierce, Moslem pride for his kismet. And by the ancient rules of single combat not one of his friends could enter the field to help him.

"Do you yield, Omar-id-din, or shall I bash out your brains with my gun barrel?" I asked, standing over him.

"I yield to you, Selim-ul-Reuben," came low but clear out of his bearded lips.

"Are you of a right mind to take oath before our God?"

"Yes, I am. I'm very weak, but in my right mind."

"Do you swear on the word of a Moslem, Allah bearing witness, that if I spare you, you'll pay the forfeits agreed, take no vengeance or seek no satisfaction on anyone for your defeat, and will take service in some remote post, not returning to Stamboul as long as I stay in the Sultan's domains?"

"All that I swear, as Allah is the only god, and Mohamet his prophet. I was betrayed by one of my own train—likely the dwarf Giafar—but I'll take no vengeance on him or anyone, only sell him to a better master than I."

Love of life came upon me in an exultant rush. "I'll not take your rifle, Omar-id-din. Its iron braces saved your life by checking the force of my bullet. And now I'll call your attendants, to carry you from the field."

"In a short time I'll be able to walk from the field."

I waved to the watchers. Timor-id-Osman, the two seconds, and the surgeon mounted their horses, and with a groom leading Omar's Arabian mare, rode into the field. Bracing with his left hand, Omar sat up.

"What's your word of the battle, if you have voice to speak?" Timor asked him.

"I've lost it, my lord, and am paroled to my conqueror."

"Allah upon you, Selim Effendi, for sparing my colonel's life," the Agazzi told me.

The surgeon cut away Omar's sleeve, located the ball against the skin on the back of his forearm, and fixed a sling. Then he gave him a lump of pure musk, a sooty substance found in the bodies of a variety of deer in the mountains of Thibet, and believed to be a powerful stimulant as well as love potion. Certainly it appeared to revive the wounded *spahis*: he declared himself able to ride his bay mare to the palace, if the grooms would hoist him on her back. This they did, and with a black *sice* leading the animal, we left the field.

While the surgeon had been treating Omar, I had reloaded my piece. I was glad of that, when I met the angry eye of the Janissaries.

"I cry foul," one of the junior officers shouted before we had hardly checked our horses. "Rustum had been given some evil potion, to inflame his heart and madden his brain against his master."

"Do you accuse me of it?" I asked sternly. "By Allah, you're privy to it, or why did you specify that neither man mount till the starting gun? You knew he'd discover the cheat, and ride the mare."

"Why, he demanded that Omar ride the stallion, when he knew well that in a fair fight he'd have twice the chance against the bay," another stormed.

"What do you say to that, Hassan Serdar?" asked Timor-id-Osman.

"I believe, with Ibrim Capudan, that the stud's been drugged. Maybe he'd been given the juice of Indian hemp, which the blacks call bhang. Perhaps Selim-ul-Reuben had knowledge of it, after the act. But Omar's spies watched his every move from the moment of the challenge until the starting gun. I bid him tell this company whether his enemy had any opportunity either to administer the potion, or to effect it by bribery."

"No, my lord, I swear before Allah. The trick was turned by one of my own slaves."

"Then mark my words," said Hassan Serdar. "Yesterday Selim rode valiantly for the Sultan, and today for his life and honor. Since when must soldiers warn their enemies that they've been betrayed in their own camp? The rules of the duel were agreed to and obeyed. So if any one charges my principal with foul crime against Omar, I myself will answer with my scimitar."

No one spoke for long seconds. Hassan Serdar was one of the most famed blades in the Ottoman Empire.

"I saw the foul dwarf, Giafar, stop him by the paddock, as though to curse him," a reed-voiced, puny-captain ventured. "If Omar-id-din doesn't whip the slave to death with his kurbash, I'll cut his throat myself."

"No, not even that," Omar said wearily. "I've sworn no vengeance shall be taken for my defeat. Pray you, gentleman, close the book."

"It's closed," declared Timor-id-Osman, "I pronounce Selim-ul-Reuben the winner, to enjoy in peace the fruit of his victory. Peace upon you all, and farewell."

"There's no majesty and no might save in Allah," came many voices.

Timor-id-Osman made off with his train. The Agazzi was next in rank, but since Omar and the surgeon were in his party, he waited until the defeated champion completed his affairs.

First he turned to his black *sice*. "You'll ride a mare and catch Rustum, and deliver him, saddled and bridled, to Selim Capudan."

"Yea, my master."

I think every eye in the company followed his as he turned to his white groom.

"Lilith, I've lost you on a wager, and you're no longer my slave."

The Circassian girl continued to look through him without the slightest recognition of his existence.

"Do you hear me, you child of Eblis, as your very name signifies?" he stormed, perhaps half in rage of her, half in pain of his wound. "If you do, speak."

"How dare you speak to my master's female slave without his consent, you lecherous Omar?" she answered. "Only yesterday you railed at the same offense, and today fought a duel to avenge it."

"By heaven, do you wonder I put her in pawn?" Omar appealed to me, greatly to my surprise. "Selim, if you're wise, you'll cut her throat here and now, ere she drives you to cut your own."

"Answer him, Lilith," I told her.

"So any donkey-driver may pay me his addresses without rebuke from you?" she turned on me, sneering. "Omar Pasha—Omar pig— was at least a man. Methinks I've been won by a eunuch."

"Do as I bade you, you misbegotten!"

"Omar-id-din, I know I'm no longer your slave. If you'd wanted to cut your throat, you'd better have done it before your right arm dangled like a pigtail. One more brave battle, and you'll have to ask your groom to cut it for you."

"I've warned you, Selim-ul-Reuben," Omar said solemnly. "Woe will be unto you, for taking this cockatrice to your bosom."

He spurred his mare and despite the pain it must have shot through his arm at every jounce, cantered toward the palace. The other Janissaries and the surgeon fell in behind him, but Hassan Serdar and some of the small fry waited in compliment to me. So shaken I could hardly sit my mare, but too exultant over my victory to heed Omar's warning, I gazed eagerly at my prize.

Like many Circassians, she was very fair. Her hair was of the hue rightly called golden, not merely a pale yellow; her skin was snowy and her eyes of a serene blue. This fairness was at odds with her severely planed face that could well belong to a daughter of Cathay.

No doubt she had the blood of Tartars in her, although not nearly enough to behave so like one.

On the whole her countenance was shaped rather like Taveoa's set off by the flowers of Hawaii. There was no deep niche at the eye, and this appeared longer, more of it visible from the side, between lids forming a far narrower angle than in European faces, slanted a little downward. Her nose was rather short, well bridged, shapely, and lifted looking because of the slightly forward thrust of her jaws. Her lips were rounded and full without being in the least coarse. Her chin was strong and the entire line from thence to the crown of her head appeared gently indented but continuous and integral, not a jagged cliff under a dome like the profiles of Westerners. On the whole its structure was doubtless somewhat primitive, but strikingly decorated with her fine, bright hair, transparent, delicate skin, deep-blue eyes, and spare, superbly molded flesh. Oddly enough she did not look in the least savage or shrewish when her face was in repose—rather innocent, in fact, and childish.

As I looked at her, her eyes turned slowly to mine. They did not turn away or fill with self-consciousness or indeed any consciousness of me. She simply became a front-view picture on a wall for me to see.

"Ride to the stables, give your horse to Omar's groom, and come to my quarters in the guest house."

"Yes, master," she answered with a still face. And then with her eyes still fixed on mine, she spat deliberately and expressively on the ground.

4.

Luckily the Janissaries had gone, for it would have been almost enough to console them for their defeat. Hassan Serdar looked at her angrily, as though he would like to slap her. But I was too tired to be either humiliated or outraged at her serpent's tooth and did not even watch her ride away.

Hassan Serdar gave me a sooty lump of musk he had got from the surgeon. "Swallow that," he told me in a fatherly tone, although he was only two or three years older than I. "It will brace you up until you can take food and rest."

My feelings welled at that—they had had so many ups and downs —and like a tosspot I was about to ask him to accept Rustum as a token of my gratitude and esteem, but held my tongue just in time. In the first place I had saved his bacon in a measure the same as my own—the new artillery corps had sharply scored over the Janissaries. In the second place, to give away a steed worth a thousand dinars was no way for an adventurer in the Sultan's court to get ahead. I thanked Hassan Serdar kindly, both for his support and his medicine. Feeling much better now, I would not accompany him to the palace, but would see to Rustum, being worried about the valuable animal when the drug given him wore off.

"I don't blame you for your concern for him," the general told me. "He's a fit reward for your victory, and unwittingly befriended you today. I wish to speak to you a moment in private."

When he had drawn me aside, I expected him to have something more to say about the horse-doctoring—perhaps far from pleasant—but I was mistaken.

"That vixen of a Circassian amuses me," he told me in low tones. "God knows she's no moon of beauty, but I tire of supine women, and she'd be a novelty. How much will you take for her?"

"Why, Hassan Serdar, I hadn't considered selling her."

"Will you set a price? I've taken a fancy to owning her, and if it's in reason, I'll pay it."

"Not now, my general, if you please. Winning her at such hard trial has made me loath to part with her, for fear my luck will turn."

"Your luck may turn if you keep her. In all frankness, Selim, you're not acquainted with some of the inhabitants of the Empire. This girl comes from the wildest fastnesses of Gunib in the heart of Daghestan. The mountaineers are wolves, not men, refusing to pay tribute to the Sultan, waging bloody vendettas with neighboring tribes, living in stone huts by their little fields hacked out of primeval forest—a life unchanged since King Suleiman. They call themselves Christians— they belong to a primitive sect of the ancient Nestorian heresy—but they're worse barbarians than the head-hunters of the Spice Isles. Moreover this girl is the wildest and most evil-tempered I've yet seen. I think she'd make your life a burden, even as Omar's."

"Still, I wouldn't want to sell her." Indeed I was less likely to than before.

"I happen to be blessed by Allah with great riches, and can indulge my foolish whims," he went on. "What if I said a thousand dinars?"

My skin prickled at this munificence. "I'll give you first refusal of her, if I decide to part with her."

"Keep it in mind. You can buy a likely female attendant for a third of that sum. And mark you, it represents her present value in my sight. A little later, I might not accept her as a gift."

"I mark you well, Hassan Serdar."

He returned my salute and rode with his aides back to the palace. Bayezid told me that he would seek me out in Constantinople by which time he hoped to find me comfortable quarters in the establishment of the *Reis* Effendi and a fairly lucrative post. I had Zimil take Amine to the stable, and rode his gelding in pursuit of Omar's black *sice*. The musk had stimulated me like a quart of black coffee and I had heard the Arab mare whinny not far off in the woods.

It turned out that the stud had run only a short distance from the field, his crazy spell passing off soon after Omar had been thrown from his back. Also he had appeared perfectly composed before Omar had mounted him. Now I had already observed that almost any kind of odd behavior in the Ottoman Empire was attributed either to potions or some kind of magic charm. Although Islamic laws and the tenets of the religion itself were admirable, high minded in the extreme, and in many ways superior to Western institutions, their exercise had been debased by corrupt hierarchies and by generations of piratical conquest. Arabic learning had been largely lost, and while a few physicians still practiced in the school of Avicenna, more that bore the name were merely nostrum-selling quacks. An enormous trade flourished in love potions, charms, and even subtle poisons. But I thought Giafar had taken revenge on Omar by more direct means. Indeed I suspected that he had turned an old Yankee trick.

"The saddlecloth is not smooth," I told the black *sice*. "Perhaps when Omar was up, the saddle rubbed and smarted. Hold the stud hard, while I straighten it."

Rustum shied from me and gave me a wicked stare, but minded his manners when I had cut him thrice across the neck hard as I could lay on Zimil's riding whip. Then I loosened his cinch and slipped my hand under the saddlecloth. The "potion," which I did not show Omar's man, was a steel rowel between his ribs, longer and sharper than had ever lost a Yankee horse race.

I did not feel equal to trying to ride Rustum home, so had the *sice* lead him behind his mare. Heartily disliking the black monster—for no apparent reason—and determined to sell him, I saw no need to risk my neck and strain my will trying to master him. I had enough before me, as it was.

I found myself hurrying to my quarters, but they were empty and lonely. Lying down on my heap of rugs, I gave up waiting and watching for anyone to come and drifted into sleep; after that my mind should be more composed and capable. Two hours later I clapped my hands for Na'od, had him bring me some cold mutton, bread, coffee, and sweets. These down, and well-fortified, I called the worthless black again.

"Bid the head eunuch of the house send to me Lilith, my Christian slave girl, with all her belongings," I instructed him. "Unless she makes haste, tell him not to spare the kurbash."

A few minutes later the girl came in the servants' door with a small portmanteau on her head. Doubtless she could carry a pail of water there without spilling a drop, and perhaps this method of burden bearing in her wild mountain village partly accounted for the extraordinary grace of her carriage. It was the first time I had seen her on foot. She moved with a long, slow stride that was like a ripple on water. She still wore the groom's habit Omar had provided her.

Putting down the leather bag, she stood before me with an empty countenance.

"Your slave obeys your command," she told me.

"Take your ease. I wish to talk to you and discover in what service I may employ you. You may be seated."

I tossed her a cushion, and she sat on it cross-legged. I remained seated on my couch.

"Tell me about your home," I proposed, to break the ice.

"I have no home, save in the baggage train of a master."

"This is your home now, and there'll be a better when I've fetched you to Constantinople."

"Truly a palace," she said, looking about her. "Omar Pasha kept his horses in better state than this."

I had expected a few minutes of fairly civil conversation with the woods waif, and could hardly believe she would turn on me this soon. Apparently she would seize any excuse for a quarrel. Perhaps because I had been through so much today I could not keep from snapping back at her.

"No doubt you'd rather go on cleaning Omar's stable."

"It was a less loathsome task than some that might be appointed me."

"For that, many a master would give you the whip. It's a wonder to me your back isn't already striped."

"Well, it's not," she told me complacently.

"You've been indulged so far, because plainly you're too young and foolish to appreciate your position. Haven't you been taught the duty of a slave? It's cheerful and prompt obedience to her master's will."

"Did you buy me for a thousand dinars, or even five hundred? No, you won me by base trickery from Omar. Sell me to the Sultan, where

I may dwell in splendor and wax fat, and I'll obey his every command."

No doubt this was the dream of the prettiest maids of Daghestan. It had been shattered in Lilith's case, and that had something to do with her wicked temper. Still I was becoming increasingly puzzled by her. There was no more natural malice in her face than in Taveoa's—not a hateful line or the track of a sullen thought—and at her last words it had lighted like an amiable child's.

"Where did you come from?" Hassan had told me, but I wanted to hear it in the girl's own words.

"From Gunib, among the fast rivers and the walnut forests." Her blue eyes suddenly glowed.

"How would I know where Gunib is? Probably the end of nowhere."

"Do you know where your nose is?" she asked, scathingly. Then patiently instructing me somewhat as a little girl her doll, "Everyone in Stamboul but blind beggars and fools knows of Gunib, the pride of God, and the real cause of the great war fought in my father's time between the Sultan and the Czar of all the Russias. Each coveted it more than crown jewels. Our holy father told us so."

She was so in earnest that I hadn't the heart to disillusion her, even if it were possible; but I could imagine the Muscovite emperor inspiring his troops with the battle cry "Gunib or die!"

"Why, do the people there pay such high taxes?"

"We won't pay one mite! If a foul tax-collector dares come through the pass, we crucify him to teach his fellows a lesson. If a governor is sent, he and all his train are shot on sight. We won't bow down to the Sultan or the Czar either, so the great war was fought in vain. If they want our jewels, they must send merchants to buy them at a fair price, then we'll treat them kindly."

"What kind of jewels? Emeralds and rubies?" But I thought I knew what she meant.

"The devil's curse is on me that I'm won by an idiot! Don't you know that the fair maids of Daghestan bring the highest price of any slave girls in the market?" She lifted her head in pride.

This I doubted greatly. "Your father sold you to a slave merchant?"

"What of it? It was his right. Like the other girls, I'd heard much of the rich haremliks of Byzantium, and I thought it would be a better life than bearing wood and drawing water for a dirty barley-grower of Daghestan. But in an evil hour kismet delivered me not to the palace of an emir, but into the tents of stinking soldiers."

I feared she would spit on the Sultan's carpet. "What do you know of kismet?" I asked to quiet her. "Omar called you a Christian."

"Yes, I'm a Christian of the only and true church, and may Saint Thomas and Nestorius have mercy on me." She crossed herself quickly.

"How old are you, Lilith?"

"I've seen fourteen winters of deep snow, and one of dirty fog and rain."

"Did the merchant sell you to Omar?"

"He? Omar couldn't buy a hag from a brothel in Batum, spending his little dinars on guns and stud horses! I was sold for five hundred dinars—the highest price of any girl in our caravan—to the *Reis* Effendi. Save for the merchant's dull wits and the Effendi's miserliness, I'd have fetched a thousand."

There came upon me a sense of ill being, of something gone wrong, as occasionally in the Adirondacks when I had taken, without noticing it yet, the wrong trail. It proved to have nothing to do with Lilith—I was only wondering what price Roxana had fetched, and whether she boasted of it among her master's other women. Five hundred dinars? Perhaps a thousand? As I knew full well, a year or two can bring great change. Pride is a tender plant, quickly withering in cold and stony ground.

"Then why aren't you in the haremlik of the *Reis* Effendi?" I went on, putting all that by.

"Because he had a jealous wife who took one look at me, and bade him get me out of his palace before evening prayers, lest she poison him. No wonder, when she had the grace of a Bactrian camel! He put me away, hoping to enjoy me in secret, but I'd have none of him save in honor in his rich household. Despairing of my favors, and pursued by the slut's vile scolding, he traded me for a jeweled scimitar Omar-id-din won in battle."

"How long ago was that?" For maybe I couldn't put by those other thoughts. Perhaps I wanted to know how long a white female slave, whether by defiance or guile, might resist her master. Anyway it would be a losing game, and a most dangerous one.

"Three months that seem since the Flood. Save for that sow, I'd now be the *Reis* Effendi's favorite, with ten serving girls at my beck and call."

My heart was not very true. Heedless of its ties, it began to quicken in perverse delight of my prize. "Are the other girls from Daghestan like you?"

"Some of them shame our tribe by vile servility. I'm the daughter of a chief, the wager of two feuds to the death, the leader in every fight against invaders of our land, a descendant of Malek Juchana [Prester John] and a true Christian."

"Then what did Omar mean, when he said you were named for a child of Eblis?"

"She was not! He ought to have his throat cut for the dirty lie!" The girl flushed with righteous indignation. "Lilith was no devil's child, but a thousand times more worthy than Lickspittle Eva and if you weren't as unlettered as a donkey you'd not have to be told."

"I know nothing of Lilith."

"Yet Omar called you a Christian!"

"Faugh! I'm a son of the Prophet."

"A foul turncoat, I don't doubt. Lilith was the first woman, but she wouldn't become Adam's *thladi Yigo roqoy*—in your vile tongue, his wife in the house. She wouldn't submit to him, he being but a gardener. Once she gave him her favor as a free gift, and bore him a beautiful daughter who in time married Cain, but she'd never bow down to him, and he cast her off."

It was the nearest to a *rapprochement* that the girl and I had established. Some of the wild, defiant look went out of her face. She had never been appealed to in the right way, I thought.

"It's true, I have my fortune to make," I told her. "But I'm young, and of great ambition—"

"I'll make it for you, if you'll let me," she cried, her eyes lighting. Her tone became childishly confiding. "I've already saved you from certain death, and won you a horse and jeweled saddle worth a thousand dinars."

"What do you mean, Lilith?"

"Did you think it was Giafar who caused Rustum to rebel against his master? It was I who thought of the plan. I could hardly keep a straight face when the silly pashas talked of potions—as though any witch's brew could so make him prance and cavort when Omar tried to shoot you, and 'twas a wonder he wasn't thrown and his vile neck broken. It was a trick I heard from an Armenian horse-dealer."

"But Giafar carried it through—"

"Yes, but only because I'd smiled on him, and balmed the stripes Omar gave him yesterday, and patted his wooly head. Rustum wouldn't let me enter his stall to put the spur under his saddlecloth. Anyway Giafar hated Omar and was glad of a chance to undo him."

"What if he'd been caught and brought before the Cadi?"

To my amazement a troubled expression flitted across her face. "He wouldn't have betrayed me," she said, "when I was his only friend in the house." She looked at me, bristling. "Yes, I liked him, even if he was black and a dwarf and ugly, mock me if you will. He was a better man than his master and most of the pashas with great, black beards—and like enough you!"

"I don't mock you for that, Lilith."

"If he'd got in trouble, I was ready with a tale," she went on, smiling to herself.

"How will you help me make my fortune?"

"First, buy me rich array—selling Omar's stallion will bring enough —then send me as a gift to the Sultan. That alone will gain his favor, and when on his royal couch I speak in your praise—"

"Foolish one," I broke in in a disgusted tone. "Hold your tongue!"

I would have given her to the Sultan's sweeper if it would promote my quest, but any Osmanli prince, let alone the Grand Seignior, would be angered at the offer, when she had ridden barefaced and behind Omar as his groom. Only highly educated and cultured slave girls entered the Seraglio. Probably the lowborn *Reis* Effendi had never seriously considered her for his haremlik: she had been one of a batch his agents had bought for him, one or two of whom he might favor, the rest to be given away to favorites or sold. Lilith was highly marketable to rich but less haughty lords; otherwise she was laboring under an illusion.

"So you don't think I'm good enough for the Sultan!" she demanded, her eyes glittering.

"It isn't that, but—"

"I'm only good enough for a stallion like Omar, more fit to wed a mare than a gentle lady, or a mere stinking captain, unheard of till yesterday. By my saints, you'll never use me. If you dare lay hand on me, one night you'll wake with a woeful pain in your skinny belly—"

"Lilith, you did me a good turn—"

"Do you know what I'd have told the Sultan's brother, if Omar hadn't sworn to take no vengeance on Giafar? I'd said that while dallying with one of Omar's spies, I'd seen you steal to the stables with a wicked potion in your hand."

"You're a child of the devil, as he told me."

"You lie in your ugly teeth. I was christened and confirmed in the holy church under the holly trees."

"Take off that groom's habit, and at least appear like womankind, even though you're an evil witch."

"Yes, master," she replied with sudden, infuriating calmness. "I'll retire to the anteroom—"

"Change your raiment here and now, so I can see you haven't the witch's mark. Don't I own you body and soul?" The Turkic thoughts came too freely to my tongue.

"No man will ever own my soul, for it's in the care of my sweet saints, and you'll never own my body, lest I slay you in your sleep. Yet—" and the last trace of anger faded from her face—"I'll obey your command."

I think she took a malicious pleasure in doing so, although the only indication was the brilliance of her eyes. With a completely casual air she removed her long woolen coat, baggy breeches, and shirt; then, as though thinking of something else, the coarse shift she wore underneath. Then she turned and faced me.

"Master, do you see the witch's mark?" she asked, turning slowly. "Look well."

"I see the temptation of the devil," I answered.

"It's in your own evil imagination. If you'll give me to the Sultan, you'll be rid of it—or sell me even, for don't you think I'd fetch a thousand dinars?"

"I've no doubt you'd bring two thousand, but I mean to keep you for my own."

"That we'll see." Calmly she opened her portmanteau, took from it a fine linen shift and a bright-colored, full-skirted costume that I supposed she had brought from the Caucasus, and smiling to herself, put them on.

CHAPTER TWELVE

Wayside Adventure

1.

There was a dark side to owning Lilith that at first made me think I must dispose of her: the reminder that someone owned Roxana. Perhaps this was the real reason, unknown to me, why I had not bought a slave girl long before now. But truly there was no use denying the pleasure I took in her: far beyond the ordinary, because of her vixen-like defiance of my power over her.

Bayezid called and we chatted about it over our coffee cups. A learned fellow, he told me that Gunib customs embraced some matriarchal vestiges growing out of an ancient connection with the Nestorian Christians of Malabar. Lilith could even have absorbed notions of female superiority. Her mother might have been prominent in a cult of female witchcraft, rather common in low civilizations, whose mystic flubdub taught a contempt for the male. Her naming her daughter Lilith supported the theme, he said with a pedantic air, since it was synonymous with womanly revolt against subjection to man.

But when he had taken himself off, pleased with himself over enlightening me, I found myself no wiser than before. Something more than these abstractions was needed to explain the pretty spitfire. I did not think she had always been one; her face told me that although high tempered, she had been a half-civilized but happy, dutiful child, with plenty of native sweetness, lately greatly wrought upon by unhappy events and inward conflict.

Perhaps no few of Omar's associates had coveted her and his fight with her at pawn had advertised her oddity. About sundown I received another, unaccountably unwelcome, sign of her dinar value. A shabby Armenian, styling himself Kagig, a sort of account-keeper at the park, salaamed to me on the terrace and called me aside. He addressed me in an excited whisper.

"A gentleman of note in the Empire has asked me to approach you on a delicate subject," he told me, after a little sparring.

"No doubt he wishes to buy Rustum," I suggested.

"No, his stable is well stocked. For that matter, so is his haremlik. But the Circassian girl has taken his eye—her shrewishness entertains him—and since Omar didn't mar her value, he's willing to pay a good price for her."

"What price will he pay? It would save time if you begin at the top."

"What would you say to five hundred dinars?"

Until now I had suspected that Kagig was an agent of Hassan Serdar. Now it appeared that another buyer had entered the market.

"Why, I wouldn't consider it."

"No doubt you've heard of girls bringing a thousand—occasionally even more. But these are invariably cultivated beauties from the more civilized regions of the Caucasus, or a veritable Queen of Sheba from Ethiopia. Five hundred is a high price for a barbarian, and I'll expect no baksheesh."

"I've already been offered a thousand, and refused it."

His small black eyes probed mine to see if I was lying.

"It doesn't seem likely that my principal would agree to such an exorbitant figure—but, unlike a rug or even a diamond, a slave girl will bring what some fool will pay. Quote me the lowest figure you'll take and I'll give you his answer before dark."

It came to me to ask two thousand dinars, to get rid of the fellow; but instead of that, the riddance might be Lilith. Nowhere in the Levant can one safely discourage a huckster by offering the most trifling price for his ware: too often he finds himself its possessor and cheated after all. The reverse might well be true if Kagig's principal strongly coveted my goods. I felt confident that no prince or great noble would employ such a low, disreputable agent; however his riches might be beyond Western counting and, according to Turkic thinking, solely for the gratification of his vanities and lusts. I could not afford to own an article worth near that sum—there would be many demands on my purse—yet did not want to know how much he would pay.

"I've decided to keep her," I said rashly.

"My friend, if I may advise you, that would be most unwise."

"I haven't asked for your advice."

"I'll give it anyway, to a once fellow-Christian. I was born in the Empire, and have learned not to oppose the will of any of the great. Think well of it, Selim-ul-Reuben."

With that, his sharp features took an odd twist from his one-

sided, ugly smile—characteristic of many Armenians—and without
bothering to salute me, he made off. I went to my apartments with
an oddly excited and troubled mind—not eased any by finding Lilith
sitting on the best cushions the place afforded, eating raisins and
tarponi dates and spitting out the seeds, and barely glancing up as I
entered. Over her scarlet jellick and yellow pantaloons—no doubt
Omar's gift—she wore a *baracan* of almost transparent silk, a sign
that she was in the company of a stranger, not her lord.

She was extraordinarily pretty and graceful. There was something
decidedly engaging in her look of a Chinese child combined with
her bright, Circassian fairness. If I asked two thousand dinars for
her, one of the two fools bidding for her might pay it. My thoughts
turned to Roxana—turned aside—and then by my will returned to
her. Over and above the fact that they were both slaves, there was
a vague, unwelcome, but fascinating linking of the two girls in my
mind, and it needed confronting.

If this were beauty in Lilith's face, and I suspected it might be,
it was as strange as Roxana's. Both countenances appeared a little
sorrowful in repose, and both flashed out a wonderful vitality and
élan when animated. I had not yet heard Lilith laugh or cry, but I
thought that both would be hearty; her voice in even temper was
quite sweet. Roxana and Lilith were alike natural, one learning to be
so by intelligence and culture, and the other never learning not to be.

Lilith's small, rounded body could not begin to be as beautiful as
Roxana's tall, somewhat gangling, highbred form with its long,
delicately molded bones; but it might bring as much from brutish
buyers. In truth it was enchanting in every sense of the word, its
joining exquisite, its voluptuous lines appealing powerfully to that
side of a man which only pious frauds need pretend to be ashamed
of. All in all, I was greatly taken with my prize and hoped I could
afford to keep her.

With hardly a word to her, I clapped my hands for Na'od, and
bade him bring my supper. This I had Lilith stand to serve me, and
afterward gave her the leavings. She accepted the post and the
pottage without much rancor.

"Now you can make my couch for the night," I told her.

"That's a task for Na'od," she replied sharply. "My father didn't
sell me to be a chamber slut."

"No, he didn't, and since it's a chilly night, you can make it wide
enough for two." I hadn't intended to propose this nearly so soon.

"I didn't bring five hundred dinars—and a piddling price at that—

to be the bedfellow of a captain of horse." She was looking over her shoulder at me with a spiteful expression. "And you'd be a *spahis* in the rank, with a coarse woolen coat, if some foul witch hadn't put *baraka* in your gun."

"Are you so fine? What gifts and accomplishments have you, to make you desirable even to a captain, let alone a pasha of one horse-tail?" I must get her over her notion of being too good for me.

She returned to her cushion, took her ease lithely as a cat, ate a date, and spat the seed halfway across the chamber.

"Why not put me on sale and see what I would bring?" she asked. "Have you received any offers for me yet?"

"Who'd want you, after Omar swore before Allah your true worth?"

"I think, master, you lie."

Maybe Kagig's lecherous master had already spoken to her, promising her a luxurious life and her weight in gold and jewels if she would assist in her delivery, intact, to him. If only a little more of a Turk, I would have wanted to cut his throat for the insult to my Moslem honor! Her blue eyes, so astonishing in her Tartar-shaped face, shone with joy to see her shot tell and with childish satisfaction over being such a hot cake at the fair.

"Perhaps you've some qualities other than you've shown me," I suggested, in an easy tone. "Can you play a dulcimer?"

"I'll leave that to your hatchet-faced Greek girls, and Jewesses from Georgia."

"Surely you can keep time on a tabor when others play."

"We held such things in scorn in Gunib—" But her face had flushed, not wholly with anger.

"Can you sing sweet songs, or only blast my ears with the wild, heathen yelpings of Daghestan?"

"You lie like a Greek! The songs of Daghestan are the sweetest on earth. And we're not heathens, or vile heretics like you. We belong to the true faith."

"Then let me hear one of those sweet songs. For it must be plain even to your dull wits that I can't set a price on you or give you to the Sultan's baker without some sense of your worth."

"At least I'd get good bread, like the first sister in the tale of Al Raschid," she answered with ready wit, "not gnaw the crusts of a trifling soldier."

"I'm glad to hear you know the stories of Scheherazade, for entertaining your lord when he lies wakeful."

It was a sorry parry of her sharp thrust, yet to my amazement her face drew and she seemed about to cry. "You mock me, and if my brother heard you, he'd tear out your tongue with red-hot pincers." One little tear got out of bounds and ran down her cheek.

"The *Reis* Effendi paid five hundred dinars for you, so you say—but he traded you to Omar for a scimitar."

"I tell you, that scimitar was of Damascus steel, into which price-less perfumes had been worked so it gave forth sweet scent even in the reek of battle!" She spoke in a tone of righteous indignation. "The jewels in the hilt alone were worth five hundred dinars, and the scabbard was of pure gold, wonderfully worked!"

"So he told you. I'd like to look at those jewels through a glass."

"If they were made of glass—and truly they were of first water and great luster—they'd still be less false than you, a *renegado*."

It was a moment before I could appreciate her quick and vigorous imagination. It came to me that if any of my countrymen had heard this conversation, they would never doubt that I was a renegade.

"I don't wish to be made the laughingstock of the merchants," I told her with a harshness needless and shameful to such a child, "so if I decide to sell you, I'll ask two hundred dinars."

I instantly regretted the brutal words, but they did not faze her. "Why, then, you can afford to kill me, when you've had your pleasure with me," she remarked, calmly.

"What do you mean, Lilith?"

"Otherwise you'd never taste meat or drink coffee again."

I took four rugs from my lavish pile and threw them on the floor about two paces distant. "There's your bed for tonight."

"Thank you, master." She looked spent and a note of wistfulness and perhaps gratitude crept into her childish tone. "Are you ready for sleep too?"

"Yes, your tongue has wearied me."

"Sometimes I speak too hastily and hotly. Will you summon your black slave, to undress you?"

"No, I'll undress myself, in the custom of my country."

"Then to save your modesty—and the joy my master takes in my innocent eyes when you sell me—" She walked quickly to the lamp and blew it out.

But I was mistaken about being ready to sleep. The winter moon shone through the latticed window as Lilith disrobed and crept between her rugs. A year and a half in the barbaric courts of Islam had not prepared me for this situation.

"Are you warm enough?" I asked, after my watch had ticked an endless thousand.

"Did you speak to me, master?" she answered in a startled tone.

I did not think she had been asleep. "I asked if you are warm."

"Yes, master."

"This couch would be warmer, and softer to your tender flesh."

"I'm well satisfied with the one you furnished me, my lord."

"Then take it into the entry, and your misbegotten self with it, and Eblis take your soul."

She rose, picked up the rugs, and started for the door. To my surprise she made no other answer until she stood in the doorway.

"Two hundred dinars," she said thoughtfully. "That's all my worth, my master declares—and yet he can't go to sleep."

2.

Early the next morning, the main of our company set out for Constantinople. Timor and some of the pashas traveled in state and luxury, by way of Karasu and the Black Sea, but I was content to ride with the middle and little fellows on Kurdistan ponies, with only Lilith and Na'od in my train. Traveling at a leisurely pace and breaking the journey at a caravanserai, the Circassian girl made no complaint, and in truth enjoyed the adventure, no doubt reminiscent of long rides in Daghestan. That she was a horse-woman born and bred I had suspected from the first, and this clinched the fact.

Bayezid had agreed to transport my nags, Amine and Rustum, with other horseflesh of their class, and deliver them to me in the city.

Lilith complained that the small, inelegant sloop that would transport us westward on the Sea of Marmora smelled like a fish boat. It was not fit to be mentioned in the same breath with the luxurious vessel on which she had sailed with Omar-id-din on the eastward journey. This off her chest, as we Yankees say, as though it were her duty, her spirits rose, and for the first ten leagues' sail I could not have asked for a more engaging traveling companion. She took a childish delight in the sights—the bright and beautiful sea with its dreamy wooded shores, the leaping fish and romping dolphins. Once she swore she saw a mermaid!

Halfway to Constantinople, as we sat in my cabin cozily enough, her tongue turned sharp again.

A tray of plums that the steward had sent me had just slid off the chest, spilling the fruit all over the floor. It was the first notice

I had taken of slightly worsening weather and a somewhat choppy sea. "Pick them up," I told her, pulling on the long stem of a houka, "and secure the tray."

"Pick them up yourself," she snapped back.

"Are you my mistress, or am I your master? You don't seem to have it straight in your thick head."

"What right have you to be my master? Save for me, the worms would have mastered you! You can't buy me one jewel bigger than a grain of millet."

Nevertheless she began picking up the fruit that was rolling all about the floor from the uneasy movements of the vessel. Chasing the plums on her hands and knees heightened her temper.

"Some enemy has looked upon me with the evil eye," she scolded. "Doubtless it was that cow of the *Reis* Effendi's who robbed me of riches and honor. Or why should that long-nosed Greek of a Julnar, bought for three hundred dinars, be traveling in splendor with her lord Timor-id-Osman, while I, who brought five hundred, should ride a spavined camel of a ship behind a beggar? Is Julnar crawling around the floor, picking up plums? No, she reclines on silk cushions, so heavy with gold and jewels she can hardly rise, with censers of gold beside her pouring forth sweet scent, and bathed in orange blossom and rose water."

"Didn't you agree to your father selling you? You've no one to blame but yourself."

"Would I'd cut off my own tongue! I wish I'd married a barley-grower of Daghestan, and carried wood and water on my back!"

She crept back to her cushion and sat brooding.

"Yes, it was great wickedness," she went on in a bitter tone. "The old priest told me so. There's only one way for a maiden to surrender her flower in honor and saintly blessing, and that's by the ancient, holy law of Gunib."

She seemed deeply depressed, and I wanted her pale cheeks to flame again, if only in anger. "Some barbarous custom, no doubt," I remarked.

"I tell you it's the true way for lovers to be joined! It was so in the days of Prester John! What right have you to call it barbarous, when you were begotten on a saddle blanket, your father paying a few coppers to a chamber slut?"

"No," I told her with unwonted forbearance. "My parents stood up before a clergyman, as was lawful."

"Stood up, did they?" she spat out. "Your mother stood up with your father, without proof of his manhood or his love! By Saint Theodore, it's not so in Gunib! Before a maiden yields her favors, she must be fought for! The greatest chief or the humblest woodcutter must fight a great fight, his friends and kinsmen battling beside him, against her friends and kinsmen."

If Lilith but knew it, she did not need jewels now. She was wearing a couple, odd-shaped and set on a slight slant, that outshone the most priceless star sapphires of a sultan's favorite.

"They come on fast horses at sundown to her father's house," she told me, quivering with excitement. "The guns shoot, and the hooves of their steeds thunder on the road. Then they rush to the door, where her kinsmen, gathered for a feast, fall upon them! Sweet Jesus knows they don't spare their rods, flailing one another's heads, and the noise of battle is terrible to hear. After half have fallen, bleeding and sore—and 'tis a wonder many aren't slain—the maiden's lover snatches her up, heedless of her wails and shriekings, hurls her to his croup, springs up before her, and spurs away. Her clan ride after him in vain, the mountains resounding with their shouts. Then when it's seen they can't overtake such a wild rider and mighty warrior—his love and valor have proved him worthy of her—then the clans make peace and feast and drink at the bride's house until dawn."

"Then all is forgiven," I proposed, getting a more secure seat against the rolling of the ship.

"Yea, soon after breakfast the pair return, he riding slowly, displaying the proofs of his conquest of her maidenhood, and she walking barefoot in the dust behind him—but that I'd never do!"

I had seen such proofs, displayed after the bridal night. The barbarous custom was not confined to Daghestan. Marriage-by-battle I had never seen, but had heard of its practice in various outlands of the earth. It was a sham battle, of course, and Lilith knew it; but no doubt the lively scene had been as dear to her girlish dreams as the veil and ring and all the rest of the dreams of little maids of my own country. And just now she was suffering from homesickness, I thought.

"If you refused to walk in the dust behind him, wouldn't he have beaten you until you did?"

"Yea, he wouldn't have cared how he striped my pretty back." Her high color faded fast.

"Then wouldn't you have been even more of a slave than you are now?"

"His beast in the field! And once he became a brother of my brother by the blood rite, I couldn't kill him with slow poison, only hate him until I withered up and died. Yet that would be better than being bought and sold by filthy soldiers. I'd have saved my honor, and gone to heaven without trial in purgatory." I thought she was about to break into tears.

"Lilith, I haven't made you a beast in the field, or even a stable-sweeper." I spoke as gently as possible, for it seemed to me that she was undergoing some quite real suffering.

"Nay, but you won't sell me to some rich pasha." Again two big tears escaped her eyes.

"And mark you, I didn't buy you with silver and gold. I fought for you, even as Gunib lovers for their sweethearts. That ought to console you for my lack of riches."

"You lie!" She hurled the words at me like a grenade, her eyes gleaming with unfeigned fury. "Your tongue was made for lies, and you've a serpent heart. Did you challenge Omar to the duel? Nay, he challenged you, and you'd have squirmed out of it like a worm save for the soldiers' eyes upon you. Only after the meet was set, did you pawn worthless Na'od against me. And even in the fight you didn't prove yourself worthy. Save for my folly—and it turns my stomach to think of it—he'd have killed you!"

Something had indeed turned her stomach. At the end of the outburst she uttered a gagging sound, and springing up, rushed onto the deck. So it was not homesickness she had been fighting with such a fiery spirit, although no doubt this had aggravated the misery. I had no inclination to laugh. Remembering my own spells on first putting out on the "Hattie"—torment just short of torture—I marveled she had fought it so long and well.

I followed her to the rail, to find her leaning over it, the picture of woe. When the spasm had passed, I picked her up, carried her to my couch, and drew curtains over the ports. The view of the rising, falling, tipping, rocking horizon is almost as sickening as the rolling waves themselves. Then I took a comfortable seat and drew her bright head onto my lap. To my astonishment she caught my hand and held it tight.

3.

While I did not and might never know the tides and gales and crosscurrents that bore Lilith's bark along, I would like to discover what cargo she had brought me. It seemed to be very rich. It was

263

happiness more real than any that had come my way in a long time, to hold her on my lap, quieted now, and sometimes kiss her eyelids and her throat.

Her clammy skin turned warm. She was sleeping like a child. Was there a place for her in my life, for the duration of my quest? I had a right to happiness on the long, perilous road. If I could win her not as my slave but my companion and delight during my Oriental exile, I would travel as fast and perhaps in better heart.

What would happen to her when I left Islam, in victory or defeat? My Turkic schooling would not let me ignore this. No doubt I could sell her to a prosperous but not princely Mussulman who would prize her highly. The fact she had been my couch mate for a year or two probably would not reduce her price as much as holding the same office for a day or two. Sensible Turks had no compunction against taking young and pretty widows—the same with sensible men everywhere.

Glowing with these good intentions—perhaps in Salem they would have seemed the quintessence of evil, but I was in Rome now—I coveted Lilith warmly, and having eaten my supper, lay down beside her. Although in deep sleep, apparently she sensed my presence, and was not ungrateful for it this cold rough night. As for me, I was mightily taken with her, sometimes dozing, more often in pleasant reverie, not greatly wrought upon by the touch of her body against mine since her innocent sleep and my sense of care and tenderness toward her became a more effective barrier than a naked scimitar. Her little hand was loath to let go of mine.

At the midnight bell I remained enough of a sailor to go out on the deck and look at the weather and our rigging. An old and leprous moon raced through ragged clouds against a stiff, crossbeam wind. The sea was choppy but not very rough and I judged we were making three or four knots. To listen to the wind and wave I made my way to the fo'c'slehead, which served me like reading poetry serves more sensitive, higher men—as sometimes it had me, when my mind was well attuned. I had no thought but to be alone as on an empty desert but to my great amazement someone followed me there.

An even greater surprise was to recognize Kagig, the Armenian who had talked to me about selling Lilith. I had not even known he had come aboard; it was queer I had not seen him in one of the boats. He gave me a rather deep salaam, for which I liked him no better, and then that one-sided smile of his that bent his face unpleasantly, for which I detested and, a little, feared him.

"Communing with nature, Selim Effendi?" he asked. Armenians of his trade did not commune with nature—they studied it searchingly, especially human nature. They lived by taking advantage of its weaknesses.

"Yes." I thought he might take from that short answer, that I wished to continue to do so.

"I've been idling about the deck, unable to sleep, and saw you go by. I thought to entreat a few minutes of your company."

"You have them, Kagig."

"Seeing you come here made me think you're reconsidering the proposal I made you. Otherwise you'd be in the company of your white slave."

"No, I haven't reconsidered it."

"Are you still determined to keep her, when a great lord of Islam, a potentially powerful friend—or, for that matter, a possibly dangerous enemy—will pay an extravagant price for her?"

I listened to the words, and more than that, to their tone and timbre. It came to me that he did not speak as urgently as before. It did not matter greatly to Kagig now whether I accepted his proposal or not. He had alternate means, almost as convenient, for winning his goal.

"Yes, I am."

Kagig yawned. "Well, then, I've wasted my time. I wish now the pasha hadn't intrusted me with the office. Rather than disappoint him entirely, I'll have to watch for every ship carrying slaves, pick them over, and try to find one that will please him."

This was not his alternate plan. He was just talking—and waiting. It occurred to me what his real plan was, but at first I had a little trouble believing it. I had not stayed long enough in Barbary and the Ottoman Empire. There were a few facts out here that I was still loath, or not quite able, to grasp.

"After all, his yearning for that particular Circassian is just a whim," he went on brightly. This could very well be true, I thought, but since my disappearance would cause no ripple in the Sea of Marmora, why shouldn't he gratify it? I knew now why I had not seen him before aboard the vessel—he had embarked secretly and been stowed away by confederates. After doing the job he was here for, he would again stow away until he could disembark secretly at Constantinople. He had hardly hoped for such an opportunity as my venturing on the fo'c'slehead in misty light and noisy weather.

Patently he had intended to go about it in some other way, but having an open mind, he had joined hands with kismet.

My heart was beating very fast but not fluttering yet or fainting. For that I could thank another scene over seawater—a dock in Salem, and Dick Featherstone sitting at ease beside me. This was an Oriental affair; and I felt almost a Turk's acceptance of fate. My show of casual conversation sounded well. Still I kept an Occidental concept of the value of human life—I could not kill him until certain that he intended to kill me. But the strain of waiting grew severe, and I decided to force his hand.

"It's a cold night, and I'm going below," I told him.

He was standing between me and the hatch. I thought his face changed expression—perhaps it was an illusion, for the moonlight was a faint mist—but his body remained relaxed and he stood lightly on his feet. My scalp felt tight and my spine began to tingle horridly, as though lightning were being aimed from a low-hanging cloud. Every movement and word seemed long drawn.

I thought he would draw back a step to let me pass him, then strike at my side or back. Prepared for these tactics, I dreaded them as the hardest to combat. He did not, perhaps because he did not trust a long stroke. Maybe he was an infighter, depending on a short, quick thrust. Perhaps he was overconfident.

"Yes, it's unseemly cold," he remarked, glad of the opening. He drew the collar of his coat higher about his throat, and his hands moved along his *baracan* as though drawing it closer about him. They did not stray toward the dagger in his belt. He had another somewhere near his left armpit, under his caftan.

His hand stole to the hilt. My hand was in position to draw my hunting knife, now with a decorated grip and worn in a Turkic scabbard to disguise its alienhood, and I was still defter with it than with any jeweled dagger. Because Kagig had hoped to conceal his murderous movement until his blade was bared, his slow start enabled me to beat him all along the line. Before he could grasp his haft, my blade was hissing from its sheath. Before his was half-drawn, mine was clear and slicing toward him. Before his point could touch my flesh, mine had plunged deep into his breast.

I had not anticipated his crying out as the cold steel pierced his heart chamber, or thought of it at all. Yet I found myself surprised that he did not—that any such vital being as Kagig, so intensely alive a second before, could die so quietly. I saw the life go out of him in a kind of shudder, and he fell so fast that only by a violent movement could I partly soften the sound of his body hitting the boards. Anyway it would not carry far above the splashing and tearing of the waves and the noises in the rigging.

There was no reason to believe that the slaying had been seen. The watch was busy on the main deck, no shout was raised, and no lantern lifted and hung still. I picked up Kagig's body, and holding it by the ankle, lowered it overside. Dangling it near the water as possible, I waited for a noisy sea, then let go. The sound changed a little, but seemed no louder, and in an instant was just one that had come and gone.

A draw bucket stood near by. This I lowered and filled to sluice away a dark spot on the boards, formed when I had withdrawn my knife. The blade I carefully washed and resheathed, before venturing down the deck to the companionway. Lilith wakened as I gently closed the door.

"Master?" she called.

"Yes?"

"Why did you leave me? I've been afraid. I'm not a mare to be left in a stable." So she spoke, in her wont, and it seemed impossible that I had just taken a human life.

"You've never shown you desired my company, and I took some air."

"Nay, you've been dallying with some female slave. Your voice betrays your guilt." But as I lighted the lantern with my tinderbox she sat up staring, her ire giving way to alarm.

"Your hands are shaking," she gasped. For the first time she felt concern for me, mainly from realizing that her fortunes were linked with mine.

"Your stomach was turning and twisting a few hours ago. How is it now?"

"What's happened? You're pale, and your eyes look black as night!"

The impulse came to me to tell her of the business. It might make her respect me more. On the other hand she might make use of it against me.

"If you must know, I've been feeding the fish." This vulgarly humorous expression was as current in Osmanli as in English. Truly I had fed them though, and horridly—sharks most likely, maybe conger eels if any dwelt in these waters, cold, creeping things on the bottom, and sea lice. Maybe I had fed kites that fly along the shore. That ought not to trouble Selim-ul-Reuben for the Koran bade the Faithful be good to bird and beast, but my skin prickled all over.

Lilith had made no immediate reply. When I looked at her, expecting an outburst of acrimony, she appeared actually a little ashamed.

"You were seasick?" she asked, looking at the wall.

"I said as much."

"Sick like me?"

"What of it?"

"You, who battled Omar and killed a tiger, made sick by the rolling of the waves?"

"Laugh at me, if you will."

"Nay," she said, after thinking it over, "I won't laugh at you for that—as you didn't at me when I said I liked Giafar the dwarf."

In the morning I stood by the rail with my fellow passengers, and as opportunity offered, studied every man's face. None betrayed the faintest surprise at finding me hale and whole in their company. Likely the Osmanli lecher who coveted Lilith had embarked on another ship. However, someone—perhaps a sailor—had helped Kagig stow away, and was no doubt wondering what in the devil had happened to the fellow.

4.

"Is this where you expect me to live?" Lilith demanded, gazing about my quarters at the Seraskierat in disdain.

"For the present, yes."

"Why, Omar's tent in the field was more richly furnished than this hovel."

"No doubt he'd buy you back from me, with a scimitar set with flawed jewels, and I've a mind to make the bargain."

"Where are your other female slaves?"

"I have none."

"By my sweet saints, do you expect me to spend my days in dreary solitude, without even one merry damsel to sport with? In the haremlik to the *Reis* Effendi, I'd had fifty."

"What you need is fifty strokes of a kurbash, and I've a mind to give them to you."

"Your words are big, but your deeds small. You'll not stripe my back and so reduce my price on the day you put me on sale, for well you know your life will be a burden to you until you do."

"No, I'll not stripe your back," I told her, in sudden fury over all the trouble I had had on her account, and at her low esteem of me. "But there's another way to teach you a lesson."

With that I seized her, pinioned her arms before she could rake me with her nails, and dropping to the floor, flung her across my knee. Perhaps I had intended to do no more than this—to scare her and demonstrate my power over her—but when she continued to resist, shrieking imprecations and threats, I could not resist finishing the business I had started. It was to fling my leg across the back of her knees to stop her wriggling and twisting, bare her spanking place, and lay on with the flat of my hand.

Although a ridiculous performance, I was enjoying it. It would do Lilith no harm, it seemed, and me a great deal of good. Then her shouts of fury turned into shrieks of seeming pain. My hand was big and hard and the smart of it plus the sharp smacking sound convinced the child that she was being tortured. She was nothing but a child in her personality, and if I would remember that, we could get along better. But her form was of budding womanhood, complicating all my relations with her, including the present one, to the ribald mirth of the gods. Spanking thus a pretty grown girl is not a wise procedure by any young man on many counts. He becomes inclined to forgive her everything.

She began to wail for mercy. "Will you stop your plagued scolding and complaining?" I demanded, still whacking her.

"Oh, truly, I'll never say another wicked word." She was blubbering like a six-year-old.

"Will you treat me with the honor due your master, and be grateful for my care and kindness?"

"Let me go, lord, and I'll be your dove."

The extremes of Ottoman expression had never struck me as so extravagant before.

"Have I given you any more than you deserved?"

"Not a tittle of my deserving, and if you took a horsewhip to me, it would be my due, but be merciful to your slave."

At that I let her go, but she was crying so hard by now that she could hardly rise from my lap. This was something more than the pain and humiliation of the spanking: she was easily persuaded to turn over and lie in my arms, her head against my shoulder. I was glad now of the preposterous incident with its low comedy: it had released some dammed-up feelings in the child and opened my eyes to her situation. She did not belong to me any more than Roxana belonged to some bearded Turk who called himself her master. I would never punish her again for her rebelliousness and spite, although even now I could not wholly account for them.

"I'm a wicked girl," she whimpered, when the storm began to pass over.

"I don't believe it. You may go to sleep there, if you like."

"I've been wicked from the start, but the worst was to do you so ill, when you've been kind to me. I'll entreat you no more to sell me to a rich pasha."

"What do you think of Hassan Serdar? He offered me a thousand dinars for you."

"And poor as you are, you refused?"

"Yes."

"Yet it was no paltry price, although I might bring more."

"Aye, as Circassian girls are counted, it was a good price."

"He too is a soldier, living half the time in camps."

"But in tents far finer than Omar's."

"Still I'd not want him to buy me, unless you want to get rid of me for my wickedness and vile tongue."

"I don't want to get rid of you, Lilith."

"Then until you do, I'll be your faithful slave, and obey your every command."

"Do you know what you're saying?"

"Yes, master." But tears filled her eyes again.

"Even against your will?"

"The will of the master should be the will of his slave. Our priest told me so, when against his entreaty and stern injunction I went away from Gunib to be sold in Byzantium."

"What if I command you to share my couch tonight?"

"To hear is to obey." She looked woebegone.

"Then will I wake with a sharp pain in my belly as you threatened?"

"No, I'll take no vengeance on you."

"Even to speak of vengeance means you'd think I'd wronged you."

"No, lord. I didn't mean to say it. You'll be in your full rights, as my master."

"I can't give you that command against your will."

I had hoped she would protest that—urge me to exercise my rights as her owner—perhaps hint that my will in the matter might easily become her own. I knew then that I wanted her more than I had ever confessed to myself. Nor was I such a fool as to be ashamed of it, when it was very life.

"Anyway, it would be better for you, if later you decide to sell me," she answered. "And I'll serve you in a hundred better ways, guarding your meat against poison, and your belongings against theft, and seeing to your wardrobe and serving your meals. I'll converse with you or be silent at your wish. And when you're weary I'll sing the songs of Gunib, most sweet songs, even though I can't play on a dulcimer."

"It will be a joy to me to have you kiss and caress me. Would that be distasteful to you?"

"No, lord, if it goes no further than is winked at in Gunib, when young men and maids make merry at harvest home, at the May pole, and such festivals. I'd take no shame in that, if it doesn't waken evil in your heart."

"I'd still consider your wishes, Lilith."

"Then that far, I'm your willing slave."

When I proposed that she kiss me, she did so, shyly and very flushed of face. It was a sweet and most welcome favor, but at my gusto in reply her eyes widened and she sprang out of my lap to her feet.

"Master, it's not well that you—" She stopped, not knowing what to say.

"Is that how you keep your word?"

"Forgive me, effendi—and be gentle with me—for I fear you'll not keep your word."

"I will, Lilith. And the rest is my business, not yours."

"Aye, it is—in anything you do to me—and it's wrong of me to cross you. Yet be merciful to me in this one thing."

She obeyed me, in childlike trust, and the hour that we idled away was my happiest and least lonely holiday since setting sail from France. There was no reason to think that Lilith found it distasteful, and some signs, patent to any lover, that she was as delighted with it as I. Without making any resistance unseemly in a slave girl, she managed to instruct me in what was and was not permissible in Gunib courtships, and to my great pleasure those wild mountaineers were by no means prudes. But she remained heart and soul unwilling to favor me beyond that point, and there was no indication whatever of future yielding.

On the following morning Bayezid called on me, faintly smiling in his fashion. He had not succeeded in obtaining for me an audience with the Sultan, nor would that sublime being take any public notice of my good race with the Cham of Tartary or my good fight with Omar. This was from political considerations: apparently he hoped to win over the recalcitrant Janissaries and did not care to rub these victories in their faces. However, the *Reis* Effendi was looking after me privately. I had been promoted two steps to lieutenant colonel in the artillery corps and would have in my charge the instruction of rapid fire at the barracks in Uskudar across the Bosporus from the capital, meanwhile of course ever on call to help entertain royal guests on the hunting field. My salary would not be large but my emoluments pretty, including well-furnished quarters.

"I thank you kindly, Bayezid Effendi."

"Furthermore, I've a good offer for Rustum from a colonel of Janissaries," he went on. "The sum named was eight hundred dinars, all the brute's worth, but if you authorize me to ask a thousand, you'll get it, out of sentimental considerations."

"I'm not yet well versed in Turkic sentiment."

"The gentlemen of the corps can't abide the sight of you astride the prize won to their woe."

"Pray you, sell the stud for what you can get. And that reminds me—I won another prize, doubtless to their mortification."

"So you did. Are you thinking of selling her? I fancy the bidding would be brisk."

"Do you think they'd feel the same about her as about Rustum?" I was trying to explore every angle of my affair with Kagig.

"The feat of equestrianship involved is not so public." The wording was very delicate for Bayezid.

Making sure that Lilith was not at the keyhole, I told him about my two meetings with Kagig. His eyes sparkled and his mustache appeared to bristle during the latter part of the recital. He rubbed his big nose and considered.

"I'd venture the affair was a private one between you and a rich, baseborn coveter of the maid's charms," he remarked. "Truly I haven't the slightest notion who the wretch might be. I do know it wasn't Hassan Serdar, who's a gentleman, and God knows it wasn't I, and since Omar is famed for keeping his given word, I'd wager my hopes of paradise that it wasn't he. It could have been the Agazzi, but I doubt it, since he's inclined to well-rounded, definite brunettes from Ethiopia. Timor-id-Osman is pleased with you and as the half-brother of the Sultan, he would not stoop to a Gunib savage. Probably it was some other rich and rash Janissary."

272

"Will he be so rash as to try again? I'm fond of sound sleep."

"If he believes the lady treats you no better than Omar, he may try again to buy her or even some other device, but there are certain inconveniences connected with committing murder, even on the Golden Horn. The sea trip furnished him with a rare opportunity. You were to disappear while he was on another ship; no doubt he had forged a contract to buy the Circassian. But if you're poisoned or stabbed, any such document will be suspect. Actually King David's crime is not winked at in Constantinople—it creates public indignation—every owner of a choice bit thinks his turn may be next. Besides, I'll breathe about the court that we know a great deal more than we let on. Provided you don't allow yourself to be decoyed alone into dark alleys—I'm speaking, mind you, only of dangers from without— I think you may enjoy your prize, and sleep soundly."

"That's good news. Now I would like to ask you one question. Do you know a slave-trader by the name of Kemal?"

"I have heard of a silk-dealer by that common cognomen." He paused, his eyes full of thoughts. "It's my turn now. You're no ordinary renegade, Selim. I ask you, before Allah, or by any god you may believe, does your real business in Islam bode harm to the Sultan, or to my Faith?"

"By Allah, or by whatever name God is called, it doesn't."

"You'll oblige me by not telling me anything more about it. Kemal, specializing in beautiful and accomplished Circassians, and private purveyor to some of the greatest lords in Islam, has a silk shop by the Mosque of the Shah Zadeh."

He had coffee with me and departed: that very afternoon I called at Kemal's bazaar. I had never seen such silks and satins, clothes of gold and silver, laces and velvets; he loved soft, beautiful textures. Kemal himself was an aesthetic, almost effeminate-looking Turk and were he not a Moslem I would have taken him for a eunuch. He did not concern himself with me at first, as he waited on a heavily-veiled woman, but turned me over to a bustling clerk. I bought enough transparent rose-colored Samarkand to make a *baracan* for Lilith.

"You have good taste, effendi," Kemal told me, when his customer had gone out. "I have more expensive fabrics, but few more beautiful."

"I've often found that the best is not the most costly—perhaps because the vulgar rich compete for the gaudy instead of the delicate and rare."

"You're a man after my own heart. I must trade with the money-bags, but my joy is to entertain a connoisseur."

"I am Selim-ul-Reuben, the Sultan's host at his hunting lodge to the Cham of Tartary. *Salem alicum!*"

"*Alicum Salem,* effendi."

"Perhaps it's a lucky thing, since my blood is nobler than my purse is heavy, that I've only one in my household beautiful enough to wear this cloth from Samarkand."

"I've no doubt that she's truly a moon of beauty." His eyes glistened.

"She would not be considered so in the eyes of the vulgar. She's not fat, nor has she a long nose. Not one of her features is perfect—yes, perhaps her brow—but each is in harmony with the other, to make as a chord of music."

"Will you join me, effendi, in a cup of coffee? My apprentices can take care of the customers."

I thanked him, and was presently seated on an alcove sofa, where he no doubt entertained his richest clients. He hoped for profit from me, but also he wanted to talk about beauty like the artist he was. I had become a little uneasy. There might be many slave merchants named Kemal in the city, and I could hardly picture this voluptuary roughing it throughout Islam buying stolen goods.

"Kemal, I know you had to go to the ends of the Empire, to procure those treasures," I proposed, gesturing toward the laden chests. "Have you ever visited the Caucasus?"

"Why, yes. Beautiful rugs are made there."

"They're not the finest things that come out of Caucasia. Why should beautiful rugs exist, save for feet of snow to walk upon them, or beautiful colors, save to set off the warm, white silk that only Allah fashions on a magic loom?"

"Why, indeed, and you put it in good words."

"Kemal Effendi, one jewel in a ring is a pretty thing, but when two are set there, or three, each differing from the other, but all of first water, then the hidden beauties of each is revealed. I'm of a mind to buy another."

"Why, that shouldn't be difficult. There are some good merchants in the city."

"I'd rather deal with the best."

Kemal put down his coffee cup. "Will you tell me, Selim Effendi, who recommended me to you?"

"Gladly. It was a gentleman I met at the caravanserai at Ada bazaar, named Timor-id-Izmid."

He clapped his hands, whereupon one of his clerks drew aside the curtain, "Ali, bring me the yellow book."

It was brought, and Kemal thumbed its pages. "I've no record of a client of that name," he said.

"I don't remember his saying that he was a client of yours. But he knew of your reliability and proposed I go to you for such cloth as I needed—and such jewels. On second thought, he said that when he called here, about two years ago, you were away on one of your journeys—to the Barbary States, if I remember correctly."

I was not looking straight at him and took a sip from my cup. Still it was made known to me that he had been in Barbary about two years ago—he did not have to think back, so well he remembered. And now I knew I was sitting beside the slave-buyer who had looked over some contraband brought into Algiers by murderers, and after close examination, had bought it. He had not wanted the three sailors but had to take them to get a tall, fair-haired Frankistan girl whose peculiar beauty appealed to his epicurean eyes. He had known it was a dangerous transaction, and might not even be very profitable, since some of his richest clients did not have such eyes. Indeed it was a lucky thing for the Turkic pirates that Kemal happened to be in Algiers at that time. He was not virile but he was brave; I doubted if he had ever bedded a beautiful female slave, but he had a connoisseur's knowledge of her parts.

In his handsome head this moment was the remembrance of that incident, one of the most exciting in his beauty-delving life. Not only that—in the forefront of his mind was the name of Roxana's buyer, the price he had paid, and his abode. All I needed to know for my last great stroke was there, a foot or two from me. But I could not strike his head open with my scimitar and read the tidings. That less than finger breadth of skin and bone remained a formidable barricade. Be patient, Roxana, for I must!

"What friends have you in the city whom I may know?" Kemal asked. For the finger-breadth thickness of my skull was alike impervious to him.

"I'm in the service of the *Reis* Effendi. My friends are Hassan Serdar of the artillery—Bayezid Effendi—"

"If you're a friend of Bayezid, you need no other recommendation. And it's true, *sahabti*, I buy a few jewels for exacting clients, although to avoid traffic with the vulgar—as well as the disfame to which brutish merchants have brought the trade—I choose to keep the matter confidential."

"I'll regard it so. But as I confessed, my purse is not heavy." I put aside my cup and rose.

"I don't choose my clients by the weight of their purses but by the discernment of their minds. I'll be happy to have you call again."

This might be great gain in the course of time, but perhaps there was a shorter road to the same end. I was not now watching his face as closely as the yellow book in his hand. As we walked together from the alcove into the bazaar he passed it to a clerk, who put it among larger books in an iron-doored open vault built into the wall.

I had perceived that it was a neatly kept record of numbered names: plainly Kemal had an orderly as well as voluptuous mind. One of the books in the vault was no doubt a day-to-day ledger of the preceding year. In it he had probably recorded every large transaction.

5.

It would be safe for me to call again in about a week, to tell Kemal how well my slave girl was pleased with the Samarkand silk, and say nothing that would remind him of Algiers. After two or three such calls, he might invite me to his *gulphor* and, amid frankincense and myrrh and the perfume of pomegranate sherbet, become more confidential. Meanwhile I might get a close look at the vault, learn something of the day and night procedure of the shop, and even pick out an apprentice or account-keeper whom, though at heavy risk, I might try to bribe.

Meanwhile I was pleased with my slave girl. On the following day she, Na'od, and I moved to our new quarters at the outskirts of Uskudar. They were fit for entertaining Kemal in return for his hospitality to me; I had plainly come up in the world. The reception rooms were ample, the haremlik large enough for a round dozen wives and female slaves, the balconies airy, the small private garden green and fruitful. With the other excellent furnishings went a eunuch steward, a capable cook, a gardener, two sweepers, and four Negresses for scullery and chamber service, all gifts from the *Reis* Effendi.

"What do you think of it?" I asked Lilith, when her keen blue eyes had taken everything in.

"There's no fountain and no fish pool," she replied, although without great reproach.

"No, there's not."

"The baths don't compare with those at the palace of the *Reis* Effendi."

"I'm only a colonel of horse, not the Grand Vizier."

"I've seen far finer couches, and the censers are of silver, not gold. Yet Omar-id-din lived in no better state, if quite as good."

"It's a pity the *Reis* Effendi failed to provide me with young female slaves. But I can buy two well-favored girls with the money I'm getting for Rustum, and later, as my purse thickens, purchase some beautiful Greeks and Georgians."

"For me to wait on, doubtless! By my saints, I'll poison 'em first!" Her breast had swelled and her eyes gleamed.

"No, you won't be called upon to serve them, or they you. You'll all be equal in my regard."

"You lie! They'll be your favorites, because they'll kneel to you. You'll put me in the scullery. You lust for a hatchet-faced Greek, or a fat Georgian Jewess. You're a lecher from crown to heel!"

"Only three days ago you scolded me for not having female slaves for you to sport with. I'm only thinking of your happiness."

"I'll make friends with the Negro women—they're a merry sort— and you may spend the money on jewels and fine raiment for me—or even put it in your purse, if you're that stingy. Mark you, your lusting for other girls is nothing to me. You can make them your favorites for all I care—I spoke in anger at the insult to a daughter of Gunib worth a thousand dinars. But since you swear you don't want them save to ease my loneliness, I'll do without their merry company, just to test the truth or falsehood of your words."

"Of course, my love for a beautiful Grecian lady would be nothing to you," I told the brat in a kindly tone. "How could it be, when you refuse the proffer?"

"That stands to reason." She turned her face from me and what served her for an Adam's apple bobbed up and down her pretty neck. "And you've a serpent's tongue!"

I petted and kissed her, and thought her response was somewhat more vehement than usual. Sweet-tempered again, she set about taking charge of the house, pointedly let my steward know that she was its mistress, and with childish delight saw to my creature comforts. I left her puttering about; and on my return from the drill field, there awaited me on the foot-high table a tasty supper.

The rules of courtship in Gunib proved somewhat more lax than she had at first confided. As we became better acquainted she assured me that such-and-such a delight would do either of us no harm, in an attempt to deceive herself and me that was far more provocative than frank desire. Her grateful surprise at the consequences always enchanted her—but raised the devil in me. Actually she had never been wooed in this fashion either at harvest home in Gunib or in the tents of Omar, but I was in my rights as her master, she told me, as long as I did not break my promise. Her cheeks would flush and her eyes sparkle or grow dreamy as little gales swept through her: in me they aroused great gales. But apparently she felt no need of surrendering all to me and did not seem to understand my growing tension.

At least this was true for our first week in our new home. Thereafter I suspected that Mother Nature had begun to plague her too, demanding of her what she would not give, to her inward stress. Her tongue that had been honeyed grew sharp again and she had a good many crying spells and fits of anger. As for me, I knew now what mankind has known ever since civilized society began—that a young man and maid of mutual attraction cannot live together and sleep in the same room for many nights without becoming either mates or nervous wrecks. Saint Anthony could not have endured the day-and-night proximity of this provocative lass; and I had never aspired to a halo.

Dealing with a fact, I deduced another fact. It was that unless Lilith consented to become my natural mate, I would have to get rid of her. I could not take the way of the high-handed Turk. I was not too kind and honorable—but Roxana too was a slave.

But I had warmed and ripened her, and when toward the end of the second week I sensed a change in her, I had good reason to hope that she had decided in my favor. She did not come as frequently into my arms and even demanded a little coaxing. She was quieter, her temper sweet again, and when unconscious of my scrutiny she moved about with a look of joyful anticipation on her face. She was like a child bride-to-be on her wedding day, I thought, and suggestive of a little girl expecting a doll for Christmas. I had sense enough not to rush matters and fell in with all her whims.

Meanwhile the young moon was rounding every night, extraordinarily brilliant this clear, winter weather. Lilith harbored a lively set of superstitions about the heavenly bodies, and I thought she might be waiting for the full moon, the climax of various rites and festivals in her savage tribe, to bring our period of courtship to a happy ending. It chanced that on that evening our corps would celebrate some bygone victory of Ottoman arms with gymkhana and feasting. I was prepared to forego the officers' fiesta if it conflicted with Lilith's plans, but she urged me to attend the games, drink sparingly of the forbidden wines, and return an hour after moonrise. I took it that she was going to spread a bridal feast for me.

While I drank syrups and jested with my comrades, the hands of my watch moved it seemed almost as tardily as when I had waited for Roxana on Gallows Hill. The remembrance was followed by a twinge of shame, but it did not bite very deep—men have to live! Fifty minutes after the moon had shown her silver rim I left the mess and rode the short distance to my house. I had thought that all the windows would be lighted and the inmates scurrying about. Instead the lamps were low and its little noises hushed, but that might be by Lilith's provision, a sweeter reception to me than I had figured on.

Na'od took my mare and the steward let me in the gallery door.

"I didn't expect you so soon, my lord," he told me, "or I'd been more generous with the oil."

"It is well. Where's your mistress?"

"She hasn't left her apartments since sundown."

"Has she had supper?"

"She ordered none, lord, or any spread for you, so I took it she intended to make a feast when you returned. I can fix some quickly."

"Wait a while."

I did not know what to expect on approaching the door of the haremlik. When alone she usually kept it bolted, admitting me at my call; when it opened readily I supposed she had one or more of the Negresses keeping her company, or had prepared some sort of "surprise." But there was no flurry when I came in, no sound of mellow voices, and as yet no sign of any reception. The rooms remained exceedingly still, and dimly lighted by a single lamp burning in the main bedchamber. Perhaps my welcome was to be made there. But my hopes had plummeted now, and I went through the curtained arch half expecting to find her asleep.

The "surprise" awaiting me was very great indeed. Lilith was not on her couch or anywhere to be seen. The bed coverings lay strewn on the floor, the fruit stand had been tipped over and its salver of apples spilled, and the casement overlooking the courtyard flung wide. Fitted to the window was an iron grate, the same with most windows of the haremliks of Byzantium. This too hung open.

My first frantic alarm instantly passed. My heart felt cold as I glanced again at the somehow orderly confusion in the room, and then examined the evidence of a robbery. It was a quick, but fruitful examination. Long before now I had observed that the iron bolt of the window grate might possibly be broken by a heavy tool of peculiar shape thrust through the bars from without, but it could not possibly be slid save from within. Tonight it had been slid.

I had no need to wonder how Lilith could be forcibly abducted, fighting and screaming for help, without alarming the house. The thing I could really wonder at was what happened inside of me. It would have amazed my Turkic friends, even broad-minded Bayezid. I felt no angry passion toward her and her fellow conspirators, only weary gratitude that they had not again sought my life. As to the troubled child from the fastnesses of Daghestan, I had only a devastating sense of failure.

I turned to leave the room, perplexed what to tell my more faithful slaves. Then, facing the curtains I had just passed through, I saw a sheet of paper pinned level with my eyes where it could not possibly be overlooked.

The handwriting was of an almost illiterate person, half the words misspelled, but in so large a script I read it with ease:

I'm one of your enemy's slaves. I hate my master and want you to avenge the evil he has done you.

He's taking your beautiful white slave worth two thousand gold dinars to his boat hidden by Seljuk quay, meaning to cross with her at midnight, he having bribed the watch, and put her in his great palace as his favorite. If you come with half a dozen of your friends and kinsmen you may get her back unharmed. We will ride slowly through lonely lanes not to raise an alarm, and if you'll make haste you may intercept us at Kubbe Bridge. The moon is nearly an hour up as I write this.

Your Unknown Friend.

6.

Rushing to the stable, I found Amine almost ready to ride. Lazy Na'od had barely loosened her cinch and slipped her bit from her jaw. Even so, I took time to hold a lantern to the mud-daubed cobblestones of the alley leading to my courtyard. At least four horses and possibly several more had come and gone within the last half-hour.

Still I did not go back for my rifle. The enemy would hardly be bold enough to defend his ill-gotten gains with musketry on the busy bridge or the well-guarded quays, and only on secluded ground make any stand at all. So I raced across the parade ground to the officers' mess, handed my reins to an orderly, and sped to the table, no higher than a stool, around which half a dozen of my junior officers were squatted, drinking fig wine.

"A slave has been stolen from my haremlik," I told them. "Will you ride with me to get her back?"

This was stronger drink than any on the board. Instantly the stout fellows were on their feet, and in a moment astride their horses. Wildly we rode, to their general and my special joy, out the cantonment gate and by the shortest cut to Kubbe Bridge. I wished that Lilith could see us, riding abreast in full dress uniform, our heads encircled with the gold-embroidered shawl fastened to our caps, our *baracans* bright with gold and silver cloth, our baggy trousers of blue cashmere, and our boots bright yellow. But it would not be long, I figured, before we afforded her the fine sight. Although my fellows would not believe it, I had every hope of intercepting the thieves before they could gain the Kubbe Bridge.

Galloping hotly from a side lane into Courier Road we found ourselves fifty paces in the van of six big fellows well mounted and no doubt well armed, and one little fellow on a lead palfrey. For the moment I was not quite sure that these were not peaceful wayfarers. If our quarry, they must have had numerous and provoking delays in their two-mile ride from my house, since they were still three furlongs short of the bridge. But we had hardly checked for a better look at them when the *baracan* covering the head of the undersized rider appeared to blow down in the brisk wind, revealing in the limpid moonlight a wealth of bright-colored hair.

Alarmed at our cavalcade, but still uncertain of our identity, the rogues had checked their horses. Perhaps they could hardly believe that their well-laid plans had gone awry, and we had overtaken them with such dispatch. But when I shouted "Have at them!" all doubt was removed. Instantly they wheeled up the road, hoping to give us the slip in the dim light or to gain more secluded ground to fight us. So everything was perfect, thus far—a fine, hot race in the making but with their escape over the bridge cut off.

We followed with lusty shoutings, spurring our horses to their fastest clip. Their hooves clattered rhythmically on the cobblestones, and our spurs and bridles and scabbard chains made a tremendous jingle. But presently the sport was spoiled for me. The halter rope leading the palfrey was too short to give the little beast his head, and already overtaxed by his taller, faster leader, he was likely to fall. Moreover, from the awkward way Lilith grasped her pommel I feared that her wrists were bound.

I had had enough, regardless of her ideas. I yearned to see her captor set her pony free. He did not at once, perhaps because he had rashly lashed the halter to his saddle. The quarry turned into a lane that led toward the great Moslem cemetery on the high ground behind the town. We thundered after them, lost sight of them in a grove of cypress trees, then saw them looming on the crest of the hill. Seeing we were overtaking them, at last their leader reached back to cut the palfrey's lead rope. But they did not try to make off. The whole passel wheeled toward us, drawing their scimitars.

Undoubtedly they were bodyguardsmen of a no inconsiderable Turk, perfectly capable of giving us a hard and bloody fight. Still it did not stand to reason that they would do more than uphold their own and their master's honor. Gunfire would summon the watch, and they could hardly hope to vanquish all of us and recapture their prize. Besides, one of their corpses left on the battleground would convict their master of the heinous crime of slave-stealing. Even so, there was no predicting the lengths the bloody belligerent Turk would go, once he smelled battle.

"*Allah Akbar!*" shouted my puny-captain, as we bared and drove at them.

When they did not draw their pistols, I had every reason to believe that they would keep their heads and be content with saving face. That was what I had hoped for, to make the entire venture an astounding success. The proof of it came when, engaging them hotly, they did not cut at us, only parried our strokes with soldierly skill. At once my men sensed in the way of soldiers that this was only a passage of arms, and no longer went for them tooth and nail. But it made a good show and a lively clatter of steel. Truly it was good sport for my lusty *spahis*, and no doubt an unspeakable delight to one onlooker. As the foe gave ground toward a grove of cypress, I hacked away my level best to increase the din.

"Hah!" cried my puny-captain, as his blade drew blood.

"Run for it, before they know my face," the leader shouted—doubtless quite a fellow at the coffee houses. They had almost gained the grove by now, and were glad enough to scamper into the dark. Some of my men followed them a distance, shouting and shooting pistols, but soon sped back to rejoice with me at regaining my prize.

As I started toward her, she was leaning forward in the saddle, her head sprightly set on her neck, and seeking a last glimpse of the flying foe. Seeing us approach, she minded her manners and began to cry a little, as was no doubt proper.

"Are you hurt, Lilith?" I asked in a gentle voice.

"Only lame and sore from struggling, and that's nothing. I was helpless against them—but sweet Jesus, what a mighty battle you and your men fought! How many are slain?"

"By a miracle, not one."

"I knew you'd ride to my help, and delayed them in a dozen ways. But how were you able to trail them so swiftly?" Her voice shook a little.

"Luckily, one of their own wicked band felt remorse for the evil, and left a letter telling me the road. But that can wait, until you're rested and refreshed."

I cut the strap that bound her wrists and gave her the reins. I did not think that her ordeal had been so trying that she could not control and stay on a horse. Hereafter she could have the trim, fleet, sure-footed, well-bred Kurd for her own, a well-deserved memento of her adventure.

It was not good manners for me to pay any more attention to her while in the company of my officers. Those rode abreast with me on the homeward jaunt; Lilith ambled behind me. Only when they pulled up at our gate to bid me good night, all of them immensely pleased to have shared in such a virtuous as well as short-order victory, feeling themselves no end of fellows for protecting the sanctity of my home and waving away my thanks, did she make bold to address me.

"Master, will you offer my thanks with yours, to your valiant friends, for saving me from a fate worse than death?" she asked.

They had of course heard of her sharp tongue and vixen defiance and could hardly believe their ears at this pretty, modest speech which they supposed filled the bill so well. Either she had been maligned, they thought, or I had done a wondrous job of taming the shrew. Every one of the rascals bowed low; and careful not to stare at her, gave me a slightly wondering but certainly flattering glance. My scamp of a puny-captain answered handsomely, his voice vibrant with emotion.

When the *spahis* had ridden away, Lilith followed me demurely to the garden door of the haremlik, which I opened with my key. "It was a dreadful ordeal for you," I told the child, "and to speak of it would only rack you further. At some other time, when the shock has passed off, you may tell me the particulars."

"You're merciful to your slave."

"Now you may set the room to rights. There's no use of setting my servants' tongues to clacking." Doubtless these were already busy with what they could surmise of the night's business.

She obeyed meekly, while I refastened the window grate. Thereafter I summoned a wide-eyed Negress and ordered a light but luxurious repast served in our rooms. It was ready by the time another of the wenches had bathed and perfumed Lilith, dressed her hair, and arrayed her in her prettiest jellick and azure pantaloons. Tonight she wore no *baracan* of transparent silk as we sat on cushions at the low table from which rose the fragrance of taponi dates, spice-cakes, sweetmeats, the nectar of pomegranates, and a long-stored flask of fig wine.

When the trays were removed, she lighted my houka for me and passed me the stem.

"Lilith, the day will come that I must leave Islam and dwell in Frankistan," I told her, while the bowl bubbled cheerfully. It was a long-awaited moment of crisis and my voice was not as calm as I had wished.

"Yes, lord," she replied with averted gaze.

"Until then you will be foremost in my train. But in Frankistan I have a wife, and it's not lawful there for a man to have more than one wife, or concubines or female slaves of his body. So when my kismet sets me on that road—after a great venture—I can't take you with me."

"What would you do with me, I make bold to ask?" Her eyes had grown big.

"I thought to sell you to some rich pasha who'd be agreeable to you, and treat you kindly."

"There's no harm in that," she answered, sweetly and cheerfully.

It was my favorite Turkic expression. I loved it now, for it allayed a deep-seated anxiety I had not confessed, born of my Western upbringing. I needed no more balm for my but feebly troubled conscience. It was easy to forget that this blue-eyed child was not competent to make a contract of such consequence in her life—that she lived from hour to hour, without thought of tomorrow. I too denied the future. The bridge could be crossed when I came on it, I thought, with a wanton leap of my heart.

"My unknown friend in the band of thieves gave your worth as two thousand dinars," I went on, unable to resist teasing her, although with a straight face, about this remarkable echo of her own opinion. For suddenly I was in that wonderful state of elation which wooers know when the prize—long-craved, hard-sought, seemingly too good to be true—comes within their grasp. "But I'll take less than that sum, when the time arrives, to see you well and happily provided for."

"Still you needn't sell me for a song, even though—" She paused, her lovely color growing.

"I know not how long it will be, but it's unwise to waste time. Even now you're a beautiful, shapely woman, ripe for love. Would there be harm in your lying in my arms?"

"It would be my pleasure, if it's yours." Trying hard to conceal her yearning, she rose and climbed into my lap.

"Perhaps there's no cause to deny ourselves any pleasure we may give or take tonight in each other. It's come to me that your saints, or a happy kismet, have brought about the performance of the sacred rites of Gunib even here on the Golden Horn."

"Why, I hadn't thought of that!" She was so happy that it was no trouble to her to look astonished.

"Yet it's true, as by a miracle."

"Yea, and I'll make grateful offerings all my days. The villains seized me, and would have undone me, but my master, leading his brethren, followed them on his steed, won the race, fought a great fight with them, and proved his valor and his care of me—even as in Gunib."

"I couldn't have won such a fight out of mere care of you, Lilith. My heart was in it."

"A lion heart, truly. And any joy that my lord takes in me, will be not my dishonor but my joy too, and pride; and there'll be no sin on my soul to be burned away in purgatory."

To the victor belongs the spoils! In this case the victory was hers as well as mine, and the prize to be blissfully shared. I could afford to abstain from the sweet offering a moment more, in breathless anticipation; and in reflecting on our troubled courtship culminating tonight, I felt for Lilith what a French king, speaking of his sweetheart, called "inflamed respect."

Her inmost being had demanded that she surrender honorably or not at all, according to what was right in her native land, but she had been no hairsplitter as to trivial detail. A bigot might point out that the ceremony had been back-end to—in Gunib the lover and his party stole the girl from her home while her kinsmen fought to retrieve her, but tonight he had been the rescuer instead of the thief.

Lilith, with fundamental common sense, had looked to the spirit and not the letter of the ritual and made the best of adverse conditions.

Her resources in the matter amazed me. Granted that the clandestine advances of some rich Turk, probably the very one that had sent Kagig to kill me, had presented the initial opportunity, she had seized and shaped it with bold and capable hands. She had consented to the abduction, set the time on the feast-night, and by some trickery found out where his boat was to be docked. I did not doubt that by devious tricks she could have prevented the crossing until midnight, in case the delays she was able to bring about did not permit me to overtake her on the road.

It was significant that she had not given me the name or the address of the wealthy pasha who coveted her. If I had failed to rescue her, her abductor would have proven his worth in her eyes; and she was too much of a child to perceive what a perilous leap in the dark she had taken. I did not doubt she would have had a rude wakening in the slave-stealer's harem and would have wished she had stayed with me, even without the benefit of the marriage-rites of Gunib. The fact remained that the reckless little savage had provided a fair fight; she had not stacked the cards although she had undoubtedly wanted me to win. In either case she would win, she had thought—the desire of every real heroine. Knowing the brutal Turk, in this case probably a cold-blooded killer, I was aghast to think that had he succeeded in the abduction, the affair would have been closed.

Could I find fault with her brave and ingenuous, although deadly dangerous, folly, when it was according to her sense of right and wrong? Thank heaven, I was not such an outlander; Roxana had taught me tolerance, the keystone of civilized thinking and feeling. Anyway I had gone to some reckless shifts myself, to adjust my scruples to my heart's desire. Instead I blessed my kismet, heeded no distant drum, and rejoiced in my strange wayside adventure.

When after due delay and many wooings I picked her up and carried her to my couch, no bride out of the West could have surrendered with more lovely ecstasy. Truly I had been enriched along the long road of my quest as I had foretold Nicodemus; and fate had dealt nobly with me thus far, in letting me win fairly a prize of such delight, and in an uphill fight.

CHAPTER THIRTEEN

The Warm Trail

I.

It happened that Lilith and I had a honeymoon. The *Reis* Effendi ordered my attendance at a military field-day in ancient Smyrna —an old-fashioned riding and shooting match save for its pomp and gaudy show—and I took her with me in good style and array. During this month I did not lift a finger for Roxana, and never let her image rise between me and—the term was fair enough—my child bride. Our absence from the capital gave my unknown rival's heat a chance to dissipate, and saved his face a little. It stood to reason he would now give up the game.

On our last day there, I bought at a bazaar a rarely beautiful prayer rug quite possibly three hundred years old. It gave me an excuse to call on Kemal immediately on our return to Stamboul; he examined it, pronounced it an excellent Ferahan, and held learnedly forth over coffee cups on the modernization and decline of the art of rug making, now that much of the product was being sold in Frankistan. Was good taste so lacking in the West, I asked? Surely there was nothing finer than the glass of Venice and the lace of Ireland.

"Those are fine, but there's one produce of the West that I consider finer," he told me.

"If it's that fine, I'll ask you to procure a bit of it for me."

"Order a roc's egg, even as did Ali-din's bride, and I'll have a better chance to serve you."

"I can't imagine what it might be—unless wonderwork in gold and ivory, with the breath of life."

"Selim, our minds meet as good companions."

"Have you ever collected jewels of that sort?"

"Only once—of the quality I'm thinking of. I've had a couple of Piedmontese—daughters of a mere trader in cutlery—and once a Navarran with hair aflame—her mother sold her to a trader in Athens

—choice but not superfine. I doubt if there are fifty Frankistani of medium quality up, in all Islam."

It was on my tongue to ask how he had made out with the jewel of first water, but a little warning bell tinkled in the fog of the unknown. Instead I pleaded being pressed for time, and would he honor me by supping in my *gulphor* on the first evening he had the leisure? He accepted gratefully for the following Thursday, the eve of the Moslem sabbath. He promised to appear an hour before sundown prayers, to see some riding and shooting on the parade ground.

Lilith liked to direct the household, so I discussed with her the repast I wished to offer a distinguished guest. It was to be exquisite rather than elaborate—a portion of the heart of date palm, multicolored, with a flavor of banana, almond, and pine, date bread of Fezzan, *kuskuku* dressed with lamb in the Arab style, and a pomegranate and raisin sherbet in which I intended to introduce some fig brandy, forbidden by the Koran but obtainable in certain bagnios in the city.

"It must be a very Osmanli, for whom you spread this feast," Lilith ventured, her eyes indrawn.

"No, only a silk merchant, Kemal by name, from whom I expect favors."

"I've a curiosity to see his face."

"Why, you may. And since he's a beauty lover, he'd like to see yours."

Kemal arrived at the appointed hour dressed in subdued but studied elegance, attended by four immense Negro slaves, looking so much alike that they could pass for brothers. Half a dozen of the best horsemen of a Kurdish squadron of *spahis* performed feats of equestrianship for his admiration—the sleek perfectly-trained ponies and their impassioned, death-contemptuous riders making a strong appeal to his sensuous nature, as I had expected. The supper on the ankle-high, gold-inlaid ivory table—a surprisingly fine piece of furniture for a house of this simple style—opened his sybaritic eyes.

"I ordered the dishes that I like best," I explained, "hoping you'd pass favorable judgment on them. Again not the most costly, but to my rude palate, the most delicious."

"I've tasted no better at the table of the *Reis* Effendi," he answered, aglow with the secret ingredient of the sherbet.

"By the same token, I didn't invite any of my officer friends to share such a simple meal. Unless there were at least a score of dishes, they would think me inhospitable."

"Anyway we could not talk so freely of our wide and wonderful world. There's no majesty or might save in Allah—but there are many narrow prejudices among His Faithful."

"You spoke once of the vulgarity of the jealous concealment of our loveliest jewels," I remarked, after sending the servants to their quarters. "For instance, it would be considered a sin against Allah for a female of my household to enter this room."

"Is it not astonishing how custom comes to wear the halo of God? It's an affront to my intelligence."

I rose, went into an anteroom, and clapped my hands. At once Lilith appeared, veiled, and wearing a *baracan* of heavy blue silk over her jellick and trousers. I had told her that I might present her to my guest in the *kiffir,* and she had arrayed herself properly for the occasion.

"You may enter and light the effendi's houka," I told her.

"But not in your *gulphor,* lord! He would think it most unseemly—"

"Do you dare question my command?"

She followed me into the apartment where Kemal kissed her hand as though she were the lady-wife of a pasha instead of my Christian slave. Then with due humility she performed the courtesy I had ordered.

"Lilith, my distinguished guest is a connoisseur of all manner of beautiful things," I told her. "He rejoices in the sight of them without an evil thought. It is from him that I bought the red silk of Samarkand. Array yourself in it, and present yourself to his eyes."

"Yes, master," she murmured, her head bowed.

"And you may unveil your face, for truly he has as much right to see it as the swains of Daghestan."

"He has more right, master." She raised her head slowly and behind her veil her eyes were fixed on mine. "To hear is to obey."

She withdrew gracefully, leaving me somewhat uneasy about what was going on in her unplumbable heart. In many parts of Islam the women went unveiled—Arabia, for instance, and in regions of Inner Asia—and Lilith was born and raised outside of the Mohammedan faith. Surely, I thought, the child should be flattered to have me show her off to a beauty expert. I had just assured myself of that when she made her astonishing entrance.

She had unveiled her face and put on the rose-colored *baracan* as I had bade her. But under the flimsy drapery she was as naked as she was born.

I could not catch my breath until, with a proud pace, she had advanced into the center of the brightly-lighted room and stood before us with a serene expression. "Your slave has obeyed your command," she told me, calmly.

Kemal gaped, then turned to me with an ecstatic look. The man was not only charmed with what he thought was a delightful surprise I had prepared: he was brimming over with gratitude at the compliment that he supposed I was paying his clean, broad artist's mind.

"You see, Kemal, the color becomes her well," I remarked, as soon as I could collect my scattered faculties.

"By my head, *sahabti*, she's like a sultana in it—and I shan't forget this respect you've shown me—this great joy you've given me—as long as I live."

"I knew you'd understand. You alone, among my friends, would conceive no grossness in my display of her graces, any more than my drawing a curtain from a beautiful painting by a master."

"What a wonderful fellow you are! It's my very thought. Did the supreme artist, Allah, paint and shape his masterpieces to be shut away in dim cells for one pair of brutish eyes? No, he fashioned them for those worthy to behold them!" Meanwhile Kemal's worthy eyes were feasting voraciously.

"Lilith, turn slowly to show how the garment becomes you from every view."

"At your pleasure, lord."

"Truly she is Kobah, the evening star," Kemal exclaimed. His eyes were moist with emotion.

Of course Lilith's graces were not rare enough to deserve all this—the sensualist's imagination had run away with him. Also the almost transparent rubicund silk served as rose-colored glasses to view her through. The fact remained that she was an enchanting sight, her hair bright gold, her blue eyes agleam with excitement now, but her severely planed face otherwise still, her small, exquisitely rounded body outlined by the clinging cloth. No wonder Kemal was carried away, and I meant to make capital of it without delay.

"Lilith, you've given pleasure to my guest, and have my leave to go."

"May I say a word to her first, Selim Effendi?"

"We'd both consider it a compliment."

"Kobah, I could not wish my friend a richer jewel to wear over his heart, or you a worthier setting."

She bowed with her hands to her forehead and withdrew. Kemal composed himself with difficulty. I struck while the iron was hot.

"I rejoice, Kemal, that you've taken favorable notice of the child. Her beauty is of an odd sort, and although not great, it seems to me quite real."

"I was enchanted by her, my fortunate friend."

"I was reluctant to display her, because you've seen some of the greatest beauties in Islam, but am glad I made so bold. She ranks, say, as a perfect sapphire, compared with a ruby of pure fire."

"That would be my opinion. I'd not hesitate to ask a thousand dinars for her."

"Will you paint for me, with words, two or three of the rarest jewels that ever passed through your hands?"

"Why, gladly. One was a Thracian maid, now the wife of one of the great nobles of Islam. She was of Lilith's size, with more red in the gold of her hair, eyes of a serene violet hue, and a wide, rosy, laughing mouth made for lovers' kisses. Her skin had the gloss of worked ivory. I'll never forget how her limbs appeared to draw the light, for there it could play wantonly, with infinite change and luster. Her belly was bright—I choose the word carefully—appearing almost luminous in a shadowy room—yet without highlights, so perfect its curves. Her fires were intense but very deep and occult—say like those of the Ak Kum ruby which perhaps you've seen, since the Cham of Tartary wears it in his turban on great occasions."

"Yes, I did see it—but I'd rather have seen the jewel that you describe so well."

"She was a houri out of paradise, I vow! *Sahabti,* do you admire a black pearl of first water?"

"Greatly."

"Then I must tell you of Chana, a Numidian maid. I have a weakness for Circassians, loving bright colors—the Master's subtle employing of yellow, blue, white, and rose—but one of the proudest moments of my life was when I delivered this latter-day Queen of Sheba to—but I must not speak his great name. She was two pics, fifteen kerat (nearly six feet) tall but did not look so because of her perfect proportions. Her countenance was amazingly like that of Aphrodite, by Praxiteles, which Selim the Grim brought from Corinthe and which stood at the Queen's entrance of the Seraglio until one of Ahmed's favorites destroyed it in a tantrum. I have kept her measurements—ankle, calf, thigh, waist, bosom, and throat—but they would not interest a layman. Her breasts were of extraordinarily beautiful development, and I was eager to weigh them, partly as a matter of record, partly to satisfy my personal curiosity. It would seem a difficult problem, but I solved it simply enough, employing Archimedes' well-known law of displacement. By immersing them in a graduated bath, I first obtained their volume. Then—reasoning that firm, boneless human flesh weighs almost the same as water, a fact patent to any swimmer—I calculated their almost exact weight. You will hardly believe me that they came to just under four okes—truly I should state it in drachmes, as we count gold. Mere bulk would be meaningless, of course, save that they were bossed like shields on a wall."

"What a magnificent description!"

"I can't begin to do her justice. I didn't presume to put a price on her—it would be almost a sacrilege to that African goddess—but the —my client, I should say—sent me a purse containing five thousand dinars."

"Why, I can almost see her," I told him, a little sick to my stomach but my heart thudding. "While, like you, my special taste is for fair women—"

"The third of the three incomparable jewels that have passed through my hands was of a countenance suggestive of Lilith's."

"That will interest me greatly." I pulled at my houka stem and was able to steady my voice. "And with something of the same bright hair?"

"Well—no. She was a Nestorian Christian from western Cathay. I could imagine her as the favorite of Kubla Khan, had she lived in his day. She seemed carved in miniature of ancient yellow ivory. You could not dream of anything more exquisite than the joining of her slender, tapering limbs on her small, perfect trunk. She was only ten when she came into my hands, and I would let no slave bathe, scent, and array her on the day I showed her to the Emir of Afghanistan. Since he is now in paradise I don't mind mentioning his name."

"So those were your three perfect jewels," I said in a sudden and dangerous frenzy of impatience. "I had fancied that one would be the girl from Frankistan of whom you spoke so glowingly before. I had a mental picture of her."

"What was it, *sahabti?*" he asked smiling.

"I thought of her as about Lilith's size—perhaps a little taller—"

"You were wrong there! She was half a head taller."

"You say *was* instead of *is.* Why, I see her as still young—not more than eighteen now—surely none of those pearls have lost their luster—"

"Selim, you have the artist's heart. Although you're a little ashamed

292

of it and try to conceal it, I can detect anxiety in your face and voice, as though you have a personal interest in these treasures."

"It's sad to think of any beautiful thing perishing. I've read, for instance, of the Greek sculptor Praxiteles—have heard of his Hermes with the godling—and was pained that another of his works—the Aphrodite you mentioned—had survived into my own time, only to be destroyed."

"I'll relieve your mind—as far as I can. All three of the divinities I mentioned are still beautiful—as far as I know. The Frankistan prize came to me only—recently. You'll oblige me, Selim, if you never mention the matter to any one, as for certain good reasons it had to be kept highly secret."

"You may trust me, my friend. I know that certain aspects of the trade are frequently ugly, but when the treasures pass through such loving hands as yours—into hands you think worthy to receive them—why, the end justifies the means."

"I try not to discover the history of some of them—it rowels my feelings."

This was a blind trail. Presently it would fetch me up in a culee. "Since my mental picture of the Frankistan girl was so far off, will you paint me a true one?"

"Gladly. You wonder I didn't count her one of my perfect three. It was because, in a way, she stands alone—her beauty was of such an unfamiliar sort that I hardly dared trust my own judgment. She was much too tall for any one but an African—rather gangling, in fact. She had a radiant smile—she gave me many a one—but when she was grave her face had a sad aspect. Her hair was peculiarly lovely, and her eyes of a deep marine blue. For such a slender girl, she had a very womanly figure."

"Was she very young?"

"As a matter of fact, much older than most of my prizes. She said she was seventeen. Since the maids of Frankistan develop later than those of southern Europe and the Orient, I judged her at nineteen or even twenty."

"Why should she attempt to deceive you?"

"She was of course eager to be sold to a rich, great lord, to have a better life. In fact she conspired with me to that end—with a frankness and boldness and indeed honesty that few Oriental maids could essay. She made a game of it, arranging with me a set of signals. If the agent represented a rich and more civilized client, I was to put two fingers on my forehead, at which she would go through her prettiest paces. If he were undesirable, I was to rub my nose. If she approved of a buyer's appearance, she winked at me. I was so charmed with her that I fell in with her game. Truly, she was a girl of amazing spirit."

"By my beard, she deserved a kind and affluent master. I hope you found her one."

"It was not easy. I'd resolved not to dispose of her to an unworthy person, if I had to give her away, yet she was extremely hard to place. Her type of beauty was unknown here and appealed only to the most educated and individual taste. Besides, almost all great nobles demanded virgins. To save the humiliation of examination by the client's female agents, she confessed to me that she had been married for a brief period. I told her on no account to tell anyone—that the Orient doesn't understand divorce—and the notion of a living husband in Frankistan would fend off all good Moslems, lest they commit adultery."

. A delicate point, truly! "What did you have her say?"

"That she'd had a lover, killed in the French wars. I think she had had one, but had tired of him. Certainly she gave no sign of grief. She remained in wonderful spirits to the very moment I parted with her."

"Do you know, Kemal, she interests me more than any of the others you've described?"

"I don't wonder at it. It was a novel experience for me, too."

"I'll confess to you that my father was an apostate, born somewhere in the West of noble family." For Kemal was likely to hear any day that *giaour* blood ran in my veins. "Although my mother was a Turkish lady and a Fatimite, I've a guilty regard for Frankistan. Some day I shall visit there."

"It's a sign of a broad mind. Both Islam and Christendom have something to give each other."

"That plucky girl! Doubtless the daughter of Richard!" *Coeur de Lion* had become a legend throughout Islam.

"At least she was nobly born."

"If I were of less stature, I'd disguise and veil myself as a female slave and visit the baths here, for a glimpse of her face."

"It would be useless, my friend. She's not in Stamboul and indeed far away."

I drank a glass of sherbet and carefully wiped my beard.

"Perhaps in some land of Islam where ladies go unveiled? In that case, I might see her on my travels."

"It's not very likely. However, if you go east, say to Tabriz, you may keep your eyes open."

The name Tabriz was an easy one for Kemal to say, but not so easy for me to contemplate. It was the second city in Persia, and nearly a thousand miles by wild-goose flight from Stamboul. To go by way of the Black Sea and thence by caravan route was more than a month's journey.

But the only question was, how soon could I start? And that depended on how soon I could read a name in a ledger in Kemal's silk bazaar.

Bitterly weary and disappointed, I gave no thought to Lilith until I saw her, feigning sleep, on our couch. Looking at her, so pretty and unique, suddenly I felt deeply grateful for her. I wondered if she thought I would beat her, and if she would try to poison me if I did. Instead I could hardly wait to take her in my arms. She had certainly broken the ice at supper tonight! She above all else had loosened Kemal's tongue, whereby I had learned Roxana's probable whereabouts and gained an immeasurable reassurance of finding her alive and well. I had thought she would know how to survive in slavery but tonight had been given proof. Instead of half a failure, the evening's venture had been wonderfully successful.

"Wake up, Lilith," I told her.

"I'm awake, lord. I was only feigning sleep."

"Why?"

"To watch your face in secret. It was sad when you entered, but not angry even then, and now at sight of me it grows bright. I'm so ashamed I wish I could die." Two big tears rolled out of her eyes.

"Why should I be angry with you, Halloowah!" This was a sweetmeat made of honey and almonds. "You only obeyed my command."

"Don't be so forgiving, or I shall weep. Or perhaps you're mocking me, more cruel than striping my back with a kurbash. Or did the effendi buy me for so much gold, that you're pleased I betrayed your honor?"

"What do you mean, Lilith?"

"Did you think I didn't know him for a slave merchant? Why, I'd heard of him before I left Gunib! I knew why you'd had him come and feasted him so richly, and when you bade me bare my face, I wanted to help you get a good price! I can't play a dulcimer or even keep time on a tabor." She was sitting up now, fighting back tears, her throat working painfully. "Even my face is that of a vile Tartar woman from the desert—I wonder you don't cover it with a cushion when you lie with me. What have I to bring gold to your purse, but my not uncomely body? So I thought to show it to him, despite the shame. I pretended to misunderstand your command—" Her voice broke, but when I moved toward her she sprang to her feet and stood trembling against the wall.

"I understand now—"

"No, you don't, for there was only evil in my heart. The rest was an excuse, to hurt you all I could. What did I care how I shamed you before your guest? I'd have come in naked, and let him try me on your own couch in wicked spite."

"I told you I had a wife in Frankistan and when the time came—"

"How much did he pay for me? If it was only a little—because of my wantonness—I'll kill myself."

"Then I'd get nothing at all," I told her, trying to smile at her, but could hardly look at her from under smarting eyelids. "And have to pay the grave-diggers besides!"

"Oh, I'll wait till he delivers the sum—" Then she ran to me, knelt at my feet, and burst into violent weeping.

"Didn't I tell you that I'd not sell you as long as I remain in Islam?" I asked her, when I had picked her up and was holding her like a child in my arms.

"I didn't believe you, lord."

"I didn't mention selling you to Kemal. If I had, he would have offered a thousand dinars for you—he was so enchanted with your beauty. But I mean to keep you for my own until the very day before I set forth on my journey." That was a rash promise, but one I would not break. "Meanwhile you and I are going together on a journey—even into the kingdom of the Shah—and see wonders you've never dreamed."

Children's tears, more hot than grown-ups'—scalding, they seem—more quickly dry. At once the sun came out after her April showers.

"A long journey, Kebbier Emir?"

"A month or more, by sea, and across the desert, visiting many cities."

"How soon shall we set forth?"

"Not tonight. Perhaps not for another month. Tonight we're going on a journey into the kingdom of delights. I'll make such love to you, and you to me by my most strict command, as the heroes and houris in paradise shall envy. You shan't wait for my addresses, but make your own, as though you were a Thibetan woman, with her favorite husband. Every little hunger shall be fed."

296

On the first of August I set sail on the Bosporus with Lilith, Zimil,
three other slaves, Zimil's gelding and my mare, and our bags and
baggage. It had taken that long to prepare for the journey to Tabriz,
and it would not have been possible at all except for the active friendship of Bayezid, whom I knew now for one of the most powerful
members of the court.

By bribery and other pressures I had learned the name of Kemal's
factor to whom Roxana had been consigned—Baidu Sa'id, a leading
slave-trader of Tabriz. I had found out that he had sold her for the
sum of sixteen hundred dinars to a yet unknown buyer. Bayezid had
obtained for me not only a firman bearing the Sultan's seal, enjoining
all his pashas to receive me kindly, and his military commanders to
take heed of what I could teach them in the way of rapid fire, but the
quietly smiling Osman had also wangled the Imperial monogram
embroidered on a dozen scarfs which I had bought from Kemal at the
reduced price of four hundred dinars. No doubt the Grand Seignior
had given his permission between cups of syrup and straightway forgot the matter—but Bayezid had been convinced I would not shame
his throne.

These scarfs I was to present on the Sultan's behalf to his emirs
along my road and to his kinsmen and vassals—at least in name—in
Persia. It was an ancient, royal expression of esteem: the recipients
were supposed to reply with gifts to his treasury and—if well presented
—baksheesh to the bearer. Therein lay my best chance of fattening
my purse. Its present hoard was hardly a thousand dinars. Bayezid had
presented me with Zimil and I had given him my eunuch steward;
others I had sold to Hassan Serdar. But I would need three thousand
before my arrival at my unknown destination, for my fondest hope
was to buy back Roxana, the safest, simplest, and most likely means of
setting her free. The sum of five thousand, not trifling even in
Golconda, might save me precious time and heavy trouble.

Only a fortnight after setting sail—we had traded at various ports
along the shore—we disembarked at Trebizond, remaining there five
days while I demonstrated rapid fire to the officers of the cantonment.
To the Turbashaw I gave one of my scarfs, adorning him in the
Sultan's name before the dressed ranks, for which he flushed with
pride and pleasure. When the parade was over he presented me with
twenty Kurd ponies, worth ten dinars apiece, enough to furnish my
attendants for their overland march, and saving me buying them at

the horse fair. It was not a bad return for a forty-dinar scarf, but I hoped to do better, later.

Here I hired baggage and horse tenders and bought supplies for the journey to Erzurum, on the ancient caravan route into Persia. We had plenty of company on the road—bands of merchants eastward bound with the trade goods of Stamboul and Europe; others westward with their desert ships rich laden with all the treasures of the Orient —spices, perfumes, fabulous cloths and rugs, bejeweled scimitars and daggers from Damascus, wonderworks in ivory, ebony, sandalwood, silver, gold, and jade. Young virgins from eastern Europe and the Caucasus, bound for the harems of Persia and Central Asia, and wrapped head to foot in woolen *baracans,* caught glimpses through their veils of girls from beyond the deserts—snow-white savages from Hindu Kush, amber-colored Kasmiri who could charm their lords with dancing and the sweet strains of dulcimer, and tender lotus blossoms from very Cathay—to be sold in the slave markets of the Golden Horn. There were wild-looking Kurds on ponies, yellow Tartars with lances, busy Jews, and mountain and desert people I could not place.

We made the journey to Erzurum in five days. There in that age-old city on a windy plain enclosed with sheer, naked mountains the khan received me in great state, for he was a pasha of two horsetails, and richer than an English duke from his tithings off the land, his toll from the coppersmiths and boot- and saddle-makers, and the hire of convoy for the caravans. Ten days I remained with my attendants as his guest. His regiments guarded the frontier, riding and shooting against wild tribes and bandit bands; and their drill-masters warmly welcomed instruction in rapid loading and fire. The time was not wasted for me, for the Serdar presented me with two Umanian camels, one a mare of great swiftness. In compliment to the bearer of a ceremonial scarf ostensibly from the Sultan, the khan made me a present of two camel-loads of tooled leather which I could sell in Tabriz for five hundred dinars.

We set out with a company of merchants over the Camel's Neck to little Kars. Here I rode and shot with the cadi—hardly more than a headman—for two days, but did not give him a scarf, he being sufficiently honored by the sight of the Sultan's seal on my firman to entertain me well, and to furnish me with supplies to the next break in my journey.

We were now crossing tangled ranges of lofty mountains, stopping at night at rest houses maintained by the governors. Snow squalls burst already on the high passes, and despite our woolen *baracans* the wind bit us to the bone. There were days of chill, melancholy rain, through which our spirits would have quailed save for our leader now, whose bright hair caught every pale glimmer of the beclouded sun. Lilith rode ahead up the stony path, delighting in every dismal forest and snowy height, because the God-forsaken wild reminded her of Gunib.

One whole day we were followed by a grisly pack of wolves. On the next we met the two-legged kind, a score of them on Tartar horses, dark, lean Yezedies who openly worshiped Satan, and save for our stout convoy they would have cut every throat but Lilith's and enriched themselves on our goods. But at last we gained the headwaters of the Araxes, and made our long way to Nakhichevan, founded by Noah according to Armenian lore. The townsmen proudly show a mound of earth as the old sailor's grave.

A pasha of two horsetails ruled the rich province, and here was my best chance to feather my nest for the remainder of the journey. We spent two weeks at his court, I hunting with him in great state in the Karabagh forests, and demonstrating rapid fire to the garrison. Mainly in respect to the Sultan's monogram on a piece of cloth, but partly because he was pleased with the way I rode and shot, he presented me on my departure with a jeweled dagger and a gold henna box set with emeralds worth close to seven hundred dinars. From thence we made Julfa in two days and there made ready for our journey across the plains of Azerbaijan to Tabriz.

Here we passed into the dominion of the Shah, yet the Sublime Porte remained a name to conjure with, and a scarf did not go begging at Marand. I had hoped to do as well at Sufian, our last lodging before Tabriz, but the little mullah proved a miser, and although I saved a scarf, we had to pay our own fare at a caravanserai. On the next day we entered the great city of the Blue Mosque, the ancient trading post between Europe and Inner Asia. That day was October 25 by my counting and, by my dreaming, the outbound journey's end.

Save for its running miles of bazaars, the wondrous temple, and the vast ruins of the castle, the main city appeared from the hilltop as a strew of yellow pebbles, differing in size but all of the same shape. But the mansions of the wealthy merchants amid outlying gardens no doubt had lavish haremliks, and the palace of the emir was said to house three hundred wives, concubines, and female slaves. I rode there, in all the state I could muster, was courteously received by the seneschal, and when my firman had been shown to the vizier, quartered luxuriously in the guest house. It came to me in solemn exultation that I might now be within a stone's throw of Roxana.

Surely Kemal's factor, Baidu Sa'id, would have shown the Frankistan girl, something of a curiosity this far from home, to his emir; and I could hardly imagine the prince not buying her for a mere two thousand or so dinars, as he would buy a diamond of rare hue from a newly discovered mine. Behind the wall and the guarded buttressed gate she might be walking among the late-blooming roses and the plum and apricot trees. She had already heard gossip of a tall, big-nosed, pale-colored Turk quartered in the guest house with his attendants and a Circassian slave girl. . . .

If she were there, I would get word to her soon.

I had flung money about for the guest-house servants so that the tale of my affluence would reach the emir's ears. The greater effendi he deemed me, the more power I could wield in the city, in case of need, and the richer his presents in the event of my journeying on. When he received me in his divan, I was at once almost certain that he did not have my girl. He wore the badge of a hadji [pilgrim to Mecca] and greeted me with a reverent "There is no God but Allah." Such a fervent Moslem prince would not likely admit into his harem a white slave who had ever been the wife or sweetheart of an Unbeliever.

On the other hand, the emir, first cousin of the Shah, was a soldier and hunter whose favors I had a good chance to win. Inventing a flowery compliment from the Ottoman Sultan to his friend and ally, I was permitted to adorn his shoulders with the ceremonial scarf, and then kiss his hand. We talked of chase and war, and on ending the audience he invited me to hunt with him in the course of the next fortnight—for axis deer, wild ass, big uriel sheep if we cared to penetrate the heights, and perhaps the small, pale-colored Persian tiger.

Meanwhile there was hunting to do in the city. In an urgency to save time that might lead to recklessness, I had decided not to try to make friends with Baidu Sa'id but to scare or diddle out of him what I had to know. In the furtherance of that premeditated scheme, I called at his bazaar, attended by one of the emir's mamelukes to give me prestige, but only looked about with a forbidding air, as though he were under suspicion of the all-powerful throne. It was a pleasure to me to rebuff his advances and see the anxiety growing in his face, since he was a coarse-faced, heavy-handed Syrian, apparently the most brutal type of slave-trader, and I could not stand to think of Roxana ever being in his power.

Then a chance came to frazzle further the nerves of Baidu Sa'id. Riding with one of the emir's viziers to see the ancient, ruined Arc I made an excuse to stop in front of the slaver's door, talk gravely with my companion, and give the effect of boding him no good. A much more telling stroke, calculated to frighten him out of his wits, I proposed to deal him in my hunting trip with my host. The moment came when we had ridden and shot for four days, taking a good bag of deer and bear, and the emir had invited me to coffee in the *gulphor* of his hunting lodge.

"I've never had better sport," he told me, "and never shot with a better team of hunters than you and your mare."

"Allah upon you, Haran Emir, for your gracious words."

"It comes to my mind that when the Cham of Tartary was guest of your Sultan, he rode against a *spahis* named Selim."

"Yes, sir, he did, to my great honor."

"He told me it was the hardest ride in his long years to beat you by one head. Selim, I want you to stay at least three weeks more—" and I had been his guest that long already—"to instruct the officers of my *lashkar* in rapid fire. My master, the Shah's devotion to your Sultan is well known, and one day they will stand side by side in a holy war against the *giaours*."

"You do me great honor, Haran Emir. What little business I have in the city is of no moment—"

"I'll see that it's done to your satisfaction, effendi."

"Why, it's only the sale of two camel-loads of dressed leather and some other trifles, and an inquiry into the honesty of a Syrian slave merchant."

"That's simple enough. If you refer to Baidu Sa'id, a Syrian who's had dealings with the court, he has a heavy hand with Christians, but is in good repute."

"A Nestorian Christian sold to one of my Sultan's viziers proved to be with child. He's not certain that Baidu was aware of the shame, or that he was the merchant that sold her to his agent—but pardon me, my lord, for wearying your ears with such a trifling matter."

"It's no trifle to me, Selim, if a merchant of my province cheated a buyer in Stamboul! My city's honor and prosperity stem from our commerce. If you've any proof that he was culpable, he shall be strangled immediately on my return to Tabriz."

"I have none, lord, and will make no charge against a presumably honest dealer. The most I ask, if you're of a mind to grant it, is your firman bearing your seal permitting me to investigate one of his deals

—its nature need not be mentioned, for I want my questions to take him by surprise—and that he's to speak truth."

"Why, that's nothing. Come to me with a larger request, my hunter *sahabti*, to test my regard for you."

The firman—actually a *dahir*—was given me the day following our return to Tabriz. I rode to Baidu Sa'id's bazaar in the company of two officers of the *Amnieh* [a kind of gendarmery] who pointedly took stations outside his door. When Baidu hurried white-faced to meet me, I sternly bade him take me at once to his most secure retreat, as the business I had with him was both grave and highly secret.

He led me into a small coffee room, gave orders for no one to disturb us, and locked the door. When I showed him the emir's firman he was so terror stricken that I almost felt sorry for him. No doubt he had turned many a shady deal, and thought that one of them had found him out.

"Baidu Sa'id, you'll come to no harm if you answer my questions honestly and fully," I told him in Turkic. "I warn you though that what is said here must never pass this door. An effort is being made by the emir himself to cover the matter up; no one but my Sultan, the Shah of Persia, and he knows what it is. If you ever mention it to your favorite wife, let alone to any officer of the court, you'll die the death. The emir is so upset that if any word of it comes back to him, your lips will be stilled forever."

"I mark you well, effendi," he told me, trembling.

"I'm the confidential agent of the Ottoman Sultan. More than two years ago a Frankistani slave girl, named Roxana, passed through your hands. It's now known that she was a kinswoman of Napoleon, conqueror of Egypt."

"Woe upon me! I remember her well but never dreamed—"

"For a long time her capture and enslavement were denied, and the truth can still be concealed with enough secrecy. You must not write or speak of this to Kemal, in all your days. For certain reasons of state, he hasn't been informed of the investigation."

"Allah, be merciful unto me! Selim Effendi, if I lie in one word—"

"I'm not afraid of that. First, who bought her, and where is she now? If the Grand Vizier of Persia has her, you must reveal the truth." It did not matter now if my voice trembled and my breath failed. He would think that I too was appalled by the business.

"Kemal didn't warn me, Allah's curse upon him. He would buy and sell the Sultan's daughter, if he liked the lift of her nipple, or the shape of her toenail! Would that someone had strangled the yellow-haired beanpole, ere I laid eyes on her!" I did not mind him saying that, for it was proof that my fish was hooked. He leaned toward me now, speaking in the deepest confidence. "This was what happened, effendi. I showed her to Haran Emir's agent, but he'd have none of her, because she wasn't a virgin. One of the buyers for the very Shah looked at her through a lattice as a woman bathed her, but said his master frowned upon tall girls, let alone skinny ones. It was the same with a dozen or more of my best customers—she had been used, or was too tall, or too thin, or did not take their eyes. Meanwhile she'd eat only the best and costliest of food, but I dared not stint her, lest she lose more weight. She couldn't sleep save on down, and I must provide her a serving maid, lest she grow ill from loneliness, and a little dog and kitten."

"That's the very one," I said, when Baidu Sa'id stopped suddenly and looked at me, to see if I were wearied by these details. "Why didn't you suspect that she was a *lilla keiberra* [great lady]?"

"Fool that I am, she tricked me. A Jew money-lender from Malta could understand her talk, and she made herself out happy in her state, only desirous of a kind and wealthy master, even as Kemal, besotted with her, bade me find for her. Yet when I had kept her for three months, with the highest offer for her only eight hundred Turkic dinars—I had to get almost twice that much to break even—she wrote a letter and dropped it with a gold pin to an urchin. Mark her cunning, effendi: on it she had drawn the picture of a temple bearing a cross. Luckily this was an honest lad, who brought me the letter instead of delivering it to a Nestorian priest, who might have smuggled it to Frankistan. The Jew who read the letter said it was to a physician of that country, bidding him be easy of mind, giving my name and city, but warning him and another—doubtless her brother, though I've forgotten the name—to take no steps for her deliverance, save to appeal to the Czar of the Muscovites."

"It is well you stopped the letter. What did you do then?"

"Thrown into a fury by her trickery—and her ingratitude at my many kindnesses—I swore to sell her to the next customer who'd name a price. Luckily the *naib* [deputy governor] of Baku, very rich, and fit to tame her *giaour* spirit, looked upon her with favor, and bought her at my asking price of sixteen hundred dinars."

"Why don't you give his name?" I asked sternly despite a twisted throat. "If you're trying to shield him—"

"By my head, effendi, I was coming to that! His name is Nazir Baba—"

"Where is Baku? Is it near by?"

"No, medium far—midway up the shore of the Caspian—but the girl's not there. Nazir Baba bought her for a gift to his patron, the Emir of Bukhara, beyond the Caspian and across the Kara Kum. I thought he'd never part with her, he was so taken with her face and form, but undoubtedly he did, because a Tartar merchant of Bukhara, journeying to Mecca, stopped here for the night, and on my asking of the woman, he told me he had seen the face of such a one, yellow-haired and a Frankistani, at the caravanserai. For there even the daughters of the Faithful are careless of their veils."

"Did the merchant tell you that she's now in the emir's harem?"

"I did not ask him, effendi. It was too delicate a question to put even to an old friend. But I did not need to ask, since Nazir Baba, knowing the emir's tastes, bought her for him."

I fetched a good imitation of a sigh of relief. Under the circumstances it was the bravest and best dissembling I had ever done.

"Then nothing will ever be heard from her, and the Emperor of Frankinstan, my Sultan's enemy, may be led to believe she never arrived in Stamboul."

"Truly, Bukhara is two months' journey posthaste even in good season, and it's as though she were in her grave."

"Yet it may be that I must go there, to warn the emir to guard her closely. If you hear of my setting forth, hold your tongue and your countenance! If all goes well, you'll never hear of this again. But if the Shah must find a scapegoat—"

"For Allah's love, protect me if you can."

"Then tell me, are you convinced beyond all doubt that the girl the merchant saw in Bukhara was the Frank Roxana?"

Baidu Sa'id thought as hard as ever in his life. "Effendi, I know Teragai well. He has great respect for his word—like all nobly born Tartars. He spoke of the girl's long neck, and the way she wore her hair—in one curl before her shoulder—and of her happy laughter at a pet monkey frolicking there. She must be the one! And somewhat to my wonder, he pronounced her very beautiful. He spoke in a glowing voice of her, and even, I thought, with pride, as though her coming had honored his native city."

4.

When I parted with Baidu Sa'id, he offered me a chest of gold and silver cloth worth five hundred dinars, patently a bribe to shield him.

I had no scruple against the swindle, but dared not perform it, lest the hurt to his purse set him wondering whether I was a fraud. That closed every door to which I had a key—beat out every bush. For the rest I had to trust to tolerably good fortune.

Near the end of my stay Haran Emir of Tabriz held a review of his *lashkar*, culminating in a picked squad's exhibition of rapid loading in the American frontier style, after which he summoned me to his post and complimented me before the dressed ranks. Although I flaunted no horsetail, he addressed me as Selim Pasha of the Faith, and truly my decorations and citations warranted the honorary title. It greased my vanity no little, but what counted more were Haran's tokens of friendship when I knelt before him in his audience chamber —his leave to journey into the Realms of Gold of further Islam, and a safe conduct and a thousand dinars in fine gold to smooth my road.

So now my purse was heavy with four thousand, enough to build and lade a good Salem ship. What would it buy in Bukhara? Perhaps not even a glimpse of a slave girl's face.

Making haste to Baku across the great Mugan Steppe, we sold all our baggage and riding beasts save Amine and Zimil's gelding, which plucky pair we would put to pasture on the eastern shore of the Caspian Sea. Over those dreary waters to a Persian fort, we bought long-furred Bactrian camels, which alone could cross the storm-bound steppes in midwinter, and began the long march to the Oxus. On that terrible treck we joined a caravan of Turkmen and Kazaks, sons of these deadly sands, who know every trick of survival; otherwise we would have perished in the first blizzard. The blown snow stung and seemed almost as dry as dust.

Our sustenance was camel's milk, occasionally fat-tailed sheep when we came upon a kibitka [a temporary village of perhaps a dozen tents], a mush called balamyk, and salt fish. At low sun every day we pitched our felt tents on willow frames, banking them well against the icy blasts, and slept on carpet floors wrapped in our *baracans*; in the dreadful dawns we struck them and strove on. But loading and unloading the camels took so long that we barely gained more than fifteen miles between dawn and dark. At night our little fires of dried dung or saksaul scrub were mighty lonely looking under the cold, white stars.

The new moon waxed to full and waned away without our passing a single permanent human habitation. The only other travelers on the road were a few nomads, caravans whom an evil kismet had driven forth at this dread season, and once a band of robbers—fire-worshipers, the Tartars said—whom we fought off with gunfire, killing a half dozen of the murderous beasts, with the loss of only two of our number. That day I gained face with our desert men for straight, fast shooting. My facial structure and dark hair were a little like theirs, they told me; perhaps I too had the blood of Tamerlane flowing in my veins.

I stalked and shot a saiga antelope at a good three hundred paces, much to the wonder of the Tartars whose smooth-bore muskets would not carry true for half that distance. That evening we feasted richly, and their elder chief visited my tent. He, like the others, spoke a Turkic dialect, but I could hardly catch its drift. So the chief talked to me through an Osmanli-speaking slave.

"Effendi, if your fate takes you to Khiva, we'd like to present you to our Cham."

"It's not in my mind to go so far, but—" The back of my neck began to prickle. "I'm a stranger to these lands, and forgive me for not knowing his name."

"Why, Timur, the same as the Lame One."

"Is he old, and small of body, and a great rider and rifleman, and lately paid a visit to the Ottoman Sultan?"

"That is the great Cham."

"It's been my ineffable honor to hunt with him, a year and some months ago."

The elder touched his hands to his forehead and I returned the salaam. "Then he'll be grieved unless you come to his court in Khiva, and again ride beside him in the chase. Although he ages fast—he has seen three score and twelve suns—he can still lay low a stag while riding full-tilt."

I could well believe it. "It would be a great joy to behold his face, but I intend to go only to Bukhara."

"That too is part of his ancient domain, as are these very sands; but for a little while a Persian emir sits upon his throne. But the foreign tyrant is wise enough to pay our Cham great honor and much gold, to buy peace with him and prevail upon him not to call forth his horde. He provides a palace for him in Bukhara, when he wishes to tarry there. It has a sunny garden, and he may be there now, the winters at Khiva being bitter to his aged bones. It's come to me that you are fated to see his face again."

It would be not only a real pleasure but a great stroke of luck. Perhaps he could be persuaded to act as intermediary between me and the emir, employing his great influence to help me buy Roxana out of the royal harem. The task before me might be far more diffi-cult than I had ever let myself believe. For I had never forgotten Baidu Sa'id's report of a Bukhara slave-trader speaking of her with seeming pride—as though her coming had honored his native city. The utterance had gratified me at the time, but had preyed on my mind ever since.

Could it mean that Roxana had become the Bukhara Emir's *saki*—the mother of his first-born son and hence heir to the throne?

"Perhaps when the emir dies, the Cham will regain his throne," I proposed. "Has the emir sons?"

"None, nor daughters. It's believed among us that Allah made him barren, so that his usurper line will perish." This was good news, but the elder's next remark made my scalp creep. "It shames him greatly, and drives him to great cruelties against the people."

"Yet he would not dare treat cruelly his wives and female slaves, lest they reject his seed."

"I know nothing of that. But when you come to Bukhara, stand at noon by his minaret, and you'll know him for what he is."

"The journey nears its end—and all of us are weary of the wastes. From henceforth, let us make haste."

On our fiftieth day on the road—three months since setting out from Tabriz—we saw the distant winter gold of the oasis. Two days more we traveled, beside its barley fields, naked vineyards, apple, apricot, and cherry orchards, and through its scattered villages, the country ever more fertile as we neared the "spreader of gold," the Zerafshan River, dying tributary of the Oxus. Then we saw the emir's minaret, two hundred or more feet high, lifting tenuous as a prayer to the pale-blue winter sky.

Night was falling as we passed through the western gate of the city wall to the caravanserai. In the morning I said farewell to my companions of the road, and the elder's parting gift was some good news—the Cham of Tartary was indeed wintering in Bukhara, at his palace among the gardens on the Shahri-Rud. The sun had come out warm, the very desert wind was gentled from blowing over growing things instead of the dead desert, as in mid-morning my little band set forth for the Cham's palace.

Lilith could not get enough of the strange sights—the seven-mile-long bazaar displaying cloth, carpets, karakul, thousands of chained slaves, and all the riches of Central Asia under clay roofs—but I looked with dread to the many-towered and buttressed palace of the emir, crowning a hand-made hill, within a mile of frowning armored

307

wall. This was the famous Ragistan, under whose stones dwelt prisoners of the state, with hope abandoned of ever seeing the light of day.

But the emir kept another prison above ground, where fountains played and incense burned, but with a like unbreakable door.

I rode once around the square looking up at the palace windows. I saw no flower box hung on the walls, but there were scores of casements opening on locked and eunuch-guarded courts. By now it was approaching noon, so I left my horse with Zimil, and drew near the emir's minaret. Close by the beautiful Mosque Kokhumbes, a throng had gathered as though waiting the muezzin's call to midday prayers. Presently it sounded, whereupon the Faithful prostrated themselves with their faces toward Mecca; and I aped them with a bitter heart. But the crowd did not disperse: they had made their orisons and now would behold the majesty and might of Allah—in the person of the Commander of the Faithful, Abdulla, Emir of Bukhara.

It was a motley crowd, gathered from all Central Asia, for Bukhara was the greatest mart between the Caspian Sea and Mongolia. There were Turkmen, Persians, dark, Indian-looking Tartars, Jews, fair-haired people from Hindu-Kush and the distant Pamirs, nomad Kazaks down from their endless steppes, hirsute Kurds, Punjabi, Afghans, and desert wanderers whose tribal names were lost. No few rich merchants fondled their golden chains, scores of slaves in gaudy dress displayed their masters' wealth, and some unveiled women of low station waited excitedly with babies and market baskets in their arms. All were gazing toward the top of the minaret, some with strained, anxious faces, now and then with horror, but mostly in what seemed pleasurable excitement. A big Negro near by showed his fine teeth in an expectant smile. A few of the expressions were hideously cruel.

Three small figures appeared far aloft. The middle one seemed to have no arms, for the reason that they were bound behind him. While the crowd watched in breathless fascination the other two seized his head and feet, swung him back and forth, and hurled him over the edge. *"Eli! Eli!"* I heard him shout, the cry it seemed endlessly repeated, horridly loudening as he careened down, but cut off at last by a squashing crash on the cobblestones below.

"Is that all?" I heard a resplendent merchant, probably from the Ukraine, ask his attendant in quite passable Turkic.

"Yes, master. Only one."

"I'm a stranger here," I said. "Is this a daily event?"

"Why, no. Often three or four days pass without anyone being thrown down, but sometimes three or four are thrown at once."

"What crime had the man committed?"

"I don't know. Doubtless some grave offense against our emir." The merchant shrugged. "Anyway he was an Unbeliever. You heard him cry out—in vain—on his false god."

I turned quickly away. My mouth was full of bitter slime, but I did not retch in this public place. I must remember that this was not the dim, silent forest of my first long hunt, and then there had been no hope. Then I had been alone; not now. Lilith gazed at me when I returned to our little caravan—started to speak—bit her lip. When I had mounted she rode out of her place behind me, to my side. She spoke in low tones.

"The business that you do here—it's life and death to you."

"Why, no. If it thrives or if it fails, I'll make many a journey yet, and see many a wonder."

"Must you hide your heart from your slave? The road ends there— or there." She pointed first to the emir's castle on its proud hill, then to the grisly cobblestones beneath the minaret.

"I have a firman bearing the Sultan's seal, and a safe conduct from Haran Emir. Those are mighty safeguards."

"Hark to me, Selim." It was the first time she had ever addressed me so. "If I'm the lightest burden on you—weakening your hand in one jot or tittle—let me go. By my soul, I don't want to stay. The slave market is only a few streets away. I'll smile at the buyers and bring a good price."

"Lilith, you don't weaken my hand. You strengthen it."

With a slight inclination of her head she drew in her riding camel behind me. We rode on toward the palace of the Cham of Tartary.

5.

It was a rambling single-storied structure of red brick, with a well-watered garden, no doubt emerald green in season, and set among ancient apricot and apple trees. There was already a vernal suggestion amid their boughs. I had forgotten that the month was nearly April.

While my caravan waited in the courtyard, I was admitted into the *kiffir* by a lean, eagle-eyed Tartar. Like the people I had seen about the gate, he was attired as a desert nomad, in a long, full, sheepskin coat caught in at the waist with a leather belt, a homespun shirt of lambswool, skullcap, and long boots of undressed leather over invisible but probably rough woolen trousers. The attendants in the *kiffir* wore no silks or satins, gold or silver cloth, and the room itself revealed that the Cham kept a comfortable and plain court. I was glad of that, since I had plain business with him. Halfway across the world, it made me think of home.

The Tartar's speech was unintelligible to me, but he understood and repeated my name, and passed through a heavy felt curtain, like those hung in winter tents, into an inner room. In a moment one of his fellows came out, looked hard at me, and then uttered *"Ai!"* in surprise and pleasure. Salaaming to me quickly he came and put his hands on my upper arms.

"Selim-ul-Reuben!" he exclaimed, his dark Tartar face lighting.

I did not remember him, but very plainly he remembered me. Without doubt he had ridden behind his master in the great race.

He gave me a little shake, which no Persian or Turkish underling would dream of doing, then rushed away behind the curtain. Presently he reappeared with three or four other excited Tartars, who escorted me through an anteroom into what, in Turkish houses, would be the master's *gulphor*. It was a long room with more light in it than in most *gulphors*, its walls hung with bright-colored tapestries and carpets, and warmly heated with braziers. At sight of me a skinny old man in a woolen robe rose from a bench. He had a noble countenance, the skin like old, beautiful leather of deep ivory color and so taut over highbred bones that it still appeared unwrinkled although the light revealed countless fine lines. When he chose, it could be as impassive as stone. Now it was eloquent with welcome.

"Selim-ul-Reuben," he pronounced in a deep, resonant tone. And he raised his long, strong, fine, old hand in greeting.

I knelt to him, not for the first time to an Oriental potentate, but for the first time with my heart in it. Gravely he gave me leave to rise. I could not catch one word but perceived his meaning. At once he gave an order to one of his slaves, who brought a bench for me. When both of us were seated, he gazed quietly into my face for several seconds.

Again he spoke, and when I shook my head, called up another attendant. The man listened to his instructions, then turned to me. "Timur, the great Cham, lord of the forest and the desert and all the land from Cathay to the Ural Mountains, makes Selim-ul-Reuben welcome." He spoke in a Turkic dialect more akin to Osmanli than that employed by my companions of the road. Although some of the words were unknown to me, the meaning was quite plain.

"I rejoice to behold again the face of the great Cham."

I spoke as slowly and plainly as possible, yet the Tartar did not understand. So I put my fingers on my eyes and then raised my hands cupped in an ancient Oriental sign of gratitude and pleasure. The old Cham nodded.

He spoke again, with a suggestion of a smile. "The Cham asks if you've had good hunting, since he saw you last." The interpreter raised an imaginary gun to his shoulder and curled his forefinger.

"It has been fair." I pointed to myself, then held my hands about two feet apart, then to the Cham and held them at arm's width. I did not think he would miss the pantomime. The old man spoke at considerable length.

"The Cham of Tartary bids me tell you he has taken a lameness in his bones, whereby he can no longer chase the tiger and the stag, and the wild ass, fleetest of all of Allah's creatures, and surely he's no longer young, but he will ride with you another day to shoot antelope on the desert. Also, when his son Hosain Khan comes from Khiva, he'll send you forth with him and show you good sport. While not your peer—so says the great Cham—Hosain Khan rides well."

"The Cham, old as he is, rides with green spurs." I used the Arabic expression and was not greatly surprised, since it was current throughout the desert kingdoms, to see his dim eyes gleam.

He spoke again, and with less reserve. "The great Cham bids you and your train be honored guests in his house as long as you remain in Bukhara."

I salaamed, and the old mogul gave orders to his attendants. A low table was placed between us, and a plain repast brought through a door opening behind me—dried beef, fried lamb, wheat cakes, and candied apricots. The pitcher brought by a eunuch in Persian dress—evidently a steward—no doubt contained mare's milk, the Tartar's mainstay and ceremonial offering at every feast, symbolic of hospitality. Rather to my surprise, as the steward bent to fill the Cham's porcelain mug, he shook his head emphatically, uttered an impatient "Buu" and gestured for him to fill mine.

It was a new thing in my experience for a king's guest to be served ahead of his royal host. Plainly the Cham felt no need of pomp and was treating me as a companion of the chase, entertained in his tent on the steppe; but the scene meant more than that. The attendants were watching closely, their faces very still. When the steward had filled my mug he again offered to fill the Cham's, and was again rebuffed. Now the old man covered his cup with his wrinkled hand and spoke imperiously.

The disconcerted steward looked toward one of the attendants who wore the scimitar and camel's-hair coat of a court official. This fine-looking Tartar approached his master, salaamed, and spoke in a deeply respectful but grave tone.

"Buu!" the Cham cried again. Then, gesturing toward the door behind me, he answered to some length and, I thought, with real majesty. I perceived now that he was speaking Turkic-Tartar, and distinctly heard him apply the term "old friend" to me. I had the impression that he was justifying some breach of custom which had shocked his minister. He was an old man set in his ways.

The official drew back and the steward set down the pitcher and went out. A moment later someone came through the door behind me with a quick, light step. It halted for an instant; the Cham looked over my head with childish pleasure and royal pride in his wonderful yellow face. The one he had waited for came to the table, smiled at him, picked up the pitcher, and filled his mug.

I sat there, biting my lips to withhold their cry, shutting my eyes to force back tears, with a torn and bounding heart. Although the Cham's white slave wore Tartar dress, I had seen her golden hair and the forlorn look of blinding beauty that followed her smile.

CHAPTER FOURTEEN

The Old Cham

1.

Roxana, do you know me? I am not Selim-ul-Reuben, a bearded Turk, a Son of the Prophet, one on whom you must not gaze, one who has not the right to look upon your face. I am the one whose grisly trophies you touched in my little deckhouse. We blessed each other in farewell where hollyhocks bloomed, but I could not let you go.

Did you begin to doubt it, in the long years between? Have your hopes soared too many times in vain at sight of tall journeyers on the caravan roads, their faces dim, half-hidden by their shawls, but yet reminding you of me? You stopped briefly behind me as though startled; but now you do not glance at me, as I sit here eating in due quiet. I am bearded and lean and brown of face, and not only my garb but my least gesture trumpets Islam. Yet if you look once into my eyes you will know me.

Perhaps you take great care not to do so. Your face is sun- and wind-tanned, for you are the slave and follower of a desert nomad, but under the ivory color you appear pale. Perhaps you are purposely doubting me, while you rally strength. You must not break into tears. When you turn your gaze upon me it must linger only an instant, then move off without betraying you.

But you cannot deny me very long. Your thoughts are rushing to meet mine, you cannot hold them back; they are changed by mine; every nerve is taut and tingling. I think that even now you are sure. There is a light in your eyes—I see it out of a side of mine as I would a distant beacon in deep dark. You stand very still beside the old Cham, waiting for him to drain his mug so you may pour it full again; but your face was always still save when you spoke or smiled; it never meant that your imagination was not soaring or your heart not glowing. It is for my sake too that you delay any sign of recognition.

I may glance at you now with such fleet glances as are permissible to your master's guest when he has brought you unveiled into my presence—with restrained curiosity and even admiration. I note changes in your face other than its richer color, and in your form. I had never expected you to look much older, and you do not. In some ways you look younger, perhaps because of your body's litheness, apparent even in your loose Tartar dress. You have the deer-like trimness of a horsewoman, as no doubt you are—wildly you have ridden behind the Cham, and perforce for days across the steppes and deserts. You're no longer gangling: your limbs are no larger but your long muscles knit with the bone. The skin is drawn a little tighter over the cheek bones, appearing to lift the corners of your long eyes; the sad look between your animations is more pronounced, more touching, although your smiles are brighter. Your beauty is more obscure, but far more rich.

Beauty is not your condition, Roxana, but yourself. It is not something you possess, but something that possesses you. I am no longer stonied to find you here, instead of in the palace of the emir.

I might have known that if Timur Cham had seen you, he would buy you, even with the ruby of Ak Kum. As the greatest of the kings, in heart and soul, he was your most likely acquisitor. I could have foreseen it by merely remembering that the merchant who spoke of you to Baidu Sa'id was a Tartar merchant. Of course his face had lighted with pride, for you rode in the train of his Cham.

It was a long ride before you came under his strong shield; since then it has been long, across the blazing sands or the winter steppe, for he would not spare you their hunger, thirst, hell heat, and wolfish cold—for you must prove worthy to keep his tent. You must not shame the dauntless heart, the bridle hand, the kingly blood, and the lance of Tamerlane. But as the first Roxana won to Alexander's couch, now you pour the mare's milk for the Cham of Tartary!

I do not know the source of bravery, the golden ore, or on what divine anvil it is hammered, but I think it goes hand in hand with beauty. I know that when the gods bend down and touch a mortal's shoulder with its magic sword, he becomes ennobled: and it is fitting that we kneel. It is at once splendid and deeply sad; the sight of it fills the eyes with stinging, ecstatic tears.

You are very brave, Roxana. It is not something you possess, but something that possesses you. I can speak out to you now.

In the Cham's *gulphor* no word had been uttered for five minutes or more. He and I were performing the rite of breaking bread together, in which speech is unseemly; the only sound was the hearty smacking of our lips and the clump of our jaws on the hard wheat cakes and lean meat. But now the Cham wiped his lips and small grizzled mustache on a napkin Roxana handed him; an attendant handed one to me. He had not washed before eating, like most Moslems, nor was any skewer of water offered to him afterward; the desert men had learned to be sparing of the spreader of gold, the elixir of life.

"It is good meat," I told the Cham's interpreter. He shook his head; he did not understand.

Still looking at him, I spoke again—in English.

"Don't start and don't look at me, or give any sign. You know who I am."

The interpreter shook his head. Then the Cham spoke.

"My lord, the Cham, asks if you know Persian. His steward speaks Persian."

I shook my head. Then I was shaken to the marrow of my bones by Roxana's voice, welling into the room. She was addressing the Cham in his own tongue and it stood to reason she was asking his leave to speak. That seemed a daring thing in the presence of the court and his guest: when another white slave, Esther, had asked the same of another king, Ahasuerus, his refusal would have decreed her death. It did not surprise me that he nodded, his dim eyes kindling. His stern face had gentled at the sound of her voice and he looked to her eagerly, for she was always saying what delighted and surprised him. The whole court cocked its ears and only the official who had protested her entrance, no doubt a master of ceremonies and duty-bound to uphold the proprieties, looked uneasy.

But what she said then almost curled my hair, in my dread of the law of purdah. Although I caught only a word or two and the proper names, I was as sure of her meaning as though she had spoken English.

"Great Cham, many of the Turkic emirs learn Frankistani," she said in effect. "If it is your wish, I will try to be your lips and ears in conversing with your guest."

The old Cham showed no sign of anger. He could hardly control his countenance, so pleased he was with the apple of his eye for the new wonder, and so anxious for her to succeed. He could not resist a great glance of pride to his attendants. The master of ceremonies was obliged to look shocked, but he was just as much fascinated as the rest.

"*Ai*," the Cham replied.

Roxana turned to me and our eyes met for the first time. I sat with a face of flint. She was very pale, and when she addressed me in English, her voice faltered, but her hearers would think she was overcome only by the honor paid her by her master, Timur, the great Cham.

"Jason, you got here sooner than I thought."

I did not know how she dared say anything like that, not that there was danger of someone here understanding English, but because of its effect on me. But perhaps she thought after coming this far and undergoing certain trials I could control my emotions.

"Why, didn't you tell me to come the first day of July—many years ago?"

I had spoken clearly and, it seemed, calmly. A dim unspeakably lovely smile began to curl her lips, but she turned quickly to the old Cham, so he would think she was giving it to him, and, in part, she was. If the others saw it, they would take it for happiness that she could fill the office he had appointed her. That smile was his most precious jewel.

She spoke to him. "Yes, my lord, he is schooled in my native tongue," was about what she told him. It seemed to me that the whole court looked proud.

The old Cham tossed his gray head, then instructed her what to say to me. She turned to me again.

"The Cham asked if the Sultan is well. You needn't take time to answer. I'll take care of both sides of the conversation. Jason, is my father alive?"

"I don't know."

"Have you ever got word to him that I'm alive?"

"No. I'll tell you why later."

She turned again to the Cham, spoke what she thought was fitting for me to say, and listened to his next remark to me.

"I'm glad you didn't," she went on. "I was terribly afraid he'd try—say something, Jason."

"I was afraid he'd appeal to the ambassadors—"

"I couldn't have made him believe I was all right—"

"Don't speak too long. He'll get suspicious."

"No, he won't. He hasn't a suspicious hair in his head. The others might, though."

She made a suitable reply to the Cham's question. He spoke at length.

"The great Cham tells me you're wearied from your journey—he can see it in your pale face—and his steward will show you quarters for you and your train."

"How soon can we talk?" I asked, looking toward the Cham.

"It won't be long. Leave it to me, Jason. There's no hurry."

"I can't say any more anyway. Thank God I found you. I love you."

"I love you, Jason—and want you. Salaam to the great Cham."

I did so, and he raised his hand in acknowledgment. He summoned the steward, and without a backward glance at Roxana I followed him into the guest house, connected with the main structure by a walled passage. No doubt these were the best guest chambers the palace offered, but I did not look at them in the brief time that I would be left alone, before my followers and companions on the long road made demands on me. But the paroxysm soon passed; I could breathe and see again and rose from the sheepswool bed restored.

Zimil reported that my beasts were well disposed, and he and the other men comfortably quartered. Lilith, flushed from sitting beside a brazier, walked about surveying the apartment. It was nothing like as luxurious as the guest house of Haran Emir but completely comfortable and indeed paradise compared to our tents on the winter desert.

"The Cham of Tartary is the most exalted personage that has ever entertained us," I told her, "but the Tartars scorn luxury."

"Greater than the emir within the high wall?"

"Far greater."

"I'm glad we're not to stay with him, after what we've seen."

"I'm glad that no one for whom I care has to stay with him."

"Do you think we'll visit here long?" She spoke a little wearily.

"We won't travel on until spring comes full."

"Do you think he'll give you a rich gift, when you depart?"

"Perhaps five hundred dinars."

"Lord, you spoke then with another voice." She stopped, her eyes wheeling slowly to mine. "It must be mighty business that you do here."

"It may be so, little one."

317

"Once you spoke of a great venture. It comes to me that its hour is striking, even now."

"It may be striking, Lilith."

"Your eyes glitter as I've never seen them. I've seen them very bright—and thought that the joy that made them so was taken in me, your slave—but never bright as this."

"I rejoice at meeting my hunting comrade. But think of the countless nights we've rejoiced in each other—"

"I've counted every one. Lord, I'll pray to my saints that your venture wins—even though I've no part in it—and it will sever your slave from you."

"You do have part in it—and in every venture of my days—and in every day I live." Deeply moved, I put my arms about her and kissed her warm, vital, lovely lips, and she was as beautiful as ever to me, and as prized. "I won't free you from your chain until I leave Islam, and then see your face in dreams."

I knew then that for me there had been two worlds, and I lived in both of them. Roxana was my sun, golden in the western skies, Lilith my moon of Ramadan.

3.

The Mohammedan institution of purdah, a word meaning a curtain—the seclusion and concealment and often life-long imprisonment of women—was not upheld as strictly in Central Asia as in the Barbary States, Persia, and the main Ottoman Empire. Even there, poor men's wives who must go to market, borrow from neighbors, and keep house only pretended to veil. The nomadic Arab women, forever pitching and striking tents, went bare faced, and since only the sheiks' wives and slaves could afford shifts under their *haracans,* with scantily covered bosom. I saw many women's faces on the streets of Bukhara, and the wives and daughters of rich merchants and even nobles made free on the terraced roofs and in their gardens. The nomadic Tartar women veiled only on ceremonial occasions.

The Cham's garden extended along one side of the guest house, and the open gate gave me frequent glimpses of the old man sitting there in the pale sunlight of dawning spring or walking about looking at the fruit trees with his favorite female slave. It was not unusual for his ministers or attendants to address him there, in which case Roxana held her ground and frequently took a lively part in the conversation. After salaaming to him once or twice from outside the gate, on a mild afternoon I made bold to call to his *Chiah*, then in attendance upon him. Roxana stood, as usual, at his side.

I had asked, in Turkic, for permission to address the Cham. The *Chiah* spread his hands and shook his head. Then I called the same in English to Roxana, who straightway turned and repeated the request to her master. He nodded and raised his hand and I approached his bench. He looked eagerly to his darling to translate for him, nor did the *Chiah* appear shocked. He too was an old man, and had long since discovered that custom and convention were not omnipotent gods, and a wife or female slave would be hard put to it to commit adultery in the time that "water may flow out of a broken vessel."

When at my direction she had paid him my obeisance and regard for his health and prosperity, she looked to me again, gravely, in the part of his dutiful slave. Her eyes were bright but he had often seen them so.

"Do you think it's safe to tell him that my travels for the Sultan will take me to Frankistan, and ask if you may be allowed to instruct me in the names of the kings and the nobles—the caravan routes and cities? Tell him I can see you're a fount of wisdom."

"I think it's safe enough—if I explain that you recognize me as a noblewoman, who in my country may talk freely with her lord's guests. He may refuse, but—"

She turned to the Cham, salaamed, and spoke at length. I could not catch the drift of her Turkic-Tartar, but heard her refer in a shy and modest tone to Morgiana, the resourceful slave girl of Ali Baba in the *Arabian Nights'* tale and a byword for womanly wisdom and fidelity throughout Islam. Obviously she was saying that I had applied the name to her, and while she could not pretend to any such worth, if the great Cham saw fit for her to try to instruct his honored guest as to her native land, it would be a great honor.

The two old men exchanged prideful glances. At once the Cham ordered a bench placed for me, and gave Roxana leave to sit on a lambswool cushion about ten feet in front of me.

"You'll have to guard your voice and expression," I told her. "I've got to find out some important things."

"Don't worry. I've had long practice at it."

"You've got to advise me what to do."

"I don't even know where to start—except tell you to be patient."

"Do you see any way—"

"Not for several months, at least. I couldn't bring myself to leave him before that long—until he could get someone to take my place.

319

I don't know how to go about it. There must be some way out, in time, but Jason, it's going to be mighty hard to find."

"Gesture a little, as though you're telling me about roads—"

"All right. He's given me a sealed parchment setting me free at his death, and enjoining every emir from here to Constantinople to see that I'm conducted safely to Malta. But—that may be five years."

"Tell the Cham you've lived in the very country the Sultan's sending me to as an envoy—you know the emirs and khans—and by his leave I'd like to have you instruct me to much greater length."

She did so, and the Cham looked pleased.

"You'd better call for a pen and inkhorn and paper, and pretend to take notes and draw maps," she said.

"Good. And show him my firman, bearing the Sultan's seal. Tell him it brings his greetings to all his kinsmen and subjects, and asks them to assist me on my travels."

I got the document from my pouch, and she rose and handed it to the Cham. He put on square spectacles with iron rims, probably made in China, and examined it gravely. She stood at his shoulder, repeating what I had said. He touched his heart, then his forehead, and returned the parchment to me. At his order, the *Chiah* dispatched a servant into the palace for writing materials.

"You've gone through no marriage ceremony with him, have you?" I asked, speaking as calmly as possible.

"No. He asked me—he has only two wives still living, both in Khiva—but I told him I couldn't renounce my God for Allah."

"But you've made yourself so necessary to him—"

"I had to, Jason, to survive. Anyway I wanted to, after what he'd done for me."

"What pressure can be brought to bear on him to let you go?"

"I don't know. It can't be very harsh."

"I suppose I've got to know just how much you owe him—"

"Don't look discouraged. Aren't we together—when—I thought—? We're sitting here, talking together. It isn't a—dream."

"Don't look so wonderstruck. Your eyes are like stars—"

Instead of dimming they filled with tears, but she turned quickly to the Cham and addressed him in a tone at once jubilant and sad. Only afterward did it occur to me what she had told him—that speaking of her native land had made her homesick, and would he forgive the unseemly display before his guest? He nodded kindly, gave her a troubled glance, and asked a question. She made a proud answer.

320

It did not greatly matter from now on what came and went in her face. A little wearied by the foreign speech, he turned a little on his bench and gazed off toward the distant Pamirs. When a servant brought a small writing stand, paper, inkhorn, and quill and placed them before me he spoke to the *Chiah* and rose. Both Roxana and I stood up, but he spoke to her in a kindly tone—amazing in a Tartar addressing a slave in public—and followed by his retainers, disappeared within the palace. The *Chiah* took a seat on a stone bench perhaps thirty feet from us. I did not think that the Cham had stooped to having him spy on us. It seemed more likely he had asked the old man to remain in respect to the proprieties. Even so, the laxness of Tartar observance of Islamic custom could not entirely explain his extremely liberal attitude. Plainly he trusted Roxana implicitly, and me to a notable degree. Perhaps too he thought that talking of her native land was giving her much innocent pleasure which had touched him. A great factor was the writing stand before me, and the quill in my hand. A simple soul, forthright, unschooled in guile, he could hardly perceive these things as a curtain behind which we might plot her escape from him.

"Of course you have to know how much I owe him," she told me. "But I can't tell you—until we're alone." Her voice faltered.

"When will that be?"

"Maybe tonight. I'll find some way to let you know."

"You belong to me, not to him. Don't ever let a doubt of that cross your mind."

"I never have and never will. When I saw you with the Cham— your back to me—I was almost sure you'd come. Then I stopped and thought, 'No, don't be a fool. He couldn't have come this soon.' I didn't dare look at you. Not because of the others—because I was so afraid—"

Tears filled her eyes again. They did no harm—the *Chiah* was half-dozing on the stone bench. Yet she seemed to think it necessary to explain them to me. She wanted me to know that they did not flow for little things.

"I'm going to tell you of the night I was captured," she went on. "You'll understand then—a little—of what his love and care have meant to me."

She was looking back at a scene in dreadful contrast to this one. Here was blue sky now, and intimation of spring; she had found safety and kindness as a slave of the Cham and I had come at last. Just to look back was nothing to one whose utmost bravery had been challenged again and again. Yet I saw bravery moving in her now, going hand in hand with beauty, and how strangely they had wrought upon each other! She was not only strangely beautiful to me, but illustrious.

"The Turkic pirates took us aboard their vessel and set sail. When they had time to look at us, they threw the old woman overboard with the baby in her arms—before my eyes. The one-armed man went next, and another man started to scream—he was the one who rushed the boat—and they cut his throat. He fell, and—"

I ached to take her hands and kiss her wide eyes. "That's enough—"

"No, I want to go through with it—but it's harder than I thought. When one of the Turks began to tear off my clothes, a French sailor snatched a sword and fought them. He killed two before someone crept up behind him and felled him. They finished killing him and threw his body overboard. It turned out they didn't—do—anything but look at me to see what I'd bring in the slave market. I'd seen the Terror in France but it wasn't like that. The French mob was insane with hate but was at least human. But that awful, animal cruelty—"

"I remember," I said, writing on the page, "an obligation you were under to a French corporal who hid you from the Terror. You gave him the reward he wanted—the only one you could give him."

She did not need to glance at me to know that I meant no more than I said—a sober meaning—and that I spoke in love of her, not in resentment for anything she gave the Cham, and was not trying to find out anything.

"This debt is far greater. I'll tell you, when we can be alone."

"Hadn't I better go now?"

"Yes. Can you see the window, third from the end, by the apricot tree?"

"Yes."

"If there's a light in it tonight, that's a warning not to come. But if it's dark, meet me in the passage leading to the guest house at midnight. I'll do it only if it's safe."

I was about to say that we should not risk it this soon, but sudden, glowing, welling confidence in Roxana made me say something else.

"I hope we can meet. I've got a plan to propose to you. It's very simple—and pretty reckless. You can tell me what you think."

As the hour drew toward midnight, the window that was to warn me remained dark. I had instructed Lilith on no account to let anyone know of my absence at that hour—my great venture and all our lives were in pawn—and there was no stir of sound or shadow as I crept into the chill hall and waited in the blind, black dark. I did not hear any footsteps but presently a hand slipped into mine.

It was a little larger than when I had held it last, and a great deal stronger and more firm. There were many callouses on the palm. But the whisper I had heard in Reil's woodshed in Salem had not changed.

"Come quickly, Jason."

But I could not obey her instantly, and perhaps she could not have let me, if I would. I heard her catch her breath, and as my arms went about her in long aching hunger her mouth leaped to mine and she kissed me in a wild storm of passion. Her face was wet with tears. But I had crossed high mountains and wide deserts to find her, traveling slow but sure. I wanted her now beyond all sense but common sense; more than that, I wanted her always. The Cham's servants traversed this passage at all hours.

"Take my hand and show me where to go."

She whispered something. I thought it was "thank you, thank you!" and hurried me through a long corridor and into a narrow door. We passed through an anteroom lighted dimly by one candle, then into a large room where at first I could see nothing but the red coals, licked by a low, blue flame, of a charcoal brazier. Roxana softly shut the door and slid a strong bolt. Then she seemed to be waiting for me to survey the scene.

Close to the brazier lay some wool sacks heaped with rugs. No doubt these were of the wonderful, living, raspberry-red of Inner Asian dye; they were picking up and warmly reflecting back the glow of the fire. I thought they would be warm to the touch, but not wholly from the burning charcoal; likely this was Roxana's bed from which she had not long risen. But about twenty feet distant there was another, higher bed, and on this someone lay asleep.

I crept nearer, expecting to see a trusted old woman or perhaps a young girl, Roxana's intimate. But now that my eyes were getting accustomed to the gloom, I could not believe them. It was an old man who lay snoring there; I saw first his gray, scant hair, then his highbred Mongolian features, and then the ancient parchment of his skin. I whirled to Roxana to see her lips curled in a faint smile.

"Don't be afraid," she murmured. "He won't wake up."

"Good God!"

"I should have warned you." Her eyes looked shiny in the charcoal blaze. "But Jason, it's the safest place to meet you—the only really safe place. He smoked opium after supper—he suffers terribly from rheumatism—and the roof would fall in without waking him."

She was speaking in low tones and without haste.

"Are you sure?"

"You can trust me, Jason—as long as you don't make love to me. Then I'm irresponsible."

"How about people coming in?"

"No one dares disturb him. It's only going back and forth that there's any danger. I'm his only woman." This last in a tone of pride.

"I don't think I can stand it."

"Believe me, Jason. No one will come. He never calls his servants at night. When he wants anything I get up and get it for him. He sleeps like a baby even if he hasn't smoked." She looked fondly toward his couch.

"Stand close to me, and whisper."

"The walls are solid brick and the door two inches of oak without a keyhole. We don't have to stay on guard." She squatted by the brazier in the way of Oriental women, especially the dwellers of tents and plyers of the cooking pots.

"Have I time to talk about something unimportant?"

"You can stay till nearly dawn."

"Did you go with the Cham to Constantinople about a year and four months ago?"

"I went only as far as Smyrna. I think he was afraid to take me to the capital—wild horses wouldn't have dragged it out of him—but he fears big cities anyway and thought he might somehow lose me—"

"He might have lost you. Of course he's told you by now that I hunted with him—"

"He told me about 'Selim Capudan' the first night of his return from Smyrna. I was only beginning to learn Tartar and didn't understand him very well. Yet when he said how his opponent rode and shot I thought of you. Selim made me think of Salem, too. Still I wouldn't let myself believe it could have been you."

I glanced again at the Cham's couch and a cold wave of fear dashed over me, but Roxana calmly warmed herself by the brazier.

"It was fate, wasn't it, that he and I should meet?" I asked.

"There was a kind of logic to it, though. You're the two best hunters in Islam."

I was still standing on the other side of the brazier, half afraid to come nearer her, or even to sit down. "I believe in fate."

"Of course. You're a gentleman." I did not know quite what she meant by that, and she had a dreamy expression.

"Hadn't I better tell you what I've been thinking about? It's not a plan—only an idea—and it seems almost hopeless—"

"Let's not talk about almost hopeless things—yet. We've got so many wonderful things to tell each other. You're here. It's really you. We're together." Tears filled her eyes.

"Don't cry, Roxana. I'll have to take you in my arms—and then—"

"I know. We must restrain ourselves, for a very good reason."

"Tell me what the Cham did for you. It will help me decide if my idea's any good."

"Anyway I want you to know. After that night on the ship I thought I could stand anything—never break again—survive at any cost until you came. I got along all right with Kemal, then Baidu Sa'id sold me to a Persian khan. He bought me as a present for the emir here. But at a caravanserai—on the Caspian shore—he decided to keep me for himself. I'd sworn I wouldn't resist, no matter who bought me—but he terrified me—he was horrible—"

She sprang up and ran to me, her hand clutching mine. She was panting and pale and I thought of the night she told me of a little Terror in Bordeaux, when the mob got out of hand and wanted another young girl on the guillotine. The fates do not often find spirits like hers to play with and to inspire their dread drama—beauty and valor to draw the lightning.

"Let it go, for now," I told her.

Instead she withdrew her hand from mine and moving away a few steps, turned and faced me. "I ask you to forgive me, Jason," she said, breathing slowly and deeply. "After what you've gone through—to find me—I'm ashamed to act like a child."

"It was not much compared to what you've gone through."

"I fought him tooth and nail," she went on, speaking slowly and in a low, level murmur. "Then I got away under the tent and ran, with him after me, and saw an old man crouching by a fire. I ran and knelt at his feet, and he rose up like an old lion and threw a fold of his *baracan* over me. I didn't know how much that meant at the

325

time." She was speaking more rapidly now, but with a proud look, her eyes fixed firmly on mine.

"The Persian khan demanded that I be turned over to him. The Cham told him—I know now about what he said—that I had touched the hem of his garment and was under the protection of Timur, Lord of Tartary. The Persian said he was nothing but an old nomad without a throne and spat on his robe. The Cham snatched a lance from one of his men and drove it clear through the Persian's chest."

"Well, I'm glad of that."

"It's true that the Cham hasn't a throne any more. The Shah—even the emir here—might have had him killed. But he sent word that if they made him any trouble he'd call out every Tartar from the Gobi to the Black Sea in a war to the death. They knew he'd do it, and the men would ride—they worship him. They'd be defeated, but Central Asia would run with blood."

Living her story with her, for the moment I had forgotten the old Cham asleep in this very room. I tiptoed to his bed and looked down at him. I had seen other sleepers in the opium trance and there was not the least danger of his waking for hours yet.

"He's wonderful looking, isn't he?" came a low murmur over my shoulder.

"Yes, Roxana."

Satisfied, she took my hand and led me back to the brazier. With light effortless movements she placed one of the wool sacks near the fire and invited me to sit beside her.

"He might live five years yet—even more," I told her.

"Maybe he can get someone to take my place—"

"If it's possible at all, it would take a long time. These are our best years. We've been parted nearly four years."

"But you've lived prodigiously, Jason, and so have I. We were apart and yet somehow—all the time—we were together."

"That doesn't satisfy me. I can't stand the thought of parting with you again."

"It didn't satisfy me. And now—" She started to say something more but was afraid.

My heart made a wanton leap, and a warm irresistible wave of desire swept slowly through me. It was as though a resolute and cunning foe had been massed and waiting for the least breach of my walls to press home his attack. It was not a foe, instead my life force, but no less dangerous now. My very breath was no more native to me, seemingly no less vital after this long deprivation. Instantly I knew it was the same with Roxana. Her eyes darkened in her pale, drawn face.

She rose slowly, trembling, and stood on the other side of the brazier. Then she looked me in the eyes.

"Jason, we can't."

"Are you sure? I can't think straight."

"I'm not too clear headed either but I know that much."

"Is it—because it's here—in this room—"

"No, I'd disregard that. I'd have to—what's scruple of that kind against a force like this? What I owe him has nothing to do with it—we've every right to have each other."

"Then—"

"Jason, I won't be able to go with you for a year or two at least, if he lives that long. If I had a baby by you, he'd know it wasn't his, and he'd have to kill me by Tartar law. It would kill him to do it. He'd die. Yet he would do it."

She did not tell me how he would know—whether by the look of the babe, or by its mere conception. Many things that would have mattered to me once—almost in a life and death degree—had lost their awful urgency.

"I'll tell you my idea—absurd as it is—and go. I can't stand this."

"I can't either, Jason. I love you. Shut up in this room with you after all these years of waiting—it's unbearable. I ought to be ashamed—"

"Why should you be?"

"Because I'll risk so much—let one kind of love prevail over all the rest—" Her hands went fiercely to a broach at her throat and began to unclasp it.

"If the danger's only—" I was beside her now, my arms about her yet not confining her.

"It's partly this country—Central Asia—the desert and the steppes. I've become a Tartar woman. It was that, or die." She was whispering in a superb intensity of life. "It's for you to say. I'm used to dangers —I've had to face them everywhere to survive—and if you care enough—"

"I care too much." I did not know where the strength came from to say that.

Her eyes, burning in her head, wheeled slowly to mine. I started to speak then, stopped because she was saying something.

"Are you in love with someone else?" she asked, suddenly rigid in my arms.

"Only with you."

"Are you sure? It could be just duty that brought you here. The women say there's a Circassian girl in the guest house who belongs to you. I wouldn't blame you for that—I've been too long in the East not to expect it. But if you're in love with her—"

"She belongs to Zimil, one of my men."

That was what I had intended to tell her, if she ever mentioned Lilith, and could think of no more likely story. Roxana's expression in the ruddy light told me that she had accepted it for the present. In this present there were only she and I and an old Tartar king in drugged sleep.

"I asked you because I could hardly believe—if you still love me —you'd deny yourself and me," she murmured. "I told you I'd become a Tartar woman. It's not in our philosophy to consider a distant danger."

She spoke not in reproach but it seemed in a strange, pagan pride.

"It's not that. It's something more shadowy, I'm afraid. You see, my plan was—all that it amounts to—was to ask the Cham to let you go."

She looked at me in disbelief. "Are you mad?" she whispered.

"Do you think I can steal you—or buy you? What chance is there of that?"

She caught her breath, hesitated, then said, "None."

"He wouldn't let you go at once, that's sure—but after a few months—"

"I can't believe it. You know what slavery means in the Orient—"

"He didn't buy you, remember. You came to him and asked his help. That might not change it, but—have you ever told him you had a lover?"

"Yes, but let him think I was forgetting you. I couldn't tell how he felt. When he wants to hide his thoughts his face seems carved of ivory."

"What is there to do but come out with it, face to face? He's a just man, isn't he? He can't blame me for coming in search of my betrothed."

"Jason, he might have you killed—or me. Anything's possible out here."

"I see no other course. And if I do have to look him in the eyes and tell him I love you and have first right to you—"

"I see now why you won't give me what I want."

"He wouldn't know, and I wouldn't feel guilty. Still I'd be playing it both ways. That doesn't make sense when you've been bought and sold—"

"I think it does, Jason—to the girl I used to be—but I've forgotten."

"Shall I put it up to him—straight?"

"I don't know. It's terribly dangerous. But we'll make the sacrifice tonight—a greater one than either of us would confess—"

"I confess it. And it may be a needless ordeal."

"We've waited this long—we can go on waiting. Jason, don't do anything for a few days. Don't try to get word to me; I'll get word to you when I've anything to tell you. Go hunting with him, if he wants you to, and with his son Hosain Khan, who's expected soon from Khiva."

"The longer I wait, the more shocked and angry—"

"Wait a reasonable time. That's expected in the Orient—it's bad manners to rush things. I'll be thinking about it—and about him."

"If you're sure he wouldn't let you go, there'd be nothing to gain and maybe—everything—to lose."

"If he refuses outright we can't meet again—as long as he lives. That's the least penalty. Yet—"

Her eyes had filled with thoughts. She lifted her head a little in a sign well remembered, greatly loved, and spoke what came to her.

"The great fact for good or ill—a frightening and yet the only hopeful fact—is—he's Timur, Cham of Tartary."

5.

Roxana took me up the passage, brushed my lips with hers, and sped back. I found Lilith awake and half expected her tongue to be sharp. It was not, though. She rose and put charcoal in the brazier and had me lie in the place she had warmed.

In a few days Hosain Khan, the Cham's son, arrived from Khiva, and when he had rested barely a day from the grueling journey, proposed that we hunt together. A notably handsome Tartar, much taller than the Cham, Hosain reminded me of a gerfalcon, and at times a young Iroquois brave in his suppleness and grace. He was much less old fashioned, too. He boasted finer raiment and more jewels, and in his train were half a dozen wives and slaves, mainly Persians but one exquisite Kashmiri and a ruddy-skinned, hazel-eyed, brown-haired, supple child from the Himalaya Mountains—not a Thibetan, Zimil told me, but a Sikkimese—who I thought would be acceptable to the Grand Seignior. He had a hearty laugh instead of the acrid bark of most Tartars, and while liking mare's milk and dried beef, had his saddlebags bulging with Persian dainties.

At first I was at a loss what to do with Lilith in my three or four days' absence. For woman's reasons Roxana might be compelled to talk to her, and the barrier of language between Turkic and Turkic-Tartar was not so great that two determined girls could not make shift to surmount it. While Roxana would not of course confide our dangerous secret, the stormy petrel's sharp eyes and lively instincts might surprise it. In doubt as to Roxana's attitude, I was quite sure of Lilith's in this event—green-eyed and perhaps calamitous jealousy.

Luckily that problem was solved by Hosain Khan's taking two of his female slaves on the hunting trip, whereby I obtained his permission to take Lilith. Since all my other attendants would accompany me, and it would be highly improper to leave her unguarded in the guest house, Roxana might not attach too much importance to her going. It was shifty and humiliating business, but could not be helped in this perilous crisis of my quest.

We started before dawn on Mongolian ponies, with thirty laden camels. Advancing spring tempered the icy blasts; that night we were snug in felt tents by a desert well of the Kara-Kalpak. A few nomads were already driving their flocks into the wastes, to take advantage of the scant herbage before it would be seared by the summer heat and smothered by the terrible waves of red sand. Herds of wild camels, asses, and saiga antelope had precoursed us, and, like us, wolves and a few leopards followed their spoor.

I slept with Lilith in a sheepskin bed, wondering at it a little but never very greatly, and took joy in her sweet warmth and nearness. The hunt that followed made friends of Hosain and me, but had only one novel feature. One morning Zimil complained of lameness—he had fallen from a camel the night before, he said—and asked to be excused from the day's hard ride. Lilith was standing about, and promptly entreated me to let her take his place as my groom and gun-bearer—the effendi would recall she had filled a similar office before. Since the long hours in camp had irked her, it seemed very likely that a piece of silver had passed from her hand to Zimil's.

Hosain thought that Lilith would slow us down—but discovered soon that he had no cause for complaint. She made a very pretty picture, her bright hair flowing like a pennant of flame, and seemed to bring us luck, since that day we shot three saiga antelope and a wickedly beautiful leopard.

On returning to Bukhara I was no nearer a decision on my great problem than before. That did not matter—it had been made for me in my absence. Openly fastened to my bed was a note in English:

Ask the Cham to receive you privately in his audience chamber after the evening meal. I'll act as interpreter. Unless you love me with a love that can never die, it's too dangerous to attempt—tell him that you resign your claim. You needn't be afraid for me in that case—I'll be set free and return to France at his death. But if you do love me with all your heart and want me for your wife, speak out like a man.

Before facing the main issue I wondered at Roxana's change and growth as evinced in these expressions and ideas. They were not only forthright and mature; she had employed a grave eloquence befitting the favorite of the great Cham. She could help me a great deal.

I sent in my petition through the *Chiah,* whose seat was in the *kiffir;* and it was straightway granted. After the evening meal I dressed in my richest Turkic raiment and slung my jeweled dagger and scimitar to my belt. When I entered the main palace, the Cham's attendants greeted me ceremoniously and escorted me to the audience chamber, a small room hung with tapestries opening from his *gulphor.* The old mogul was seated on a dais, but his throne was no more than a bench, with lambskin cushions. He wore a white robe and on his turban blazed the great ruby of Ak Kum.

I knelt and kissed the hem of his garment. He at once ordered a bench placed for me, then raised his hand for his attendants to leave the room. When they had shut the heavy door, the Cham clapped his hands. Roxana entered through the *gulphor* and took her stand just below the dais. She was dressed in very bright colors and wore a necklace of amethysts. She appeared very grave but I could not see that she was frightened.

He spoke to her in his native tongue, and then, with his eyes on mine, to me. Her voice flowed out into the hushed room.

"The great Cham will hear the petition of his friend, Selim-ul-Reuben."

"Great Cham, I seek *Shair Allah* [Justice in the name of God]." I used the Arabic expression, current throughout Islam.

". . . . If a wrong has been done you, I will seek to redress it."

"A great wrong has been done me. The lady betrothed to me was stolen from her father's side by Turkic corsairs and sold into slavery."

I could not see a flicker of expression across his face.

331

". . . . Truly that was a great wrong. Did it occur in my domains?"

"No, great Cham. She was sold in Algiers to a Turkic merchant, and dispatched to Persia, where she was again sold. But she is now in your domains."

". . . . Has she become the wife of one of the Faithful? If so, it is Allah's will and I can do nothing to deliver her unto you."

"No, great Cham. She's held in slavery."

". . . . By whom?" The Cham's voice dropped very low; Roxana's trembled a little.

"By my lord, the Cham of Tartary."

The old parchment of his face become a little lighter in hue, I thought, but on it there was no writing I could read.

". . . . You've come to Bukhara in search of her?"

"Yes, great Cham."

". . . . The woman you speak of has been in my train about two suns. Why did you wait so long to follow her here?"

"I've searched for her for three suns. It was a long and weary search."

He bowed his head slightly. ". . . . What in your mortal sight is the justice of God in this matter?"

"That you, great Cham, deliver her to me to take to wife and bear to my own country."

". . . . I am not bound to do so, Selim-ul-Reuben, either by the law of Allah or by the ancient law of Tartary. It is written there that if a maiden be not well guarded by her kinsmen or betrothed, not defended to the flow of blood against those who would seize her, and is thereafter sold into slavery, neither her kinsmen or her betrothed may demand redress. It has come to me that such is the case here."

"Great Cham, you do not know all. It was my fate to be far from her when she was stolen, but she was guarded as well as was in her kinsmen's power, and one of them, like her a descendant of Charlemagne, king of the Franks, fought for her not only to the flow of blood but to the death." And I did not have to wring that out of my surging brain: it came clear as writing on the wall.

". . . . I am not bound to deliver her to you, Selim-ul-Reuben," he said after a slight pause. "Granted that she was well guarded and bravely defended, yet she came to my tent on the desert seeking help, and I slew her pursuer, and she came willingly into my house and under my shield."

"For that, great Cham, I'm ever in debt and fealty to you. But before then, she was betrothed to me in honor and in love. I had lain with her in the embrace of love, and by *Shair Allah* that is above the law of Tartary. I ask that you be merciful and restore her to my arms."

If he were going to order my death, he would do so now. His hands moved a little and I thought he was going to clap them to summon his attendants. Instead they went slowly to his knees. His eyes lifted a little, as though to appeal to Allah. There was no sound in the room.

". . . . Since it is not a matter of law, and I know not the justice of Allah in this thing, I will do my will. Into that enters not only my happiness and welfare, but the happiness and welfare of my dearly beloved slave." It was a concession I had never dreamed that an Oriental despot would make openly. "Do you think that my Christian slave Roxana wishes to be returned to you?"

"I think, great Cham, that after a few months for taking farewell of you, in spite of her love and gratitude for you, she will wish to go with me."

I thought of asking to have her speak for herself, but I did not dare. I did not know what he would do, if he heard the truth from her own lips. Then my heart stopped, for I knew that he commanded that very thing. Beads of sweat came out on the carven ivory of his countenance and his eyes were sunk in his head.

Roxana knelt quickly, kissed his hand, and made her answer. I could not doubt what it was.

I looked at him and thought of a wounded eagle.

". . . . Selim Effendi, do you swear to me, Allah bearing witness, or in the name of the God of Frankistan, that since your coming here you have not committed fornication with my beloved slave?"

"I swear I have not, by the true God."

". . . . Then the Cham of Tartary will answer the petition of his friend Selim-ul-Reuben. . . . I will not let her go in a few months. . . . She is the apple of my dimming eye. . . . She is the moon of beauty upon which I gaze from the desert of my old age. . . . She is the new moon, after the fast of Ramadan; she is the well amid the wastes after my weary march. . . . Her hair is of the spring sun and her eyes of the sky at sunrise. . . . On her perfumed breast I lay my gray head and in her tender arms I come unto paradise. . . . She alone pours the mare's milk into my bowl."

The old Cham was speaking as the Scythian Horde might send up

333

flights of arrows. The pauses between his sentences were long, charged it seemed with menace, then they flowed with arrow smoothness, without apparent haste or passion, but with dread import. His voice was low, his face expressionless; there was no wasted power; all of it was in the winged shafts themselves. He was the bow, Roxana the cord. For the moment it seemed that she had ceased to exist save as his instrument. Her face was still as his; her mind transformed, transferred, and applied his raw power. Her voice echoed his majesty.

". . . . But although I am now old and enfeebled," he went on, "once I was a lion of the desert. . . . I have slain the lion, even the black-maned lion in his rage. . . . I have crossed the Kara Kum under the summer sun. . . . I have lived when the camels died, and the sand shifted between the white ribs of the once-fierce wolves. . . . I have seen the sand dunes march like kings' elephants before the desert wind, and did battle with them, and did not die. . . . I have passed the Great Pamir and shot the giant sheep, tumbling him from his heaven-jutting crag. . . . I have slain the worshipers of Eblis, the fair-haired warriors of the Hindu Kush, Kossacks without number, and no few Persians who gazed at me with insolent eyes!"

Roxana had turned very pale, but it did not seem with the dread of what was coming. I had the strange, fleeting impression that her thoughts were not now racing ahead of his words, and that she would accept the judgment he was about to speak with the same sense of fate as Omar-id-din would have once accepted death at my hands. I could not reach her where she now stood, beside the throne of Tartary, its ambassador, its very voice. She was caught up in a drama of which our love for each other became only an instrument of destiny—the will of the gods opposed to the will of its aged hero.

". . . . Although I am old it is not meet that I bow to infirmity," he decreed, wrapt in an impenetrable dignity. "To yield my due from my Christian slave would be such base submission, so I will not let her go in a few moons. . . . Yet to deprive her of her due too long would be likewise base submission, to the desires of my heart. . . . She has served me well. . . . She has not flinched from the thirst of my deserts, or the icy blasts of my steppes. . . . It is not meet that she wait beside me while I wither away, when her youth and her beauty long for their fulfillment."

His dim eyes began to glitter under his grizzled brows. The cords of his hands stood out.

". . . . Selim-ul-Reuben, hear my *dahir* [decree from the throne]. For twelve moons shall my Christian slave Roxana remain in attendance upon me, and you will be to her as one who has drunk the Cup of Death, and she unto you. . . . Near the close of the year it is in my heart to go on a pilgrimage to Mecca, to kiss the Black Stone of the Ka'ba, to stand on Arafa shouting 'Labbeyka' unto God, and, I pray, to end my days on the Hill of Mercy. . . . I had thought to take Roxana with me, to pour my mare's milk, and to smile upon me when the sun is hidden in the black storm of sand, and to refresh me with her kisses like the dew of dawn. . . . But I will not; I will journey there without her hand upon my heart. . . . And I will not go by way of Bushire and the Persian Gulf but by Baku and the Black Sea, Suez and Jidda, so that I may touch Stamboul. . . . There you may come on our Day of Deliverance, one sun from now, and there I will set free my beloved slave Roxana, and deliver her unto your love and care."

He drew his breath sharply and then rose slowly to his feet. He was rising not from a throne but only from a bench of lambswool; he had no throne. He was an old man, and small; although his face remained impassive his voice trembled with emotion. But as a man thinketh, so is he. Roxana translated his declaration in a low but regal tone while tears rolled down her face, and the ruby of Ak Kum burned on his turban with solemn ceremonial fire.

"For I am the lord of the desert and the steppe, master of the mountains, sovereign of a hundred cities and king of a hundred kings, the son of Tamerlane twenty sons removed—*Timur! Cham of Tartary!*"

CHAPTER FIFTEEN

Old Rendezvous

I.

Roxana and I parted without a word. She gave me one proud glance, plighting our love and our reunion; then I went out the door and, as far as communication with her was concerned, out of her life. That night I told Lilith that we were returning at once to Constantinople. My venture had not failed but would not be completed until the Moslem Day of Delivery, almost a year from now.

Cham's word was pledged again by his son Hosain on the day of our departure. He said that he would meet me on the Uskudar quay on the appointed day and deliver to me a white female slave to whom I had certain claims. In case of his father's death prior to that time he promised to safeguard her for me and in case of my death see that she was safely conducted to France. If kismet caused me to be late for the appointment, he would put her in the charge of the *Reis* Effendi.

The Cham made no mention of the matter when I bade him farewell in his *gulphor*—on this occasion his Turkic-speaking son acted as interpreter—but, grave and very dignified, he treated me with notable courtesy, asked for Allah's peace between us, and seemed sorry to part with me. I presented him one of the ceremonial scarfs and he gave me an amulet containing a fine turquoise supposed to bring me safely to my journey's end.

Such haste we made that in the first golden days of June we saw the towers of the Seraglio agleam on the Golden Horn. Bayezid received me alone in his *kiffir*, as good a friend as when I had bade him goodbye. It made me proud, but he should have been prouder of his native constancy.

"By Allah," he burst out at sight of me. "You haven't gone a-begging! I'd take you for a pasha of at least one horsetail."

"Thanks to you, I've been hospitably received along the road, and have prospered reasonably," I replied, thinking of the more than three thousand dinars in my money bag.

"Where in Eblis have you been? We've heard nothing from you, since you left Tabriz."

"I visited, as a poor pilgrim, some distant shrines. Did the reports do me honor, or bring me to disfame?"

"In replying to your presentation of the scarfs, your hosts spoke of you not unkindly, and better yet, sent some handsome presents to the Sultan."

"I'm glad of that, since I've come to entreat his consent to another voyage."

"Are you an afrit, accursed of God, who can never rest? I'd hoped you'd stay a while, in our not dull town, and court the Sultan's favors. To speak plainly, I've missed our occasional cup of coffee together. Also I found you a tolerably interesting study."

"Will you tell me why?"

"I'm familiar with renegades, and despise them I thought you were one man who'd gained your mess of pottage without selling your birthright." He smiled and puffed lazily on his houka. "Where do you want to go?"

"Westward, for a journey of perhaps nine months. My male slaves, including Zimil, can't accompany me and I want them well disposed before I embark. Will you do me the honor of accepting them as a token of my esteem?"

"I'm enlarging my establishment—rather against my own tastes, but to match a new honor or two—and could use them handily, if I may make you a gift of a thousand dinars."

"Why, you may, provided you'll also accept Amine, that I had from you, and fit to be served by Borak." Al Borak was the stallion that bore Mohamet to paradise.

"Why, gladly."

"On my return here I must part with my female slave Lilith. If her kismet ordains that she be offered as a gift to you, will you accept her?" My voice held well—like a lordly Turk's—but there was a sudden palsy in my heart.

"There's no harm in that. I've found her most engaging. But perhaps she'd prefer a younger, lustier fellow."

A younger and lustier fellow to whom she had surrendered in loveliness—yielded all her beauty without stint—was a Yankee renegade called Selim-ul-Reuben. She loved him fiercely and headlong. I wanted to tell Bayezid that Lilith would be happy with him, for the sake of his native kindness and his high place, but my tongue stuck.

When I rose to go, he put his hand on my shoulder. "I have an inkling we'll not meet again."

"I hope for a happier fate, Bayezid."

"No, Selim *Sahabti*, these sands are running out. Parting with Lilith means that you mean to part with Islam."

We touched our breasts and foreheads, and I kissed the back of his hand, a gesture of deep meaning in the Orient and no shame upon me. I would not have found Roxana nearly this soon, save for his friendship and trust, and few men I had ever known were of bigger parts.

With Lilith and one young Negress named 'Stantina to attend and keep her company, I sailed to Malta, the ancient sentry box between Christendom and Islam. There the unofficial Turbashaw of its large Turkic settlement obtained for me most welcome, but not at all astonishing, information. My Uncle Dan'l Todkill and his good ship the "Hope" had indeed come to the Barbary War nine months before, and had received letters of marque as a Yankee privateer. Tough, slippery Nicodemus was presumably aboard.

My uncle would certainly report to our naval headquarters in Syracuse before long, and was likely to put into Malta any time. He was known to have a fondness for Maltese oranges, a sure prevention against scurvy, and his crew liked the small, graceful, shining-eyed Maltese women. Since Syracuse was only a hundred miles by sea, I did not trust my tidings to perfidious ink, but engaged the captain of a sardine boat to watch for his vessel there, and to come for me and my goods and chattels as soon as he spied her.

"Where are you going to take me, lord, on the ship you're waiting for?" Lilith asked, sucking an orange in the garden of the comfortable house we had leased. Of late she had been in good spirits and sweetly disposed toward me, oblivious to my worries about her future, and harboring none herself.

"What business is that of yours?" I replied in the masterful tone she liked. "Your place is beside me, wherever I go, until we part. But to gratify your childish curiosity, I'm going beyond the Gates of Hercules and down the coast of Africa."

During the present lull in the Barbary War and in my own emprize, I thought it a good time for my uncle and myself to stand off the Gold Coast, lay for Captain Joshua Radcliffe, and settle the business of the "Happy Chance," now the "Saint Agatha." It would be a fine thing to come for Roxana in my own ship, then have her to ply the seas, bringing up their treasures to my girl and me in a safe, dry house in Salem. True, there was business to settle there as well, before we could settle down in the old witchridden town. Dick Featherstone had hardly crossed my mind during my eastward journey, but of late he had begun to loom large in the distance.

"Will we sail to Africa on an elegant ship, such as the *Reis* Effendi and his favorites enjoy, or will it be a stinking fishboat?" Lilith asked.

"The fare will be plain and the beds hard. There will be storms to buffet, and danger of reefs and battles with cannibals. Perhaps you will be carried off as a slave to a black king, and maybe eaten. But if you're not equal to the honor, I'll leave you here, for hire as a scullery maid, and take 'Stantina in your place."

She looked me full in the eyes and spoke quietly. "I'd be equal to a greater honor than that, lord."

"What do you mean?"

"So far I have cheated nature as you bade me, lest when you leave me I be burdened with your babe. But now I know it was not the burden on me that you feared, but on your own heart. You've deprived me of my due and made me a mockery to other women so you can go your way without pain."

"It will be pain enough, Lilith, leaving one, not two of my own."

"You mock me still." Suddenly she dropped on her knees before me, and touched my foot with her forehead. "I pray you, Selim Pasha, let me bear your babe."

2.

I carried the child into our bedroom and cuddled her in my arms. But I could hardly bare to look into her imploring eyes. No doubt she yearned for a baby as plowed land for seed and rain. "Your prayer may not be granted," I told her.

"Consider well, lord." A desperate cunning crept into her face. "Many buyers will pay more for me if I'm with child—it would mean two slaves instead of one—and have greater care for me—if that's of care to you."

Her tone became very dry and she swallowed painfully. "If it's your wish that I be happy—a great honor to pay your slave—I'll be more happy with a laden womb. Until I find bliss in my new master's arms —for mark you, I'm only a mountain woman, without constancy, fickle as the wind—I'll have his sweet company in my belly. I'll rejoice in its swelling, to mean he grows whole and lusty, and in the swelling of my breasts, so when the time's out, he may suck. When he gains strength to kick me, I'll waken my new lord with a cry of joy."

"Be still," I cried to her, greatly overwrought. "Or when my time is out—I can't go."

She fled from me, weeping. The best I could do was to close my mind to her plea, go on from day to day, and trust to fate to provide some reasonably happy solution. Luckily within the week my Syracuse boatman brought word that the "Hope" had docked there to revictual. So now I dared write the letter dreamed up so long—to Dr. Reil in Lorient—and dwelling on the happiness it would give him I was able to shunt aside my own fears of the future. In veiled language I conveyed to him that a wonderful thing would come to pass within a year, to bless all the remainder of his days, provided he did not, in fatal folly, try to hasten it or indeed confide these tidings to anyone. This I dispatched on a Genoese brig, to be delivered through the prefect at Brest.

It would be great sport, I thought, to appear before my uncle in Turkic beard and garb and have him guess where he had seen me before, but this whimsy I put by, for discretion's sake. When his crew frolicked in port, tots of rum would loosen tongues, and I wanted no one to know that Jason Starbuck and Selim-ul-Reuben were one and the same until all my stakes in Islam were pulled up. So I bought a razor, and some decent Maltese attire for Lilith, 'Stantina, and myself, and although sailing from Malta as a Mussulman, I meant to arrive in Syracuse as a *giaour*.

The Sicilian was being well paid for his transport and for swallowing any yarn I told him. Warning Lilith of the impending transformation, I asked her that when she saw my face bare as a baby's bottom, not to desert me for another lover. So that the shock would not be too great, I had her clip my beard with scissors, and stand beside me as I shaved. For a few minutes she gazed in disbelief, almost embarrassed to find herself in the intimate presence of such a stranger, then her eyes grew big and sorrowful to vision what this meant.

She needed coaxing to kiss me, but had no complaint thereat, and then found a certain comfort in my looking like a Tartar, for apparently the wild desert nomads she had seen in Bukhara had captured her fancy. On my furnishing her and 'Stantina with Maltese dress, the two girls whispered and giggled while donning the things, and seemed greatly taken with the effect. One was hardly less a child, or more a savage, than the other.

We disembarked from the sardine boat under the very bows of the "Hope," looming trim and pretty as when I had parted with her in Massachusetts Bay. In the shadow of a dream I walked up the plank. Two hands leaned over the rail, but I did not recognize them, and they hardly glanced at me, the young lusty fellows having eyes only for the two pearls, white and black, setting each other off so well, sedate behind me.

"Is Cap'n Todkill aboard?" I asked, my heart standing still.

"Aye, sir, having breakfast in his cabin."

My face must have changed then, because one of the sailors stared hard at it. His hand went up to touch his cap before any sign of recognition came into his eyes. I knew him now for a good hand named Winkle.

"Sir, I've seen ye somewhere before—"

I nodded, but had no time to explain. "Wait here," I told Lilith in Turkic, as I dashed for the companionway. My uncle was sitting at a fine, carved table he had lifted off some tall ship since I had seen him last, eating white-and-yellow eggs and curly bacon. He looked at me standing in the opened door; his weathered face flushed, but he secured his fork on his plate before he rose. His eyes were lighting up and they were young eyes yet. Having to maintain his calm throughout so many storms, he appeared to maintain it now.

"Jason, or ye can blow me down," he remarked distinctly.

I said, "Uncle Dan'l!" and that was the extent of our conversation for half a minute. We shook hands, then stood looking at each other, and grinning. Something hard to handle rose inside of him; he took care of it by giving me a hard lick with his arm near my shoulder. Old Pierre had given me a little lick with his wooden arm when he had bade me goodbye.

"Is Nicodemus all right?" I asked.

"Fine as a fiddle."

"Does he still give you his counsel, to keep you out of trouble?" I spoke gayly, but my throat filled.

"He can't figure how I got along without him, nigh three years."

"Have you sunk the 'Zainab' yet?" Merely thinking of her, steadied me. If she were still afloat, her deck yet stained with the blood of a heroic Frenchman who had died for Roxana, we would search for her instead of for Captain Radcliffe and his ill-gotten slaver.

"I figured ye'd want to know that, straight off. It was no easy chore, or short watch. She'd changed her name to the 'Halluma,' for she had bad dreams. We laid for her, and spoke her off Samos."

I had thought my Uncle Dan'l would speak before he fired on her, despite my request to sink her without warning.

"What did you tell her?" I asked.

"I spoke to her captain and told him lifting a Yankee girl and selling her into slavery was the worst mistake he ever made, and throwing an old woman and a baby overboard made it worse. He had a renegade aboard who spoke Spanish well."

"What happened then?"

"He denied it, as Allah was his judge, but I knew ye wouldn't have set me on him, if ye wasn't sure."

"Yes, I was sure."

"Well, we run up the flag Nicodemus had fixed—the same I saw flown in the war with England, a coiled snake on it, and reading, 'Don't Tread on Me.' Then I told him I meant to sink him, and he'd better man his guns. He fought well, when he knew he had to, but it did him no good."

"Did many get off?"

"A lot got off, but I don't know how many lived. There was a heavy sea running."

I found myself rubbing my hands, not with gloating as much as in absolution. Then I stopped rubbing them, for thinking of another problem on them.

"Have you heard any news from Salem?" I asked.

"It's no trick to hear that, with Yankee frigates all about these seas. I broke a bottle with a Salem skipper, new out from the Bay, only a month gone at Messina."

"I suppose he didn't mention Dick Featherstone."

"Sink me if he didn't—at the fourth glass. I led him up to it on a larboard tack—hoping and reckoning you'd soon be back from Turkey. Dick has been gone from Salem nigh three years. No one's heard from him since, to the skipper's knowledge, and he may be dead."

"I hope so, but I doubt it." And what was he up to, full of avid life?

"Speaking of old acquaintances, there's someone ye want to see."

My uncle bawled out his door. It must be that the sailor Winkle had recalled by now where he had seen me last and spread the word, for Nicodemus was waiting in the companionway and instantly appeared. He came in with his freckles standing out, his nose very pointed, his demeanor perfect. He saluted his captain, and then me.

"Well, sir, I see ye got back safe," he observed.

"Yes, by following your good advice and not carrying too much sail." We shook hands with proper restraint.

"Ye're looking well, and I doubt not your venture prospered."

"Yes, and I'll tell you about it later."

"While ye was talking to the Cap'n, I made bold to go up and speak to the young lady, thinking she was the one, but when she didn't know no English, and had what ye might call a foreign look, I took it I was mistaken."

"Nicodemus, you were. I'll explain later. I'm eager to know if you've heard any news of Cap'n Radcliffe and the 'Saint Agatha.'"

My uncle and his old cabin boy exchanged quick glances.

"We heard he'd sailed from Havana shortly 'fore we put out from Le Cap," my uncle told me. "He's had time to get back there, and sail again. He might be still at Bristol, selling his sugar, but more likely he's off the Guinea Coast by now. The slavers rendezvous off Cape Three Points in the late fall of the year."

"Well, we'd have plenty of time to meet him there, if you and Nicodemus are ready to help me take over the ship. I'd like to get her, before the slaver stink works into her timbers."

My uncle scratched his head, "Well, the war with Tripoli is slacked off right now. The pasha's afraid to send out his ships. 'Twould be a good venture."

"How about you, Nicodemus?"

"I'd favor it highly."

"We'll chart the course later. The girls I brought with me may be getting uneasy. Uncle Dan'l, would you have any objection to their making the voyage with us?"

"Why, if they're respectable young ladies—"

"One's my sweetheart, and the other her maid." I thought best not to mention slaves to my liberty-loving uncle.

"I've plenty of room. My hands know their duty, and aren't superstitious about women aboard."

Anyway, my uncle could refuse me hardly anything. He came with me to be presented to the girls—the shoe was on that foot, now that they were in Christendom and on a Yankee ship besides; they were not now chattels who must ask leave to speak—and he bowed to them with an old-fashioned courtesy that warmed my heart. Then he had Nicodemus show them their cabins, a fairly large and pleasant one for Lilith to share with me, and a cubby close by for the Negress.

"I've seen finer ships," Lilith told me, "and the naked-faced men look like eunuchs." Meanwhile the little gypsy was not able to conceal the luminosity of her blue eyes.

My uncle's crew welcomed the adventure, especially since I promised them a third share in the prize, Nicodemus to have a sixth, and I content with one half. They would earn their wage, my uncle told me, if Captain Radcliffe chose to fight for his heavy-gunned slaver, instead of settling our just claim for a bag of infidel gold.

In fine fettle we weighed anchor, but heaved the big hook overside before we had hardly wet our stem in the green Atlantic. The cause was some tidings that we heard from a Bristol slaver spoken just outside the straits. We had asked her buckram skipper, looking more like a deacon than a dealer in black cargo, had he clapped eyes lately on the "Saint Agatha?"

"Do you mean to do her good or harm?" the Englishman called back, his voice carrying well across a cable's length of slick-calm sea.

"Good," my uncle replied.

"'Tis naught to me either way. She served the Lord in fetching niggers from savagery, and making Christians of 'em, and for that I'd do her a good turn. But Yankees have got no business selling 'em outside their own country, for 'tis ag'in Yankee law, and brings down the price in Cuby. For that you can sink her, for all I care."

"Where can we come across her?"

"She was all but laden when we set sail from Avenmouth, and won't be a week behind us. 'Tis her custom to put into Tangier, to stow a few fine Borkus that a catcher there has for her, every trip. But with Yankee frigates thick as fleas, she may not risk it."

We thanked him for the intelligence, and stood in close to the port. At least Captain Radcliffe would venture near to see if the coast was clear, my uncle reckoned; with fair luck we could save the long voyage to the 'Shanti country, where he laded his main cargo. As luck had it, we caught a glimpse of him on the fifth day, but the light was failing, and we had no chance to get him under our guns before he could make the harbor. So we hung off, not showing our colors, until he had finished his trading in Tangier and again took his south'ard course.

We raised the stinking bitch putting out of the bay, ran up to her, and hailed her. It was well that we looked like a peaceful trader, perhaps seeking black cargo ourselves though we did not smell of it yet, or she might have given us a race. Yankee frigates had orders to seize any Americans engaged in transporting slaves to foreign ports. Radcliffe either did not know the "Hope" by sight or name—he had never seen her to my uncle's knowledge—or else he considered himself our match. Heaving to hardly a hundred fathoms on her weather

344

quarter—the afternoon was still and fine—Captain Todkill stood on our quarter-deck and cupped his hands.

"Cap'n Radcliffe!" he bawled. "Where's Cap'n Joshua Radcliffe?"

I saw a squat, gray-haired man, naked save for breeches, hasten to the rail.

"I'm Joshua Radcliffe," he called back. "Who are ye?"

"I'm Cap'n Dan'l Todkill, of the 'Hope,' and I've business with ye."

"I do vum! My old matey Dan'l Todkill! I thought ye'd gone to hell, long 'fore now." But he did not sound greatly astonished.

"I'm on business of Cap'n Barnaby, and we'll come aboard."

At once he had a boat put over, and after giving certain orders to the gunners, he, Nicodemus, and I were ferried across and climbed the Jacob's ladder. Although my uncle and Joshua Radcliffe were sworn foes, I was a little surprised at the lack of ceremony of our reception. Radcliffe did not put on his coat or any insignia of captaincy, or have us piped aboard. The crew stood about on the main deck, staring at us insolently; and I was glad now of the provision my uncle had taken for our safety, for a more brutalized, malignant passel of cutthroats never sailed with Teach on the Spanish Main. I had visited some of the worst bagnios in Islam but had never ventured upon such a foul-smelling spot as this infamous deck.

It was hard to think of the befouled "Saint Agatha" as once a clean Salem trader, the "Happy Chance." I would never sail her, could not abide the thought of sleeping one night in her loathsome cabin—I would have to sell her for the dirty trade she was fit for—yet now we had come this far, there was nothing to do but go ahead with the sorry business.

"In the name of my benefactor, Cap'n Barnaby, I welcome ye," said Captain Radcliffe. "What can I do for ye?"

"I'll deal plain with ye. Though you don't see so many, my ship has sixteen guns, six of 'em trained on your water line, shotted, and primed."

"Distrustful as ever, I see. Why, I've no thought—"

"I don't trust ye, Joshua Radcliffe, far as I can spit. Ye'll set a table on the quarter-deck, and provide us chairs out of hearing of your crew, and in plain sight of mine. At the first sign of treachery, they'll blow ye to hell. I've bade 'em sink ye first, and have care of us afterward, for I'd rather be at the bottom than at the mercy of ye and your blackleg crew."

"Well, as to that, I'll have to ask the cap'n. He told me to bring you to his cabin."

"What's that ye say?"

"Are you deaf, since I seen you last?"

"Aren't ye the cap'n of this stinker?"

"Why, no. I'm first officer. I sold the ship and her new owner's master. Our papers are all in order, as he'll prove to ye."

Radcliffe vanished down the companionway. A moment later a young, tall, powerfully built man in elegant Spanish attire appeared on the quarter-deck. I saw this much about him, as well as the odd pallor of his handsome face, but at what else there was to see I could hardly believe my eyes.

But I had come to it, despite the ice and fire along my backbone. I was not suffering a hallucination. The new captain of the "Saint Agatha" was Dick Featherstone.

3.

"Welcome aboard my ship, Cap'n Todkill," came his deep, easy voice. And he gave my uncle a bow patently histrionic, but indubitably graceful.

"And who might ye be?"

"Richard Featherstone of Salem."

"Belike the son of Elisha Featherstone, clerk to Mr. Cabot?"

"Your tone of contempt for him gives me no offense. A meaner toady and skinflint I never knew. Don't bother to introduce me to your nephew. We've met before."

"Why, yes," I said. "So we have."

Dick turned to me. "Jason, you seem a little astonished to find me here."

"I wasn't expecting you, I confess, although I might've. I knew the Featherstones were behind Radcliffe's steal."

"There was no stealing done, as I'll show you shortly. For once the Featherstone Company wasn't up to its old tricks. But even if I'd had no finger in the pie, you should have foreseen the possibility of finding me here."

"I don't know why."

"Didn't you believe what I told you that day on the wharf? I felt sure you'd never return to Salem, but thought likely you'd get in touch with Mate Radcliffe." He was smiling his quiet, thoughtful smile.

"To gratify my curiosity, will you tell me how you knew I had business with him?"

"It was as simple as A-B-C. Having no more pressing affairs, I visited the scene of your escapade in Charleston—looking for such business as I could do with you. Perhaps you'll remember the turnkey to whom you gave five dollars—he'd stood outside your uncle's cell during your visit. The conversation was cryptic enough to the poor oaf, but fragments of it that aroused his curiosity were quite revealing to me. Your uncle spoke of Captain Radcliffe and the 'Saint Agatha'—and a paper in his chest. I suspected—was almost sure—what that paper was. On seeking capital for his venture, Mr. Radcliffe had shown our company his title to the ship, including Barnaby's new will revoking one in favor of Captain Todkill. Apparently your uncle thought that the other will was valid and meant to give the ship to you. It was a fair assumption you'd come for her in time."

"Dick, you've gone mad. It was only a chance—and to wait for me two years on a dirty slaver—"

"At first I meant only to talk to Radcliffe and provide a suitable reception for you, in case you boarded his ship. I found him in Havana—too late to find you—and after watching him discharge his cargo, I decided to sail with him. These two years have been the most satisfactory of my life. I've found my true calling—the most worthwhile, profitable, and interesting I could desire."

"I see now you'd take to it naturally."

"I lost interest in every kind of gold but the black kind. Lately, I've almost lost interest in you." He turned to Radcliffe, standing like an old, gray jackal at his side. "Order a table and four chairs, a flask of my best Santiago rum, and glasses. Then bring out our papers for Captain Todkill's inspection."

"You'll need five chairs, Cap'n Featherstone," I told him. "My friend Nicodemus is part owner of this ship."

"Five chairs, Mr. Radcliffe. If Cap'n Todkill will sit with a man 'fore the mast, so will I, and tell the hands to take their big ears off."

This was provided quickly. "I've no longer any claim on her," my uncle told him, "having deeded her to my nephew Jason. I'll sit with ye and Joshua to see the business fairly done, but I'll not drink with ye."

"You'll not?" Dick asked, his pale eyes gleaming.

"No, or with any slaver."

"For that, Dan'l Todkill—" Radcliffe began ominously.

"Hold your tongue," Dick commanded him. "You know as well as I do it's the dirtiest trade this side of hell. Will you drink with us, Jason?"

I shook my head.

"How about you, Nicodemus."

"Nay, sir."

"May I ask, Captain, if you, not Jason, provided that we be covered with your guns? Mr. Radcliffe said it was you, but I still thought it might have been Jason, and he had dissembled his surprise at seeing me."

"It was by my provision, knowing Joshua well."

Radcliffe went to the cabin after the documents, and Dick looked thoughtfully to sea. Presently he turned to me with a faint smile.

"So, Jason, you came only to seize the ship, with no thought of encountering me."

"I was very short sighted," I answered.

"Well, for a year or more I've not given much thought to encountering you—nor taken my former pleasure in the prospect. So if you're willing to make our meeting strictly business, I might be the like. You see, you've come almost too late."

"I don't know what you mean."

"The great issue between us—compared to which this stinking scow is a sorry stake—no longer exists."

"Roxana?"

"Of course." Not his manner but himself changed briefly. My ear could catch nothing different in his voice or my eye in his countenance, save that he looked a little whiter under the bright sun; yet his posturing and histrionics had faded away. "I'm sorry she died, not only for our lack of something to live and fight for. Neither of us will ever see her like."

"You've spoken one true word."

"And the business will be a disappointment to you." Radcliffe had returned with the papers, and Dick handed them to me. "Read these."

One was a rambling letter from Captain Barnaby to Radcliffe, in much the same repentant tone as the one my uncle had received, and the other was his will. This was dated January 30, 1794, revoking a will written a month before in favor of Daniel Todkill. Therein he left his ship, the "Happy Chance," to his former first mate, Joshua Radcliffe. Captain Todkill's only legacy was a punch bowl in massive gold, lifted off an Indiaman, with the bitter injunction that he drink himself to death.

I handed the will to my uncle. "Is this Captain Barnaby's handwriting?"

"I'll compare it to the other will, but there's no doubt of it."

"Look carefully at the date. Has it been set forward?"

"No, for it's written three times in the document. Sure as God it's a later will. If ye want to know the truth, Cap'n Barnaby never meant my will to stand. He hated me, and baited me even on his deathbed. But I thought he hated Joshua Radcliffe nigh as much."

"He did, till I'd brought him a 'Shanti girl o' thirteen, to warm an iceberg," Radcliffe said. "Then we made peace."

"Well, then, what's our course?" I asked my uncle.

"It's for you to say."

"Why not take your bowl, and both go our ways?" Dick broke in. "Granted it's a poor prize for the trouble you've gone to, yet it's worth a thousand pesos, and I've kept it for Captain Todkill, as his right. Mark you, I'll fight you if you please. Just now we're under your guns, but so are your persons; when that's fixed we'll be so close matched that one or both ships will go down, profiting neither. Now that Roxana's gone, it's hardly worth it."

"There's sense to that," said my uncle. Perhaps he too remembered Lilith and 'Stantina, whose lives would be pawned on the outcome of a close, needless fight.

"Whatever you decide, it had better be quick," Dick said. "The weather's changing, and we can't lay here long."

"Dick, I don't want your stinking ship," I told him. "I would have taken her if I owned her, for the price she'd bring, but it would be dirty money which I don't need. All she's fit for now, is lading slaves, and I'd as soon you go to hell captaining her as anyone else. As for fighting you, there's too much risk for too little gain."

Dick bowed to me slightly.

"Will you send for my uncle's punch bowl? Then we'll set sail."

For I did not want to be aboard his evil ship when the squall broke. I had seen it making the same as he; then the "Hope" would not be able to protect us with her guns. Perhaps this fact had hurried and perhaps helped shape my decision to abandon our venture; still I did not see what else I could have done. The bowl, a pretty bauble, was brought from the cabin; while Dick stood smiling by the rail, our party boarded our boat and put out for the "Hope."

Only then it struck me how strange it was that Dick and I had met and parted in peace. There was no likelihood of his shooting me on our short row to the ship; our trained and shotted guns looked after that. As I glanced at him, tall and fine in his cocked hat, he raised his hand.

"We may never meet again, Jason," he called, "and it's better so. But I wish you luck."

What kind of luck, and what would he do to bring it on, when he heard that Roxana was alive and in my arms?

"And I the same to you."

Soon or late, we would meet again. The worsening weather when the day had broke so fine seemed a very augury of some final, fateful meeting in raging storm. A black cloud spread rapidly in the northwest. Still the strange parting progressed. No sea to speak of was running yet, and we had no trouble boarding our vessel. At once my uncle ordered the boat secured, the hatches battened down, and a cross wind course that would stand us to sea from the breakers. I watched Dick's departing ship as in a dream.

He had run a distance westward and had now turned south, apparently bound for Guinea. But suddenly he veered westward again, and for a moment I did not know why.

"Sail on our larboard beam," a sailor called from our rigging.

"What do you make her out?" Captain Todkill asked.

The man scampered to the tops. "Yankee frigate, and she's changing her course to meet the 'Agatha.'"

"He's new passed the straits, and going to search her for black cargo, I'll bet my ship," my uncle told me gleefully.

"Maybe we'd better make tracks ourselves."

"Why, Jason, we're an honest privateer, under letter o' marque! We need only run up the Stars and Stripes. But the 'Agatha's' an outlaw, and doubtless he knows her by the smell."

"Then Dick's praying for that squall to strike, so he can give her the slip."

But the weather remained wonderfully crystal clear. The "Agatha" was a good league off, but we saw her small but plain, little but stencil sharp, and now plainly made out the topgallants of the frigate, at least a league beyond her. The air seemed to have a telescopic quality, as it might have in heaven or in the land of faery—all the more weird for the low sun being hidden behind purple rack, and the light flooding from a huge pearly mass, too bright to gaze upon, clean across the sky. The purple cloud slowly darkened. It was churning slowly, powerfully, ominously. The wind blew soft and low, waiting for a signal. The waves rolled slowly, with long pauses between them, and made an uneasy sound.

Cap'n Dan'l Todkill called for a more westerly course, to maintain about the same distance between us and the slaver, and then called for his glass. His eyes had been glistening before he raised the magic tube, as though he felt things that would make no sense to tell; and now he spoke, deep in his throat.

"Some of her crew are busy at something by her starboard rail." That was the rail nearest us, opposite and concealed from the frigate by her deckhouse. "Your eyes are younger than mine."

I took the glass, focused it to my vision, and steadied it with my elbows on the rail. Against the "Agatha's" deckhouse wall appeared a number of what seemed little black sticks, standing in a line. Half a dozen little white sticks, very lively, were moving abaft the line, would stop an instant, appearing to stand together by the rail, and move on. The curious thing was, after this maneuver the number of little black sticks was always one less. There had been about nine when I first took the glass, then eight, and now there were only seven.

As the seventh disappeared I noticed a glimmer against the ship's side that might be splashing water.

"Am I right?" my uncle asked me in a low voice.

"Yes."

"It don't surprise me. Jettisoning contraband is nothing new. I've known of slavers to put their whole cargo overside, to lighten a ship in the gale. The frigate will have no evidence against her, now."

"If one could live until we got there and picked him up—"

"What chance of that? Aren't they bound hand and foot?"

My eyes strengthened, as by a miracle, and I saw that the black men appeared to have no arms, the same as the prisoner who cried *"Eli! Eli!"* as he careened down from the minaret of the Emir of Bukhara. Each waited for his turn with a mighty patience, it seemed, not stirring from his place, so it stood to reason that his feet were likewise bound. Indeed as I caught a glimpse of one of them being rolled over the rail, he continued to look like a little black stick, bending in that brief glimpse, but with no splinters sticking out.

There were five left, and then four. I moved my glass until I found a finer figure than the rest, standing almost as still as the patient black ones, but grandly and apart on the quarter-deck. From where he stood he could watch how the work was going. Every splash cost him something like a hundred dollars in trade goods but the crew could not see that it worried him a whit. No cucumber was cooler than he!

When I looked again to the rail there were only two little black sticks. The lively little white ones stood still, looking toward their captain, so I looked toward him and half saw, half surmised, that he had raised his glass for another view of the frigate.

"Wait a minute," I could imagine Dick saying in his deep, masterful voice. "I believe he's turning off from us."

"Aye, aye, sir," the petty officer in charge of the detail had doubtless replied.

If he spared those twain or even one of them the situation and my whole life might be changed. I did not know what I would do in that case or, for that matter, in case he made a clean sweep, but the course of action would be different. My left eye took in a considerable reach of sea beyond the "Agatha" and it had seemed to me, too, that the frigate was changing her course, but the veering was as yet too slight, too likely imaginary, for me to be sure. I went back to watching the scene by the rail. The still white figures got into motion and grouped again.

"It may be a feint," their captain might have said, shrewd and long headed that he was. Then in a philosophical tone, "We'd better be safe than sorry, so get on with your work."

There was only one, little, lone, black stick beside the deckhouse wall, alone in all God's world, and then the wall showed white and bare.

"Is the frigate turning off?" I asked my uncle.

"I think so. I can't tell yet."

"Do you reckon he's guessed what happened?"

"He'd likely guess it. He knows she hasn't a whole cargo, or she'd run for a squall, and if only a few head, he'd not find 'em."

"There's no squall for him to run to, yet."

"There'll be one, presently. Aye, he's making off! And that's the likelier reason—by the time he runs up to her, he'll not be able to launch a boat, to go aboard her."

True, the wind was rising. There was a loudening song in our rigging. But it did not rise nearly as fast as the waves, as though a gale were blowing beyond our sight at sea. Captain Todkill's prophecy that in a few minutes no ship's boat could be launched appeared well founded.

"Yes, the frigate's going about her business," I told him.

I had lowered the glass now, and his eyes met mine. But he waited for me to say something more.

"Uncle Dan'l, will you keep the 'Agatha' in sight awhile? You might have to change your course, if the weather thickens."

"It's going to thicken." He called orders to the helmsman. "What's in your mind, Jason?"

"I don't know yet. The frigate's running 'fore the wind and'll soon be out of sight."

"There's a squall making south'ard too. We'll soon lose her."

"Well, that's handy."

My uncle's eyes burned into mine. "I know what you're thinking of. It came to me, the same, but my heart's not young and strong enough to act on it by my own will. I couldn't anyhow without putting it up to my crew—a deal such as that. It's a Yankee vessel, slaver or no. But if you want to, and the crew agrees, I will."

"I don't know that mine is strong enough, but I wish it were."

I looked at the men on the main deck. Only a moment before they had been busy, aloft and below, getting ready for the blow; but it happened that nothing needed doing just now; Mate Dawson bawled no command, and he and everyone stood still, gazing on Captain Todkill. Doubtless they had heard some of our talk. Mr. Shawe, the gunner's mate, had watched through a spyglass the distant scene, and a whisper had passed about. Also they knew their captain well.

"If it's mainly business between Cap'n Featherstone and ye, don't ask me to do it," my uncle said.

"That's the trouble," I replied. "I know he'll never rest, and I'm mighty afraid of him. But the other slaver—the 'Zainab'—spared four of her catch, yet you sunk her without mercy. Dick didn't spare one."

I thought this would not make very good sense to my uncle—that there was no real connection between the two affairs—yet Cap'n Dan'l Todkill nodded slowly, waiting for me to speak on.

"The frigate's out of sight," I said.

"She'd hear the guns this wind, but they're common on the seas these days. It won't matter."

"The 'Agatha' has fewer guns than we, but heavier."

"Twelve, I believe. Aye, we're well matched. She's armed against the Portugee that covet her trade. But mark ye, there's a heavy sea running a'ready. At this rate soon no man can get off a stricken ship."

I had marked it well. If, despite it, I went ahead, something more than hate and fear of Dick had worked on me. Both of those motives would tend to have me wait for a safer time, a less even match, a better opportunity to kill with less risk of being killed—the same favorable odds that Dick would wait and scheme for. I would not pick a fight wherein people I loved would fall with me if I fell—my uncle, Lilith, and Nicodemus—or people not close in my life, such as Captain Todkill's crew.

"If we don't do it," I went on, "likely no one ever will."

"That's to be thought of. What if I sound out my crew? We can't do much yelling back and forth, when yon squall hits us."

"All right, but tell them it's not settled yet."

Captain Todkill stepped to the break of the poop. "All hands attention," he called.

"Aye, aye, sir," Mate Dawson replied.

"I'm thinking of engaging the 'Agatha,' to send her to the bottom. She's about our match, and may send us there with all hands. My own feeling is, 'twould be worthwhile work. But if one of ye is adverse, speak out like a man and say so, for ye all are men, or I'd not have ye aboard my ship."

There was no sound but the long tearing of the waves and the wind's noise in our rigging.

"Mate Dawson, what say ye?" my uncle went on.

"Why, 'twould be good riddance to God and man," Mate Dawson answered.

"What's your opinion, Mr. Shawe?"

"I'm for blowing her out of the water, and ye can lay to that."

"Peter Davies, ye pray to God before ye sleep, and are of noble mind. What say ye?"

A small man, who looked like a farmer, saluted. "I say to send the slimy bitch to hell," he answered in the voice of Joshua, avenger of the Lord.

"If any man knows any reason why we shouldn't fight her to the death, let him speak now, or forever hold his peace!"

My uncle waited a long-drawn half minute, then he turned to me. "Jason, ye're of my blood, and ye saved me from the hangman. But that's not why I resign this unto ye. Ye're of deeper mind than me, and more learned in the thoughts and actions of great men living and dead. Shall we stand this trial before the Lord?"

If it had not been for a great gust of wind that appeared to sweep out of the high sky, roaring up the deck and shrieking in the rigging, I might not have known what to say. It was a savage wind, yet fair. It swelled every sail iron hard to beat us toward our foe. It seemed to swell my heart.

"Aye, aye, sir," I answered Captain Todkill.

He turned again to the crew, roaring louder than the storm. "Helmsman, fly her with the wind. Mr. Shawe, blanket your magazines and fill your fire buckets, and fire a warning gun, for we'll fight her fair. Gunners, take your posts. Mate Dawson, run up our flag."

There was a vein of heroic poetry running through my uncle. His eyes kindled as the Revolutionary flag, with its savage emblem and defiant motto, went springing to our masthead and stood straight before the wind. The fire in his heart was the same that had kindled Anthony Wayne and John Paul Jones. Famine can not starve that Promethean flame, or the cold breath of hovering death blow it out. The wild tempest causes it to leap. It warms the chill of penury and often ennobles the base born.

Don't Tread on Me!

I had felt its fierce heat in Nicodemus, Zimil, Omar-id-din, the Negro Jehu who rode behind me in Charleston, the dwarf Giafar, and a hundred others. Pierre had been instinct with it. It had glowed in Roxana's tale of a heroic French sailor. In the deep breast of the Cham of Tartary it was incandescent. It did not make men good but it made them brave and, in some measure, beautiful. I could not deny beholding it in Dick; it inflamed the heart to evil deeds as readily as good. Indeed in the run and ruck of men, of which I was one, it was rarely nobly struck: we used it to fight our fellows, feed our revenge, fulfill our evil dreams, and flaunt our false prides. Only a few giants forged weapons in its heat in defense of mankind—in my own time Washington who had died without my seeing his face, John Howard, John Wilkes, Edward Jenner, Franklin, Robert Burns and Thomas Gray, Lafayette and other scholars, saints, and heroes. Yet it alone redeemed our sorry world; alone it endowed it with real beauty or more often a showy semblance that delighted our childish eyes.

Up the mainmast of the "Saint Agatha" leaped joyfully an ensign replying to our challenge. My glass made it out a black inverted cross on a red field. I had no doubt whose dark, mocking mind and blasphemous heart had devised it, and whose exultant voice had ordered it be flown. But it was no less heathen, hardly more impious, than ours.

I sped below to warn Lilith and 'Stantina of the joining battle. To my great joy I found them cheerful despite the storm—gallant sailor girls, fit voyagers for a fighting ship. But Lilith's eyes widened as she gazed into my face.

"What's the matter?" she burst out.

"I've found my old enemy, and our ships are going to fight in just a minute." For she could understand a blood-feud far easier than the present cause.

Lilith turned white but did not flinch. "Is it—great danger?"

"Yes. One of us will sink the other—perhaps both will go down. You'd better say your prayers."

"Can we go out on deck? I'd be afraid to die in this little room."

"You'll be safer here from flying shot—"

"I've been in danger before, master—in the flying snow of Kara Kum."

"You may both go to the captain's cabin. Whatever happens, be proud you are with us today."

I caught Lilith briefly in my arms and raced to the deck. By now the crystalline light had changed to a weird, dark green and the wind was whipping off the crests of the waves, but we sped so swiftly before it that the flying spume and spray appeared to move slowly beside us and drift down. We would have lost the "Agatha" save that the storm had not struck her yet—we were running in its very van of blinding gusts. The distance between us swiftly narrowed. The slaver was not running from us—not she!—but maneuvering to get us under her guns.

We fired our bow guns much too soon, and could not wait for likely range to deliver our first broadside. We learned better then, but now the squall had struck her, and although hardly a cable's length on her starboard beam, we saw her as a ghost ship through the smoking scud and blinding rain, dimly looming a few fleet seconds, then fading from sight. Now that we had closed, she too raced before the wind. No other course was open to either of us, if we were to remain engaged. So it came to pass that this was truly a running fight, side by side, that carried me back to my race of death with Omar. Yet so nearly equal were our speeds that at our occasional hurried cross shots it was as though both ships were at anchor, our only movement a slow rise and fall with the swells.

"Aim for her hull," Captain Todkill bawled. "Sink her, don't cripple her, or we'll lose her in the storm."

He ordered the gunners to fire at will. Had he called for volleys, the foe would have melted in the rain before the words were out of his mouth. The trouble with it was, the men were too avid. They took snap shots at her mere flicker in the mists, and sometimes fired blindly. We had not yet stopped a single ball ourselves, but had no cause to believe that we had sped one home.

We were firing solid shot, mainly eighteen pounders, which must strike fairly or fail. My uncle had ordered grape to be broken out and readied, but had forbidden its use unless the enemy employed it first. Later I would wonder at this seeming chivalry, but in the heat of battle it seemed a sane and fitting thing, since his crew was not fighting Dick's crew, but the "Hope" and all she stood for had engaged the "Saint Agatha." Grapeshot was made to scatter and to kill men or pass them by with a horrid impartiality, a logical part of the impersonal business of war, but we were out to sink a slaver or be sunk. If bowling over part of her gun crews might serve that end, it cut no ice with him. He lived or died, conquered or suffered defeat, by his own law.

In the smoke of battle, many truths fade from view, but many that in our daily lives are obscured by common sense blaze up like cannon mouths.

So far no grapeshot flailed our decks. It was by no mercy on Dick's part, God knew; so if it were not by his strange heart fire, a satanic pride or even a kind of poetry—whereby he consented to our terms of ship against ship, ball against ball, all or nothing, clean-cut victory or death to all hands—I did not know what it was.

In the first part of the fight I swabbed and passed powder and balls with a gun crew amidships, good work for my hands. Then a sixteen pounder ripped through our afterhold, too high to do us much harm, and a few minutes later what might have been a ball of twice that weight from a two-ton gun shrieked across our main deck, barely missed the mizzen, and carried away a davit. The boat was jerked into the air, flew wildly a distance of forty feet beyond the rail, and then fell in little chips. Only then did I see Peter Davies lying almost at my feet, which his breast torn open. His blue eyes that had reminded me of a farm boy's were wide and without light.

He had been struck by a flying fragment of the davit. If the ball had hit close to our water line the ship would have sunk like a stone. So I moved from gun to gun—six of our sixteen we could bring to bear—proposing a stratagem. Rather, I gave orders that three of the guns must at all times be shotted and primed. I would designate the three that were free to fire, always keeping the others in reserve for a victorious volley. For any moment now the blinding squall might blow over, or else a wide rift in the blown rain and flying spume afford us a clear, sustained target. When that moment arrived I did not want to be caught with empty tubes.

The men did not have to obey me, but seeing the sense of it, they did so. Some of them cursed when it was their turn to hold fire—they couldn't have missed her that time, they'd have sunk her sure, she'd shown plain as a pikestaff under their muzzles—then cheerfully waited another chance.

Instead of slackening off, the storm increased in fury. The sky darkened, save when weirdly glimmered by long, white gashes of lightning. The thunder outroared our guns, the deck was flaked with foam and the wind raised a prolonged, unvarying, wolfish howl. But we were running with the seas, and not one broke over our decks. We must have shown ourselves baldly once through the veil of rain, for the "Agatha" gave us a broadside. Blessedly she had lifted on a swell a moment too soon; and all but one of the balls screamed through our rigging, carrying away our naked topgallant mast and piercing our mainsail although without crippling us in the least. But one ball, about a fourteen pounder, made a clean hit. It struck amidships, smashing the cart of an empty gun, killing three of its crew of nine, and missing by a handsbreadth a wet-blanketed barrel of gunpowder. The rest could not look at or even identify the dead, for the sea rushed in through the rent in every swell, and they were busy thrusting in a tarpaulin and bracing it with timbers.

Their fellows at the other guns gave them hardly a glance. With calm indrawn eyes they watched for the foe to show herself, clear and long; at least four of their tubes were shotted, ready to roar; they could take careful aim, knowing that after her volley she could not at once reply. The chance did not come but they saw the worth of teamwork in a run and blaze fight in the dark like this. They were more confident of victory.

A weatherwise tar named Griggs, whose knees ached before every rain, went to report to the captain. He had sensed a lightening inside of him—his heart and head felt different—he did not know—often he was wrong—but it might be that the weather would clear in the next half hour.

"Well," my uncle asked Mate Dawson, "why not try it?" The sun was already low; in another hour the falling night would end the fight. The mate agreed to the stratagem they had already discussed. The weather was now two points off our starboard quarter, and when the helmsman had put the wheel hard over, only a little abaft of our larboard beam. The "Agatha," unseen in the storm, was flying from us fast, and we were in danger of heeling over or of our sails being carried away, but our rudder chains held as we crossed the enemy's stern, when once more we resumed our course. And now the men made all the sail that the quivering masts could carry. Indeed if the gale rose higher instead of falling off we might capsize. The cold rain had changed to sleet that filled the sky.

The crews moved to our starboard guns. No shout must be raised on the deck lest the wind carry it to our foe's ears; no man must bring fire to touchhole till the word was given. A man aloft, clinging for his life to a spar, kept a close and deadly watch. In about twenty minutes he came down and reported in a low voice that he had caught a glimpse of the "Agatha" about sixty fathoms on our starboard beam. Captain Todkill ordered our topsails reefed—a dreadful trick in this weather—and there was nothing to do but wait.

Suddenly the sky began to lighten, the sleet changed to a downpour of big drops of rain, threshing the sea; and this a gust of wind scattered and swept away. Out of the parting mists stood the "Saint Agatha," every sail clean cut against the dark rack beyond, her pennant blood-red save for its black, blasphemous cross, her gun crews straining, with matches ready, for a sight of us where they had seen us last—on her starboad beam. A bearded man on the quarter-deck peered in vain, then heaved him clear around in sudden terror of his ancient foe. But his shout of warning came too late.

Our gunners had their aim by now, and six cannon roared almost as one. Our ship reeled keelwise from the blast and heeled almost on our beam-ends. By the time she righted herself, the slaver's men had rushed to their larboard guns, and these too were shotted and primed. But the stricken ship was already listing to larboard from the sea pouring into her shattered hull at the water line, and the brave crews could not lift their mouths of death to speak to us. The balls fell short and crashed into the sea twenty fathoms beyond our rail.

"Ram her and board, Mr. Radcliffe," a strong voice shouted.

But that was a useless command. The ship's way was sweeping her on and down; her bows were already almost under and she would not answer the helm. Then her stern began to settle, perhaps from the weight of her after guns, and in a moment more her main deck was awash. Her hands stood straight an instant, then one after another or in whirling clusters they were lifted on the swells and swept away.

The last I saw was a tall man on the quarter-deck who by supreme strength clung to the deckhouse cleat. When a great wave broke over him I thought he was gone, but in the hollow saw him clamber to his feet. For an instant he seemed to be standing on the level water. Another sea rushed headlong to swallow him up, but ere it crashed he freed one hand, raised it high, and waved. All that remained were the masts, the sagging sails, and a slaver's defiance of God, stiff streaming in the wind.

CHAPTER SIXTEEN

The Lash of Kismet

I.

We had buried our dead, and treated the vessel's wounds. On the following night I showed Lilith three horrid-looking objects I usually kept in a buckskin pouch. At once she was childishly interested in them and then pleasantly excited as she began to guess their nature. Had I bought them from an apothecary to make medicine against my enemy? She knew well the magic potions were frequently made from human hair, fingernails, and urine, but the best for a borning was the hand of an unborn child.

"Why, no," I said. "These are no good for medicine. I cut them off the heads of three Indians a good many years ago." The word "Indians" meant to her inhabitants of India, as it should mean.

"Three that you killed in a great battle?" she asked, greatly proud of me.

"In a way of speaking. They belonged to a war party that had killed my mother and father, and an old man I loved."

"A blood-feud!" she cried. "Why, it's the same in Gunib. In a great feud, my father's clan killed all of the enemy clan that pisseth against the wall." She did not word it quite as it is thus worded in the Bible but her expression meant that, and had the same Mosaic origin.

"One of these was worn by a woman. She'd led the party to our house."

"You shot her with your gun?"

"No, I cut her throat."

"That was good." Lilith's eyes gleamed. "Women who help their men in a feud should be treated the same." She was impelled to throw her arms about my neck and kiss me passionately.

"I've carried them a long time, now, and am going to throw them overboard."

She looked dumfounded. "Why, master? They're trophies of your victory. And it's said in Gunib that the spirits of the dead are helpless to harm their slayer unless their bodies are whole. I don't believe such childish tales, but—haven't they brought you luck?"

"I've had wonderful luck, still I'm going to throw them away."

"If you give them to me, I'll keep them in your memory. I will hide them from the sight of my new lord."

"No, moon of delight. They're too ugly."

I went to the rail and dropped them overside.

They had been only matted locks of hair and pieces of dried skin. Now they floated a little while, fluffing out like seaweed, ere they became water-soaked and sank. It might be I was a sort of hadji now [one who had made a pilgrimage to Mecca] and no man is ever the same afterward, so the Moslems say. Among other mercies of Allah, the scales fall from the pilgrim's eyes so that he knows his debts to his fellow-men.

As I stood sick and dizzy by the rail, it had come to me clearly at last that I knew no way of parting with Lilith, my child-bride and faithful slave, at the journey's end.

We ran to Syracuse, and while my mates hunted for Tripolitan pirates, Lilith and I took comfortable quarters near the water front. Within those walls we lived and loved like a pasha and his *saki*, for all that a Christian merchant and his shrewish wife dwelt next door, and the Moslem Day of Delivery drew nearer every dawn. I tried not to gaze forward to that day, because I did not know what it would bring. The very qualities that I found so entrancing in Lilith—her wildness and childishness and fire—put her in grave danger and thus put a heavy charge on me. She might be a diverting plaything, for a while, to a brutal Turk; most Mussulman lords, demanding supine women, would merely break the spirit of such a defiant slave, and with a broken spirit Lilith would straightway die. I could imagine her safe and kindly treated in quiet Bayezid's harem, but to save me I could not picture her as happy there—and it seemed I owed her happiness even more than security, a due and honest debt.

Otherwise my homeward way was open wide. Commodore Robert Morris, commander of the American fleet, had already obtained pardon for my uncle and immunity for his crew against charges of piracy pending at home, because of their services in the war: they could anchor the "Hope" in Charleston harbor and drink deep in Tavey's tavern with impunity. Although I had not signed on or manned a gun, a little figuring and forgery would have turned the trick for me; however, Commodore Morris delivered to my uncle a dispatch from Richard O'Brien, still consul at Algiers, that more than filled the bill. It contained not only a pardon for my part in the Charleston affair, but a sword, and a citation. Mr. O'Brien had written Washington about the saving of the "Trenton" from the French sloop, and Captain West had verified my claim. The consul had delivered these good tidings to Captain Todkill, thinking that, if I yet lived, I would surely hunt him up and, if I were dead, he could keep them in my memory.

After capturing a Moroccan ketch off Tripoli Bay, the "Hope" put into Syracuse in early February. On the twenty-second, George Washington's birthday, I went aboard with Lilith, 'Stantina, and my other goods and chattels. Captain Todkill set his course for Constantinople. The Moslem Day of Delivery was three weeks away.

When we were only one night out from Uskudar, my question was still unanswered. I had made love to Lilith, in blind, raging passion, but afterward she caught my aching gaze upon her face.

"Why do you look at me so, lord?" she asked.

"Why not? Aren't you my bringer of delights?"

"It was a look of pity, not love. I beseech you, Selim Pasha, hide all tenderness from me. Or when this moon wanes, I shall die."

"What if I should set you free?"

"What good is freedom to me, lord? Am I to beg my way back to Daghestan, and entreat some barley-grower to make me his field-worker? I who have crossed the Kara Kum in the dead of winter? I who have shared your couch nearly a thousand nights? Only sell me to some rich lord with a bolted door. Rich or poor, a pasha or a donkey-driver, sell me quickly."

"What do you think of Bayezid?"

"He has a great house and name, and many female slaves for me to sport with. Surely it will be a great honor to your mountain woman. So why do your eyes turn dark, and your face be white as the Yankis'?"

"I grieve at parting with you, my Moon of Ramadan."

But I could hardly believe it, as I entered my uncle's cabin. I had lived in two worlds, and perhaps the penalty would be greater than I dreamed. Was I fated, for Lilith's sake, to remain in exile as a Christian renegade, saying farewell to Roxana, and sending her to France in my uncle's care? There was a deadly logic in it as well as poetic retribution—or so it seemed to my stunned mind. Roxana was tall, proud, and resourceful. She would grieve for me, then fight for, and win, a rich, full, and ultimately happy life. She would not submit to it being barren and halfway. But that was one more reason why I loved her and wanted her to bear my sons and daughters. There was a justice to that too, although I was too perplexed to think it through.

My uncle looked at me and asked, "What's your decision?"

"I haven't reached any. It seems on the lap of fate." But for once in my life I avoided his straight glance.

"If this should prove to be our last night together, let's spend it like two sailors ought." He removed from his chest a bowl of massy gold, decorated with figures of elephants, tigers, and Hindu deities in *repoussé* work. Into it he poured two flagons of Medford rum, and hot water, spices, and melted butter from the galley. Then he ladled a good pint of the mixture into a drinking mug and handed it to me.

"To Dick Featherstone, in hell," he proposed, lifting his own cup.

"He'll do well down there," I replied. "One of the devil's pashas in no time. To his good health!"

We touched our mugs and drank deep.

"He decided to go there, in due course, and went," my uncle said thoughtfully. "Nobody made the decision for him."

It was not the rum that set my blood a-tingle. "He was a man, all right."

"You told me a remark Roxana made, when you said you believed in fate. 'Of course. You are a gentleman.' She meant you don't want to take credit for your chance victories, or blame God for your chance defeats. You perceive the poetry of life, without which it's not worth living. Of course you—and other gentlemen—invented that poetry. English gentlemen choose to believe in kings. But when that king turns tyrant, they send him to the block."

"I think I know what you mean."

"It's an Oriental view that no man can fight his fate, but you're not Selim-ul-Reuben, you're Jason Starbuck, born to Reuben Starbuck and his wife Prue, and you went to school to old Pierre. You're a rifleman from U.S.A. So I ask you again, what's your decision as to Roxana, your betrothed, and your slave girl, Lilith?"

We looked into each other's eyes and I answered without trouble or delay.

"I'm going to provide for Lilith as well as I can, and take Roxana home to Salem."

363

We tied up at Uskudar Quay and the sands of my five years' emprize ran out fast. Bayezid had gone to Smyrna and was not expected back for ten days; but it was known in every coffee bazaar that Royal Tartary and his son were guests of the Grand Seignior, the old Cham on his way to Mecca. Had they brought a large entourage? Not large—only two score or so of wild-eyed Tartars and, it was said, a small number of female slaves.

I had asked Bayezid's dragoman to inform the Cham's son, Hosain Pasha, that Selim-ul-Reuben was aboard the Frankistan vessel "Hope" and to discover when I could wait upon him at the palace. Instead, the Tartar prince, attended by three of his nomads, visited me on the ship. I saw nothing in his face to frighten me—although that proved nothing—and I could not believe he would have appeared so lighthearted had I made the journey in vain.

"How is your royal father?" I asked, after receiving him with due Turkic ceremony in my uncle's cabin.

"Still able to level a piece and ride a camel. By Allah's will, he'll live to shout 'Labbeyka!' on the Hill of Mercy. And he's reconciled to parting with his Frankistan slave."

"Allah upon him, Hosain Pasha, and upon you, for bringing that good word!" I said it with a brimming heart, and His name could be Allah as well as Jehovah, for all I knew or cared.

"He'll restore her to you on the Day of Delivery, and on the same day take ship for Alexandria, it being a most auspicious day to begin a voyage."

"I have two female slaves that I wish delivered to Bayezid Effendi" —'Stantina had chosen to stay with Lilith—"but at present he's not here to receive them. So on the day before the Day of Delivery I'd like to put them in your care, to keep for him until he returns."

Hosain looked at me as one man of the world to another. "I myself have seen fit to send my wives and other female slaves away for a week in the country, when I received a new and beautiful addition to the number," he confessed, a sly finger beside his nose. "A man should not be so chickenhearted, but valor is ever tempered by discretion. But as for getting rid of them entirely—"

"It's necessary in this case, Hosain Pasha."

"Every man has to decide such things for himself. I'll be glad to oblige you in this matter, and keep the girls safely. I'm going only this far with my royal father, as I must return next month to Khiva. Would you like to have me deliver them personally to Bayezid Effendi, or will you see to it yourself?"

"By your great kindness, I'll take them from your care when Bayezid returns, as I wish to make certain arrangements with him. Lilith, who rode with us one day on our hunt, is my *cobah*. The Numidian is her attendant."

"Now you speak of Lilith, I recall her vaguely."

We talked a few minutes of war and sport, and then I accompanied him to the deck. A cold fog had been lowering over the Bosporus when he had come aboard, and now it lay thick on the harbor and its gray folds shrouded the ship, so that her masts appeared the wraiths of naked trees, as in the mists off the lakes in the Adirondack forest. I did not look closely enough to identify two vague figures on the main deck until we were almost to the gangplank. Then I saw that they were Lilith and 'Stantina; and to my amazement, Lilith had withdrawn her veil.

"Why, this is the Circassian you spoke of," Hosain remarked to me. "I remember her well, now."

"Yes, she brought us good luck that day." But I wondered what luck she might bring us now.

"Have I your leave to speak to her?"

"It would honor both of us."

"Moon of beauty, my eyes rejoice to behold you again."

Lilith's eyes were indrawn and very bright as she salaamed. "May the Pasha *Kieber* forgive my unveiling in his sublime presence, but the cloth blinds me, and I longed to look well upon the face of my master's bride."

"Lilith, is this meet?" I asked.

"Why not, lord? Surely you can grant that favor to the once mistress of your house. Why is the great pasha here, except to bring you the woman for whom you journeyed even across the Kara Kum? Do you think I didn't know? Before you sell me to Bayezid Effendi —or to any other who'll pay ten dinars for an ill-favored slut, unable to play a dulcimer or to keep time on a tabor—before I go, surely I may look upon, humbly and from a distance, the lady *Kieber*."

"She won't be delivered here for some days. I'll entreat the pasha's pardon for your unseemly display."

"Nay, hear one word more. If you won't grant the boon, grant I may go now to the slave-market—or where else?—so you may be

365

fresh and lusty to welcome your bride. The sight of me will sicken you, in these days of waiting. Will not the least of the pasha's followers stoop to lead me through the streets to the place you appoint me?"

"Pardon, Hosain Pasha. Lilith, go to our cabin. It's my kismet to part with you, as you well know, and I'll see you well disposed, but not in shame and anger—"

"I pray you, let me go now." She whirled to the Tartar prince. "Great lord, you've spoken good words to this lowly one. Now will you bid your meanest attendant take me where I'm to go? I'll kiss the dust beneath your feet."

"Why, I'll take charge of you, as I told your master, until you're delivered to your new master. Selim *Sahabti*, it's for you to say—"

"Let me go, lord." Lilith ran to me, and knelt at my feet. I raised her up quickly, greatly wrought upon, and was thankful that my countrymen were below, in sailor hate of the cold and clammy fog, and did not see her there. My arms went about her in an instinctive effort to quiet her. The mists swirled around us.

"Will you let me go?" she gasped.

"Not now, Lilith. Be still."

"Then it's too late. Now you'll be still."

Her left arm encircled my neck, but I felt the tension in her right arm just in time, checked its violent movement with my elbow, and then caught her wrist. The wicked little Persian knife that she had concealed under her *baracan* fell from her hand.

She tried to pull away from me, perhaps to fling herself over the rail, but when I lifted her in my arms she burst into violent weeping. Calling to 'Stantina to follow, I ran with her to our bed, ordered the Negress on pain of the kurbash not to let her harm herself or anyone, and locked them both in the cabin. Then I rushed back to take leave of Hosain, for he must not think I would scant my courtesies to him because of a rebellious slave girl.

"I entreat your pardon, Hosain Pasha, for this shameful scene, but Lilith is a *gibbeleen* [mountain savage] and of fiery temper."

"She's also of strong spirit," he remarked thoughtfully, picking up the knife. "By Allah, she'd have had this in your ribs, were you not on guard."

"She's half-child, half-vixen."

"I remember now how she rode behind us—and we took a good bag that day." He stroked his wisp of beard.

My cold heart began to leap again. "Four saiga and a leopard."

"Nor is she uncomely. Effendi, are you departing from Stamboul for many years?"

"It's my kismet to spend the rest of my days in Frankistan."

"Then it's in my mind to ask you if you've already bargained for her with Bayezid Effendi?"

"Why, no, but I promised Lilith, Allah bearing witness, that if she wishes Bayezid for her master, she may have him."

"To be plain with you, she's taken my eye. I've never seen a wench of stouter spirit. If the price is in reason, I'll buy her."

There passed before my eyes the winter wastes of the Kara Kum, with its blown snow dry as sand, where in spring the nomads brought fat-tailed sheep to gnaw its scanty herbage, and Tartar horsemen hunted the wild ass. Hosain Pasha was a good rider and hunter. He would prize only those who could follow him across the deserts and the steppes, starve or thirst at need, ride on through the hell of heat, buffet the blizzard; but those he would prize highly, as his companions rather than his chattels.

"Hosain Pasha, she's a child in mind and heart, and it may be she'll be frightened of going so far, and hold me to my promise that she may remain in Stamboul, in the house of Bayezid."

"If so, it will be only proof that she's not the daughter of Rustum, and unfit to keep my tent and milk my mares."

"She has been my only couchmate these many moons and is greatly loved, so he who buys her must swear by Allah to set free, and raise in the Faith, any son or daughter she may bear him."

"They would be stout sons, and moon-faced daughters. 'Tis agreed."

"Then I'll find out if she has the mettle to cross the Kara Kum again, and give you the answer tomorrow."

"If she has that mettle, she'll know her mind now. I'll wait in the captain's cabin while you question her."

"To hear is to obey."

I went to my cabin and unlocked the door. Lilith was out of her storm of weeping and got quickly to her feet. Her face was as still as when I had first seen it, when she rode as Omar's groom, and very pale. It was hard to believe that she had tried to knife me only a few minutes before.

"Master, have you come to slay me?" she asked. "It is your right."

"No, for an evil jinni possessed your heart."

"Will you hate the nights we have lain together, for this sake? If so, bind fast my throat with the scarf, and draw tight the ends."

"I'll treasure them greatly, but you will not, for long, unless you tame your hawk's heart. How do I know that when your new master looks with favor upon his *saki*, you'll not turn on him like a mountain lynx, and have your throat cut?"

"Lord, I swear by Saint Thomas and Theodore, I'll be his dove."

"Take no oath you can't keep, Lilith, but keep yourself safe for my sake. I came to ask you to choose between Bayezid, for your master, or Hosain Pasha, but lo, I'll do with you as I see fit. So you'll keep the tent of the son of the great Cham."

It behooved her to appear meek or at least to look solemn at these tidings, but she was too much of a child to accomplish it. Her eyes began to kindle and she was struggling between hope and disbelief. Knowing, never doubting her passionate love for me, I could hardly believe my own eyes.

"Belike he won't have me, lord, now he's seen—"

"He's forgiven the great sin, since the steel struck at my heart, not his, but if you ever raise a hand against him—"

"Lord, I never will! Why, I'd not dare give him a spiteful look or shrewish word, for there's a man who—" She caught her breath and I thought bit her tongue.

"Aye, he won't give you the flat of his hand but lay on the kurbash, as a man should."

"Why, lord, I'd rather share his love with fifty women than have all of Bayezid Effendi's. I thought the great pasha looked at me unseemly on the day I rode behind you—when he slew the leopard on the desert—but the Gypsy soothsayer never told me—"

It was I who slew the leopard—but no matter.

"Hold your tongue, and array yourself quickly, in your best attire, and with the *baracan* of Samarkand silk. When you're ready, send 'Stantina to me, and I'll meet you in the companionway."

I hastened to rejoin Hosain, meanwhile trying to keep my countenance. This was easier than composing my mind, bewildered by the events of the last hour including my stormy petrel's joyful acceptance of the new arrangement. I could reason only that her attack on me had been the culmination of days of jealous brooding, and in ridding her of her malice it had also relieved some of the passions that fed it. These she could switch before many days to Hosain, and it seemed likely that she would learn to love him more than she had me, as I understood the word, for in some respects I had remained an outlander. Fortunately for her he had none of his father's greatness, or Bayezid's. Such men she might idolize, but this desert nomad could give her tit for tat.

"Hosain Pasha, my slave girl Lilith rejoices she's found favor in your sight, and aspires to the honor of keeping your tent."

His handsome black eyes sparkled. He was a singularly handsome man.

"What would you count a fair price for her?" he asked.

"I aspire to the honor of presenting her to you, as well as her attendant 'Stantina, as a token of my esteem."

"It's a great compliment I may not refuse. But it will be my pleasure to send you a purse containing fifteen hundred dinars, as a token of my gratitude."

"Allah upon you, great prince. I'll accept the lavish gift, but only to put with it three thousand dinars, all as a farewell gift to my *cobah*. Thus she comes not to you as a penniless slave, but more like a young widow, of good estate."

"By Mohammet's Beard, you prize her highly, and I'll show you I'm not an ingrate. The money shall be kept in her own name, in case I am slain or beggared, and for that I shall give bond before a cadi, witnessed by three noblemen. More than that, when she has followed me to Khiva, I shall take her to wife, one of my very four permitted by the Koran. Then if she bears me a stout and bouncing son—for my other sons are by slave girls only, not by my princesses—lo, he may some day wear the ruby of Ak Kum, and be lord of Tartary!"

"*Kief, kief.* And to him I'll leave my jeweled scimitar and dagger."

We discussed other matters, including the conducting of Roxana aboard the ship, and then 'Stantina appeared with word that Lilith was attired and waiting in the companionway. I went there to tell her goodbye and escort her to the cabin. She was wearing her jellick of gold cloth, blue trousers, little yellow slippers, and a *baracan* of rose-colored silk.

"Raise your veil, Lilith," I ordered. She was wearing it as properly as a Sultan's daughter on the way to the Mosque.

"To hear is to obey."

"I bid you kiss me, as sweetly as you're able, forgetting what's better forgotten, and remembering our multiple and great joys."

She did so, with passion and deep tenderness, her face wet with tears.

"We've journeyed a weary way together, but you made the days bright and the nights blissful," I told her.

369

"It was not a weary way for me, Selim, and I'll pray to my saints for you to be happy always, and unless they defend me from the wickedness, I'll long for you as for the Moon of Ramadan."

"You are my *cobah*—morning star—and whenever I gaze eastward, I will behold you beautiful and shining."

She dried her eyes and her head had a sprightly set on her neck that I had seen before. "Lord, will you grant me one favor?"

"If it's in my means."

"I'd not dare ask the great pasha, so will you tell me how much he's going to pay for me?"

I was not much taken aback and in some curious way relieved.

"It's no concern of yours, yet so you'll strive to prove yourself worthy—well over a thousand dinars and precious gifts besides."

"Why, that's no paltry price, for a Circassian woman who can't play a dulcimer or keep time on a tabor, and with maidenhead nigh three years broken," she remarked with radiant eyes.

"Drop your veil and follow me."

Hosain appeared not to see her enter the cabin and stand demurely by the wall, but plainly he did not regret the bargain. Unless his blood was tingling pleasantly in his veins, I missed my guess.

"Lilith, pay respect to your master, Hosain Pasha," I commanded.

She salaamed deeply to the Tartar prince and then gazed straight ahead.

"I sorrow to part with you, but rejoice you've come under the shield of such a mighty chieftain and illustrious prince."

She did not even glance in my direction.

"Has the cat got your tongue?" I asked.

"Master, have I your leave to speak?" she asked Hosain.

"Why, yes."

"Your slave is grateful to the effendi for putting me in your service, and he means no disrespect in addressing me without your consent." After this mealy-mouthed exhibition of propriety, she gave me a sly, triumphant glance through her veil.

Hosain ordered her to pack her wardrobe and belongings for one of his attendants to carry to his apartments. I thought I saw her quiver a little at his masterly tone and perhaps at his ill-concealed impatience. She had hardly gone, well escorted and heavily veiled, 'Stantina in excited attendance, when the Tartar prince gave an excuse for a quick departure. I felt no qualms or the least wonder: I knew that breed by now. What I did feel was a curious regret, unseemly in a moral and civilized age, and yet, beneath all sentimental attitudes, completely natural in me and, I believe, shamelessly human.

I wished I had had a son by Lilith while I had the chance. He would have been no puny brat: Hosain would proudly have passed him through his wife's shift, the rite of adoption in Islam, and I would have left him Pierre's rifle. He would have learned to ride a horse before he could walk. At ten he might have felled his first saiga, the kick of the big piece knocking him head over heels; at sixteen he would have exacted his first revenge and begat his first heir.

I could picture him—he who had been cheated out of his birthright by tame peoples' scruple—leading a troop of the Horde. He outflies the wind in chase of the wild ass, spears the wild boar in the Caspian fens, turns not from the shaggy bear or the raging tiger at bay, and lays low those who gaze at him with insolent eyes! Allah bear witness that he be named Bairam, even as the great hunted of old. *Shair Allah! Allah Akbar!*

But it was only a dream of what might have been. Thank my stars, I was not always a shirker, and had made greater dreams come true.

3.

I had gone into the battle wounded, but came back whole. Roxana's and my reunion on the deck of the "Hope" was sedate, almost ceremonious, since Hosain was looking on, but it would have been sober in any case, with many hidden but few shed tears, in this high, deep tide. We had been apart, but yet together, for so long.

She and I had had only a few minutes alone in my uncle's cabin when she asked me to go with her to a near-by quay to say farewell to the old Cham, setting sail for Alexandria on the road to Mecca. Foremost among the other leave-takers was Hosain Pasha with full regalia and retinue: he had brought his loved ones to do honor to Royal Tartary and gaze upon him for the last time in case his prayer to Allah were answered and he died on the homeward journey. Thus it chanced that I saw Lilith once more. Although she was heavily veiled, I recognized her among Hosain's female slaves by her form, her buoyant carriage, and the alert set of her head. 'Stantina gave her proud attendance. Lilith stood close behind the Prince's *saki*—and was edging up.

For her it was the beginning of a new and adventurous chapter; but the old Cham's book was closing, with its large writing and illustrious history. He was plainly dressed, but in his white turban glowed the great ruby of Ak Kum. About the old man was gathered a score of his nomads, bidding him farewell ere they returned to the steppes. I did not know until that moment that Tartars knew how to weep.

Roxana took my hand and led me into his presence, where both of us knelt. He gave me his hand as a friend, but Roxana he raised up, and kissed between the eyes, and spoke to her words I did not know, but which caused her to kiss the hem of his garment and her tear-wet face to grow luminous. Then he spoke to his son, who spoke to me.

"Timur, Cham of Tartary, bids me tell thee that he entrusts to thee his heart's beat and treasure," he told me in classic Osmanli.

"Wilt thou tell Timur, the great Cham, that within my power, it is met?"

We went out of his sight, and aboard the "Hope," and at last were in each other's arms. The vessel set sail on the midnight tide, and although we could hear the wind in our rigging and the ripple of water against the hull, we could not believe it yet, for it meant we were going home, and that was more strange than a dream. Then the gentle rocking of the ship began to remind us of a moonlit scene on Massachusetts Bay. Three score moons had waxed and waned since then, and we could never bring them back to shine above us, but we would hoard all that remained, and not abjure their magic.

Time and event moved; and I shaved my beard, and both Roxana and I resumed the appearance and soon the ways of the West. The day came that I saw the face of Doctor Francis Reil with Roxana in his arms. He had aged greatly in these four years, but appeared to grow notably younger in four hours.

Roxana's mother had died two years before, he told us, no doubt in a stifling odor of sanctity, and Roxana was sad a little while, for the sake of a love and loss that might have been. But the way had now cleared for him to return with us to Salem, and she could not shut out the joy of that. She and I were married in an ancient church in Lorient, the ceremony performed by a venerable priest who had baptized and shrived every Reil d'Oglivy who could get to him, but we intended to take another turn at it, in the Congregational Church in Salem, not for need of any further clerical blessing, but to show the good people of the town we had the right to have children.

"But we'd better hold our horses," Roxana told me, employing an old Yankee expression, and with a ribald sparkle in her eyes I had seen before, "or my figure won't be fit for a bride."

At Brest we expected to part with the "Hope" so that she could return to the war, we three continuing our homeward journey on another vessel. But on hearing that the American fleet had been greatly augmented, and perhaps wearied of the waves and yearning for the harbor, my uncle decided to sail on to Salem, discharge his passengers there, drop his own anchor in his native Medford, and bid his ship and shipmates goodbye and a fair wind.

"Ye'll pay me a bottom price for the old hooker," he told his mustered crew, "and ye'll not take her slaving or freebooting, but put her into honest trade on the Seven Seas. Then ye can victual her in Medford, where the rum's the best, when ye pass that way, and I can see she's clean and seaworthy, or know the reason why."

"She'll be tidy and stout as a Dutch bride, and ye can lay to that," Mate Dawson assured him.

"Or ye can blow me down," said Mr. Shawe.

Other old skippers had anchored there, so my uncle would not be lonesome. Indeed the bluff sailor and the cultured doctor had learned to enjoy each other's company on the voyage home and took many a nip together. Since the grandnephew of one would be the grandson of the other, soon there should be an occasion for more cups of cheer. Also they planned to go fishing together, when the tide and moon were right, and the weather good.

Roxana and I had more serious business ahead of us, but not until we raised Nantucket did we give it much thought. My purse was thinner than when we had first met, and although she had an emerald and a turquoise necklace worth a good ship, both gifts from the Cham, she hoped to leave them as heirlooms to our oldest daughter. I felt pride-bound, if not duty-bound, to make that come true.

Our prospects brightened amazingly when, shortly after docking in Salem, I called at Mr. Derby's countinghouse. He had already heard of our arrival—he missed very little that moved on Massachusetts Bay—and like all the town was agog over Roxana's being aboard, when a report of her death had been brought, talked over and out, and nearly forgotten three years before. But sometimes ships long given up for lost, the insurance paid, the sailors' wives taken new husbands, lift their old sails on the sea rim of mossy Salem. Mr. Derby greeted me not only cordially but with boyish delight, for he had news for me not nearly as strange as this, although odd enough, a little whimsical, and surely welcome.

In Cathay there is a saying, "Time is a gentleman." It means, I take it, Time has a way of spreading oil on the troubled seas of life, and behaving in a gentle manner to his slaves. By and large I took no stock in it, more inclined to credit the dreadful legend on a sundial in Italy. "Every hour wounds, the last hour kills." If the Chinese believe it, it may be because the lot of old men is a relatively happy one in a land where age is venerated, and the grandsire has the easiest chair and first turn at the victuals.

The fact remained that Time, as used by Mr. Derby, had done well by me. Of the tidy fortune I had made in my travels—once enough to buy the finest house in Salem—not one gold piece remained. My chattels here had numbered ten shares of stock in Mr. Derby's company, worth hardly a hundred dollars on my departure, and a boat worth about five hundred, which I had chartered to two Frenchmen in Haiti, to be delivered with her rental to Mr. Derby to use as he saw fit. With the latter he had bought me more stock when it was down—a total of seventy shares—which had since come up. With its accumulated earnings these shares were worth the stallion Rustum and the mare Amine combined, and perhaps some camels and Kurdish ponies thrown in—six thousand Yankee dollars if a penny.

So it was my first voyage on the "Hattie," as a green hand 'fore the mast, that had made me a man of some property and hence of position. Sea otters wore warm furs in the cold seas, got from eating fish and clams, and redskins gladly traded them for warming rum bought with some other furs from the Adirondacks, and somehow in the process a poke had got in my pocket filled with gold. I had seen the Blue Mosque since then, and crossed the Kara Kum, but the sale of salt herring and hides had feathered my nest.

To him that hath, shall be given. In that strange way of good men, Mr. Derby was greatly pleased with me for having himself done so handsomely by me, for very God seems to love those He serves more than those who serve Him. I helped it along by telling the grizzled merchant some of my travels, whereby he was self-persuaded that my knowledge of foreign markets—of which I was as innocent as a princeling in Lilith's womb—would benefit his business. Actually I had Uncle Dan'l's file to put to good use and definite information that one of his competitor's ships, the "Saint Agatha," need no longer be reckoned with. Also I knew something else of immense value to him—that our little western nation was fated for greatness, because of the hardihood and incredible dash of our people. Strong England and mighty France must look to their laurels soon! Thereby I would be on the side of boldness in all his ventures. Catching and skinning, trading horses, putting our trust in God but keeping our powder dry, the United States of America would grow rich, vain, powerful, and mayhap in time fat, but this last, by my calculations, I would not live to see.

Aware of my uselessness at account books, Mr. Derby was compelled to give me a better post—glad of the excuse, perhaps—and so made me second boss of his shipyard. I rejoiced to see a keel laid and marvelously grow into a ship, since I did not have to sail her on the wintry seas. The pious were at first perturbed to behold their gallows' bird so prettily perched, but did not fail to attend Roxana's and my American wedding, celebrated about a month after our arrival. Indeed the town was at fever pitch, hoping for something sensational, but when it went off solemnly and well, Roxana's beauty escaping their minds but touching their inward hearts, I think we were forgiven everything, as a prodigal son and daughter returned to our own.

I stood gloried beside her. She was with child, and the wonder of it bound me. I hardly heard the minister's words, pronounced with a solemnity at odds with his Yankee twang, for listening to echoes out of the past—wind in the rigging, the rustle of wind-blown sand on the desert, the soft pad of camels' feet or the drum of hooves, and the muezzin's call to prayers. I thought of equally noble words, written by one who had heard all this in divine fancy, and there seen cloud-capped towers and gorgeous palaces:

Here is my butt,
The very sea-mark of my utmost sail.

All this was because Life and I are lovers. It seems to me that angels who have not come down for earthly birth and death do not know what they have missed! Mean, dusty little world, with your high-held torches, when if ever I gaze down upon you from beyond your troubled skies, I'll long for you as for the Moon of Ramadan.

THE END